P9-DOC-783

Bᵗᴰ

The

MORNING SHOW

Murders

A NOVEL

AL ROKER
and Dick Lochte

DELACORTE PRESS
NEW YORK

The Morning Show Murders is a work of fiction. Names, characters, places, and incidents either are the product of the authors' imagination or are used fictitiously. Any resemblance to actual persons, living or dead, events, or locales is entirely coincidental.

Copyright © 2009 by Al Roker Entertainment

All rights reserved.

Published in the United States by Delacorte Press, an imprint of The Random House Publishing Group, a division of Random House, Inc., New York.

DELACORTE PRESS is a registered trademark of Random House, Inc., and the colophon is a trademark of Random House, Inc.

ISBN 978-0-385-34368-8

Printed in the United States of America

Book design by Christopher M. Zucker

One of the few good things about modern times:
If you die horribly on television, you will not have died in
vain. You will have entertained us.

—KURT VONNEGUT

The
MORNING
SHOW
Murders

Chapter

ONE

The big guy lumbered toward me, waving the cleaver. Weeping like a baby.

"Take it easy, buddy," I said. "No harm done."

"I d–d–didn't mean to do it. I swear to God I didn't."

"I hope not," I said, looking at the mangled, bloody mess he'd caused. "Why don't you give me that cleaver before you make this any worse?"

"I'm a screwup," the big guy said. He was close enough for me to read the little name tag on his white coat. Eldon Something with Too Many Consonants.

"We all have bad days, Eldon," I told him. "Just hand me the cleaver."

He hesitated, then handed over the knife. He made a loud sniff to clear his sinuses, then used the sleeve of his white jacket to wipe the moisture from his eyes and the sweat from the rest of his face.

I was sweating, too. It could have been the heat from the television lights. Or the steamers. Or Eldon's incompetence with the cleaver. Probably all three.

"I'm sorry, chief," Eldon mumbled.

"Chef," I corrected him.

"Oh, right. Chef."

Actually, it's Chef Billy Blessing. If you recognize the name, and I sincerely hope you do, you'll understand that I don't engage in a whole lot of on-the-job chef-ing these days, though I do run a popular restaurant on the Lower East Side in Manhattan, Blessing's Bistro. (A *New York* magazine pick. Tops in food and service per *Zagat,* thank you very much.) I have a line of savory prepared meals (which you can find in the frozen-food sections of the better supermarkets). And there's a series of cookbooks (the latest of which, *Blessing's Best: Brunches,* just went into a second printing, a *New York Times* Bestseller).

But people usually know me because I'm on TV. My own show, *Blessing's in the Kitchen,* appears on the Wine & Dine Cable Network, Thursdays at four p.m. EST, and, for reasons I've never understood, repeated at two a.m. on Saturdays. I guess if you come home drunk, the first thing you want to do is turn on the forty-two-inch LCD and watch me cook. And, crucial to the whole Blessing mini-empire, I'm a regular on *Wake Up, America!,* the morning news show airing weekdays on the Worldwide Broadcasting Company. I'm the guy with the food features, interviews, and the joke of the day. Viewers tell me I remind them of a stocky Eddie Murphy, minus the mustache, the honking laugh, and the leather pants. I prefer to think of myself as a more accessible, less intense version of Denzel Washington.

They also assume, because our producer, Arnie Epps, has instructed me to keep a smile on my face whenever I'm on camera, that I'm always cheery. I'm not. At the particular moment I am describing, in the midst of a disastrous trial run for a new Wine & Dine series, I was one hundred and eighty degrees from cheery.

I turned to survey the other nine inhabitants of the soundstage kitchen. They, like Eldon, were dressed in chef coats, with most of their hair tucked under white caps. Also like Eldon, they were all very young, the exception being a beady-eyed fortysomething gent who had the appearance and the odor of a greasy-spoon fry cook.

They'd separated themselves by gender. A male with acne was staring at me with the goofy adoration of a dependent dog. Another was nervously rubbing a mustache that looked like anchovies attacking his upper lip. I spied a brown Mohawk partially tucked under a cap, the oily bottom spikes sticking out over the collar of his coat like the tail of a dirty bird. *Yuchhh!*

One of the very young women—girls, actually—chomped on gum. A pretty brown-skinned sister who might qualify as a super-model trainee seemed more interested in protecting her long fingernails than in food preparation. A girl with a sallow complexion had little pieces of metal piercing her brows and ears, and every time she nodded her head, which was often, they caught the light and reflected it into the camera, causing a flare. God help her if she was ever trapped outdoors in a lightning storm.

Breakfast was obviously the most important meal of the day for a fourth girl, judging by the tattoo of a fried egg on her neck. A fifth, another black woman, was showing more attitude than Wanda Sykes but none of her humor.

All were supposed to have had at least an introduction to the preparation of food, but my guess was that they wouldn't have known how to toast up a Pop-Tart.

"Is there anybody here who can split a duck?" I asked.

The fry cook stepped forward. "*No problema,* boss," he said, taking the cleaver from my fingers.

He approached the countertop chopping block, where three medium-size ducks rested. Two of them were picture-perfect. The third had an ugly gouged and mangled breast, thanks to Eldon's half-hearted use of the cleaver. The ducks had been cleaned and were ready to be seasoned with salt and pepper, rubbed with olive oil, and then placed in a steamer with chopped scallions, shredded ginger, six tablespoons of dry sherry, and oil.

But first they had to be split.

"Make it a good, clean whack," I told him.

"Easy as spankin' the baby," the man said. He drew back the cleaver and brought it down on one of the perfect birds. A clean severing.

"Excellent," I said. "Continue."

The man shrugged and raised the cleaver again. He removed the neck and wings.

"Fine," I said.

But instead of stepping away, he raised the cleaver again and cut off a leg. He'd lopped off the other leg before I could shout "Stop!"

His brow furrowed in confusion.

"The legs are supposed to stay on," I said.

"Sorry there, boss," the man said. "Guess I'm kinda used to how we cut 'em at work."

"Where would that be?"

"KFC on Forty-second."

"Of course," I said. I turned to squint into the darkness beyond the lighted soundstage and called out, "Lily, if you're out there hiding, may we speak?"

The show's director and my coproducer, Lily Conover, moved past the camera crew and emerged into the light. Lily was a small, wiry woman in her forties, with highlighted blonde hair cut in a short fluff. She wore cat's-eye glasses, a plaid shirt, tight black jeans, and cowboy-style boots made from the hide of some no doubt nearly extinct reptile.

"Pretty ugly, huh?" she said as I rested my arm over her shoulders and led her to the rear of the studio.

"You think? *Food School 101.* A concept right up there with a singing cop show, *Who's Your Daddy?*, and *Britney and Kevin: Chaotic.*"

"The idea isn't totally awful," Lily said. "But we needed more time. This bunch is the best we could find on such short notice."

"These kids would have trouble microwaving soup," I said.

"They'd probably leave it in the can," Lily said.

"And the so-called celebrity judges?"

We turned to the table where the three judges sat, looking hot and restless. The most famous, an aging former sex kitten whose only lingering fame was due to her vociferous disbelief in global warming, was trying unsuccessfully to keep the unpopular, and some might say repulsive, insult comedian from invading her personal space. The final judge, a three-hundred-plus-pound food writer, was staring wistfully at the raw ducks.

"Let's dump the concept and send this crew back to KFC and points south."

"Rudy won't like that."

"Rudy," I said, sighing. "Why did we even consider his lame idea?"

"Why? Let me count the ways," Lily said. "One, Rudy Gallagher is a Di Voss Industries vice president, and executive producer of a morning news show we all know and love, *Wake Up, America!* You may remember the name from your W-2 forms.

"Two, while Rudy isn't directly in charge of our little cable network, his fiancée, Gretchen Di Voss, is. That would be the same Gretchen Di Voss who is the daughter of the owner of Di Voss Industries. I know you've heard of her, because you and she used to . . . How do the kids put it? . . . Knock boots."

"Okay," I said.

"And three," Lily said, not to be denied, "your old flame has given the lovable Rudy's independent production company the green light on this pilot. So . . ."

"Okay, okay," I said. "Points made. Rudy is to be obeyed."

"We can sort of work around him, I think," she said.

"Let's try. And could we possibly set our celebrity standards a little higher than the D-list?"

"Sure," she said. "Of course, that would mean paying them a little more. And the money would have to come from our end. . . ."

"That's one of the things I love about you, Lily. The subtle-but-powerful quality of your arguments. So we stick with these turkeys. But can't we at least find apprentices who don't look like fugitives from the Syfy Network?"

"Rudy wants the show to skew young," Lily said. "And he wants eccentric."

I rarely get headaches but felt one coming on. "These kids can't even turn on a stovetop. How can we expect them to cook a meal? And the bozo with the Mohawk, what's that all about?"

"I repeat, Rudy wants eccentric," Lily said.

"Which explains the gal with the egg tattoo on her neck."

"As I understand it, that's just the start of her body menu."

Having no interest in the special of the day, I smiled but only fleetingly. "How serious is this youth-demographic thing? Are they gonna ask for changes on *Blessing's in the Kitchen*?"

"You know the game, Billy. But for now at least they're focusing on *Food School 101*. Yet another reason not to just blow it off."

"You're right," I agreed, glancing at my watch. Nearly six-thirty. "Let's call this a wrap and head back to the old drawing board. Priority one: better students."

"I'll put somebody on canvassing real cooking schools and colleges," Lily promised.

"And forget the eccentric stuff. I can be eccentric enough for all of us."

"Your call. But Rudy won't like it."

"Let me worry about Rudy."

"Well, now's your chance," Lily said, using her chin to point across the soundstage. "But you may have to wait in line."

Rudy Gallagher, tall, trim, immaculately dressed, was deep in conversation with the black pre-supermodel, his TV camera–handsome face registering concern at whatever she was telling him.

"What's her name again?" I asked Lily.

"Melody Moon."

"Of course it is. Another of Rudy's protégés?"

"I don't think so, though it looks like it might turn out that way."

Rudy had the girl's right hand sandwiched between both of his and was saying something that brought a stunningly bright smile to her face.

"Do you remember Ms. Moon's age, by any chance?" I asked.

"Eighteen," Lily said.

"Think I should go break it up?"

"She's past the age of consent."

"Barely," I said.

"You should meet my gramps, Billy. You two think alike. Today's eighteen-year-old girl is the equivalent of a debauched forty-year-old when you were a kid."

"I thought forty was supposed to be the new thirty," I said.

"That's the deal. Teens are older and fortysomethings are younger. Now we all meet in the middle. Like Ms. Moon and Rudy."

Melody Moon was handing Rudy Gallagher a tiny white card. He slipped it into his coat pocket and watched her walk away, a wolfish grin on his face. As soon as she joined the other contestants, he dropped the grin, turned, and stormed toward us.

"Why the hell is everybody just standing around, Blessing? Time is money."

"Yeah, and a penny saved is a penny earned. We can throw clichés back and forth all evening, Rudy, but it doesn't change the fact that it's not working."

"What's not working, besides you?"

"These would-be apprentices. They're doofuses."

"That's exactly what we need," Rudy insisted. "For Christ's sweet sake, don't you get it? I want *American Idol* in the kitchen. I want the contestants to look like idiots during the tryouts. The dumber and more inexperienced they are, the better. If there's one thing viewers love to watch, it's extroverted idiots who don't care if they look like assholes."

I was too surprised to reply. I'd been imagining a sort of game show where people might actually learn something about preparing food—and Rudy's so-called mind was on *American Idol*.

Lily jumped into the void. "The problem, Rudy, is that these contestants are just boring fence post dumb, not funny dumb or charming dumb. We didn't have enough time to round up the right kind of extroverted idiot."

Rudy stared at her, thinking about it. "That could be," he mused. "I didn't hear any thick foreign accents. Accents kill. That goofy kid on *Idol* you could barely understand, the viewers loved him."

"Accents," Lily said, getting out a pen and jotting down the word in her notebook. Not for the first time, I marveled at her ability to involve herself in such nonsense without breaking.

"So what you people are telling me is that the concept is solid," Rudy said. "You just screwed the pooch by rushing it."

"You wanted us to get a pilot going by the time you were back from Afghanistan," Lily said. "But you came home early." Rudy had traveled to Kabul to oversee a week of live evening news broadcasts on the WBC network, bigfooting the evening news producer to accompany the show's square-jawed voice-in-the-well evening news anchor, Jim Bridewell, and a bare-bones production team. The others were still there, but for some reason Rudy had returned after just a few days.

"How was it over there, anyway?" Lily asked.

Rudy straightened. His handsome mug tightened into a parody of seriousness. "It was ghastly, Lily. Real, gut-level suffering and pain everywhere you looked. And bloodshed. A fellow at our dinner table had his throat cut by terrorists."

"My God, that's horrible," Lily said.

"Not one of our staff?" I asked.

Rudy waved a hand airily. "Oh, no. He was . . . just somebody we met over there."

"And he was murdered right in front of you?" I couldn't believe he was being so blasé about it.

"As close to me as you are now. My God, it was horrible."

"What was the deal?" Lily asked. "Why'd they kill him?"

He shrugged, opened his mouth as if to say something, then fell silent.

We waited, expecting him to tell us more, but, being Rudy, his thoughts had turned inward. "You know, back when I was a fledgling, in the eighties, I cut my production eyeteeth gofering *Cease Fire*. Don't know if you remember it, but it was the only series about 'Nam that went into a second season. That was gritty stuff. But the real thing makes *Cease Fire* look like *Hogan's Heroes*."

He punctuated the statement with a deep breath and, with a shake of his head, seemed to call a mental "Cut!" to his war-torn memories. Then it was on to the business at hand. "Okay, suppose we hold a couple of citywide auditions. How much time do you need?"

Without batting an eye, Lily answered, "A month for the auditions, maybe three weeks to edit the footage into two or three half-hours. Then another couple of weeks to shoot the first show."

Rudy turned to me. "No way to speed it up a little?"

"Lily's the boss when it comes to scheduling," I said.

"Okay," Rudy said. "But don't let me down again."

He turned, started to go, then said over his shoulder, "Billy, walk with me."

I looked at Lily, rolled my eyes, then followed him on his way out of the studio.

"I'm an old hand at what works on the box, Billy," he told me. "They call it reality TV, but that's just another name for game show. And I know how the game show is played, from the days of *Let's Make a Deal* to *The Biggest Loser*. Viewers love to watch the crazies, but they also want a display of skill. We'll need a couple of kids good enough in the kitchen to make a contest of it."

"Uh-huh," I said, sensing where this was going.

"I was just talking with this gal, Melody, I think she said her name was. One of your people."

My people. Ignoring the racist remark, I said, "Melody, the pretty eighteen-year-old."

"Eighteen? Really. I'd have thought nineteen at least. Anyway, she's exactly the kind of final contestant we need. Beautiful. Poised. Ethnic. I'd go so far as to suggest she should be a finalist. One of the serious contenders for the grand prize."

"She didn't seem to be serious about anything but her fingernails," I pointed out.

"Maybe. But if she were to get some practical experience . . . at a restaurant, say . . . for the next month . . . ?"

"You asking me to put this kid in my kitchen?"

"Just a thought. Like an apprentice's apprentice. Work it out so she can do some simple stuff. Broil a steak. Scramble eggs."

"Gee, Rudy. Putting aside the obvious fact that I'm running a four-star restaurant and can't afford to serve burnt steaks or insult my professional kitchen staff, there's also the legal and ethical problems of training somebody for a cash-prize TV show that I'm coproducing and hosting."

"Damn if you're not right, Billy. Now that I think about it, it would be a lousy idea." A frown barely disturbed his almost ridiculously handsome face. "God, what was I thinking? Putting them together . . . No. No. Definitely forget the restaurant. But keep her in mind as a contestant."

I found Lily in the cafeteria, playing with her laptop. She looked up as I approached the table, a diet soda in hand. "What'd the great idea man have to say?" she asked.

"Not much. What a jerk."

"Either that or he's a genius," she said. "*American Idol* in the kitchen."

"Our own Simon Cowell," I said.

Chapter

TWO

Lily left at eight to attend an experimental video show in SoHo. Having had enough experimental video in my own studio, I called it quits a half-hour later. I was standing by the glass doors at the building's entrance, waiting for my driver, when I heard my name being called.

Gretchen Di Voss had just exited the elevator. She was in her brisk, all-business mode, wearing a black suit with gray stripes and a taupe silk blouse. She was carrying a gray cashmere coat and a black leather briefcase.

"Gretch, you're looking even more beautiful than usual," I said.

"I do my best," she said. "I'm glad I bumped into you, Billy. Saves me a phone call."

"A last-minute invitation to an intimate dinner tonight?"

"Our intimate dinners are over, Billy. But, as a matter of fact, I am headed to your restaurant."

"I'm not surprised. Your fiancé is a big fan of the Bistro."

"Really? Well, unfortunately, Rudy won't be enjoying it tonight. He had a last-minute conflict."

I thought I knew what, or rather who, the conflict might be.

"What's the problem with *Food School 101*?" she said. "Rudy tells me you canceled the pilot."

"Not canceled. Just postponed. It wasn't working. Lily and I spent the last couple of hours putting it back on track."

"I hope you didn't treat Rudy to your usual sarcasm and rudeness?"

"Gretch, this evening, I actually bumped it up a notch."

"You should give him the respect he deserves."

I was tempted to tell her that her weasel fiancé was, at the moment, probably clinking wineglasses with a bimbette young enough to be her daughter, but there was no percentage in that. Instead I said, "I do give him the respect he deserves."

She studied me closely for signs of sarcasm or rudeness. "Billy, I hope our . . . former relationship isn't causing any animosity . . ."

"Gretch, I swear, if you and I had never met, I'd still feel the way I do about Rudy."

She gave me another suspicious look, but I was too good a poker player to let her see how I really felt about her fiancé.

"It wouldn't have worked with us," she said.

"I know. But we had a pretty good time finding that out."

"I guess we did," she said, relaxing. She held out her coat. "Help me with this?"

It was a familiar feeling, standing close to her as she slid into the coat. We paused for a few seconds, my arm around her. Then she pulled away. "Want to share a cab to the Bistro?" she asked.

"Thanks, but Joe should be here any minute with the car," I said. "We can give *you* a lift."

"I'm already late," she said. "Billy, you'd be doing yourself a favor if you keep on Rudy's good side."

"We're okay, Rudy and I." I sang, *"Eb-ony and i-vory—"*

She gave me a wan smile. "I hope that's true," she said.

I watched her exit the building and glide down the front steps, her long, dark hair swaying against the gray cashmere coat. She hailed a passing cab, and I continued watching until it carried her out of view down Ninth Avenue.

THREE

My driver is a diminutive Asian named Joe Yeung. I like to think of him as "Mighty" Joe Yeung, a reference amusing only to those of a certain age, but, hey, we take the grins where we can get them. "Front door or rear, Billy?" Joe asked as we neared the Bistro.

It had been a long, difficult day, and tomorrow would start very early. I wanted with all my heart to say "rear," which would have meant ignoring the restaurant and using the hidden entrance and the stairwell that led directly to my office and living quarters on the second floor. But it's good business to put in at least a brief appearance each night. And Cassandra Shaw, the Bistro's manager, hostess, and, on occasion, bouncer, had text-messaged me earlier, *"ned to tlk."* Since Cassandra is as self-sufficient as a wilderness survivor, this was like a *cri de coeur.*

Joe braked the dust-crusted dark-blue Volvo about ten feet from the Bistro's front door. "That all for tonight, Billy?" he asked. "Miz Joe on my ass to see the new Richard Gere movie. He tight with the Dalai Lama, and she like his tiny eyes."

"Take off. But don't forget to be here early tomorrow."

"I know, I know," Joe said. "Take you to Glass Tower. Or as they say in my country, Grass Towah." The reference was to the skyscraper that housed the Worldwide Broadcasting Company.

"Give Mrs. Joe and Mr. Gere my best," I said, and headed into the Bistro.

The restaurant's second seating had just started and the main room appeared to be at full capacity, which, considering the economic climate, filled my heart with joy.

Cassandra was in her Gwen Stefani mode, heavy on the eye makeup and bright red lipstick, her blonde hair pulled back in a bun so tight her cheekbones looked like they could cut glass. She was wearing a short black knit dress that showed off her splendid legs and hugged her equally splendid figure like a second skin. If that weren't intimidating enough, her spike heels lifted her an inch or two above my five-eleven.

"Time you showed up," she said, exhibiting her constant ill humor. For some strange reason, our customers seemed to love her snarky personality. Maybe they thought she was kidding. Maybe they were too awed by her physical presence to notice her attitude.

"What's the problem?" I asked.

"Prob*lems*. Better if we discussed them in your office, Billy," she replied. "After you've put in your face time."

I began my slow trek through the main room, nodding to some diners, shaking the hands of others, and leaving still others with a quick quip. A British actress, an Academy Award winner, reminded me of a dinner I'd prepared for her ten years ago when I was a working chef at a private club in Aspen. At another table, a former Yankees second baseman, so sloshed I could almost see the scotch-and-waterline in his bleary eyes, told me a pointless story about a pizza he'd had at St. Barth's that included fish tongues.

A large, bullet-headed black man in his sixties wearing a midnight-blue suit and dark horn-rimmed glasses waved to me from a table in a corner of the room. He was dining with his wife, a thin, fashionably dressed woman with a steel-gray close-cropped Afro, and three preteen children, two girls and a boy, who squirmed on their chairs and looked like they were more than ready to get back to their Nintendos, or whatever the hell kids got back to these days.

His name was Henry Julian, and a generation ago he had controlled most of the major crime that took place in Brooklyn. His two sons, Jayson and Adam, ran the family business now, which, prior to the recent downturn in the economy, had been focusing on several slightly more legitimate enterprises, like real estate and banking.

Henry had grown up in the same apartment building on 127th Street as my foster father and mentor, Paul Lamont, and theirs was a friendship that had lasted long past boyhood. I'd discovered that fact over a decade ago, at Paul's funeral, when Henry introduced himself and, in a quiet room at the rear of the church, talked me out of going vigilante on those responsible for Paul's death. A few years later, I found out that Henry had taken care of them himself.

A week after I'd opened the Bistro, he came in and reintroduced himself, and we spent the evening drinking and reminiscing about Paul. After that, he dropped by every few months, sometimes alone, sometimes not.

He started to get up, but I waved him down.

"You know my wife, Sarina, don't you, Billy?" he said.

"Of course," I said.

"And these are my grandkids. Little Jason, Rasheeda, and Adama. Kids, I want you to meet the man who owns this palace of fine food—Mr. Blessing."

Little Jason and Adama gave me bored-kid looks, but Rasheeda fixed me with her alert brown eyes and said, "I've seen you on *Wake Up, America!* You smile too much."

"Ra, be polite," her grandmother said.

Rasheeda cocked her head and said, "You're more handsome when you don't smile."

"Tell that to my producer," I said.

Henry Julian chuckled. "She's the one, ain't she, Billy?"

I told him I thought she was. In fact, I was wondering how long it would be before she put her father and uncle out to pasture with her grandfather.

Henry asked his wife to take the children to the powder rooms and suggested I sit for a moment beside him. Naturally, Rasheeda wanted to stay, but her grandmother dragged her away.

"You're a man about town, Billy, and you're in the news business at Worldwide Broadcasting," Henry said when they'd departed. "What do you hear about Felix the Cat?"

"Not much," I said. "But I do try to keep up with Bugs Bunny."

"Ain't talkin' 'bout any cartoon character," he growled. "This Felix ain't all that funny, know what I mean?"

I gave him my blankest look.

"This Felix supposedly lives in Par-ee, though nobody knows for sure, and when he shows up in any other city, the population decreases. It worries me he might be coming to town."

"What makes you think so?"

Henry shifted his shoulders, moving his neck around in his shirt, turtle-style, like the late Rodney Dangerfield. "I may be retired, Billy, but I still got my sources. This guy Felix plays it pretty close—nobody still alive even knows what he looks like. But as quietly as he moves, he makes some waves. There's this dude the really high rollers use to keep track of trends and the shifting moods of people worldwide. I pay him to be my danger spotter. He swears Felix is on his way to the Big Apple."

"To see you?"

"I don't think so," Henry said. "I wouldn't be sittin' here jawin' with you without a couple uglies watching my back, that be the case. But between us, not that long ago I had a very minor business arrangement in Nigeria that was, ah, protected by the late General Santomacha. Know who he was?"

"Another in a long line of brutal dictators," I said.

"Well, this Felix put an end to the general's reign in a very nasty way. Ever since, I been keepin' track of the man. So if he's in my town, even if he's here on business got nothing to do with me, I like to know about it. Which is my point in askin' you what you've heard."

"Why would I have heard anything?"

"My spotter says Felix's target got something to do with the media. Couldn't get any more specific than that. But you a member of the media in good standing."

This really wasn't a conversation I wanted to be having. In spite of the things the old man had done, I liked Henry, and he'd stopped me from making a terrible mistake. But talking about a mysterious hit man flying in from Paris to take out somebody in the media? Murdered dictators? Much too complicated for my simple life. "I'm sorry I can't help you, Henry," I said, getting to my feet. "I've never heard of this Felix guy."

"Yeah, well, I figured I'd ask. If you do hear of anything . . ."

"You know it," I promised, shaking his callused hand.

Cassandra was waiting at the rear of the room, near the exit. "Finally," she said.

Moving down the hall to the stairwell, we passed the open door to a private dining room. I made the mistake of looking in and catching the eye of Gretchen Di Voss.

She was seated at a table with two other women and one man. She waved me in.

"Billy, come say hello to my friends," she called out.

I looked at Cassandra, who sighed in exasperation.

"I think you know everybody," Gretchen said as I entered the room.

I knew them. The gamine, red-haired Gin McCauley was a comrade-in-arms, a coanchor on *Wake Up, America!* She was flanked by her short, plump manager, Hildegard Fonsica, and Frederick Spence, her agent. Hildy's ruthlessness in fighting for her clients had earned her a certain infamy, but as far as I knew she played it straight, and I found her lack of bullshit admirable. I hadn't made up my mind about Spence. He seemed affable enough but was a little shy in the sincerity department.

"Any menu suggestions, Billy?" Gretchen asked.

I spent a few minutes plotting their meals, then excused myself to join the impatient Cassandra, who was hovering just outside the door. As we headed for the stairs to my office, she said, "I'm surprised the TV princess didn't ask you to toss the salad for them."

"That reminds me," I said. "Send them a bottle of Dom '98 with my compliments."

"I thought it was all over between you and Miz Di Voss," Cassandra said.

"If I was still in love, I'd have sent the Cristal '99."

Chapter

FOUR

Finally in my office with the door closed, Cassandra said, "Do you want the bad news, the badder news, or the baddest news?"

"Isn't that supposed to be the bad news or the good news?"

"Not tonight," she said.

"Start with the bad and build up."

"Okay. Mr. Politano informed me this afternoon that he was doubling the price of corn. He gave me some bullshit about crops being depleted because they're being used for ethanol."

"That may be true," I said. "But doubling is a little much."

"I told him he could stick his corn up his ass," she said.

"It might be more practical to make ethanol with it," I said. "How much corn do we use, anyway?"

"That's beside the point," she said. "May I continue?"

"If I said no, would you stop?"

"When Mr. Politano got tired of shouting Sicilian curses at me, he said he wouldn't sell us any more produce at any price. So I was forced to phone an acquaintance, Mr. Tamonia."

"The one who runs the book on Forty-fourth and breaks kneecaps?"

"Exactly. I got him to convince Mr. Politano to continue providing us with produce, including corn. The corn would be at a forty percent hike, from which, I presume, Mr. Tamonia will take his cut. It's still less than we'd be paying if I'd just bent over and spread for Mr. Politano. I hope all of this is okay with you."

"Sounds fine," I said. "Is Mr. Tamonia the badder news?"

"No. It's that dickwad Philip Rodell. . . ."

"The dickwad who happens to be the number-one hotshot in the district attorney's office. The dickwad who put the Calibrio Family in the jug."

"Whatever. He threw a hissy out front tonight."

"Because . . . ?"

"He waltzes in with his crew a little after eight. Three couples. No reservation. Just, 'Seat us in a private room, sugar tits.' Classy, huh? I tell him the private rooms are occupied, as is the main room, and, though it galls the crap out of me, I offer to set something up in the lounge for him. He tells me he doesn't eat in lounges. He *orders* me to move one of our private-room parties to the lounge and give him *that* room."

"I hope you didn't suggest *he* shove anything up his ass."

"Of course not. I told him to fuck off."

"How'd that work out?"

She blinked her sky-blue eyes. "He called me a few names and demanded to talk with you. I told him you weren't around and suggested he move on. He, in turn, threatened to keep sending health and fire inspectors until they find some reason to close us down."

"That *could* be a problem."

"I . . . don't think so. I showed him the security camera we have over the front door. I asked if he thought his wife might like a copy of his entrance with his crew."

"He wasn't with his wife," I said.

"Not unless he's married to a thousand-dollar-a-night hooker."

"What is it with these fighting lawmen, can't keep it zipped? Well, you seem to have things in hand, Cassandra. Why'd you text me?"

"Because of the baddest news," she said. "Juan hit Bridget."

Juan Lorinda had spent two tours in Iraq with the other members of his National Guard unit. During the second, he'd lost his right leg to a suicide bomber. He'd been working behind the bar for five months. Bridget Innes had been waitressing at the Bistro for more than a year. She was not a bad server, but she regularly ignored a rule I'd established about not dating customers.

"She okay?" I asked.

"Just a slap," Cassandra said. "But enough to leave a red splotch on her cheek. She cried and tried to hit him with her tray, but I intervened."

"This happen in the bar, in front of customers?"

"It was early. Just a couple of martini drinkers. They seemed to like the show. I told Bridget she could take the night off, but she preferred to stay. So I sent Juan home and put Josef on bar detail. Didn't want whatever it was to start up again."

"Juan go quietly?"

"Like a lamb. He tried to apologize to her, but Bridget wasn't in a forgiving mood. Some temper on that girl."

"Lovers' quarrel?" I asked.

Cassandra held up a hand. "When you hired me, Billy, I told you I'd take care of every aspect of the Bistro except for one. I do not get involved in HR matters."

"Forget human relations. Were they sleeping together? Or was it something else?"

"I don't know. I don't care. I have presented you with the problem, which is as far as I go."

"Well, hell . . . I guess you'd better send her up," I said. "And while you're at it, have her bring me a roast beef on rye and a glass of merlot. The Altadon 2002."

"Sure you wouldn't rather the Cristal '99?" she asked.

I stuck my tongue out at her departing back.

Fearless, that's me.

Chapter

FIVE

I was perusing Bridget's file when there was a tentative knock on the door.

Assuming it was she with my supper, I placed the file in a desk drawer and said, "Come on in."

The tiny woman with a mop of red hair and an uncharacteristically sheepish grin was definitely not Bridget. "Hope you don't mind my droppin' in like this, Billy," Gin McCauley, the morning-show coanchor, said. "Hildy and Spence suggested I get lost while they have a little chat with Gretchen about mah contract." Her Greenville, Mississippi, accent, usually subdued except in moments of stress, was in full bloom.

"Glad to have the company, Gin," I said, rising and gesturing toward a chair. "Sit. Please. Want me to order something up?"

"No, thank you. Sure ah'm not distractin' you from somethin' important?"

"What could be more important than being distracted by you?"

She smiled. "Fact is, Billy, I been meanin' to ask yo' advice about somethin'. You were sweet enough to help me get loose from that son of a bitch Bobby Lee."

The reference was to a relationship that had turned ugly when Gin refused to "lend" her then boyfriend, Robert Lee Ferell, seventy thousand dollars to semi-finance a documentary on media bias in America. His fallback position was to threaten her. He'd secretly filmed one of their more intimate couplings and told her that unless she paid him the seventy thou, he would give the TMZ and Gawker websites something to make their day.

She hadn't known what to do. Going to the police was out of the question. Ditto the network. She didn't even trust her manager or her agent to keep the secret. Instead she'd settled on me.

I wasn't surprised. When I was younger, I realized that I possessed something rare: Because of the way I looked or talked or because of my body language or manner, people trusted me. Men, women, black, white, or in between. Didn't matter.

In my teens, I misused this gift. But the karmic danger of that to body and soul had been brought home to me in a particularly brutal and violent way. I'll save the details of that part of my life for another time when we've known each other a little better.

Let's just say that for nearly two decades I've done penance for my misdeeds by justifying the faith that people seem to have in me. The closest I've come to falling back on my old ways was in getting Gin out of her bind. I conned her ex-boyfriend into a situation, filmed by his own camera, resulting in a short movie that, if unspooled, would have led to his spending time in prison. He and I settled on a mutual agreement to let Net cruisers find something more positive to watch.

"What's the problem, Gin?"

"Nothin' like the last one," she said. "That was mah first and last cougah moment. As I hope you know, ah've been totally faithful to Ted evah since we met, even with him away so much."

"Ted" would be Theodore O. Parkhurst, byline "TOP," an investigative reporter for *Now Magazine* who'd spent nearly a year covering the progress of the war in Afghanistan. He seemed like a nice guy and an excellent journalist, and I hoped that Gin really was being faithful to him. And vice versa.

"My problem this time is strictly business, Billy. About my future on *Wake Up.*"

She had my full attention now. The morning show was important to me. I was about to urge her on when Bridget arrived with my dinner, announcing her presence with a loud clearing of her throat.

The physical result of Juan's slap was no longer in evidence. Natural healing or makeup artfully applied. Bridget was a tall, handsome ash-blonde with the look of a college football cheerleader who'd added a few years and enough curves to move on to the pros. The Bistro's uniform of khaki pants and pink men's dress shirt did very little for her full figure. That was the point. I was running a restaurant, not a wet-T-shirt bar. Still, there was a sensuality about her that even a clown suit would not have subdued. "You wanted to see me?" she asked.

"I do, Bridget. But not right now. Give me a half-hour?"

"Sure." She turned to go.

"Whoa," I said. "You can leave my dinner."

"Oh, 'course."

She took her time walking to the desk and depositing her tray. "Can I get *you* something?" she asked Gin.

"No, thank ya. Ah'm fine."

Bridget gave me a fleeting smile and departed, closing the door behind her.

"Wow. Bridget, huh?" Gin said. "You ever fool around with the waitresses, Billy?"

"Nope. And I hope I'll always be smart enough not to, even if there was no risk of losing this place to a harassment suit. But we were talking about you and *Wake Up, America!*"

"Right. The morning show. That must go on. Billy, I don't know what to do."

"What's the problem?"

"I've been on *WUA!* for almost seven years. People have forgotten I started out as a standup."

"I certainly haven't. I remember seeing you at Carolines. You killed. But I still don't get—"

"I've been offered my own comedy series," she interrupted. Her usually pale face flushed with excitement.

"Great. And the problem is what, that it's on the CW?"

"It's CBS, honey. Prime time, between *CSI: Atlantic City* and *M*A*S*H in Mosul.*"

"Sounds like a great slot," I said, trying not to look too longingly at my roast-beef sandwich. "You going to be able to fit it in with *Wake Up?*"

"That's the problem. See, *The Gin Fizz Show* is gonna be kinda like a once-a-week version of *The Daily Show.* Comedy news, heavy on the politics. Only we can't do it here in the city because, well, *The Daily Show* is here. And also, we're gonna be in prime time on network, which means instead of usin' really clever unknowns that go on to be big stars, we're gonna start off with big stars. To do that, we've gotta tape it on the Coast. So it'll be bye-bye to *Wake Up* when my contract runs out."

"When will that be?"

"Next month. Unless I just blow off the series. What do you think I should do?"

"What do your people say?"

"Frank and Hildy are . . . not crazy about me leaving *Wake Up*. It's a big, big risk leaving an important, successful show for a series that has about a five percent chance of makin' it. If it flops, I'll be used merchandise.

"And there's Ted. He says we'll be able to work it out somehow. I mean, I probably won't be seeing any less of him on the West Coast than I am now. Still, one of these days, he'll be back and then . . ."

"Sounds like you've already made up your mind," I said.

"The thing is, I like comedy," she said. "And I'm funny. I don't get the chance for funny on *Wake Up*."

"Okay . . ."

"But I think I'm turnin' into a pretty fair newswoman," she said. "You know, I do a lot of mah own research and I write mah own material. And that gives me great satisfaction. I don't know if I want to go from real news to fake news."

"Then . . ."

"But Rudy has been givin' the gets to Lance." Lance Tuttle was her slightly pompous but sincere coanchor on our show. "Ah'm real tired of interviewin' *Dancin' with the Stars* losers and novelists."

I decided not to remind her of the interviews *I* was assigned: cookbook authors, faddists, diet doctors, and their ilk. "Have you talked to Rudy about it?" I asked.

"Uh-huh. He said he admires Lance. They have this frat-boy thing goin' on, you know?"

I knew. "You tell Gretchen about the series offer?"

She nodded. "Yesterday. That's when she suggested we all meet for dinnah."

The mention of dinner reminded me of the sandwich. It had been eight hours since lunch at the studio. But it didn't seem polite for me to start wolfing it down. "If Gretch is putting on the feedbag, that's got to be a good sign," I told Gin. "My guess is at the least, she'll offer a pay bump."

"This isn't about money, Billy."

"Of course it isn't," I said, and gave in to the gnawing in my stomach. "You mind if I have a bite to eat while we talk?"

"Oh, Billy, ah'm keeping you from your dinnah. Please eat."

It was more encouragement than I needed.

"So you think Gretchen might agree to me getting some of the first-half-hour interviews?"

The question caught me mid-chew. Instead of speaking with my mouth full or rushing to swallow and risking the need for a Heimlich, I gave her a noncommittal shrug.

Gin seemed to interpret this as a "yes."

"But I may not get another chance at a prime-time series."

I swallowed, savoring the aftertaste, then followed it with a sip of wine. It whet my appetite to the point where I wanted nothing more in the world than to enjoy the rest of my sandwich. Alone and unobserved.

"You're right, Billy," she said, again interpreting my food-induced silence as encouragement. "It's a win-win situation. If Gretchen gives me what I want, that's fine. If she doesn't, I get to do the series."

Standing up and striding to the door with purpose, Gin looked back at me and said, "Thanks so much for . . . clarifyin' everything." Then she blew me a kiss and was gone.

I hadn't done a thing except listen to her. I raised the sandwich, opened my mouth, and was about to take my second bite of the evening when Bridget Innes said from the doorway, "Do you want to see me now?"

"Sure," I lied. "Come in and sit."

She took the chair that had been occupied by Gin. She sat rigidly, leaning forward, as if she expected to be fired or worse.

"So what's the deal with Juan?" I asked.

"Just a mistake," she said.

"There are degrees of mistakes," I said. "Sprinkling cayenne pepper on sweet rolls instead of cinnamon. The invasion of Iraq."

"This is closer to the cayenne-pepper example," she said. "Juan and I . . . had a thing. I guess he was into it a little more than I was."

"I guess. When did the breakup occur?"

"Well, five days ago I realized I'd fallen in love with somebody else. And when I told Juan, he closed down. You know how he gets."

"No, I don't," I said. "But so I understand the situation, you told him about your new romance tonight and he swung on you?"

"No. I told him, oh, three days ago," she said. "And I could see he didn't like it, but he just moped and walked away."

"What got him going tonight?"

"Well, when I went in the bar with a drinks order, he called me a *puta*. And I called him a one-legged asshole. And that's when he slapped me. But it's okay now. It was just a flash anger thing. I like Juan. I didn't want to hurt him, but the heart knows what the heart needs."

Holy heartburn and thank you, Dr. Phil!

"Okay," I told her, "I think I've got the picture. You feeling okay?"

"Oh, yeah. Sure. My face stung for a few minutes is all. But I'm fine."

"Good. Then you'd better get back to work."

She stood. "You're not going to fire Juan? He really needs the job."

"I hope I won't have to," I said, liking her a little better for having said that.

Alone at last, I turned my attention to the sandwich. It looked a little soggy now, but I ate it anyway. Then I drank the wine and thought about love and all its vagaries.

Then I went to bed.

Chapter

SIX

"Pick you up at eleven?" my driver Joe asked as he braked near the elevator bank in the Glass Tower's Midtown underground parking area. "Or is this day not usual?"

"It's very usual," I said, exiting the Volvo, blissfully unaware of what a lousy prophet I was. "You think you might get the car washed?"

"No. It start looking too good, somebody steals it."

He didn't wait for an argument, not that I had one.

As he aimed the dirtmobile toward the exit, he swerved to avoid a rider in yellow leather zooming in on a motorcycle. The newcomer parked a few feet from me, dismounted, and removed his black helmet. He peeled off a glove and hand-combed his long blond locks, regarding me with sleepy blue eyes. He put a grin on his pale poet's face and said, "Yo, Bless-*sing,* wha's happ-a-*ning*?"

Chuck Slater was *Wake Up, America!*'s new film and television critic. Barely in his twenties, Chuck had gained fame as an Internet blogger and host of the popular website Flicpic.com. He was an arrogant, impatient young movie nut, either overly effusive in his reviews or devastatingly brutal. Quite the opposite of our former entertainment critic, George Miles, a Pulitzer Prize–winning twenty-year veteran of the *Washington Post,* whose critiques were thoughtful and informed. Unfortunately, all that experience meant nothing to management except that George was getting on in years. Which in turn meant that he had to be out of touch with our audience. Unlike Mr. Slater.

"Nice bike, Chuck," I said.

"Sy-kel, baby, not bike. Ka-wa-saki Z One Thousand. A kick-ass machine. You oughta get yourself one, Bless-sing."

"I'll go out right after the show and buy one," I said, pressing the button for the elevator, "if you can name the director of *The Seventh Seal.*"

He frowned. "Real cute, Bless-sing. You know I don't waste my time on kiddie flicks."

We were among the last to arrive at Studio 2.

Stepping into the vast array of sets, wires, cameras, monitors, and bustling people, Chuck took one look at anchorman Lance Tuttle and said, "Damn. I forgot it's Western Day."

Lance was wearing a fake handlebar mustache, a ten-gallon hat, a starched white shirt, black trousers as tight as Gene Autry's, and hand-tooled boots with heels that brought him nearly up to six feet. He waved to us and yelled, "Howdy, pod-ners."

On occasion, usually a holiday like Halloween or St. Pat's, the show took on a special look, with decorations, costumes, and theme-appropriate guests. That day we were celebrating the old Wild West. Why? The ostensible reason was that the Professional Bull Riders were in town holding an exhibition at Madison Square Garden; some of them would be dropping by to talk up the contest and shake hands with the street crowd. But more important to the network, we would be promoting *The Golden Lady,* a dramedy set in a San Francisco casino during the 1849 gold rush that, judging by its ratings, needed all the publicity it could get.

"I hate this bullshit," Chuck grumbled. "They're making me dress up like an Indian. Hell, you'd make a better Indian, Blessing."

"Thank you, Chuck, but they see me as more of a General Custer type."

"You're shitting me, right?"

"Yes, I am shitting you, Chuck," I said, and headed for my dressing room/office.

Before I could get there, Gin McCauley, done up in Ultrasuede pants and shirt, Calamity Jane–style, called out, "Billy, mah hero!" She ran to me, hugged me, and kissed me on the cheek. "Thank you, thank you," she whispered in my ear.

"For what?" I asked.

"For bein' you," she said.

Before I could press for a slightly more specific answer, she was on her way across the floor to where our producer, Arnie Epps, was chatting with Lance. Both men stopped talking, looked at Gin, then at me, and frowned. Actually, it was more of a scowl. Two scowls.

Puzzling over that, I wandered into the dressing room my assistant, Kiki Owens, had been slowly transforming into an office over the past few years. She was seated at a Formica-topped desk, typing away at a computer.

Kiki is a tiny, thin, seemingly fragile black woman who, though attractive, consists primarily of brain, bone, and muscle. She can get any job done if she puts her mind to it. Her role in life was helped by a British accent, earned by birthright, that, depending on her mood, fluctuated from charming to brutally intimidating.

She gave me a disappointed look and said, "Today's a 'special' costume show, Billy. And you're late."

"My bad. I sort of put it out of my head."

"I got Arnie to sign off on your cowboy costume," she told me. "He gave someone else the Indian outfit."

"I know," I said, smiling. "Thanks."

"I told him about your feather allergy. But I don't think he believes it any more than I do."

"It's just the whole deal—the paint on the face, the feather headdress. I think it's demeaning to Indians. Like asking me to wear a bone in my nose."

"We'll save that worry for Jungle Day," Kiki said. "Now I think you should change into your outfit and go to makeup as quickly as you can. Lo and Jolly have been popping in and out for the last twenty minutes, looking ever more anxious." Lo and Jolly were our cosmetics artistes.

The costume that I'd handpicked consisted of a white ten-gallon hat, a black shirt and white string tie, tight gray pants, and black boots. And, of course, a black leather holster with twin shootin' irons. When Lo, a very round Jamaican-American woman who had been with the show longer than I, finished removing my facial sheen and applying a thin mustache, I purposely avoided looking in the mirror. I wanted to preserve the mental image of myself as Herbert Jeffrey, the handsome cowboy star of the old movies my father would pop into the video player when I was a kid. The actor went on to sing with Duke Ellington's band as Herb Jeffries and become one of the top vocalists of the forties, but to me, he'll always be the heroic "Bronze Buckaroo" and "Two-Gun Man from Harlem" who rode the plains on a small black-and-white TV set in our living room.

Channeling the non-singing Herbert, I galloped through the morning, palavering with the bull riders while howdying the visitors lined up outside on the street, joining trail cook Buck Parminter in rustlin' up some gold-rush griddle cakes, and introducing the C&W singing group The Sons of Sacramento.

We were nearing the end of our third half-hour segment when I sensed a shift in the on-set atmosphere. Usually, we're crisp, fresh, and a little brittle at the start of the show, unless there's breaking news or a special guest to create an immediate burst of energy. Toward the end of the first half-hour segment, we've loosened up a bit. During the third half-hour we're relaxed enough to goof around.

But not that day.

I noticed there was whispering among the crew members and a tension in the air. At the start of the show, coanchors Lance and Gin had been gleefully outdrawing each other. Now it looked as if they wished they were carrying real guns. When news anchor Tori Dillard delivered a report on progress in the Middle East peace talks, she sounded so glum, you'd have thought a new war had broken out. Chuck Slater, interviewing a starlet from *The Golden Lady* show, angrily tore off his Indian headdress on camera and then tossed a wet blanket over the actress's effervescence by reminding her of the show's low ratings.

But it was our eccentric, usually genial meteorologist, Professor Lloyd Sebastian, transformed by Lo and Jolly's magic into Randolph Scott's crusty old sidekick, Gabby Hayes, who made me realize something was definitely amiss. Lloyd approached me, even more sour-faced than Gabby, and said, "I thought we were friends, Billy."

"We are friends, Lloyd."

"Actions speak louder than words," he said, before returning to his green screen.

What the what?

The show's closing theme had barely stopped playing when Kiki informed me that Gretchen Di Voss wanted me in the conference room immediately.

"What's up?" I asked.

"Her assistant didn't say. But . . ."

"What?"

"I've heard grumbling about . . . you and Gin." Kiki looked at me expectantly.

"What about us?"

"I assumed you'd know."

"Well, I don't."

She shrugged. "I imagine Gretchen will clear it up," she said.

Chapter

SEVEN

It was Rudy Gallagher who did the clearing.

He and Gretch were in the conference room with the old man himself, the company's CEO Commander Vernon Di Voss. None of them seemed too happy to see me. I didn't think it was because my costume reminded them of Herb Jeffries. Gretch was scowling. The commander, in obvious discomfort, studied an unlighted cigar as intently as if it contained tomorrow's overnights.

Rudy looked like he was about to start foaming at the mouth.

"Who the hell told you to stick your nose in this company's business?" he roared.

"What are you talking about?"

"You're gonna deny you put her up to it?"

"Put who up to what?" I asked.

"I'd worked out a reasonable deal with Fred and Hildy," Gretchen said. "And then you had to put your oar in the water."

Fred and Hildy. Gin's agent and manager. *My nose. My oar.* I was starting to get the drift of things. "This is about the conversation I had with Gin last night at the Bistro?"

"Conversation?" Rudy yelled. "I'd call it a goddamned *battle plan.*"

"That's a little dramatic, isn't it, Rudy? All I did was listen to what she had to say and nod from time to time."

"That was some fu—" Rudy glanced at the old man and self-censored. "Some bloody expensive nodding."

"The little lady hardballed us but good," the commander said, shifting his attention from the cigar to me.

"How hard?" I asked.

There was a sudden silence. Gretch broke it. "It's no longer a secret. Fifteen million a year for the next three years."

I blinked at her in disbelief. "Fifteen million dollars? Nobody's worth that kind of loot, unless they're wearing a sports jersey and testing negative."

"You're beautiful, Blessing," Rudy said. "First you instruct that little bi—*witch* to hold us up, then you have the gall to criticize Gretchen for making the deal."

"I didn't tell Gin to hold you up. And I'm not criticizing anybody, except maybe you for calling your very valuable superstar a bi—*witch*."

"It's not just the fifteen mil," Rudy continued, as if I hadn't spoken. "It's what this does to the budget of a show I'm exec-producing. Everybody thinks the contract bar has been raised. They must've speed-dialed their agents as soon as the word spread. I've been fielding calls for the last hour, explaining that nobody else is getting a bump.

"But I do know how we're gonna save a few bucks. You're through here, Blessing. Pack up your pots and pans and get the hell out."

"Hold on there, Rudy," the commander said. "Let's just cool down a little and let Billy explain himself."

I gave them a quick rundown of my chat with Gin. "If I'd mentioned the words 'fifteen million dollars,' they would have stuck in my throat, Commander, especially considering what *I'm* being paid."

The old man gave me his paternal grin. "Well, I'm not sure your participation in this matter merits a *raise,* but neither do I think it merits a dismissal."

He turned to his daughter. "Gretchen, my sweet, I hope you've alerted Heck Cochran about the new contract." Hector Cochran was the VP in charge of promotion and public relations. "I want Gin on every talk show in the free world, even Howard Stern's, and I expect to see her charming freckled mug smiling back at me from magazine racks everywhere. In other words, I will be quite vexed if we do not get a dollar-per-dollar value back in publicity."

It was his exit speech, but before he and Gretchen could make it to the door, Rudy said, "Just a second, Commander. That's it? Blessing cost this company millions and we just blow it off?"

"Weren't you listening, Rudy?" the old man said. "Billy just told us that he did not advise Gin to ask for more money."

"You believe that?"

"You're a relative newcomer to our operation, my boy," the commander told him. "Billy's been with us long enough he's like one of the family. Shouldn't one trust members of one's family?"

As soon as the commander and his daughter had exited the conference room, Rudy spun around facing me and said through clenched teeth, "Well, you're not part of my fuckin' family, Blessing. I'm disowning your ass. You can forget about the *Food School* pilot."

"It's your show, but Lily and I have worked out some of the kinks and—"

"I also plan to take a long, hard look at *Blessing's in the Kitchen,*" he said, interrupting me. "There are definitely some changes to be made there. Maybe we should get one of the hot new chefs to share the kitchen, one of the shaved-head muscle boys who do tae kwon do while filleting a sole. Bring in a younger demo."

He gave me a zero-mirth grin. "The old man won't let me can your ass, but there are lots of ways to cook a goose, right, chef?"

"That's true, Rudy," I said. "But unless you know what you're doing, you just might get burned." A careless comment that would come back to haunt me.

Chapter

EIGHT

Gin's new proactive positioning on the morning show did away with the spare moments in the past when we'd both been free to do quick coffee catch-ups between segments. And as soon as the closing credits rolled each day, Heck Cochran's people whisked her off on publicity errands. So after the first week, I stopped trying to link up with her to find out why she'd embroiled me in her now-infamous contract negotiations.

Time had made the point moot, anyway. My on-camera associates apparently had been arm-wrestled by Rudy into staying satisfied with their admittedly lucrative lots. And their old self-involved but generally pleasant attitudes returned. Even Rudy seemed to have reached the stage where he could look at me without frowning.

As best I could tell, he'd not followed through on his threat to banish me from the *Food School* pilot or to mess with *Blessing's in the Kitchen*. I suspected the commander may have had something to do with that. Or maybe Rudy had just been too busy with other matters to bother. He certainly seemed distracted.

By the time I finally did bump into Gin one morning, minutes before the start of *WUA!,* her contract was old news. The blogosphere blaze had cooled down and her picture no longer graced newspaper front pages, though the tag "The Fifteen-Million-Dollar Woman," bestowed on her by the *Post,* lived on.

"It's been a while since we talked," I said.

"I know, Billy. It's been so hectic. But I love it."

At six-forty-three a.m. Gin was glowing like the midday sun. And it wasn't the makeup. Her boyfriend, Ted Parkhurst, was a lucky buck but also, I thought, something of an idiot for continuing to work on other continents when his rep as a journalist was such that he could probably have found something closer to Manhattan to write about.

"I'm getting everything I've always wanted, Billy," she said. "And it's all because of you." She warmed me with a look that, to my jaded eyes, came damn close to adoration. "My guru."

"That's very flattering, Gin. But I really didn't do anything. I certainly didn't tell you to hit them for fifteen mil."

"You gave me confidence."

"Didn't you tell me it wasn't about money?" I said.

"Well, it wasn't when *we* talked. But then Gretchen seemed really set on keepin' me on *Wake Up!* She asked me what it would take for me to stick aroun' for another three years, and I kinda flashed on Katie Couric gettin' fifteen million from CBS and thought, heck, she's only on for a half-hour every evenin'."

"Gretchen didn't even blink?" I asked.

"Oh, she went through the usual. 'There's not enough in the budget.' 'These are times of economic uncertainty.' Bla-bla-bla. That's when my team started remindin' Gretchen of my TVQ and threatenin' her with the possibility of my poppin' up opposite *WUA!* on *The Early Show* or *Good Morning America.* Then they played with the numbers a little. The thing that finally turned the trick was my agreein' to read ad copy."

Way back when John Chancellor anchored the *Today* show, he established a rule that anchors remain apart from any form of commercial activity. He thought it undercut their effectiveness as objective observers of daily events. Other network news executives agreed, apparently, because it became a sort of industry standard. But that razor-thin line, like the one separating reportage from opinion, has worn away.

"So now you're making twice as much as Charlie Gibson," I said.

Gin beamed. "And three times as much as macho-man Lance. And you know what, Billy? With the money comes respect."

"Who'd have thought?" I said.

"I definitely would not be doing the interview with Carl Kelstoe this morning if I weren't the fifteen-million-dollar woman. And I owe it all to you." She gave me a brief hug and literally danced across the floor to get ready for the start of the show.

There seemed to be no way of convincing her that I'd had little to do with her good fortune. It would have served no purpose for me to mention that she'd unknowingly put my career in jeopardy. She was floating on air, and I didn't want her to feel any guilt if Rudy did decide to cook my goose.

I was surprised that he wasn't on the set, spreading his usual malcontent. When I mentioned it to Kiki, she said, "I sensed there was a lightness to the day. Was there something you wanted from him?"

"Not in this lifetime," I said, and left my dressing room to check the progress of the barbecued ribs I'd be playing with near the end of the hour.

Gin's interview with Carl Kelstoe, the president of Touchstone International, considered by some to be the world's largest security company, took place shortly after the news segment that kicked off the second hour of the show.

Touchstone mercenaries working for this country had been accused of starting a riot eleven months ago in Afghanistan's Helmand Province that resulted in the deaths of seven NATO soldiers and five Afghan soldiers, with nineteen pedestrians left wounded. Kelstoe was making the rounds on the news shows, doing public-relations damage control, before heading to D.C. to appear before a congressional committee studying the cause of the riot.

Watching the interview from the control booth, I was fascinated by the merc master. He must have been six-four, with a crew-cut king-size head atop a thick neck and a body that resembled Superman's, clothed in a gray gabardine suit that had been perfectly tailored to fit his v-shaped physique. According to stereotype, a guy that big should have been slow and maybe even a little mentally deficient. But Kelstoe was agile, of both body and mind.

As Camera 2 zoomed in for a close-up, the monitor picked up eyes so light brown they were almost golden. Kelstoe focused them on Gin as if she was the center of his universe.

Looking at his rugged mug, I guessed that most men would want to be his friend and most women would at least think about being his lover. Thanks to my misspent youth, I had a different take. I pegged him right off as a sociopath, the kind Shakespeare said "would smile, and smile, and be a villain."

In his seemingly guileless way, and in a whispery voice that might have been distinctive if Clint Eastwood had never gone to Italy, Kelstoe told Gin and our viewers that it would have been impossible for his expertly trained men to have acted the way the province officials claimed.

"The incident occurred just weeks after the end of Operation Mountain Thrust," he said, "and there was a high degree of confusion and tension in the province." His was the soft but mesmerizing voice of a snake oil salesman shrewd enough to make it sound like the voice of reason. "The so-called 'innocent civilian' my men had stopped was in fact an armed Taliban insurgent who was there to cause trouble. My men stopped him, ordered him to surrender his weapon. He refused, shouting and cursing them. It was a tense situation. And then someone in the crowd—I think we can safely assume it was another Taliban member—threw a rock that hit one of my men. His gun went off and regrettably killed the man they had stopped.

"That's when all hell broke loose. I'm sorry—can I say 'hell' on television?"

"It's your story," Gin said.

"Well, anyway, the crowd started stoning my guys, and two of them fell. Their weapons were yanked from their hands and used on the arriving troops. It was a terrible tragedy, but I'm not sure what else my guys could have done once that rock was thrown."

At that point Lance would probably have closed down the interview and wished Kelstoe well. Gin may have done that, too, a few weeks ago. But no longer. Not since she'd become the Fifteen-Million-Dollar Woman.

"It's been reported that your mercenary soldier fired the shot before the rock was thrown, that it was thrown because he'd used his gun on a man who was doing nothing more incendiary than brushing against him on a narrow walkway."

"I've had over a year to investigate this," Kelstoe replied, "to study exactly what transpired every single second of that deadly event. If I had discovered one thing to make me believe any of my men were responsible for that tragedy, I would say so."

"The congressional committee may see things differently," Gin said. "Am I right in assuming that whichever way the decision goes, you could wind up losing the lucrative contract Touchstone has with our State Department?"

"I don't see that happening." Kelstoe's smile started to harden, and his whispery voice showed a hint of anger.

"But you have lost important contracts since the incident, right?" Gin asked.

"I'm not sure exactly what you're referencing. . . ."

"I'm thinking of Markham Books," Gin said. "Until recently, the publisher has used Touchstone to ensure the safety of its more controversial authors on their book tours. But when ex–Mossad agent Goyal Aharon arrives later this week to promote his debut spy thriller, your main competitor, InterTec, will be guarding him. Isn't this a result of the investigation into Touchstone?"

That wiped the smile from Kelstoe's face. "It's just business," he replied tersely. "You win some and you lose some. With our operations in Afghanistan and Iraq, and an unmatched success rate, we've got quite a lot on our plate right now."

"But you can't deny that a negative report from the committee would clean that plate a little?"

Kelstoe glared at her and, just for an instant, dropped his protective shield and exposed a naked ruthlessness. Then the shield snapped back in place and he said, "More likely, when Congress hears the full story, Touchstone will be needing a nice, big platter."

I'd had enough of the dishware metaphor, and of him. As I turned away, I saw that the commander had made one of his rare visits to the control booth. He was staring at Kelstoe with such intensity that I asked if he was all right.

It took him a few seconds to break loose from his thoughts. "I'm fine," he said with uncharacteristic annoyance. "Why shouldn't I be? And where the hell is Rudy?"

Ah, if we'd only known.

Chapter

NINE

"I'm sorry, Billy, sorry I hurt Bridget, sorry I let you down," Juan Lorinda said with what appeared to be sincerity. We were in my office at the restaurant several hours shy of the time Juan was hoping to be shaking and stirring his first cocktails of the evening at the bar downstairs. He'd certainly prepped for the job. His cheeks were clean of stubble, his brown eyes bright and imploring. His hair was freshly cut close to the scalp. His shirt was starched and a brilliant white; the pleats of his black trousers were razor-sharp. I caught the scent of bay rum in the air.

It had been two weeks since he'd slapped my waitress and his former girlfriend, Bridget Innes. He'd said he wanted to "spend some time getting my head back on straight" before returning to work. The two weeks had been his annual paid vacation. If he took a third, he'd be on his own.

"You sure you're ready?" I asked. "As much as our customers might enjoy a little violence with their pear martinis, I don't want any more of it."

"I . . . I know. It was . . . It won't happen again."

"Bridget gave me her version of the situation. I never did hear yours."

He cleared his throat and sat straighter in the chair. "No big story. I jus' had feelings for her. I *have* feelings for her. But she don't have the same feelings for me anymore. She's makin' it with some other dude. And I know I got to get past that."

"Identifying the problem is a good first step," I said. "But I want you to be straight with me. And yourself. Getting past a busted romance can take a while."

"I'm ready, Billy. I really wanna work, to keep busy. That way, I don't think about . . . you know."

Like most recovering romantics, I was familiar with what he was going through. But unlike most of us, he wanted to do it in my bar. "What happens tonight when Bridget comes in with her first drink order?"

He took a deep breath. "I suck it up and fill the order," he said. "The next time, and the next, and the next, it'll get easier."

"And when you start feeling sorry for yourself, or you see her being nice to a customer? You call her a *puta* again?"

"No, sir," he said. "I got control now. I can do this, Billy. I'll be strong. I've handled worse things."

Indeed he had.

"Okay, Juan, let's see how it goes," I said, and watched him make his exit with the awkward lurch of a man whose right leg was metal from the thigh down.

A few minutes later, with nothing on my mind except the profit-and-loss numbers dancing across my computer monitor and the haunting melody of Billy Strayhorn's "Waters of March" on my iPod, I looked up in surprise to see Cassandra standing a few feet from my desk with two burly strangers.

I blacked out the monitor screen and popped out the ear buds in time to hear her say, ". . . detectives Joshua Solomon and Norman Butker."

Solomon was in his late forties, a few inches shorter than his partner, with a gray bulldog face and full lips that looked incomplete without a chewed cigar. Near his right eye was a scar containing black specks that might have been the result of gunpowder burns. He was wearing a dark-brown leather driving jacket over his shirt and tie.

Butker, a decade or more younger, was a black man with an un-pruned mustache, matching eyebrows, and a scalp full of shiny, curly hair. He was wearing a dark suit that fit him well. He stayed a half-step back from Solomon, clearly identifying Solomon as the alpha dog of the partnership.

The alpha dog flashed his badge but showed no interest in any pleasantry like shaking hands, so I remained seated. I assumed that their visit had been prompted by the Juan-Bridget spat, but I couldn't imagine who'd made the complaint. I put a curious look on my face and asked, "Detectives, what can I do for you?"

"We've got some questions about you and your restaurant here," Solomon said matter-of-factly.

I felt a twinge of annoyance but kept my face blank. "Don't tell me they've passed a law against serving gourmet meals?" I asked.

"Interesting you should bring up your meals," Solomon said. "We're not the Food Police, Mr. Blessing. We're from Homicide West."

"Who's dead?" I asked, Juan and Bridget still on my mind.

Solomon looked at Cassandra and said, "Thanks for your help, honey. We can take it from here."

"Ms. Shaw is my trusted assistant, detective," I said quickly, before Cassandra had a chance to respond. "I'd like her to hear whatever you have to say." One of the life lessons I've learned is that when conversing with homicide detectives, it's always a good idea to have a witness who's not on their team.

Solomon shrugged and said, "We understand you were an associate of one Rudyard M. Gallagher?"

"Were?"

"Yeah. That association went past tense last night when somebody murdered Mr. Gallagher."

No matter how hard you try to remain cool, there are times when you just can't keep your jaw from dropping.

"When did you see him last?" Solomon asked.

"He wasn't at work this morning." I paused to think. "Yesterday, I guess. Around ten or so."

"Ten at night?" Butker asked.

"No. In the morning, just after our show went off the air. When did it hap—?"

"You didn't see him last night?" Solomon interrupted me to ask.

"No."

"He wasn't in this restaurant last night?" Butker asked.

"That I don't know," I said. "If he was, I didn't see him. Cassandra?"

She shook her head no. "He comes in . . . came in from time to time," she said. "But not last night."

"Where were you last night, Mr. Blessing?" Butker asked. "Between six and, let's say, midnight?"

"Here. I was in the building from about four p.m., when I got back from various errands. I was downstairs or in this office until about ten-thirty, when I went to bed. I'm on television very early in the morning."

Solomon turned to Cassandra. "That about right?"

She nodded. I could tell by her frown that she was still simmering from his referring to her as "honey."

"You testify to that?" Solomon asked her.

"Hang on for a minute," I said. "I'm a suspect?"

"Like they say in every crappy cop show on the TV, we're just trying to eliminate everybody we can," Solomon said. "So, ma'am, was Mr. Blessing in this building between six and midnight?"

"Yes. I did not actually see him go to sleep, but I can and will testify that I did not see him leave the building during the hours you mentioned."

"How'd Rudy die?" I asked.

"He was . . ." Butker began, but stopped when the alpha dog nearly bit him.

"How would you have killed him, Mr. Blessing?" Solomon asked.

"I don't kill people," I said. "Murder's a crime and a sin."

"Good answer," Solomon said. "Oh, I almost forgot to mention: We're closing your restaurant down, as of now."

"What are you talking about?"

He pulled a folded sheet of paper from an inside breast pocket of his jacket and dropped it on my desk. "This is a warrant for us to search the building, stem to stern," Solomon said.

"Why, in God's name?"

"Because, according to Mr. Gallagher's fiancée, you and he weren't exactly the best of friends. And according to the plastic carryout containers at his condo, which is where a cleaning lady found his body this afternoon, he was probably poisoned by food from this joint."

Chapter

TEN

I spent the next couple of hours in a sort of nightmarish stupor, watching uniform and plainclothes cops and a cadre of technicians, geeky and coolly impersonal, trooping through my restaurant. Some probed the nooks and crannies, while others eagle-eyed members of the staff who were doing what they could to refrigerate the unprepared ingredients and foods that would have been used for the night's servings—servings that were now officially canceled.

Once the salvage operation was complete, the interrogations began. First the kitchen staff, and then, as they arrived, the waiters, bartenders, and busboys.

Solomon and Butker focused on me.

They took me through an hour-by-hour chronology of how I'd spent the previous night, which they would later compare to similar chronologies taken from Cassandra and the others. Then the detectives moved on to more specific questions.

Could I have left the building for just a few minutes? Long enough to hand-deliver Gallagher's dinner?

"Neither I nor anybody working here hand-delivers dinners to anybody," I informed them.

Did I have any idea how the food could have been transported from the restaurant to Gallagher's apartment?

"We do offer a takeout service," I said. "I suppose Rudy might have come in without Cassandra noticing. Or maybe he had a friend pick it up for him. Did it look like he had a friend for dinner?"

"Naw, looks like he ate by himself," Butker said. "But somebody made a mess of the condo. Place was seriously trash—"

"We ask the questions, Mr. Blessing," Solomon said, scowling at his partner.

"Okay, ask away," I said.

"You ever been in the victim's apartment?" Solomon wanted to know.

"No."

"Weren't there last night, throwing books around, cutting up the furniture, looking for something?"

"I've never been in his apartment," I said. " 'Never' would include last night."

"Think of any reason why your fingerprints might have been found there?"

"They could have been on some object I touched at the studio that Mr. Gallagher took home. Did you find my prints on something?"

"You kill him, Mr. Blessing?" Butker asked, ignoring my question.

"No."

"That's it for now, then," Solomon said.

"Great," I said. "No apologies?"

"For what?" Solomon asked.

"You have any idea how many thousands of dollars you're gonna cost me in food and customers?"

"I'd be worrying about other things, I was you."

"Like what?"

"Like the rat poison we found in your kitchen," Solomon said.

"We use traps," I said. "Not poison."

"Yeah, well, this stuff was taken off the market a while ago, so maybe you haven't been using it lately. Least not on rats. The fact that it's so old should help the lab figure out if it's the same Squill that spiced up Gallagher's last meal. That'll be when you got real worries."

"What was his last meal?" I asked.

Solomon hesitated, then said, "No harm in tellin' you, I guess. Looked like chicken in some kinda gravy, what was left of it."

"Coq au vin," I said, remembering it was one of last night's specials.

"If that's what you call it," Solomon said.

"What was he drinking?"

Another pause. "Red wine."

"Couldn't the poison have been in the wine?"

Solomon frowned. "Hell, I don't know. Won't, until the lab tells me."

"But you're assuming it was in the food from my restaurant," I said.

"Who's to say the wine didn't come from here, too?"

"How long before you're finished in my kitchen?"

"We won't be able to free it up for another . . . I don't know, twenty-four hours."

"In other words, no lunch or dinner tomorrow, either," I said.

"Could be worse," Solomon told me. "Oh, by the way, not that it's any big shocker, but there's no record of Gallagher's takeout. No credit card receipt at his place. You didn't happen to see it when you tore up his apartment?"

I didn't bother to respond to the question. "Check our receipts here," I said.

"We did. Nothing with his name on it from last night. Nobody remembers seeing him in the restaurant. We've got the hard drives from your security-camera setup. We'll check the footage for people coming in for takeout. Maybe we'll see a familiar face. Have a pleasant evening, Mr. Blessing."

As soon as they left, I went looking for Cassandra. She was in the bar area, being ogled by two uniformed cops who didn't seem to have anything better to do with their time. She was ignoring them while phoning customers who'd made reservations for dinner that night.

I informed her that she'd have to add tomorrow's lunch and dinner reservation holders to the list. She gave me an annoyed look, then turned to the cops and gave them the finger. Misplaced aggression.

Cutting through the main dining room, I saw that the police had finished interviewing about half the staff. The remaining members were seated at tables, waiting to be called.

Juan and Bridget were sitting side by side. He gawked at her lovingly. She seemed either distracted or apprehensive. I watched him reach over and take her hand. She didn't seem to mind. Even gave him a sweet smile. For a reward like that, I guessed he'd be willing to have a police interrogation every day.

When I got back to my desk, the digital clock indicated it was a little after six, but I put in a call to my attorney anyway. Wallace A. Wing picked up on the second ring. His assistant probably left at five. "Yo, Billy," he said, motormouthing as always. "Like I told you, don't worry about the pilot. Way I structured the contracts, even if the son of a bitch decides to try, he can't dump you or Lily without paying some heavy coin."

"The son of a bitch isn't going to be dumping me or anyone, Wally. He's dead. Murdered. And they've locked down my restaurant."

"Murdered? Holy shit. And they locked you down? Why? It can't have anything to do with him kicking you from the pilot?"

It's funny the way people get stuck on a subject, especially when they get ten percent of that subject. "Forget the pilot, Wally. I don't think the detectives know anything about it. At least, they didn't mention it."

"Then . . . ?"

I told him what little I knew about the situation.

"That's it? You and Gallagher weren't best buds and it was your takeout the killer doctored? Doesn't sound like much of a case."

"They don't have any case that I can see," I told him. "But they've closed me down tonight, and they want to keep me closed all day tomorrow. Is there anything you can do?"

"Call you back," he said.

Half an hour later, Wally returned the call.

"You only gave me half the story, dude. It's not just a couple cops closing the restaurant. DA Philip Rodell is riding herd on this, and he is one angry buckaroo. How'd you piss him off?"

"Short story not worth mentioning," I said. "How much trouble am I in?"

"If they get anything remotely resembling hard evidence, Rodell will move to indict. Billy, I'm out of my depth in a criminal case. Why don't we put Fritz Brocton on standby?" Brocton, Barger, and McAllister was the firm of choice for top-of-the-news murder suspects.

"How much will it cost me?"

"Not much. Unless you have to use him. Then you can dust off your white jacket, dude. Because Fritz does not play for pennies. You could wind up out on the street, or working in my dad's kitchen."

"I've seen your dad's kitchen. The street is cleaner."

"You got that right," he agreed. "I'll alert Fritz. What you do now is sit tight and put your faith in truth, justice, and the American way. And Fritz."

The hell with that, I thought as I replaced the receiver. I'm not about to let some half-smart killer and a pissed-off DA stick me with the tab for a murder I didn't commit.

I grabbed the phone and dialed a number I knew by heart. When a familiar voice answered, I said, "Hi, Gretchen. How are you holding up?"

"What do you want, Billy?" The words were as cold as gazpacho.

"To offer my condolences."

"Thank you," she said. "Now, if you'll excuse me . . ."

"Gretch, you told the police that Rudy and I didn't get along."

"Well, you didn't."

"We had disagreements," I said, "but they weren't the kind of things that lead to murder, for God's sake. I don't have a violent bone in my body. But now the cops are all over me. They closed down the Bistro."

"The police, a boorish detective named Solomon, said that the poisoned coq au vin came from the Bistro," she said. "That seems reason enough for them to close it down."

"They're not even sure it was the food that was poisoned," I said. "And even if it was, anybody could have done that after it left here. Maybe somebody who was with him."

"Rudy dined alone last night."

"How do you know that?"

"I . . . I called him earlier in the evening. Maybe six-thirty. He'd just arrived home. He said he was worn out, that he was looking forward to a good night's sleep."

"He didn't say anything about his plans for dinner?"

"No. Just that he was exhausted. He'd been feeling tired ever since he returned from the Middle East. And then there was the pressure from all the damned agents wanting to renegotiate contracts. Which he blamed on you, with good reason."

"Gretch, you can't really believe I murdered Rudy."

There was silence on the line for a few beats. Then: "No. Of course not, Billy. I just don't want to think about it at all. I don't even know what I'm saying anymore. I'm going to stay with Dad at the manor house for a while. It's not good my being here alone."

"I'm really sorry you have to go through this."

"I . . . I shouldn't have told that detective about you and Rudy," she said. "It was spiteful."

"Don't worry about it," I said. "Just take care of yourself. I'll be fine."

I cradled the phone and considered what I should do to make that last statement ring true.

Gretch's comment about her fiancé feeling tired every night prompted me to drag the *Food School 101* file from the desk drawer. I'd been keeping it handy ever since Rudy said he was going to can me from the pilot. I flipped through it until I found the address I wanted.

I was putting the file away when Cassandra entered the office. "This place is a frigging mess, Billy. And it's like low tide out on the street. Paparazzi and reporters and gawkers."

"Perfect," I said. "Just the kind of publicity we need. How'd things go with the reservation crowd?"

"I caught most of them. A lot of unhappy customers. The ones I couldn't reach are going to be even more unhappy when they arrive. Especially when they find unwashed paparazzi instead of dinner."

"I guess you'll have to stay at the door," I said. "Tell the customers who do make it past the press gauntlet that we're sorry. And try to sound like you mean it."

"Everybody's asking why we're closed. I've been stonewalling them, telling them I don't know."

"Might as well tell them the truth. You can bet it's already on TV and the Web. And the papers will have it by morning. Just say we're cooperating with the NYPD on a criminal investigation. If they ask for specifics, refer them to the cops and your buddy District Attorney Rodell."

"Rodell? Oh, shit. Is it my fault they closed us down?"

"Not unless you poisoned Gallagher," I said. "Rodell is just a self-important little weasel, taking advantage of the situation. I don't suppose you made a copy of that front-door footage with him and the hooker?"

"No copy. But it's on the security disks."

"The detectives took the disks," I said, standing and grabbing my coat. "I want you to do a couple of things. I need an exact count of how many coq au vin dinners were served last night and a list of who paid for 'em. Meanwhile, keep trying to reach the reservation holders you missed."

"Where are you going?" she asked as I headed for the door.

"You don't expect me to just sit here and let Rodell and his pals build a case against me? I'm going to try and find some other suspects to throw at 'em."

Cassandra frowned. "There are people you hire to do that, Billy. Private investigators. Pros who know what they're doing."

I considered telling her that I was not exactly a novice at reading the signs of guilt. That shortly after my mother's death, my unofficial stepfather, Paul Lamont, the wily confidence man, and I had traveled the country, living off of the gullibility of the greedy and the dishonest. I could have explained that my teens had been filled not merely with the education received at a long list of ever-changing schools but with Paul's lectures and on-the-job training in discovering the evil hidden in some human hearts.

But these were my secrets to keep hidden, so instead I said, "Hiring an investigator costs money. And at the rate things are going, money may be in short supply around here. Anyway, it's all a matter of prying information out of people, which is what I do every morning on *Wake Up*."

"The people you interview aren't potential murderers, Billy."

"You should watch the show more often," I told her.

Chapter

ELEVEN

To avoid the crowd out front, I used the rear exit.

Night had just fallen, and I strolled through it for a block before flagging a cab.

The address I gave the driver belonged to a pale-orange brick apartment building in the West Fifties. The green awning was faded and, judging by the debris gathered in the stairwell to the basement entrance, the smudges on the glass front door left by a hundred fingers, the junk mail and freebie tabloids cluttering the tiny vestibule, and the burnt-out bulbs in its cheap chandelier, the superintendent of the Corey Apartments wasn't very house-proud.

That made me wonder if instead of pressing a lot of buzzers and getting residents all stirred up I shouldn't just check to see if the door separating the apartments from the vestibule might be unlocked.

It was.

I decided to avoid the tiny and undoubtedly dangerous elevator. Instead, I climbed up three flights of carpeted stairwell. I arrived gasping from the exercise and the dust. I swore that as soon as this was over, I'd start working out. No joke.

According to her employment form, Melody Moon lived in apartment 319. The improbably named Ms. Moon was the beautiful black teenage chef wannabe who'd caught the eye of Rudy Gallagher at our ill-fated *Food School* pilot shoot.

There was a cartoon daisy painted at eye level on the dark wooden door to 319. I pressed the buzzer and almost immediately heard the slap of approaching feet.

"Who's there?" a feminine voice inquired.

"Billy Blessing."

There was a metallic click, and the bright-yellow center of the cartoon daisy was replaced by an eyeball.

"Wow," the voice said. "It *is* you."

Chains rattled. Locks unclicked. Eventually the door opened on an undernourished, milk-pale young woman in her twenties with spiked, dark-blue hair and a tattoo of the Batman logo on her arm. She was wearing a tattered tee featuring the cat and dog from the *Get Fuzzy* comic strip, pink cargo shorts, and matching flip-flops.

Definitely not Melody Moon.

"Wow," she said again. "Chef Billy Blessing. Come on in."

I entered a bright room with royal-blue walls trimmed in butter yellow. Rainbow-hued shag carpets were scattered on a light hardwood floor. Twin pink stuffed chairs flanked a large flat-screen TV/DVD player combo that had been trimmed in press-on zebra-striped paper. On the walls were anime cells and original comic art in frames that picked up the TV's zebra-stripe motif.

It was like walking onto a set at Cartoon Network.

"I guess you're looking for Melody," the young woman told me. "That's so sweet of you. She's out on a grocery run, but she'll be back soon. I'm her roommate, Rita Margolis."

She extended an ink-and-paint-stained hand with nails bitten to the quick. Her grip was firm and no-nonsense.

"Sit down," she suggested, indicating a maroon couch that seemed to have been made from densely packed sheets of cardboard. It was more comfortable than it looked, but then, it would have had to be.

"We don't really need the groceries," Rita said. "I just thought it was a good idea to keep Melody occupied. She's taking her fiancé's death really hard."

I let the fiancé comment go unquestioned. Instead I asked, "When did she find out?"

"It popped on the news a couple of hours ago. Melody freaked, but in a scary way. No tears. Just sort of froze, staring at the TV, even after I turned it off. Then she started talking, only, like, to herself, not to me."

"What was she saying?"

" 'This isn't happening. Rudy and I are in love.' Stuff like that. I feel so bad for her."

"Sounds like she might be in shock," I said.

"No. I know shock. I studied nursing, back before I began my creative phase. Melody's tough. I think she's just working it out.

"Like something to drink, chef? A cosmo? A negroni? Test me. I used to tend bar at Ganglion."

I'd never heard of Ganglion, which I suspected was a good thing. "I'm fine," I said.

In front of me was an antique footlocker standing in for a coffee table. Painted powder blue. Magazines and books and CDs were spread across its surface. I spied Rita's name on the cover of a comic book titled *Funny Girls*. "This yours?" I asked, picking it up.

"Yep," Rita said. "My little baby. I've been selling it on my website. Moved nearly two thousand copies at twelve ninety-five per, not including tax or postage. The girls on the cover, the three girls, have crazy adventures all over the world. They're bisexual, which adds to the fun. Both Eclipse Comics and HBO are very interested."

"Who wouldn't be?" I said. "You have a shot at twice the audience."

"I'm very proud of my work." She sat beside me and took the book from me. "Let me show you a few things." She sobered suddenly and gave me a hopeful look. "Assuming you really are interested."

"Beautiful and bisexual? Sounds like a party."

Though I'm no better judge of comic art than fine art, it seemed to me that Rita's work was professional and commercial. Her funny girls were drawn in an enhanced realistic style. Very beautiful, very shapely. Very, very bisexual. We were in the middle of an adventure in Rome, with Rita providing me with a detailed verbal annotation, when Melody Moon returned.

She was wearing jeans, a gray sweatshirt, and bright red tennis shoes. She stared at us blankly over the huge brown grocery bag she was carrying. She seemed neither surprised to find me in her living room nor curious about why I might be there.

"Look who's here to see you, Melody," Rita said, nervously breaking the silence.

"Let me get that," I said, relieving Melody of the heavy bag.

"Thank you," she said flatly, without affect. "I'll show you where it goes."

Walking stiffly, she led me to a tiny kitchenette just off the living room. It featured a two-burner, a microwave, a small fridge, a sink, and, squeezed beneath it, a mini-dishwasher. After I'd placed the bag on a narrow counter, I noticed the wallpaper—white with little dark illustrations that upon closer examination turned out to be early black-and-white cartoon characters. Bimbo. Koko. Felix the Cat. Betty Boop.

"Comic art is Rita's life," Melody said as she put the perishables away.

"Caught that," I said.

"I appreciate your coming here, chef," she said, shuffling objects in the small freezer to make room for a quart of butter-pecan ice cream, "but I'm doing fine. I'll be okay."

I felt like a louse. She and her roommate were assuming I'd come to lift her spirits, when, in fact, I was there looking for someone to take my place as murder suspect number one. It hadn't even occurred to me that she might be in mourning.

"I'm a little surprised you knew about Rudy and me," she said, folding the now-empty brown bag and placing it with other folded bags in a narrow cabinet. "He told me he was keeping it a secret from the people he worked with. But I guess there are some things you don't hide from friends."

Friends? How low could I feel?

When we returned to the living room, Rita was slipping into what looked like a shiny Day-Glo yellow plastic pea jacket. "Mello," she addressed her roommate, "since the chef's here to keep you company, would it be okay if I ducked out for an hour or so? There's a Love and Rockets retro at a gallery in the Village. Los Bros are supposed to be there."

I hadn't a clue as to what Rita was talking about, but Melody just said, "Go. I'm good."

Rita hugged her. "It'll get better," I heard her whisper.

Then she hugged me. "You're a lovely man to have come here," she said.

If I was so lovely, why was I feeling like a first-class creep?

As soon as Rita closed the door behind her, whatever had been keeping Melody going suddenly gave up the ghost. Her rigidity dissolved and her legs buckled.

I caught her before she fell onto the footlocker coffee table and helped her to the couch. "You're worn out," I said, sitting beside her. "You need sleep."

"I don't think I can. My head is full of jumbles."

"Why don't I fix you some warm milk?"

"No. Really. I'm okay. I just keep asking myself why somebody would do such a terrible thing. I don't understand it."

"Neither do I," I said truthfully. The guy had been a dick, but that shouldn't have cost him his life.

She looked like she was about to cry, but she took a deep breath and got herself under control. "He was so wonderful to me," she said. "I can't believe he's gone. I've been with . . . other guys, but he was the only man I really gave myself to."

Need-to-know basis. Please!

"He was so sweet. He worried that I'd think he was too old, but that didn't matter. For me, it was love at first sight that day at the tryouts."

"He told me he thought you were something special," I said.

She smiled. "I couldn't believe it when he asked me out that night. This great-looking man of the world, who'd been to so many places and done so many things. And he was interested in *me*. Not just in having sex with me. There've been nights when all we did was talk and laugh and not make love at all.

"Did Rudy tell you we were going to be married?"

The question caught me off guard. Luckily, before I could decide whether or not to lie, her mood turned down again and she began to weep. I'd never thought of myself as a father figure, not to mention a grief counselor, but I had no problem putting my arm around her and giving her my Zegna pocket square to mop up her tears.

"He's gone forever," she moaned.

I let her cry against my shoulder and stared at a comic-book room that, in spite of its eccentric touches and bursts of color, had grown quite dreary.

Eventually her body stiffened and she pulled away, moving into another stage of grief. She used my sixty-five-dollar pocket square to blow her nose furiously. "Some bastard took Rudy from me," she said, anger distorting her lovely face. "Business deal, bullshit. Murder business."

"I don't understand," I said.

"He was working on some deal that he said would make it possible for us to get married."

"What kind of deal?" I asked.

"Television, I guess. Rudy didn't say."

"But you think it could have had something to do with his murder?"

"We were supposed to have dinner at his place last night. Like we'd been doing just about every night. But Rudy called and said we couldn't because this important meeting came up. He said he'd phone me if we could get together later. I waited up until midnight, but . . . Oh, God. I was even sort of angry with him because he didn't call."

She began crying again.

I let the questions pile up in my head and waited silently for her to cry herself out.

When she did, I asked if I could get her something. Water? Aspirin?

She shook her head no.

"You must miss him, too," she said.

Before I had to lie and say "Yes," she suddenly reached out and plucked something from the coffee table, a thin, transparent jewel box housing a silver disk. "For a cool guy in his forties," she said, "he could be like a little boy at times. You know what he really loved to do in bed?"

I bit my tongue, shook my head, and hoped for the best.

"Watch TV," she said, pressing the jewel box to her chest. "Old shows that he'd had transferred to DVD. Black-and-white, some of 'em. He loved to lie in bed and watch old TV. Had shelves full of disks. He was in a lot of the shows."

"I guess he was," I said, remembering that Rudy's early career had been on-camera. "Melody, when you spoke with him last night, did he mention any details about the meeting? Where it was? Who'd be there?"

She thought for a moment. "It was at his condo, I'm pretty sure he said. But that's about it."

"Was he meeting with a man or a woman?"

"I got the impression it was a man, but I don't know that he said, really."

"You should probably tell all this to the police," I said.

"Oh, God. No police. I can't go to the police."

"Why not?"

She slid away from me against the sofa, arms crossed, chin tucked, shaking her head back and forth. Totally spooked.

"Okay," I said. "No police."

"It's . . . I don't want . . . some people to know where I am. And if I go to the police . . ."

"What people?"

No answer.

"Your mother?"

Hesitation, then the decision to remain silent.

"Father?"

"He's not my father," she almost shouted. "My father died. This one's not much older than my brother. He thinks 'cause he gave my mother a ring, he can do anything he wants to me."

"Okay," I said softly. "I've got the picture. How much does Rita know about it?"

"Not a lot. Doesn't take much to put Rita into attack mode. I'm not lookin' for any payback. I just want that whole part of my life gone and forgotten."

She looked even younger than eighteen. Maybe she was. People have been known to lie about their ages on their contracts, though usually it's in the other direction.

"Melody Moon your real name?"

"It is now," she said. "Aw, hell. Everything would have been so perfect if only Rudy and I could've . . ."

She drew her legs up and hugged them.

She must have seen the concern on my face, because she attempted a grin and said, "I'll be okay."

She looked at the disk in her hands. "We would have had a happy family. Rudy loved kids, you know."

"He had children?"

"Oh, not any of his own. He never was married. But when he was starting out he hosted a kids' show on a local station in Cleveland. That's where he's from."

I guess I didn't know very much about Rudy. Maybe I should have been more curious about the guy who'd won Gretchen's heart and, assuming he'd been straight with Melody, had decided to break it.

"He gave me this," she said, indicating the disk. "Four of his shows. You can see he really cared for the kids. Didn't talk down to them at all. He was so nice to them. Like a real dad.

"You mind if I put this on? It makes me happy to watch it."

"Please," I said.

It was a standard videotaped kids' show circa the 1980s. Produced on the cheap. A youthful, skinny Rudy Gallagher, decked out in what looked like an old brass-buttoned Sergeant Pepper coat and a yachts-man's cap, and operating under the nom de video of Cap'n Rudy, set sail in the good ship USS *Huckleberry* with ten or so kids on board.

The ship's bulkheads were black muslin, the portholes cardboard with cartoon waves. Rudy and the kids sat on fold-up chairs while some unidentified hapless station gofer, whom the cap'n called Yeo-man Yuckie, pretended to operate an ancient motion-picture projec-tor ostensibly showing Hanna-Barbera cartoons that suddenly filled the screen. Chief among the characters was Huckleberry Hound, hence the show's title.

Melody fast-forwarded through the cartoon segments, making the usually lethargic, blue-coated Huckleberry move faster than the Road Runner. Then she hit the play button and we watched young Rudy bonding with the kids, listening to their stories, singing sea chanteys and employing a truly awful "Avast ye, mateys" old-salt growl to spin tall tales that were rewarded with youthful cheers and laughter.

While I found these blasts from the past initially interesting, they quickly lost their charm for anyone who'd not been in love with Rudy Gallagher. By the time I'd endured two of the thirty-minute episodes, my eyes were starting to roll back in my skull.

To keep from screaming, I excused myself and went to the kitch-enette, where I found an assortment of booze. I selected a half-full pint bottle of bourbon, took a sip to make sure it wasn't turpentine, and used another inch of it to fashion a medicinal warm-milk punch for Melody.

She accepted it, took a tentative sip, and pronounced it "delicious," taking a larger swallow. "Do you think any of Rudy's old shows might be for sale on eBay?" she asked. "Maybe more of these *Huck-leberry*s?"

"Wouldn't hurt to check," I said.

The possibility of owning more video minutes of Rudy seemed to please her immensely. She settled back against the couch and drank more of the milk punch.

We were halfway through yet another *Huckleberry* episode when Melody put the empty glass on the coffee table and stood up, unsteadily. "Excuse me for a minute?" she mumbled and tottered off.

When fifteen minutes had passed, I put the TV and myself out of our shared misery and went looking for her.

There were two bedrooms just past the kitchenette. The first had, in addition to the usual bedroom furniture, an artboard, inks, paints, and a floor littered with discarded sketches.

I moved on to the second. A bedside lamp was lit, but Melody was fast asleep. There was a pink woolen coverlet folded at the foot of the bed. As I eased it from under her legs, I noticed that a red-leather wallet had worked its way free of her jeans pocket. I picked it up and draped the coverlet over her.

I scanned the room, saw nothing more interesting than the wallet, which I took to the living room. I plopped down on one of the soft, pink chairs to do some snooping. At first I found nothing of consequence. A credit card in her name, a reminder of a hair appointment at Roland's in the Village, two ten-dollar bills, a five, two ones, a receipt from a neighborhood dry-cleaning establishment named Pressing Matters, and several business cards.

My big discovery was an Illinois driver's license with her photo, which was tucked in one of the wallet's folds. It had been issued eight months before to a Mary Lou Meeshon, then a resident of 1312½ North Welles Street in Chicago. According to Mary Lou's birth date, she was still a few months shy of eighteen.

I pawed through the rest of the wallet, but the only other things of note were two photos: a creased snapshot of a little female toddler being held by a black man, his bearded face softened by a grin of parental pride, and a more recent version of that same toddler, all grown up or nearly so, sharing a love seat with Rudy Gallagher, staring at a camera that Rudy was holding up in front of them. Mary Lou and her real father, and Melody and her father figure.

I took the wallet back to Melody's room and placed it under the coverlet near her. She was still sleeping comfortably. I was reluctant to leave her alone in the apartment. I doubted she needed babysitting, but I didn't know her well enough to make that call. I'd been wrong about her before; at the *Food School* tryouts, she'd struck me as nothing more than a pampered, self-centered bubblehead, albeit a pretty one. So though I had no reason to suppose she might wake up depressed enough to do damage to herself, I didn't want to risk it.

I thought about searching the place, checking the medicine cabinet, the closets, but I could think of no good reason to invade their privacy further. Instead I went back to the pink chair in the living room and waited for Rita Margolis to return.

It wasn't a long wait.

She rushed in, saw me, did a quick scan of the room, then demanded, "Where's Melody?"

"In her room, asleep."

She double-timed it in the direction of the bedrooms, slipping out of her plastic coat as she went. I watched her as she tossed the coat into her bedroom without pausing and rushed into Melody's.

I moved closer.

Rita was standing beside Melody's bed, looking down at the sleeping girl with such adoration I felt uncomfortable enough to back away before being seen.

I was seated on the pink chair again when Rita finally joined me. "How long ago did she fade?" she asked.

"Less than an hour," I said.

"You put her to bed?" It was almost an accusation.

"No. She did that herself. I did put the coverlet over her."

"Well, thanks for your help, chef. I can take it from here."

Her mood was so brusque, I asked, "Do we have a problem?"

She frowned. "They were talking about the murder at the gallery. You and Rudy Gallagher weren't friends. In fact, the cops think you killed him."

"It's true Rudy and I weren't exactly drinking buddies," I said, "but I had nothing to do with his death."

"Really? That must be why the cops have closed down your restaurant," she said. "And don't tell me they haven't. I went by there and saw the crowd. It was your food that killed him."

"It wasn't my food," I said. "It was poison. The killer might have put it in my food. Or in whatever Rudy was drinking. Or in his saltshaker. Or his toothpaste."

"But you and he had been fighting."

"Who told you that?"

"It's on the news," she said.

Great. Just what I needed. Infamy.

"What are you doing here, chef?" she asked. "Why did you come here?"

There are times when you should clear the air with truth. This wasn't one of them. "I knew Rudy had been seeing Melody. I didn't know if she had anyone to help her through her grief."

"Uh-huh. Well, she does."

"How long have you two been roommates?"

"Long enough. Look, Melody is . . . She's bright but she's also young, the kind of beautiful and naive girl that some guys like to play."

"Is that what you thought Rudy was doing, playing her?"

Her eyes flashed. "I don't know what Rudy was doing. I wasn't talking about Rudy. I think it's time you left."

"Past time," I agreed.

Chapter

TWELVE

The doorman in the lobby of Rudy's apartment building was short, plump, and in his middle years, dressed in a smartly appointed uniform of midnight blue, with three shiny brass buttons straining to keep the jacket closed over his belly. The gray piping on the jacket's collar matched the trefoil trim on the sleeves and the cloth portion of his officer's cap. His striped tie picked up both colors.

He was wearing bright white gloves, highly polished black cap-toed shoes, and a loopy smile on his round, cleanly shaved black face.

"Welcome to the Hogarth Apartments, Chef Blessing," he said. "You're making a liar out of a brutha."

"Do I know you?"

"No, and that's my point," he said. "I tole the cops that even though I've watched you many times on the box—my wife loves your cooking show, by the way—I have never seen you in this building, in person. Now you've gone and made a liar of me."

I couldn't tell if he was busting my chops or if, as is sometimes the case, he was babbling because of nervousness. "What exactly did the police ask you?"

"If I'd seen you last night, which I didn't." He looked past me and added, "'Scuse me a second, chef."

He stepped around me to drag open the thick glass front door for a white guy in his forties with dyed white spiked hair, a dark soul patch, and several gold rings in his left ear. He was wearing an AC/DC sweatshirt and blue gangsta pants, hanging so low on his hips you could see a strip of his red ant–patterned underwear.

"Yo', Maxwell," he said to the doorman, "mah man. Cops still ugly-ing up the building?"

"They left hours ago, Mr. Washburn."

"My-t-fine," the white-haired man said, winking at me in passing, as if we were sharing some joke on the doorman.

I waited until the elevator door had closed behind him to ask, "Record producer?"

"Wall Street broker," the doorman said.

"Figures. So your name's Maxwell."

"Maxwell Sucony. Always been. Always will be."

"Glad to know you, Maxwell," I said, offering my hand. He peeled off his white glove before shaking it.

"How may I be of service, chef?"

I took my wallet from my coat pocket, but he waved his hand from side to side. "Not necessary. Like I say, my wife's a fan."

I accepted that, but I didn't put the wallet away.

"Since the police questioned you," I said, "I assume you were on duty last night."

"Six to two, five nights a week. And they didn't just question me, they sat me down and I had to identify everybody on the tape." He used his chin to gesture to a small camera secured to the ceiling and covering the front-door area. Including us.

You may have thought that appearing on television as often as I do would have inured me to camera discomfort, but I find secret taping, for whatever purpose, and that includes the cameras at the Bistro, inarguably creepy. So I shifted my back to the camera before asking, "What time did Rudy Gallagher check in last night?"

"Around six-thirty."

"Was he carrying anything with him?"

"Just a briefcase," Maxwell said.

"No big white bag, maybe a bunch of takeout cartons?"

"Nothin' like that. Was a time he'd show up some nights arms fulla takeout. Not for a while."

"He have any visitors last night?"

"No, sir."

"Maybe a delivery guy with that white bag?"

"You sure you're not the law? You askin' the same questions they did, only a lot nicer than that Detective Solomon." Maxwell lowered his voice. "What an asshole."

I knew I liked Maxwell.

"So no delivery guy?" I said.

"Like I told the cops, none I saw. Sometimes a tenant needs help and I'm gone for a bit. But last night I was right here ninety-nine percent of the time. And the time I was gone, nobody came in, according to the tape."

"Did he usually have visitors?" I asked.

"Not that many regulars. There's his fiancée, Miz Di Voss. Nice lady. She's here sometimes, but not so much last few weeks. He was out of town a while ago. Helped him with his luggage, coming and going, and the man did not travel light."

"Any other female visitors?"

Maxwell checked the lobby to make sure we were alone. Even though we were, he lowered his voice. "Mr. Gallagher was definitely a playa. Seen him take on two a night. Wore me out just thinkin' about it. Last couple of months, though, he slowed down. Aside from Miz De Voss, had just two repeaters."

"Tell me about them."

"For a while, before he took his trip, it was a blonde lady. But since he's been back, it's been this sweet-looking young black lady. Nice and polite. I don't get a lot of polite."

"Describe the blonde."

"Five-nine or -ten, blue-eyed, hair short but not goofy short. No buzz or nothin'. Well equipped. But she didn't show off the goods. Dressed down. Still, there's some curves too wide to hide, if you hear what I'm sayin'."

"I hear you. Don't suppose you caught her name?"

"Mr. Gallagher wasn't big on names."

"Anything distinctive about her? Tattoos or piercings?"

"Like I say, she wasn't flash. Least not where it showed."

"She come by cab or car?"

"Not that I noticed."

I opened my wallet and forced two twenties on him with my thanks.

"Uh, about Miz Di Voss," he said, folding the bills in half and slipping them into his pants pocket. "I saw her last night."

"I thought you said Gallagher didn't have any visitors."

"He didn't. She wasn't in the building. I saw her walking by across the street."

"When was this?"

"Aroun' ten."

"You sure she didn't come in?"

"Sure enough."

I thanked him again and, braving the nighttime traffic, jaywalked across the street and stood where Maxwell had seen Gretch the previous night. I looked up and down the street, but, with what meager information I possessed, I could see nothing that would have been of interest to her.

Except for Rudy's building.

Chapter

THIRTEEN

It was a little after ten-thirty when my cab arrived at the Bistro.

Usually at that time of night, the lights would be burning brightly inside and out. Diners would be exiting. The valet guys would be on the run, retrieving vehicles. It would be a happy, welcome sight—a busy restaurant at nearly the end of another successful night. Ching ching!

Instead the building was in darkness except for a security light under the awning. It shone down on a couple of paparazzi with nothing better to do on a no-news night than to keep vigil at the lair of a suspected murderer.

I instructed the Middle Eastern cabbie to keep going to the corner and turn left. He did that. But when I asked him to pull over near the building's rear door, he refused, saying he would not "perform an act of illegality." Instead he continued on for about two car lengths along the deserted street, then made an equally illegal U-turn to deposit me by the door.

I increased his tip by an extra couple of dollars as a reward for his eccentric observance of the rules of the road. Then as he zoomed away leaving me in a cloud of carcinogenic exhaust, I approached the building with weariness and no small amount of depression.

I unlocked the door and went in just as the alarm system began to beep its one-minute warning. I turned on the light in the alcove and tapped the access code on the keypad beside the door. The beeping stopped.

I hesitated, wondering if I wanted to go directly to bed or stop off at the kitchen to see if the cops had found the slice of peach pie I'd hidden at the back of the reach-in fridge.

A third possibility came to mind when something cold and hard was pressed against the back of my neck and a gruff voice said, "Turn around and you die."

I got a whiff of clove breath. Could have been worse.

"You're the man," I said.

"Up to the office."

He may have been following me close enough that I could have pushed backward and knocked him down the stairs. But that sort of heroic/foolish move works only in the movies.

"Turn on the lights," he said.

I did that.

The office looked messier than usual, but I wasn't sure if Clove Boy was responsible or if it was the police who'd been poking around all day.

"Open the goddamned safe," he said, with enough anger that I assumed he'd already tried to do that and failed.

The safe was an eighteen-inch-high Sentry resting on the carpet under a two-drawer filing cabinet. I saw that the tubular key that I kept in my desk drawer was already in the lock.

"You need the combination, too," I said.

"No shit," he said. "Open it up."

I hunkered down, punched in the five numbers of my zip code, not the most secure combination but one I could remember, and heard the confirming click. I turned the key, opened the heavy metal door, and started to rise.

"Get on your hands and knees and keep facing the wall," Clove Boy said.

I took some comfort in the fact that he did not want me to see him. I hoped that meant he didn't plan on killing me. Or maybe he didn't want to look his murder victims in the eye.

Or maybe it meant nothing.

Using my peripheral vision, I saw him rooting around in the safe.

He was wearing a short-sleeve dark-blue shirt and dark-blue trousers. A uniform. And judging by the slightly rounded triangle patch on his sleeve, it was a policeman's uniform. Not good.

I wondered what would happen if I suddenly flopped on my back and kicked the heavy safe door into him. Then, while he was trying to recover, I could throw myself onto him, grab his weapon, and . . . Enough with the James Bond nonsense.

Clove Boy cursed and threw a metal box at the wall. It was the one in which I kept petty cash. Not much. A couple hundred dollars. Judging by the tens and twenties on the floor, it wasn't chicken feed he was after.

"Where the hell is it?" he demanded, standing up.

"There's no big stash," I said. "We don't usually keep much cash, and we weren't even open today."

"I don't give a shit about money." He grabbed the back of my coat collar and yanked me to my feet. I felt his gun prod my back as he said, close to my ear, "Where is it?"

"Where is what?"

"The thing you took from Gallagher's."

"Gallagher's? Rudy Gallagher's? I've never been there." I was trying, unsuccessfully, not to whine.

"Bullshit," he said. "You tell me where it is or, so fucking help me, I'll put one right through your spine."

"What is it you want?" I yelled. "Tell me, and if I've got it, it's yours."

"What did you take from Gallagher's?"

"Nothing. I've never been there. I swear to God."

Something in the way I said that, or maybe the way my body was shaking in fear, must have made him a believer. He released my collar. "Another stupid fucking waste of time," he mumbled to himself. I felt the gun leave my back. Then it crashed against the back of my head.

I fell to the carpet, woozy but still semiconscious.

Looking across the carpet, I saw him running away, a big man with dark hair showing beneath a policeman's cap. From that angle, I was also able to see that his shoes were dark brown, not black. Maybe not a cop after all. Maybe just a thug who'd used the uniform to wander freely around a building filled with real cops, imitating them as they pawed through my belongings. They'd been looking for evidence.

He'd been looking for something that he hadn't found in Rudy's apartment.

What made him think I might have it?

I got to my feet, shuffled into my living quarters and, specifically, to the bathroom, where I plucked a bottle of aspirin from the medicine cabinet and shot a couple with a tumbler of water. The man in the mirror didn't look all that battered. There'd probably be a welt on the top-right quadrant of my skull, but since there was still some hair growth up there, it wouldn't be that noticeable on camera.

The things that worry us.

I turned a light on in the bedroom.

Clove Boy had been in there, pulling the bed apart, yanking my suits and pants from the closet, opening the dresser drawers, the better to fondle my underwear and socks. Well, the hell with it all. I'd get the cleanup service to take care of it.

I was suddenly struck by the understandably paranoid thought that the thug cop might come back for another go-round. As he'd said, he'd already wasted a lot of time. Why wouldn't he come back to make sure I didn't have whatever precious item he sought? A Maltese falcon, a Spanish doubloon, a rare manuscript. Since it was my story, it might be a gold pork chop.

Work tomorrow. At five-thirty a.m. Barely six hours away if I went to bed immediately.

I trudged down the stairs, wondering where the thug cop had hidden while Cassandra and my kitchen chief made their final walk-through before closing up. I supposed he could have been stretched out on my bed. They usually just checked the upstairs dining room and the office.

Yawning, I reset the alarm.

Then I decided I'd sleep much better if I had a little something in my stomach. But as soon as I stepped into the kitchen I smelled stale clove cigarette smoke. With anger rising, I turned on the overhead light and saw the empty tin plate on the tile floor, surrounded by crumbs and cigarette butts. While waiting for me, Clove Boy, that son of a bitch, had eaten my peach pie. Perfect.

Chapter

FOURTEEN

When I climbed into the Volvo dirtmobile the next morning, Joe narrowed his eyes at the coffee container and Danish I'd just picked up at the bakery down the street.

"Billy, you know rule one: no food or drink in Volvo."

"Have mercy on me, Joe. I had a very rough night."

"Yeah. You look all rumpled and used up."

"When I got up there wasn't a doughnut in the whole kitchen, and the cops hid my coffeepot somewhere."

"My father taught me there is no excuse for lack of preparation," Joe said. "Also no excuse for confusing vehicle for breakfast nook."

"I don't understand you, Joe," I said as we headed toward the Glass Tower. "This car's a rolling pigsty and you're busting me about coffee and a pastry."

"Dirt outside the Volvo, no problem," he said. "Spilled coffee and crumbs inside, smells bad and I get ants, roaches. Even rats, maybe. But okay, this once I let it pass. Mrs. Joe say I should be nice to you today, because everybody say you kill people."

"Jesus! Don't tell me Mrs. Joe thinks I'm a murderer?"

"No. She knows better. But she say some people probably believe everything they hear or read, which must make you very unhappy, which is why I should be nice. So enjoy your sweet roll."

My cohorts at *Wake Up!,* with whom I'd been working five days a week for years, should have known me a little better than Mrs. Joe, whom I saw maybe twice a year at seasonal Bistro family parties. But judging by their looks of surprise, and even fear, on my arrival that morning, they did not share her belief in my innocence.

Even my assistant Kiki's eyes widened when she saw me. "Out on bail, Billy?" she asked.

"Please don't tell me they're saying I was arrested?"

"No. Just that you probably killed Rudy. I assumed you were in the nick, because you haven't been answering your cellular."

"Yeah," I said. "I left it on my desk when I went out, and when I got back last night . . . I was attacked and beaten by a guy wearing a cop uniform."

She raised her eyes and stared at me. "Really?" she said, drawing out the word to give it that touch of snarky sarcasm.

"Really. Want to feel the bump on my head?"

"Feeling head bumps is not my style, Billy." She continued to stare at me. "You're serious about this, right?"

"As serious as a brain hemorrhage," I said.

"Why did he hit you?"

"He thought I had something he wanted."

"What?"

"I don't know, but, whatever, he decided I didn't have it and he went away."

"What did the police say?"

"I . . . didn't call 'em."

"Why the hell not?"

"I spent enough time with the police yesterday to realize they're not going to do anything for me. And I don't even know what I'd want them to do. The guy didn't take anything. Of course, he did hit me in the head. And worse, bastard ate my pie. But . . . screw it."

"Okay. Fine. We'll just pretend it never happened," she said, turning away. "I won't even worry about you suffering some sort of horrible aftereffects. Concussion, that sort of thing."

"I'm okay," I said. "What's my schedule look like today?"

"I would call it light," she said. "You're not on the show. It wasn't just my phone messages you ignored last night. Some were from Arnie. He wants to see you."

Our producer, Arnie Epps, was on the set. His tall, thin body, garbed in a faded sunset Hawaiian luau shirt and pale-green trousers, was hunched like a gaudy buzzard. On anybody less clueless, a funereal black armband pinned to the short sleeve of an orange-and-yellow-and-green shirt might have seemed a display of cynicism.

He was deep in conversation with a stunning brunette. She stood a few inches lower than his bent form, which was in the six-foot range, looking trainer-toned in a tailored black suit. Her gorgeous face was deeply tanned, bringing out the ocean blueness of her eyes and a dramatic white streak in artfully tousled black hair. At the moment all I could think of was a beautiful female version of Pepé Le Pew.

They were discussing the logistics for an upcoming interview with the former Mossad-agent-turned-novelist Goyal Aharon. When Arnie finally sensed someone was sharing their space, he forced himself to break contact with those remarkable blue eyes. Discovering it was me standing there, he stopped mid-sentence, blinked, and said, "Billy, I . . . uh, this is Trina Lomax."

Trina Lomax gave me her full sapphire-eyed whammy, and it was potent. "Chef Blessing, it's a pleasure," she said, extending a thin but surprisingly strong hand. She did not have a French accent like Pepé, but there was something unusual about her speech. It was too precisely correct for her to be American.

"Likewise, but please, make it Billy," I said.

"Trina is—" Arnie began what I guessed would be the usual credit rundown, but I knew who Trina was. I'd seen her special reports on INN, the International News Network. Her beat was the world, and she hopped from continent to continent, country to country, interviewing the great and the near-great, the famous and the infamous.

"I'm a big fan," I said, interrupting Arnie. "When you had that sit-down with Ahmadinejad, was it my imagination or was he flirting with your cameraman?"

"Sorry, Billy, I'm saving that for the book," she said.

"What I was trying to tell you, Billy," Arnie said, in a rare display of impatience, "Trina's going to be filling Rudy's shoes until the commander figures out something permanent."

"Welcome aboard, Trina," I said.

"I'm looking forward to working with you good people," she said. "But I am a little confused about why you're here today, Billy. Especially after I was told your segs had been reassigned."

"They have been," Arnie said. "I've been trying to reach Billy by phone since eight o'clock last night to tell him."

"My fault," I said. "Phone was off." I didn't even think twice about mentioning my night visitor to them. Nothing short of a slit throat would have had any effect.

"We fully understand the pressure you must be under, Billy," Trina said. "That's precisely why I assumed you'd want to take some time off. Out of respect for Rudy's . . . friends and fans, I've canceled today's meet-in-the-street segment. And the humor segs seem inappropriate. As for your book review and the mock-apple-pie demo, I thought we could let Chuck Slater spread his wings a bit."

"Boy Wonder Chuck? He has trouble reading the credits at the end of a movie. How'd you get him to read a book?"

"The only thing he has to read is the review," she said.

"So I'm off the show?"

"Only temporarily, Billy," Trina said. "In our news segment, we are reporting the fact that the food that poisoned Rudy came from your Bistro. Your appearance on the show would seem a little . . . awkward."

"The police don't know the poison was in our dinner," I said.

"The official word from the police lab, Billy," Arnie said, "is that the poison was in the sauce prepared at your restaurant."

"I hadn't heard that good news," I said.

"Arnie, Billy might want to make a statement about the lab report. We should wire him up right now and—"

"No statement," I said. "I wouldn't want to interfere with whatever you've got scheduled."

"Actually, it might clash with the remembrance piece we've put together," Trina said, making me wonder if I'd lost my gift for sarcasm.

"Lance is doing a live narration over a docu-obit cobbled from footage from Rudy's on-camera career," Arnie told me. "The guy had been working in the business for decades, on camera as well as behind."

"So I keep hearing," I said. "Do I come in tomorrow?"

Arnie blinked as if my question caught him off guard. "Uh, tomorrow? Sure, Billy. I guess." He looked to Trina for support.

"Better run it past Gretchen first," she said.

"Gretchen? She's the one who gave me the boot?"

"Nobody's giving you the boot, Billy," Trina said. "You're much too valuable to the show." Those blue eyes looked into mine, and she flashed me a comforting smile that I wished had been sincere.

"Anyway," she continued, "I'd better go check in with the news anchor. What's her name again, Arnie?"

"Tori Dillard," Arnie said.

"Tori, right. My God, what's that on her neck? A hickey? Do your makeup people even bother to look?"

We watched her stride away to an unsuspecting Tori. Arnie sighed. Then he said, "Why is it this job never gets easier?"

"At least you're still working," I said. "I'm going up to see Gretchen."

"Do what you've got to, Billy."

Turning to leave, I saw that others—a couple of stagehands, a page, Lance's assistant—had been standing around observing our conversation. As I passed, they looked away and quickly dispersed.

Yesterday I'd been a relatively successful performer and restaurateur. Well liked, if not beloved. Today people ran away from me. Was the thread holding it all together so thin that all it took was a sliver of circumstantial evidence to break everything loose?

As I reached the stage door, Gin was heading in.

She stopped, reached out to touch my arm. "God, Billy, I've been trying to phone you. How are you holding up?"

"Well, let's see. My restaurant's been padlocked by the cops, I've been attacked by a thug, and I've just been sent home by the new executive producer."

"You're not on the show today?" she said. "Wait! You were attacked?"

"Just joking," I said, sorry now that I'd mentioned it.

"Oh. Then you are on the show?"

"No. I'm not on the show. I was just joking about being attacked."

"I bet it's that Trina that bumped you," Gin said. "Isn't she somethin'?"

"She is that."

"This is all jus' temporary bad luck, Billy. It'll get straightened out.

They'll find out who really killed Rudy and everything'll be back to normal."

I flashed on Detectives Solomon and Butker. They weren't going to be finding any real killer. Not while they had me. But why get into that? "You're right, Gin," I said.

"Oh, guess what? Ted's flyin' in this evening. It's been four months since he's been home."

As I mentioned, Gin's paramour, Ted Parkhurst, had been working the Middle East beat.

"Couldn't stay away from you a minute longer?" I said.

"Well, I hope," she said. "But he's also coming in for Rudy's funeral."

"I didn't know they were that close," I said.

"They weren't until recently. They hung out a little when Rudy was in Kabul."

"Well, give Ted my best. Maybe we can get together while he's here."

"You'll see him at the funeral tomorrow, right?"

The funeral. Tomorrow. I hadn't thought about the funeral. Should I go? I may not have loved the guy, but we'd been associates. If the goddamn takeout had come from the Gotham or Town, there'd have been no question about my attending the funeral. What was the protocol for going to the funeral of the guy you're accused of offing?

"Sure," I said to Gin. "I'll see you both there."

Chapter

FIFTEEN

The executive offices of Di Voss Industries were on the sixth floor of the Glass Tower. In the carefree days prior to 9/11, they had been on the sixty-fourth floor, just beneath Sky, the penthouse restaurant that charges nearly twice as much for the exact strip steak we serve at the Bistro. (I know this for a fact; our meat comes from the same slaughterhouse.)

Anyway, concerned about the time it would take for the commander and his VIPs to clear the building in an emergency, it was decided that expediency trumped cityscapes, and down they all came to six, exchanging floors with the drones who worked in public relations, publicity, and research, and the ever-increasing IT gremlins responsible for the multivarious corporate websites.

Gretchen was rounding the desk of a terrified assistant and heading toward her office with the grim determination and speed of a ballplayer with shin splints trying to beat the throw to home plate. When I called her name, she halted and turned. She looked weary and frustrated and definitely out of sorts, so I didn't take it personally when she snapped, "Billy, I have no time today for whatever the problem is."

"It's important."

She stared at me for a beat, then said, "Five minutes."

I followed her past her assistant's desk and into her office, closed the door, and waited until I was sure I had her full attention. "Are you kicking me off *Wake Up!*, Gretch?"

"What are you talking about, Billy?" She seemed genuinely confused.

I explained that I'd been bumped from that morning's show, presumably at her request.

"This is the first I'm hearing of it. Maybe Trina Lomax . . . Has anyone told you that Trina—?"

"The new executive producer? Yeah. Met her right before coming here."

"Well, I'm not sure it's such a bad idea, you taking a few days off," Gretchen said. "It's definitely not a permanent situation. Daddy wouldn't let me fire you, even if I wanted to. And I don't want to . . . unless you keep me here wasting my time."

"I guess I was worried that you were believing all the crap in the news about me being the prime suspect. . . ."

"Oh, Christ, Billy, there are a hundred things going on in my head right now. And as hard as it must be for you to believe, you're not even in the first ninety-nine." She wavered and leaned against her desk for support.

I crossed the room to her and put my arm around her. "Take it easy, Gretch. Mustn't let 'em see you sweat."

I moved her to the couch and semi-forced her onto it. "It's all getting to me, Billy. Ever since Dad turned the news division and the cable networks over to me after Bud died, I've been barely able to keep my head above water." Bud was her late brother, Lieutenant Commander Vernon Di Voss Jr. He'd been killed five years before in Baghdad when his vehicle rolled over a land mine.

"Now Rudy's lawyers tell me he made me the executrix of his estate. So along with having to shout at *Nightline* and *60 Minutes* for trying to break our exclusive first shot at the ex–Mossad guy, and dealing with our programming idiots and, in general, running two fucking television networks, I'm making the arrangements for Rudy's funeral service at Saint Pat's, of all places, and the burial, *and* his estate sale."

"You don't have to do all this yourself, Gretch. You've got a full staff out there. And you can put Rudy's lawyers to work. They're taking their cut of the estate anyway. Make 'em earn it."

"I know you're right, Billy. But things never seem to get done unless I do them myself. God, I woke up this morning worrying about who I should hire to auction off Rudy's furnishings."

"He had a lot of his old shows on DVD," I said. "If they're going to be on sale, I'd like to pick up a few."

"Why would you want them?" she asked.

"Mementos."

"You men are so strange. Actually, those DVDs are here. We needed to sample some of Rudy's early TV work on our send-off this morning, so I got permission from the NYPD to remove them from his condo. They should still be in editing. I'll probably donate them to the Museum of Television and Radio. Take what you want."

Her eyes were suddenly damp.

Then she broke down, and, for the second time in two days, my lapels were collecting tears of grief for Rudy Gallagher.

Or so I thought.

After a few seconds, Gretch pulled away from me and stood. "He was a son of a bitch," she said, snapping a Kleenex angrily from a box on her desk. "Did you know he was screwing around on me?"

"What makes you think that?" I said, not wanting to lie to her.

She circled her desk, opened a drawer, and plucked from it a small black phone book. "This retro piece of macho bullshit."

She threw it at me. "I'm sure you've seen them before," she said.

"Since BlackBerrys, not so much." I flipped through the pages. There were no names, just initials, followed by several sets of numbers—phone numbers and ratings for "beauty," "breasts," "butts," and "bedroom."

"This book could be from years ago," I told Gretchen. "Long before you two met."

"Rudy listed his 'conquests' on a first-come basis, if you'll excuse the expression. You'll note that GDV is not the final entry. There are dozens more."

"There's this in his favor," I said. "He gave you straight tens."

"Not funny, Billy." She grabbed the black book from my fingers.

"I'm surprised the police let you have that," I said.

She made no response, merely put the book back in her desk drawer.

"The police did see it, right?" I asked.

"I can't speak for their efficiency. It arrived here with Rudy's DVD collection. I assume they've seen it and considered it unimportant to their investigation."

"A bachelor's little black book? C'mon, Gretchen. How could this not be important? You need to show it to them."

"If I make a big thing about it with the police, some sleazy individual will find a way to steal it or copy it, and in the blink of an eye it will wind up on every gossip website in the world. I'll just hang on to it, if you don't mind. In fact, I'm thinking of burning the damn thing."

"You're joking, right? The cops are convinced I killed Rudy," I said. "That black book might put just a tiny doubt in their minds."

"How can you be so sure they haven't looked through it?"

"Because it's the kind of thing they love to dig into. And I know it didn't come with the DVDs."

"Really? Suddenly you're the Mentalist? Then how did it get here?"

We had finally arrived at the real point of my visit.

"My guess is you took it from Rudy's apartment the night he died."

Gretchen paled. "That's ridiculous, Billy. I was nowhere near . . . How desperate do you have to be to make a statement like that?"

"How did you know his last dinner was coq au vin?" I asked.

"How? That detective. Solomon. He told me when he called with the news of Rudy's death."

I shook my head. "Solomon came to the Bistro almost immediately after he'd talked with you. When he and I got into a discussion of Rudy's last meal, he'd never heard of coq au vin. It was just chicken and gravy to him. Then, only minutes later, during our phone conversation you identified the dish by name."

"I guess I assumed—"

"What? That since it was from the Bistro, it had to be coq au vin? Why not Chicken Florentine or Pompadour or Fricassee?"

"That's ridiculous."

"You were seen at his place, Gretch. Right around the time of the murder."

"Oh, God." She backed against the desk, using it to give her the strength to continue standing. "Billy, he was already dead when I got there, I swear."

"What the hell were you doing there?"

"Behaving like a fool. A jealous fool. It had been over a week since we'd spent any time together. That night, I insisted. He told me he had a business meeting. Said it was something he had to do for my father and then it was dinner and bed. He'd call me the next day."

"What was he doing for the commander?"

"I phoned Dad to ask. He said he didn't know what Rudy was talking about. The last task he'd entrusted to him was a fait accompli. And a very unsatisfactory one, he said."

"I wanted to get to the bottom of this, so I called Rudy back. This time I got his voice mail. I sat around simmering, dialing him every so often and growing more and more infuriated. Finally I drove over there."

"How'd you get past the doorman and the lobby camera?" I asked.

"There's a thing Rudy did. If he was expecting someone he didn't want the doorman or anyone else to see, he'd leave the alley door unbolted."

"And you discovered this how?"

She hesitated, then said, "Once upon a time, I was his back-door romance. If you recall, Rudy was still engaged to that British bitch Samantha Prentice when he and I started up."

Recall? Hell, that was back when I harbored the foolish notion that Gretchen and I were still a couple. I didn't linger on that. "So the night he died, you found the rear door open?"

"Yes. I cut through the walkway beside the building, entered through the unlocked door, and went up the service stairs to his condo. I knew he kept an extra key under the carpet at the far end of the hall. But I didn't need it. His door was ajar.

"I went in, expecting to find him in bed with some tramp. Instead he was . . . God, it was horrible! His face twisted and grotesque. He'd relieved himself and that smell, with the vomit . . ."

"But you were able to find the black book and take it."

"I went to call the police. The black book was on the table beside the phone. I looked through it and . . ."

"And you realized how bad it might look for the fiancée of a sleep-around guy to be in his apartment with his dead body."

"I'm not that cold and calculating, Billy. I didn't dream he'd been murdered. I assumed he'd had a heart attack. Rudy was beyond anything I could do for him. I didn't see any reason not to remove the black book and save him from seeming like the letch that he was. I took it and left the way I'd come in."

"Let me get this straight," I said. "You're standing there with the carpet ripped up and the books pulled off the shelves and the place an unholy mess, and you think he's had a heart attack?"

"What are you talking about? There were no books on the floor, no torn carpet. With the exception of the space where Rudy died, the apartment was as neat as always."

"The detectives told me it was a mess," I said.

"A mess they made," Gretchen said firmly.

"Maybe," I said. I had a pretty good idea who'd made the mess, but I was having trouble working out the chronology. Rudy was poisoned by a person or persons unknown. Gretchen arrived and the place had not been searched. But by the next day, when the housekeeper found Rudy's corpse and the cops got there, the place had been ransacked, probably by Clove Boy. Ergo, Clove Boy had not killed Rudy? Or maybe he had and then was sent back to find the secret thing. The black book, maybe?

"I suppose you think I should tell the police the truth," Gretchen said.

Ding! Ding! Ding! We have a winner, I thought. What I said was "It's your decision."

"I don't want to," she said. "But what if the person who saw me tells the police?"

"I sorta fudged on that," I said. "You weren't seen in the building, just in the neighborhood. If the cops don't know that by now, they probably never will."

She seemed relieved for about five seconds, then tensed and said, "Unless you tell them."

"Did you kill him, Gretch?"

"No. Of course not."

"Then what's to tell?" I said.

I moved around her desk, opened the drawer, and took out the little black book. "I'm going to hang on to this," I said.

"W-why?"

"I wouldn't want it burned," I said. "If the DA and the police have their way and I wind up defending my life, it'll be something we can throw at the jury to confuse them."

"I don't believe it will come to that, Billy, but if it does, I'll be in your corner."

"Good to know," I said, slipping the book into my pocket.

Chapter

SIXTEEN

When I arrived at the Bistro, my new BFFs from the media were snarling and snapping at me like a pack of rabid dogs and I had Milk-Bones in my pockets. In their midst, I spied a reluctant Worldwide Broadcasting cameraman in khaki who actually was a friend. Phil Bruno was one of the guys you wanted on your team—smart, inventive, even-tempered, who always knew precisely how to get the best shot.

I waved him in, prompting even louder howls from the rest of the pack.

"Sorry about this, Billy," Phil said as I led him through the restaurant in its second day of commercial inactivity. "I wanted to call you to tell you I'd been assigned to get footage for tonight's evening news, but the new honchette, Trina, said no calls. She believes in the confrontational approach, even when it comes to friends and coworkers."

"Don't worry about it," I said. "Shoot whatever interiors you need. But do me a favor: Keep what's about to take place out of the frame."

My reference was to Solomon and Butker, who were heading our way from the rear of the building.

"It wasn't your rat poison that was used on Gallagher," Solomon said, ignoring Phil.

"Then why are you people still here?"

"We're back to square one, Blessing," the detective said, with a grin that wrinkled his face, hiding some of the black scar. "This time we're looking for . . . What is it, Butker?"

"Benzethonium chloride," his bored partner replied. "A detergent used to clean cooking equipment, among other things. Very toxic."

"My guess is: If we use it, it'll be right in the open with the other detergents," I said.

"Nothing's ever that simple," Solomon said. "Your help says they only use standard stuff. But if they did use the benzo-whatever on your ovens, then I guess you wouldn't have used it on your pal Gallagher. Anyway, it's gonna take us all day at least, pokin' around. So many hidey-holes. And you never know, we might just turn up something else that'll hook you up to the murder."

With a sinking feeling, I realized I had Rudy's little black book in my pocket. That's all the connection Solomon would need. Keeping a poker face, I asked, "I don't suppose you left one of your officers here last night?"

"No. Why?"

"A guy with a cop suit was seen on the premises."

"Seen by who?"

"Me."

"What bullshit story are you leading up to, Blessing? This 'policeman' tell you he killed Gallagher? Something like that?"

"No," I said.

"Then what *was* he doing here? Fill me in. I love stories."

I knew it would be a mistake to bring up the incident to Solomon. Telling him why the fake cop had dropped by would be futile. Or worse. Either he wouldn't believe me or, if he did, he'd assume I really had taken something from Gallagher's apartment and initiate an even more detailed search. He might even find the little black book I had in my pocket. And that would be a Go Directly to Jail card.

"You're too clever for me, Detective," I said. "Forget I mentioned it."

Solomon stared at me. "Now you're starting to piss me off. Was there somebody here impersonating one of my men or not?"

"Maybe it was just a bad dream."

"Well, if you change your mind again, I'll be around, seeing if the benzo-whatever turns up."

"I suppose this means the restaurant will be dark another night."

"Afraid so, chef," Solomon said.

"Some of the food will be going bad. I can't refreeze it."

"Butker and I and the other officers would be happy to help you out with that. I saw some mighty fine porterhouse back there, all thawed and nice and bloody."

"Bon appétit," I said, heading for my office with Phil Bruno.

"You really have a break-in here last night?" Phil asked me.

"No big deal," I said. "I should just keep my mouth shut around Solomon."

"He's a sweetheart, for sure," Phil said. "He reminds me of Rudy, may God rest his black soul."

"You didn't think much of our late executive producer?"

"You should have seen him in Kabul, Billy, in his Abercrombie and Fitch great-white-hunter garb."

"I didn't know you'd made that trip."

"Oh, yeah. Me and"—Phil deepened his voice theatrically to imitate the WBC evening news anchor—"Jim Bridewell."

"Sounds just like him," I said. "Who else was over there?"

"Rudy brought a couple of crew guys in from the L.A. bureau. Damn, but he loved to throw his weight around. In just a few days, he had the noncoms hating his ass and the officers going out of their way to avoid him. I wished I'd had that luxury. Bridewell is like a Calvinist or something, but he doesn't bother anybody with it. Rudy was a demanding, rude-as-hell asshole."

"What was that trip all about, anyway?" I asked. "There wasn't any special story, as far as I could see."

"It was the commander's idea," Phil said. "At least it was according to the late unlamented. Our first night there, Rudy got plowed at dinner. He told me Commander Di Voss had sent him there on a special mission."

"He say what the mission was?"

"No. Made out like it was a big secret, strictly need-to-know. Then why bring it up, asshole?"

"He didn't even drop a clue?"

Phil thought about it. "You know, I've been wondering if it could have had something to do with this thing that happened the next night when a bunch of us were in an Irish pub near the Mustafa Hotel. These Afghanis showed up at the pub, looking for trouble. They picked a fight with two of our security guards. A third guard got us out of there pronto and back to the hotel. The next day we found out that one of the remaining guards, a guy named Deacon Hall, got his throat cut."

"Rudy mentioned that," I said. "But he claimed he was there when it happened."

"No way." Phil shook his head. "Rudy was with me, safe and secure back at the hotel. But he freaked big-time when he heard about Hall. Took it surprisingly hard. In fact, he caught the next flight out. Bridewell and the rest of us had to stay and finish up the week. In that heat. With bombs going off. Still, conditions improved one hundred percent without Rudy."

"What makes you think the bar fight might have had something to do with Rudy's so-called mission?"

"After they brought us the news about Hall, and Rudy got over his freak and decided to head for home, he said, 'My business here is finished anyway.' Since he hadn't been planning to leave *before* he heard about Hall, I guess that made me think Hall might have had something to do with his 'mission.' "

His failed mission, according to the commander.

"They catch the killers?" I asked.

"Billy, that sort of shit goes on all the time over there. Those guys don't know from *Law & Order*. My guess is the surviving guard took care of the two Afghanis. Those Touchstone mercs don't take it well when you kill one of their buddies."

"There must have been some talk about it."

"Talk? Yeah. The Army general's office informed us we were to keep the murder off the newscast until Hall's relatives could be notified. The Touchstone security rep would tell us when we could run the story. That didn't happen while we were there. Far as I know, it never happened."

"You shoot a lot of footage?"

"That's how I roll, Billy."

"What about off-duty action? Like the night in the Irish pub?"

"I got some stuff. Nothing on the murder, though, since they dragged us out of there."

"I'd still like to see what you shot," I said.

"Anytime, Billy."

"How about after you're finished here?"

"Sure," Phil said.

"I'll see if I can sneak a few of those steaks away from the cops," I told him.

While Phil roamed the restaurant with his camera, I shut the door to my office, then took Rudy's black book from my pocket. I started at the first page and worked toward the last, looking at the initials of the dead man's sexual partners. I wondered what their full names might be and if any of them might have caused Rudy's death and sent Clove Boy to my building to retrieve the black book.

I briefly considered picking up the phone and starting to dial numbers and see who answered. But there were hundreds of entries. Even if I had the time and the patience to run the numbers through a reverse directory, I'd come up with only a percentage of the names. And then what? The bottom line was that I simply hadn't the heart to invade the privacy of so many women, especially since I doubted it would accomplish anything. The odds of my discovering a homicidal needle in this haystack of one-night stands and best-forgotten seductions and broken affairs were too long.

I was about to toss the book back into my desk drawer when the office door was flung open and Solomon and Butker sauntered in.

"Whatcha got there, Blessing?" Solomon asked. He quickened his pace to the desk and snatched the black book from my unresisting fingers.

I felt like screaming, but developing a mental method of staying cool under stress had been the first thing my mentor Paul Lamont had demanded of me before he took me on the road. "Thanks to you, I've got the night off, Detective," I said. "I don't plan on spending it alone."

Solomon flipped a few pages. "Damn, Blessing. You're the original sexist pig, aren't you? Look at this, Butker. He even grades the dumb broads who fall for his crap."

Butker gave the book a quick once-over. He seemed impressed.

"Can I help you, Detectives? Maybe you need a date for tonight?"

"Hardly," Solomon said. He grabbed the book from Butker's fingers and tossed it onto my desk. "There are some locked cabinets downstairs. Before we tear the doors off, I thought I'd ask if you had keys."

I picked up the phone, dialed Cassandra, and asked her to provide the detectives with whatever keys they needed. "Anything else?" I asked Solomon.

His answer was to leave the room. Following, Butker did not bother to shut the door.

I sighed and looked at the little black book. If Rudy's name had been in it, I'd have been cooked. But while Solomon was pawing through the damned thing, I'd calmed my panic mode with the thought that a player who'd used only the initials of his conquests probably wouldn't have put anything in the book that might identify himself.

"My God," Cassandra said from the door, "a little black book, Billy? I'd never have taken you for an ass man. When do you have the time?"

"We ass men make the time," I said, opening a desk drawer and tossing in the book. Now that the detectives believed it to be mine, I suppose it was, officially.

"Those insufferable cops are driving me crazy," she said. "You think you're rid of them, then they return. They're like the silverfish in my apartment."

"What can I do for you, Cassandra?"

"You wanted a report on the coq au vin dinners?"

"Right."

"It is one of our most requested meals. And as Maurice reminded me"—Maurice Terrebone being the kitchen supervisor—"it's all but impossible to account for every single entrée if it's on the specials list."

I understood what she was saying. Because the specials are often partially prepared in advance, and because it is impossible to accurately predict how many will be ordered on any given night, even with the waiters pushing them a bit, there may be as many as five or more left over at the end of the evening. These are often devoured by staff.

"I've accounted for the served entrées," Cassandra said, "and the takeouts. That only cost me an hour and a half studying receipts, which in turn led to my developing a killer headache. I think I may need glasses. Are contacts covered by our health insurance?"

"You'd know more about that than I," I said. "Thank you for the coq au vin report, Cassandra. And would you do me a big favor? Before the silverfish cops take all the steaks from kitchen, set two aside for me."

She rolled her eyes. "My boss, an ass man."

"Spread the word," I said. "But mention I'm not so jaded I'd turn my nose up at a pair of nice round breasts."

"Sometimes, Billy, you really disgust me."

"Don't forget the steaks," I reminded her.

Chapter

SEVENTEEN

New York's Finest had snagged all the steaks by the time Cassandra went looking for my deuce. So I wound up working a little harder than I'd planned that night at Phil Bruno's, building a dinner around a two-pound rack of lamb. While I put Phil's Viking stove to use roasting the lamb, simmering a ginger-mint sauce, and creating a potato-leek soup, he occupied himself by putting together a presentation of the footage he'd shot in Kabul.

The kitchen was impressive, better equipped and better-looking than the one we used on set at the Wine & Dine. The onyx sink and built-ins, and the leather, chrome, and smoked-glass dining-room furniture, all rested on a sparkling black-tile platform. It was a sort of freestanding set piece for a huge living space that occupied the complete upper floor of a converted warehouse in the Meatpacking District, south of West Fourteenth Street, just a few blocks from Pastis and PM and the other hot restaurants and clubs.

The walls were a dark wood, the floor covered by a deep sea-green carpet that added timbre to the voice of Frank Sinatra, who at the moment was singing about the Isle of Capri from some hidden stereo source.

I enjoyed the kitchen time: I found it very therapeutic to perform familiar tasks that I was confident would be completed successfully within a relatively short period of time. Sinatra had made his vocal tour of vacation spots and we'd moved to another Jersey Frankie, Valli, by the time I laid out the lamb en croute on the dinner table, along with the potato-leek soup, hot dinner rolls, and, to slosh it all down, a tasty, Bordeaux-styled Corbières.

Phil took one look at the spread and said, "Fuck you, Blessing, where's the ketchup?"

For a while we were too busy eating to talk. Then, hunger satisfied, we polished off what remained of the wine and sampled the lemon tarts I'd rescued from the Bistro's freezer and discussed an assortment of things unrelated to why I was there.

Phil told me a little about his late father, the famous *Life* photographer Claudio Bruno. One of his most recognizable black-and-white pictures, blown up about four times the size of a magazine page, occupied a section of the loft's rear wall, between Phil's bedroom and office. If you're old enough, you may remember the photo. It captured in crisp detail a puffed-up, then-still-ambulatory Alabama Governor George Corley Wallace Jr., strutting in some gala state parade, blissfully unaware that a little black boy in pressed white shirt, short white pants, and saddle oxfords was sticking out his tongue, razzing him from the sidelines.

Old Claudio had been a real pro with a camera but not much of a dad, as Phil saw it. Usually away from home on assignment and when at home preoccupied and distant, the elder Bruno wasn't exactly Cliff Huxtable. When Phil's mother died from cancer, he and his sister, Gina, were left to fend for themselves. Years of therapy had led Phil to believe that his father's rejection was why he'd settled for a bachelor's life.

"What exactly are you hoping to find on my footage?" he asked me, when we came to the end of the lemon tarts.

"I don't know. I may not even know it when I see it."

"Well, let's take a look," he said, picking up our coffees and leading me from the raised platform to the living-room area at the front of the former warehouse. A plush, dark-green leather sofa and chairs looked across a smoked glass–topped coffee table and an expanse of soft carpet to a large shiny black slab approximately nine feet high, ten feet wide, and two feet deep that rested near the wall. From it came the electronically subdued voices of Louis Prima and Keely Smith, dueting on "Banana Split for My Baby."

Phil placed my coffee near the chair on the right and his close to the left side of the couch. "I had wireless controls built into the left armrest," he explained. To illustrate, he pressed a button and Louis and Keely were immediately silenced. Another button and the front of the slab split apart, its sides sliding silently to the left and right, exposing an elaborate entertainment unit consisting of a large flat monitor and an assortment of decks with blinking lights—God knows what leisure-time delights they all delivered.

"I designed the case myself," Phil said, his grin a clear indication of the pride he had in his creative furniture, his electronic gizmos, and his whole setup.

"You should be working for Sharp or Sony or launching the Space Shuttle," I said. "On the other hand, looking at this place, I guess you're doing pretty well at the network."

"Oh, the building was my inheritance," he said. "The old man finally came through. When *Life* closed shop and he got hit so bad by arthritis he couldn't keep running around, he bought this warehouse for studio work. Portraits. Some ad stuff. The irony was, by the time he finally settled down in one place where we might have been able to connect, I was beginning my career at KCBS on the West Coast. He had one foot on a cloud when I started the gig here at WBC. We had just a few weeks to get to know one another.

"After he died, I took this building and my sister took the house in Long Island. She wanted to get away from winter and the Northeast, so she sold it right off. That was back when property values were up. Gina's a Miami girl now."

He'd been sorting through a stack of DVDs that he'd assembled, studying the labels as we talked. He selected one and, holding it, clawlike, by outer edge and center hole, fed it into one of the glowing decks. Then he returned to the couch, where, using his wireless armrest, he lowered the room lights, turned on the monitor, and played the DVD.

The image on the monitor was high-def sharp and crisp, a handheld scene of a poorly lit secluded street in, Phil informed me, central Kabul. Five men were walking, mainly in shadow, not talking. You could hear distant gunfire and shouts on the soundtrack.

"There we are, approaching the Irish pub," Phil said.

The quintet was suddenly illuminated by a streetlamp. The three armed security guys dressed in camouflage clothing were strangers to me, but I knew the others. Rudy Gallagher, slightly in the bag, and Gin's boyfriend, Ted Parkhurst, looking wary but game and performing a familiar gesture, using his hand to comb back a hank of the fine light-brown hair that was forever falling across his forehead.

"Ted could use a little gel," I said.

"Or find a better barber," Phil said. "But that might not be necessary. My guess is he'll be bald by the time he's forty. Hell of a nice dude, though."

"Yeah, he is. He spend a lot of time with you guys?"

"Hung out with us most nights," Phil said.

"Which one of the camo guys is the one who was murdered, Hall?" I asked.

"The biggest one, with the buzz cut. The guy with the 'stache is Gault. The one with glasses is Fredricks. He was almost human. The others were pricks. Standard merc meatheads."

The men looked as if they were headed for a concrete wall, then veered left and walked around it to the lighted but unmarked door of a mock-Tudor two-story. Hall opened the door and the others followed him inside, Gault remaining behind until even Phil and his camera entered.

They wound up in an Irish pub that couldn't have been any more festive if it had been St. Patrick's Day. Bono was wailing from the loudspeakers. Afghani waiters in white shirts, black bow ties, and black pants moved through the crowd with trays carrying bottles and mugs of beer to mercenaries, soldiers, and men and women in civilian garb.

Phil's camera panned the room, the people, the Afghan carpets covering the floor, the Guinness ads on the walls, the lanterns on the tables ("In case of power failure," Phil explained), and the bar with its green-marble top ("Imported from Ireland").

A giant Afghani who looked like he was about to bust out of his tux stood near the front door. "The dude's a bouncer to keep the natives out," Phil told me. "That's the deal the owners, a couple of Sinn Féin rejects, cut with the local militia: The bar is for the use of foreign visitors only."

"Then how did the guys who started the fight get in?" I asked.

"They were dressed like waiters."

On the screen, Gallagher, Parkhurst, and the Touchstone guards were seated at a long table. Deacon Hall, the soon-to-be victim, gestured for Phil to turn off the camera.

The screen went to black. Then almost immediately it popped back to life, this time from a fixed angle facing down the table. "If he'd asked nicely, I might have kept the camera off," Phil said. "But I don't like muscle boys ordering me around."

Nothing much happened on-screen.

The men talked, mainly about the war, drank, and discussed women, not always in gentlemanly language. Rudy spilled beer on his pressed khaki jacket and emitted a few curses. Ted joined the recorded Clancy Brothers in a stirring rendition of "Fighters and Biters." I was getting bored.

I was about to suggest that Phil use one of his famous wireless buttons to speed up the action when something caught my eye.

"You see that?" I asked.

"What?"

"Reverse it? Great. Now . . . stop . . . THERE."

The action froze on a still image of Hall leaning toward Rudy, who was seated to his left. "I see it," Phil said. "Their hands. Hall's slipping Rudy something. Something shiny that's causing a little flare-up."

"What's it look like to you?" I asked.

"A Zippo lighter, maybe. No. Thinner. Because of the flare, it's hard to tell."

"Any way you could magnify the image?"

"Maybe," Phil said. "But regardless of what you see on *24,* we can't just zoom in on it now. It'd pixilate into nothing. I'll have to put it through a computer and play around a bit. I don't know if that'll make it any easier to identify the object. You think it's important, Billy?"

"Hall gets murdered in Kabul and Rudy gets murdered here. So . . . it just might be very important."

"It'll take some work, and ordinarily I'd tell you to go screw yourself. But that was a hell of a meal, Billy. Let me futz around with it, see what miracles I can make."

I thanked him and thanked him once again when he said he didn't need any help loading the dishwasher and scrubbing up. I lowered myself to ground level via the warehouse's ancient open-sided pulley-operated lift, took a quick jog over to Ninth Avenue, and caught a cab near one of the flash clubs.

On the way to my building I was feeling pretty good about my chances of sliding down a few notches on Solomon's list of suspects. In less than forty-eight hours, I'd turned up a little black book with the phone numbers of an assortment of women who had far better motives for murder than I, and now a bit of intrigue linking Rudy to a murder in Kabul.

My mood remained high until I arrived at my darkened building. Was my old visitor, Clove Boy, waiting for me inside?

I unlocked the rear door, turned off the alarm, and immediately reset it. Then I prowled around the building. The only thing I found of note was a message Cassandra had tacked to my office door. Our new E.P., Trina Lomax, had called at six-fifteen. An executive decision had been made: I was to remain on leave from the show until further notice. She'd let me know if and how my series on the Wine & Dine Network might be affected.

Great.

Dispirited, I changed into my pajamas and flopped on the bed.

I lay there, evaluating my situation. I was still at the top of the suspect list. I was out of work. And my restaurant was in lockdown. Not to mention the usual depressing thoughts that pop into your head at that time of night. The concerns about growing old alone, and that chest pain that may not be indigestion, and the fact that you haven't really done much with your life.

It took two hours and half a bottle of Glenmorangie, pride of the Highland peats, to rock me to sleep.

EIGHTEEN

"Why are you going to the weasel's funeral, Billy?" my lawyer Wally Wing asked.

"I worked with the guy."

"Hell, I worked with the guy, too. On your contracts. But you won't catch me anywhere near Saint Pat's. Too nice a day to tempt the fates."

"Tempt what fates? It's a Catholic funeral service."

"You and I know, my brown brother, that as we speak, Gallagher's getting his ass tanned by Satan's furnace. Yet in less than an hour, people are going to be lying through their teeth about what a swell human being he was. In a house of God, no less. I don't need to be soaking up that kind of bad karma."

We were in Wally's office on Mott Street in Chinatown, a few doors down from the Peking Duck House. It was an oddly comfortable room with dark, polished furnishings—black and red lacquered chairs, a black leather couch with legs like lion paws, and Wally's sleek black desk, the size of a dining-room table.

Brightening things up was a large Oriental rug the color of pink rose petals mixed with sky blue. To our right was an altar hosting a foot-high statue of a Chinese god with a furious face, holding a hammer in his right hand. His name was Lei Kung, Wally had informed me on my first visit to the office. He was the god of retribution, who makes thunder with his hammer and punishes criminals who have escaped the legal system. At the moment, his hammer was quiet, which I took as a sign of affirmation of my innocence. A brass pot near the god's sandaled feet filled the room with the soft scent of sandalwood.

With us was Wally's clerk-assistant, a young woman of heartbreaking loveliness named Tina, who was a recent graduate of the Columbia Law School. Dressed in a dark business suit and pale-pink blouse, she sat nearby with an open steno pad, as if she fervently expected the noted contract attorney Wallace A. Wing to say something worth recording.

Wally, handsome, well-preserved in his early fifties, was garbed in a casual broad-shouldered black cashmere jacket, a black silk shirt with a Mandarin collar, floppy gray linen trousers, and gray silk socks with red clocks on them. His gray suede loafers, which rested just outside the office door, were probably twin brothers of the shoes I considered buying at Ferragamo until I saw the six-hundred-fifty-dollar price tag.

He wore small, round glasses tinted a pale blue and framed in silver. His hair was long, mainly black but with dramatic strands of gray, tied in a ponytail that didn't quite hide the cue underneath. He was a little bit trad, a little bit rock and roll.

"I didn't think you believed in stuff like karma," I told him.

"I do, when I've got a client who can get a seven-figure advance for a book titled *You Can Change Your Karma*."

"At the risk of bringing you down to earth with my petty problems," I said, "why am I here?"

"When you told me what they're trying to pull over at the Glass Tower, I had Tina dust off your contracts. Tell him the good news, hon."

"Bottom line," she said, "they don't have to use you, but they do have to pay you. You've got another three years to run at *WUA!*, with a slight annual bump, and two years on your contract with Wine and Dine. The deal we made for the new series, *Food School 101*, appears to be moot, since they will not be proceeding with the pilot."

"Nice of them to tell me about it."

"I think they either have notified or are about to notify your partner in the project, Lily Conover," Tina said. "In any case, there is a generous kill fee now due."

"So I just sit out the other jobs?" I asked Wally.

"If you want," Wally said. "But I gave Gretchen a jingle, and she says you can come back to work whenever you so desire."

"Just like that?"

"I had to sell her, of course," he said. "I told her how much the show sucked this morning without you. And she agreed."

"You watched the show?"

"Billy, on the rare occasion I'm up at seven a.m., I watch the *Today* show. Or maybe, if I'm feeling just a little too upbeat, CNBC, to see how much loot I'm losing."

"So you never watch my show?"

"Say the word and I'll watch it every morning and just add the hours to your bill."

"Stick with the *Today* show," I said, standing. "Although I'm not so crazy about the weather guy, the rest of them are pretty good. I'll be going to church now, where I will pray for your enlightenment. Tina, a pleasure seeing you, as always."

"Hold on," Wally said, hopping to his sock feet. He circled the desk and walked me to the door, saying, "There's more good news. My source at the DA's office says they're letting you get back to business at the Bistro."

"That is good news," I said.

"In the words of my glorious ancestor, Charlie Chan, 'Settle one difficulty, and you keep a hundred others away.' Go forth, my brown brother, and remain difficulty-free."

Chapter

NINETEEN

If I really was free from difficulties, most of the mourners at Rudy's funeral hadn't gotten the word. They were gathered, some fifty strong, near a side altar in the massive cathedral. In any normal-size church, they would have seemed a crowd. In that huge, high-domed, white-marble edifice, they barely qualified as a gathering.

In any case, it was a gathering where I was clearly persona non grata. But not a total outcast. My coproducer Lily Conover seemed glad to see me. She'd been standing at the rear of the church, checking things out before committing herself to a pew.

"I'd have thought the crowd would be bigger," she whispered.

"You're thinking of those movies with half the church filled with the deceased's mistresses in black, weeping," I said.

"No. I'm thinking of Red Skelton's quip at Harry Cohn's packed funeral: 'Give the people what they want . . .'"

"I hear our *Food School* pilot has been given an Incomplete," I said.

"Yeah," Lily said. "I got the call yesterday. Just as well. At the risk of speaking ill of the departed, it was a frigging boneheaded concept."

We were about to slink into an empty pew when the commander spied us and waved us to his, urging Gretchen and the row of other executives to squeeze together to make room.

"Feeling better, Billy?" he asked.

An odd question, but I replied, "Feeling fine. And you?"

"Tip-top. So you'll be back at work tomorrow?"

Gretchen was observing us anxiously, and I realized she must have told the old man I'd been absent because of my health.

"Back tomorrow, with bells on," I said, smiling at his daughter.

"Good, good. That young hippy with the long hair, Slater, or whatever his name is, was supposed to be reviewing a book this morning, and he was holding the goddamned thing upside down."

"Dad, please," Gretchen said. "We are in church."

"Well, I don't like the little cretin," the commander said. I suspected he knew Chuck Slater was sitting right behind us, turning a lovely shade of crimson.

The funeral mass was delivered by a monsignor. Gretchen had probably tried for the new archbishop, then the rector, and then settled for a monsignor. He wasn't a bad choice, tall, graying, and stately in his white vestments, which, according to the handout, symbolized the Resurrection of the Spirit. Good luck with that, Rudy.

The monsignor moved the service along smartly, allowing only one chorus of "The Hymn of Saint Patrick" and the Offertory hymn, "There Is a Wideness in God's Mercy." His sermon, in which he praised Rudy's "lifetime of service to a community that depended on him for entertainment and information," lasted twelve minutes by my watch. Very few mourners took Communion. It wasn't that kind of crowd.

According to the handout, we were asked to save our eulogies for the more private gathering at the gravesite, which took care of Wally's concern about karma and made the whole service—from "Welcome" to *"Requiescat in pace!"*—clock in at just under forty-five minutes. If there had been commercials, we could've sold it as an hour. Rudy would've been pleased.

As I left the pew I caught sight of another outcast heading to the door. Melody Moon, in a simple light-gray dress with long sleeves and a white collar and cuffs, had been sitting at the rear of the church.

"Isn't that the cutie from the pilot?" Lily asked.

I nodded.

Accompanying Melody was her cartoonist roommate, Rita Margolis, dressed in her bright-yellow pea jacket, gray slacks, and a gray beret. Rita saw me, scowled, and took Melody's arm, moving her quickly from the church.

"Who's the girl in yellow, Billy?" Gretchen asked, before Lily could.

"Just another fan," I said.

"Was she one of Rudy's?"

"How would I know?"

"She seemed to know you."

"I'm on TV, Gretch," I said.

"Her friend's beautiful."

I stared at Gretchen, wondering if she was a better actress than I thought.

"Let's not dawdle," the commander said behind me.

Outside, he asked Lily and me if we wanted to accompany them in their limo to the cemetery. Lily, caught off guard, accepted the chauffeur's hand and entered the vehicle. I thanked the commander and begged off, saying I had work to do at the restaurant, which was true. While he waited for his daughter to get into the limo, I asked, "Commander, why did you send Rudy to Afghanistan?"

He blinked in surprise, hesitated, then said, "I don't know why it would be of any interest to you, Billy. It was just a father's foolish mistake. Nothing more."

Before I could think of a follow-up question, he was in the limo. The chauffeur closed the door with a click and moved swiftly to his position behind the wheel.

I watched the limo glide down Fifth, then pause at the corner for Melody Moon and Rita Margolis to cross the street. There may be eight million people in the naked city, but paths keep crossing all the same.

I was reminding myself to pick up some of Rudy's DVDs for Melody, when Gin shouted my name. She was with her traveling boyfriend, Ted Parkhurst, who offered a hearty handshake and asked if I needed a ride to the cemetery.

Once again, I declined the chance to see Rudy get buried six feet under. "But I would like to sit down and have a talk, at your convenience," I told him.

He raised an eyebrow. "Not going to ask me about my intentions, I hope."

"Everybody's been wondering," I said. "But no. I'd like to hear about the night you spent with Rudy in Kabul."

"God, yeah. Weird night, especially with that merc getting killed. Sure. What do you want to know?"

"Why don't you have dinner with us at my place, Billy?" Gin suggested. "Can you get away from the Bistro, around eight-thirty?"

"I'll make a point of it," I said.

Chapter

TWENTY

I won't bore you with the myriad details of getting the Bistro open for dinner that night. Let it suffice to say that, what with instructing the staff that Maurice Terrebone, my kitchen master, had assembled, planning a limited menu, checking the restocking operations, observing the restaurant scrubdown, phoning customers, and keeping Cassandra's acerbic attitude in check, my work was cut out for me.

We opened the doors at five-thirty p.m. By then, thanks to a Manhattan-based movie starlet who'd hired an undercover cop to murder her socialite husband, the restaurant and I were old news and the sidewalk in front of the Bistro was relatively media-free. Regrettably, as the hour progressed, it was also customer-free.

Eventually they began to trickle in, some to drink, some to dine. By eight, the main dining room, the only one we'd opened, was at about one-third capacity. Which I suppose wasn't bad, all things considered.

"I'm outta here," I told Cassandra.

"The rat deserts the sinking ship," she said.

"The ship is not sinking," I said. "And, I should note, this rat doesn't desert. Further, he pays your very handsome salary."

"But for how long?"

"Until you start to lose that happy glow," I said.

She rolled her eyes and asked if I remembered my cellular. I showed it to her, and she said she'd give me a call if anything disastrous occurred.

It was fortunate that Gin McCauley was now filthy rich, because, while she may have been a good comedienne and a fair newswoman, the only way anything edible would emerge from her kitchen was if she paid for it. It was even more fortunate that the loot she lavished on a large Cuban cook named Estella was money well spent. We enjoyed shrimp and saffron rice, black beans, and fried plantains, served with a crisp white wine so chilled it nearly caused brain freeze.

I hadn't paid attention to the bottle when Ted poured, so my first sip surprised me. "Vionta?" I asked Gin. "A 2004?"

"From the Rias Baixas region of Spain," she said. "Just like I read about in this wonderful book that was full of wine history and lore and advice on what to drink with what. It was written by an acknowledged expert in the field."

I half smiled and put on the fake humble look most authors use when complimented. "A wise man said, 'Write what you know.' "

Ted raised his glass. "To Billy," he said, "a man who knows his vino."

"A man I can always count on," Gin added.

I sampled the Vionta again, then shifted the subject by asking Gin if she was enjoying her new status on the show. She had just learned that in spite of her cohost Lance Tuttle's big push to interview Goyal Aharon, the ex–Mossad agent had asked for her, the fifteen-million-dollar woman.

"I tell you, Billy, it's like ah'm playin' in a whole new league."

"With the loot you're making, Gin, you could buy your own league," I said.

"The rich get richer," Ted said with a smile, clinking his wineglass against his paramour's.

"Oh," she said. "Do I have to start worryin' about you lovin' me for mah money?"

"I loved you before," he said. "But now that you're disgustingly rich . . . wow, just feel the beat of my heart."

"Mah boy toy want me to buy him somethin' special?"

The conversation was turning a little too cute, or too creepy. I decided to shift gears by asking, "Is Aharon's book any good?"

"*Dark Command* is a spy thrillah that's either bad le Carré or good Ludlum," Gin said. "Frankly, I couldn't care less about his dumb old novel. His publicist says everything's on the table. I can ask him about Israeli assassination squads, torture, letter bombs. Anything."

"Let the good times roll," I said. "What about your plans, Ted? You sticking around for a while?"

"Maybe. I've missed this crazy woman, so I'm trying to convince my editor to let me snoop into a few local things. Rudy's murder being one of them."

"Any idea what he was doing in Kabul?" I asked.

"Riding herd on Jim Bridewell's evening newscasts," Ted said, brushing back his pale brown forelock.

"No other agenda?"

"Not that I know of. What have you heard?"

Instead of answering, I said, "Tell me about that night the Touchstone guard, Deacon Hall, was killed."

"In the Irish pub. How'd you know I was there?"

"Phil Bruno," I said.

"Right. The cameraman. But he and Rudy left before the guard was killed."

"You stayed?"

"Jesus, yeah. It was a hell of a thing. The others split as soon as the two Afghanis started shouting and making threatening gestures. But it looked like something to write about, so I saw it through. It was grim." He pushed back the unruly forelock again. "The Afghanis went for the bouncer, who tossed 'em around a little. Then they drew these knives and the bouncer backed off, no fool he. They charged our table and hit Hall like a pair of raptors, one from each side. He got his gun out, blasted one to hell, but the other slit his throat. The killer headed for the door, and Hall's partner took him out. Head exploded like a melon. There was blood everywhere."

"Holy crap," Gin said. "Some of us are still eating here, Vlad."

"Sorry, hon," Ted said. "But Billy asked."

"Just one more thing," I said. "Before all the bloodshed, did you happen to see Hall hand anything to Gallagher? A shiny object of some kind?"

"No. Tell me more."

"Well, from what you say, it sounds like those guys were there specifically to kill Hall."

"That's how it looked," Ted said.

"So Rudy goes to Kabul," I said. "He has drinks with a merc. The merc's murdered. Rudy comes back home and he's murdered. Maybe it's a coincidence, but a pretty big one. If Hall passed something to Rudy in the Irish pub, that would take it out of the coincidence category entirely."

"Was it Phil who saw the pass?" Ted asked.

"Not at the time," I said. "But he got it on camera."

"He was taping in the club?"

"Yeah. He was showing me the footage, and we both thought it looked like Hall handed something to Rudy. But we couldn't quite make out what it was."

"Isn't there some way to clear up the image?" Gin asked.

"Phil's been working on it," I said.

"Well, jeez, Billy," Ted said. "Get on the horn and see if he's got anything. This could be the story I'm looking for."

Phil Bruno picked up on the fifth ring, sounding annoyed. "Billy," he said, "you caught me on the computer, right in the middle of the cleanup."

"How's it coming?"

"It was just a matter of finding the right filtering program. One or two more passes and we'll have a pretty good look at the thing, whatever it is."

"I'm with Gin and Ted Parkhurst," I said, noticing that they had taken some of the dirty dishes into the kitchen. "Could we come over for the unveiling?"

"I guess so," Phil said. "Wine and cheese is about the best I can offer on short notice."

"More than we deserve," I said. "We've already eaten."

"How far away are you?"

I had to stop and think. Gin's apartment was on Riverside Drive. "Maybe twenty minutes with the traffic. Might take us another ten or fifteen to get moving."

"If you let me get back to it, I'll probably have it ready when you get here."

Ted stuck his head into the dining room. "What's the word?"

"We should go over to his place," I said.

"Great. I'll go move the little lady along."

Waiting for them, I put in a call to Cassandra and discovered that business was off by sixty-five percent. About as expected. "I did comp a few friends," she said. "Just so the paying customers wouldn't feel too lonely. I hope that's okay."

"It's fine," I said, curious about what her friends might be like. In fact, I was a little surprised that she had any.

"What about reservations?" I asked.

"Dribs and drabs, but they're coming in."

"Everybody happy?"

"Happiness is relative," she said, and hung up.

Chapter

TWENTY-ONE

Our cab took us past the bustling nightlife in what, some said, had become a much-too-gentrified section of the Meatpacking District. The noise and the traffic were only a few streets deep, and by the time we got out of the cab at Phil's converted warehouse, the glitz had been replaced by true city grit. The area was dark and deserted and almost quiet, except for the faint sounds of distant club babble.

The light over Phil's front door, which had been burning brightly for my last visit, was now dark. That's why, when the door opened, I couldn't quite make out the figure that emerged from the building.

"Phil?" I called out.

Instead of replying, the figure darted to the right, then disappeared down an alley beside the warehouse.

"Guess it wasn't Phil," Gin said, with a nervous giggle.

The person who wasn't Phil had left the front door ajar.

"Should we just go in?" Ted asked.

I entered the building and called out Phil's name.

No reply, but there was the sound of loud voices and ricky-tick music from up above, and light flashed in the open elevator shaft.

I called again. Same lack of reply.

I led the way to the old elevator and put it in motion. Wheels grinding, it took us up a flight to Phil's living space. The lights and the voices and the music were coming from the large TV monitor in the living room. Daffy Duck was in a spaceship, trying to avoid Marvin the Martian, who was wearing a helmet with a scrub brush sticking from the top. *Duck Dodgers in the Twenty-fifth and a Half Century.* A classic.

"Phil must be in his office," I said.

I took a step from the elevator and a strong, almost toxic, chemical odor stung my nostrils. The carpet was squishy wet underfoot. The whole floor seemed to have been doused in fluid.

"What the hell?"

Before my mind clicked in on what was happening, there was a loud WHOMP and the door to what I remembered as Phil's office blew open. A ball of flame leaped through it and began to consume that side of the large room, tongues of fire licking the walls, descending to the floor.

"Come back, Billy," Ted called. "This place is going!"

I watched the flame eat through Claudio Bruno's famous photograph. "Phil," I shouted.

"Billy, we're almost on fire," Gin screamed.

The flames hit the carpet and began dancing in our direction at incredible speed. Smoke clotted the air. Daffy Duck's raspy voice was being drowned out by the sudden intense sound of the fire, like a huge popcorn-making machine in overdrive.

"Billy! No time!" Ted yelled.

He was right. Ours were the only lives left to save in that building.

I jumped back on the elevator, and Ted sent it downward. We hit ground level just as the flames spilled over into the elevator shaft and started to travel down the oiled wooden sides.

We rushed from the warehouse. Luckily, we'd left the front door open. We barely made our frantic exit when the heat from the fire blew out the second-floor windows, scattering little shards of glass over us like snow.

From a safe distance, I stared in horror and, I hate to admit, fascination as the fire toyed with the building. I was aware of both Gin and Ted, drawing their phones like journalist gunfighters, calling in the story to their night staffs.

I was glad to have them there, glad I wouldn't have to be the one to summon the firemen. My conscience wouldn't allow me to just walk away, but I didn't want to be the spokesperson for the group. I was still Solomon's primary suspect in the Gallagher murder. My involvement in a new murder—and I was certain Phil Bruno's body was inside the burning building—would only add to the detective's belief in my homicidal tendencies.

With luck, Gin, the fifteen-million-dollar woman, would be the main-ring attraction of the soon-to-arrive media circus, and I could stay a few steps away from the action.

Just a thought.

Chapter

TWENTY-TWO

By the time the firefighters arrived with their hoses and axes, and the NYPD officers established a crowd barrier, a number of club crawlers had drifted our way like Kamikaze-soaked moths drawn to flame. The media crowd had been gathering, too, their interest divided between a burning building and Gin McCauley, who was being singularly ineffective in trying to convince the gawkers to go home.

"How much do you get to keep after taxes?" someone asked her, maybe a journo, maybe a drunk; it was hard to tell the difference.

Once the firemen went into action, they became the focus of attention.

Gin drifted across the street to where Ted and I had been standing, he nattering incessantly into his cellular, I keeping on the down low. We had decided we would stick to a very simple story. Phil was a coworker and friend who'd invited us to his loft for wine and cheese. When we arrived we saw someone leave the building and run away as we approached. We went inside, called Phil, and received no answer. We saw that the loft was on fire and we ran from the building. Both Gin and Ted called their offices, who in turn alerted the NYFD.

That's essentially what we told the pair of fire department investigators. They had a string of additional questions. Did we see Phil in the burning building? No. Could Phil have been the person we saw leaving? *Hmmm*. Maybe. Was I sure the rug was soaked with some chemical? Definitely. Did we know of any reason why Phil would want to set fire to his loft? No. Did we know if the building was insured? Isn't everything? Any idea where they might find Phil? Inside the building.

It took the firefighters several hours to control and extinguish the flames. The building hadn't burned to the ground, but it would have to be gutted and rebuilt.

"The place is just a concrete slab attached to steel girders," one of the FD investigators told us shortly before midnight after he and his partner had checked out the interior. "Everything else is ashes and charred wood and hunks of melted plastic."

"What about . . . Phil Bruno?" Gin asked.

The investigator's sooty face registered dismay. "There's a charred human body in there. Could be your friend. It'll be up to forensics to make an ID."

"Everything else is gone?" Ted asked.

"Pretty much. Looks like there was a lot of electronic equipment, cameras—all melted and burned to hell. Furniture, nothing but piles of ash. Porcelain sink, toilet, stove, all recognizable, but I'm not sure they can be reused. Same for the refrigerator-freezer. The heat buckled it but didn't break it exactly."

"Anything inside the fridge?" Ted asked.

"Melted and fried goo. Looks like the fire started in a small room to the right of what used to be the kitchen. The body was in that room. You say your friend was a photographer?"

"A television cameraman," I said.

"Oh. Then I don't suppose he worked with photographic chemicals."

"He inherited the building from his father, who was a still photographer," I said, "so there may have been chemicals."

"Even with that, I don't see this as an accident." The investigator shook his head. "Somebody splashed combustible fluid all over the loft area."

"Look this way, Gin," someone called, and I saw a WBC news cameraman moving in our direction. I took a few quick backward steps out of the shot line. Gin was caught in the bright light, but she didn't seem to mind at all.

I watched her field a few questions with a friendliness and poise that was both professional and a little chilling, considering what we'd just been through. I took another step back and stumbled over somebody hunkering close to the ground.

"Wha—?" I said as Ted jumped up, steadying himself enough to stop me from falling to the pavement.

"Billy," he said. "I'm so sorry."

"What were you doing down there?" I asked, once the surprise had worn off.

"There's something odd there on the sidewalk," he said.

I looked down.

On the pavement in front of Phil's building was a childlike chalk drawing. Water from the fire hoses and the scuffling of gawkers' shoes had done damage to the scrawled lines. But in the light from the cameras trained on Gin, I could easily make out the artist's intent. It was an animal with matchstick legs, a tiny tail, pointy ears, black dots for eyes, and a tiny nose over three sets of whiskers.

A crude drawing of a cat.

"This isn't exactly a neighborhood where kids play," Ted said. "And I can't be sure, but I don't remember seeing it when we first got here. You make anything of it?"

"Not really," I lied.

Chapter

TWENTY-THREE

It was clear that the members of the King of Prussia High School Glee Club hadn't spent the very-early-morning hours watching the opening of our show, reading the papers, or cruising the Internet. If they had, they'd have seen news items, blogs, videos, and Twitters about my involvement in the unnatural deaths of two of my Worldwide Broadcasting Company associates. That might have made them at least a little less eager to shake my hand as I greeted them on the sidewalk in front of the *Wake Up!* window on the city. Instead most of the fresh-faced, high-spirited young Pennsylvanians were yahooing and screaming and laughing.

One of them, a cheery young female, somehow managed to bridle her enthusiasm long enough to inform our viewing audience how much they were enjoying their visit to New York City and how grateful they were to have been invited to participate in the All-American Sing-off that would take place at Carnegie Hall on Saturday night at seven p.m.

That gave me the opportunity to trot out one of my all-time faves, "Do you know how to get to Carnegie Hall?" When the young girl said no, the crew and I shouted in unison, "PRACTICE!" Gets 'em every time.

Near the gleeful glee clubbers was a quartet of Asian women wearing large, lumpy, but colorful costumes, their lovely faces partially covered by bright orange and yellow and green masks that included brown papier-mâché animal horns that curved down to their shoulders. "Chef Blessing," one of them called out.

"Hi, ladies," I said. "What's the story on your wardrobe?"

"We're in oxen costumes," their apparent spokeswoman explained.

"You certainly are," I said. "What's your name?"

"I am Tina. With me are Lotus and Lucy. We here to remind everyone that this is the Chinese Year of the Ox and"—she reached down with black gloved hands to retrieve from the sidewalk a huge can labeled CHINA KITCHEN OXBLOOD SOUP—"for you," she said, handing me the can, which, judging by its weight, may have contained a complete ox simmering in its own juices.

"We call this special soup *seonjitguk*."

"*Seonjitguk*," I thought I repeated.

"No, no," she said. "*Seonjitguk*. Anyway, you try soup. It is delicious. And . . . it is a wonderful way to rid the body of the toxins from overindulgence."

"Good to know," I said. "Thank you."

I was about to move on when she reached out and touched my arm. "Chef, we were concerned by your absences on *Wake Up, America!* We are so happy to see you back. You are our favorite. You are why we watch the show each morning."

"Thank you so much," I said. I could have added a special thank-you to Tina's boss, Wally Wing, my lawyer, for concocting the whole Year of the Ox sham just to send the message to the WBC brass that I had been missed. But that would have been self-defeating. Instead I said, "Thank you, I'm very happy to be back."

Which was the truth. Even though the start of the show had been a bit uncomfortable.

The local news lead-in at six-forty-five a.m. had been all about the fire, the charred victim, presumed to be WBC cameraman Phil Bruno, and the fact that two other employees of the network, Gin McCauley and myself, had reported the conflagration. The beautiful, unblinking, and inexperienced talking head had then added that Gin and I would be discussing the fire immediately after the newscast on *Wake Up!* It was, in effect, a promo plug tagged to a hard-news bulletin, a cheesy exploitation method that must have had legends like Ed Murrow and Chet Huntley doing flip-flops in their tombs.

It was the inspiration of our temporary executive producer, Trina Lomax. She had insisted that *Wake Up!* begin with Lance Tuttle seated in what I called the "restricted men's-club set," a faux-book-lined oiled-wood study. Using his most sincere delivery, Lance informed our viewers that a second member of the WBC family had died at the hands of a vicious killer.

It was an audacious statement. The body had not yet been officially identified as Phil's. And even if it had been, the suggestion that a serial killer was setting us up like prospective victims in an Agatha Christie novel was nothing if not premature. And unsettling. Especially if one was to make the connection between a cat drawing at the scene of the fire and Felix the Cat, the hit man original gangster Henry Julian had warned me would be coming to New York to kill someone in the media.

"I'm now being joined by our good friends Gin McCauley and Bill Blessing, who were both on the scene last night when Phil was murdered and his elegant town house burned to the ground."

Feeling a little light-headed, I followed Gin onto the set, where we sat, flanking Lance. A male model in butler's livery, the living embodiment of The Daily Brew's Billionaire Blend logo, suddenly appeared, filling china cups with our sponsor's product. This was supposed to create the impression that we were having an off-the-cuff coffee klatch, unaware that the world was looking in, all in a nice tight three-shot.

"Guys, that must have been horrendous," Lance said, "seeing those flames coming toward you and running for your lives from the building. And then having to stand by, helplessly, while our pal Phil Bruno burned to a crisp."

My immediate thought was to smash this pompous ass in the face for referring to our friend like a slab of bacon. I replaced that thought with an urge to remind him that the DNA analysts were still a few days away from an official identification of the corpse. But I knew the rules of the game and so, like Gin, I kept up my end of the discussion by finding new ways of paraphrasing the fear and frustration I'd honestly felt.

The segment ended. During the ensuing three and a half minutes of commercials, Trina and Arnie gave us attaboys, Lance and Gin headed for the anchor desk, and, with the help of my assistant, Kiki, I got ready for my people-in-the street segment.

That segment, after nine minutes, was nearing its close.

I was talking with three gentlemen in formal kilts, representing the Jackson Hole, Wyoming, Scottish Festival to be held in three weeks. Two of the men carried bagpipes and seemed ready to wail. The third presented me with a basket containing an assortment of pastries. "I bet you were expecting haggis, Chef Blessing," he said. "But we decided on something different. These are Forfar bridies."

"Meat pies, right?"

"Right, chef. Mince meat, onions. Delicious. Just one of the delicacies we'll be having at the festival. Along with bagpipe bands, dancing, athletics. Try a bridie."

A mincemeat pie wasn't exactly my idea of breakfast food, but what the hell, it beat haggis. I lifted one of the pastries from the basket, took a bite.

It stuck in my throat. Nothing to do with the bridie, which was no doubt delicious. I'd let my eyes drift past the Scotsmen to two grim figures standing across the street. Detectives Solomon and Butker. Staring at me with all the intensity of wolves zeroing in on their prey.

I coughed.

"You all right, chef?" the Wyoming Scott asked.

"Fine," I said, turning to Kiki, who, ever alert, handed me the remains of her mug of Billionaire Blend.

I took a swallow, cleared my throat again, and asked the Scotsman, "Don't suppose you have any single malt in that basket?"

"Just bridies," he said. "But at the festival . . ."

Chapter

TWENTY-FOUR

"What exactly were you doing at Bruno's place last night?" Solomon asked about twenty minutes later.

The detectives and I were in my dressing room, along with Kiki, who silently and unobtrusively observed the Q&A while keeping track of the minutes and seconds I had left before my next on-camera appearance. Solomon had browbeaten Arnie Epps into shifting a couple of segments to make time for the interrogation, simultaneously reminding all present that the NYPD still considered me to be a one-man Murder Incorporated.

"Phil invited Ms. McCauley, Mr. Parkhurst, and me to visit," I said in answer to his question.

"Just phoned you out of the blue?" Butker asked.

"I phoned him, actually," I said.

"Out of the blue?" Butker asked.

For some reason, his repetition of the phrase annoyed the hell out of me. "No, not out of the blue," I said. And I told them my theory about the connection between Rudy Gallagher and the murdered Touchstone guard in Kabul.

"So Bruno had this video of the guard passing some object to

Gallagher on the QT?" Solomon asked. "Only you couldn't make out the object?"

"It was a blur."

"But he told you he was clearing it up, and that's the real reason you and your friends went to his place? To see the footage?"

I nodded.

"So let's say the stiff in the fire is definitely Bruno," Solomon said. "That'd make three guys at that Irish pub in Kabul now murdered. And they're connected by this unknown missing object."

"That's what I think," I said.

The two detectives exchanged looks. Butker appeared thoughtful. Solomon frowned and went *"Hmmm."*

I could've asked Solomon if he shared my deduction but instead tried a different approach. "What do you think?" I asked eagerly.

He stared at me for a few beats, then said, "That's just about the biggest pile of horse crap anybody ever tried to sell me."

"What?" I was thunderstruck.

"Some merc in Afghanistan, who's hated by ninety-eight percent of the population and barely tolerated by the rest, gets his throat cut," Solomon said. "Wow, what a surprise! A TV asshole in New York pisses off one of his business associates and is poisoned. A third guy dies in a fire, and, for all we know, he may have been trapped trying to burn down the place for the insurance. But everything's connected. Mystery solved by Sherlock Homey here."

"You don't find it odd that three men who had drinks together in Kabul just a few weeks ago have been murdered?" I asked Solomon.

"Maybe odd," Solomon said. "If it really happened."

"Of course it happened," I said. "Ask Ted Parkhurst. He was there."

"That being the case, I imagine he'd be a little spooked right now," Solomon said. "He didn't sound spooked when I talked to him on the phone. He didn't mention any drinks with the dead guys, either."

"Why would I make up something like that?"

"Oh, I don't know. Why would he do that, Butker?"

"To get the pressure off him," Butker drawled. "Divert us from the real situation."

"I'm just a simple working detective," Solomon said. "I look at evidence. I look at facts. I look at motives. You know a Franz Paska, Blessing?"

"Of course. He's one of the great young chefs. He's at Saint Julienne."

"Well, it seems that Gallagher talked with him a couple of hours before he was murdered," Solomon said. "Told him he was dropping your cable show and offered Paska the time slot. I'd been thinking jealousy was your motive, Gallagher busting up your romance with Ms. Di Voss. Now I've got a double motive. I've got the means, the poisoned food from your eatery. And I'm moving closer every day to the opportunity.

"So excuse me if I don't just go running off to check on some secret bullshit over in the Middle East when I should be here concentrating on the plain and simple fact that you hated the victim's guts."

He gave me a fake smile, turned, and sauntered from the room with Butker at his heels like a good dog. "Enjoy your freedom, chef," Solomon threw over his shoulder. "It's not gonna last much longer."

"Whoo-eee," Kiki said when they'd left. "That gent's mind isn't just closed, it's locked up tighter than a Flatbush bank. And you've got three minutes to get ready with the joke of the day."

I took out my cellular phone and pulled up the snapshot I'd taken last night, the drawing in front of Phil's destroyed building. I'd assumed it would be the pièce de résistance that would move Solomon to look into the whereabouts of the hit man known as Felix.

That optimistic assumption was my own personal joke of the day.

Chapter

TWENTY-FIVE

"See, this the reason I don't wash car," my driver Joe was saying as we bounced along a potholed section of Brooklyn far from the borough's pockets of yuppie gentrification. The parked cars had broken headlamps or were missing wheels. Trash littered the street and the sidewalks. Young brothers and a few sisters sat unmoving as statues on the steps of mottled brownstone apartment buildings, following us with their eyes.

"Even with the dirt camo, we're still not exactly blending in, Joe."

"Maybe not. But we not making anybody mad enough to throw rocks, neither."

One block farther, the atmosphere did a 180. The street was clean, the buildings well tended and slacker-free. It was like finding a model-neighborhood color photo in the middle of a black-and-white panorama of life's defeat.

The reason was Glory's Doughnut Shoppe, a freshly painted storefront with a bright-red awning that was on the ground floor of a well-cared-for building in the middle of the block. I told Joe to park directly in front.

"You not be long, right?" he asked.

"Relax," I said. "This is the safest place in all of Crooklyn."

I pointed to a bicycle with a large front basket that rested on its kickstand near the door. A metal sign attached to the basket read: GLORY'S—FOR THE BEST BREAKFASTS AND LUNCHES IN BROOKLYN.

"Do you see a lock and chain on that bicycle?" I asked Joe.

"No."

"That's because it, the shop, and the building are owned by a friend of mine, Henry Julian. You know the name?"

"Maybe. Old gangsta. Scary."

"More or less," I said, getting out of the car. "Glory's was his mother's place. It's run now by Henry's sister and her daughter, Ramona. Nobody in their right mind is going to be stealing anything that belongs to Henry or bothering anyone who's visiting Henry's shop."

Joe blinked and said, "Okay. But you still not be long, right?"

Henry spent most of his mornings at Glory's, arriving just after the breakfast customers and leaving just before the lunchtime crowd. He sat at "his" table at the rear of the shop, dressed in suit and tie, shoes polished to a sheen, sipping coffee, reading newspapers and magazines, and, on occasion, sharing some time with a friend who dropped by.

"This glazed doughnut hits the spot," I said.

"It better," Henry said. "Call your place a doughnut shop, better have some damn fine doughnuts."

"And the coffee's excellent."

"Robusta brew," he said. "Six dollars a pound wholesale, not that the poor brothers in the Congo who do the harvestin' get more than a few pennies of that. But you didn't drive all the way to Brooklyn to talk about pastry and fair trade."

"I wanted to show you this," I said, handing him my cellular with the photo of the cat drawing.

"My, my, my," he said. "Felix's calling card. These new boys got more vanity than opera singers. My man sent me a fax of a drawing that was found near the Nigerian general's dissected corpse. This looks like the real deal. When d'you take this?"

"Last night in the Meatpacking District," I said. "In front of a building that caught fire and killed a man."

"Just read about it," Henry said, pointing to the pile of papers. "They ID the victim?"

"Not officially. But every news source except the papers thinks it must've been the guy who lived there, a friend of mine named Phil Bruno, who worked for the network."

Henry took one more look at the photo and returned the phone. "Yeah, well, that's what I'd been told. Felix's interest was somebody in the media."

"Might have been a double," I said, and reminded him of Rudy Gallagher.

"Any idea who sicced Felix on 'em?" Henry asked.

"Not who but why, maybe." I told him about the night at the pub in Kabul and the mysterious object that seemed to link three deaths.

Henry nodded. "Probably something political at the heart of it," he said. "From what I unnerstand, Felix's early success kicked him up into the bigs, where the real money is. Political assassinations. He hopscotches the world for his clients." He smiled. "You're much too young to remember, but there used to be a TV newsman. Dapper little white dude. Always began his show with, 'This is John Cameron Swayze, hopscotching the world for headlines.'

"But I digress. Mos' likely there was a cat drawing somewhere in that Irish barroom that ever'body ignored."

"I don't see how Felix could have had anything to do with the death of the Touchstone mercenary in Kabul," I said. "Witnesses saw the killers. Two Afghanis."

Henry smiled at me as if I were a naive child. "Billy, you ever hear the term 'murder by proxy'? The way it used to be done, back in the sixties, you sent some hop head at your vic with a speedball full of death. How hard it be to talk some Afginnie crazies into cutting the throat of an American who was bein' paid a fortune to mess up their country?"

"The two killers were definitely focused on that particular target," I said.

"Hell, probably a cat drawing at the apartment of the news guy who got poisoned," Henry said. "Could be restin' in a police evidence room."

"The guys they've got investigating the murder might have thrown it away," I said.

Henry chuckled. "Take it from me, Billy. No matter how stupid, cops never throw nothin' away."

"What else can you tell me about Felix, Henry?"

"Jus' one thing: Leave him be."

"I'm not sure I can."

"Oh?" He was sitting upright now, frowning. "Why's that?"

"Because right now I'm still the main suspect in Rudy Gallagher's murder."

"And you're doing what?" Henry said. "Tryin' to solve the murder yourself? Son, that's about as smart as carrying a hair-trigger piece stuck down your pants. Didn't work so well for that dumb shit played for the Giants, and it won't turn out any better for you. My lawyers got excellent investigators who do that kind of stuff."

"I'm not planning on hunting the guy down," I said. "I just want to gather enough evidence to turn over to the cops. Let them take it from there."

He reached out and placed a large hand on my arm. "I always figured you as bein' bright, a man who knows the way the world works. You're not seeing this situation clearly. If you do succeed in pointing the cops in Felix's direction, it'll be like poking a bear with a stick. A big-ass, dangerous bear. You think you got trouble now. Imagine what it'll be like if you attract that bad boy's full attention."

"Point made and taken," I said.

"I sincerely hope so, Billy," the old man said. "Because of my profession and my age, I have become accustomed to losing friends. But I sure wouldn't want to lose a good restaurant."

Chapter TWENTY-SIX

"This seem like not long to you?" Joe asked when I returned to the car.

"I couldn't have been more than twenty minutes."

"An eternity," he said, "waiting here like lamb tied to tree with tigers all around."

"I'm sorry," I said. "Fear's no fun." I was feeling the effect of Henry's warning.

"Where you want to go now? Flatbush? Iraq? Camden, New Jersey?"

"Let's try someplace a little safer," I said. "The Glass Tower."

"Okay," Joe said. "But I park underground, not on street."

My first errand at the WBC building took me to a no-frills, windowless section at the rear of the nineteenth floor, where the editors worked their digital magic. It was like entering a workplace for low-ranking city-government employees. Gray carpet. Gray metal cubicles where the editors slouched on gray metal chairs, working at monitors resting on gray metal desks.

The walls were painted an ashlike smudge, their dullness unrelieved by any hanging art, even the color portraits of the network's performers that graced many a wall in the rest of the building.

Judy Alridge, whose elevated position of senior editor merited a cubicle a few square feet bigger than the others and her very own ficus tree, was focused on her monitor, mixing and matching footage from a collapsed-bridge disaster in the Midwest. She was a full-figured woman, dressed casually in denim pants and a plaid woolen shirt cut large enough to hide the result of her fast-food addiction.

In response to her name, she spun around in her gray chair, saw it was me, frowned, and said, "Hey, Blessing. Fess up now. Did you poison that prick Gallagher?"

"No way," I said. "I'm a live-and-let-live advocate."

"And I was all set to reward you with a big wet one."

"My loss," I said. "Judy, I'm looking for some DVDs of Gallagher's that you guys used in putting together his obit doc. Specifically a show he hosted called *USS Huckleberry*."

"I did the obit myself," Judy said. "I used a minute or two from that show. The son of a bitch actually seemed charming dealing with those kids. He shoulda stuck to his on-camera work. Then I wouldn't have had to put up with his obnoxious real personality, not to mention his constant bitching and moaning."

"And the disks are . . . ?"

"We tossed all of his crap into a big cardboard box in the storeroom. Right down the hall on the left. Knock yourself out."

The room was where she said it would be. Ditto the cardboard box and DVDs. There were about seventy-five of the silver disks in neatly labeled slim jewel cases. I shuffled through them and came up with a half-dozen labeled USS HUCKLEBERRY. Twelve full hours of stone-age TV animation interspersed with young Rudy Gallagher making nice with tots. Quite a treasure trove.

I jammed the six jewel cases into my coat pockets and moved on to the main reason I'd returned to the Glass Tower. For that I had to ascend much higher, to the sixty-fourth floor that pre-9/11 had been the exclusive aerie of the network's top executives. Now it was a windows-to-the-world nesting place for publicists, promotion copywriters, some advertising salespersons, researchers, the editors and maintainers of the company's Internet websites, and an elderly coot known simply as Marvin.

"Yo, Billy, what's the hap?" Marvin asked from behind his desk, staring out of the always-open door to his spacious office. He was wearing his usual sea-green warm-up togs and white cap with a flying dolphin logo, leaning back in his executive chair, long fingers interlocked across his flat tummy, huge feet snug in New Balance runners resting on top of his big, bare desk.

"Nothing much to report, Marvin," I said, before moving on to a large room filled with a long U-shaped table on which rested computer monitors, keyboards, and mice. The room was empty. I backtracked to Marvin. "Any idea where the research people are?" I asked.

"Taking an early lunch," he said, scratching his gray whiskers. "Violet—you know, the cute brunette with the ring stuck in her eyebrow—it's her twenty-second birthday, and they all went to this new place opened on East Fifty-ninth. Nanu."

"Any idea when they'll be back?"

"They're young," he said. "Sometimes they don't bother to come back. What do you need, Billy? Maybe I can help."

Maybe. I was never quite sure what Marvin did at WBC, only that he'd been employed there long enough to have been hired by the commander's father, Harold Di Voss. Marvin once told me he'd started in the business at NBC in the early 1950s, during the reign of Sylvester "Pat" Weaver, the genius who created the *Today* show and *The Tonight Show* and still had found the time to inaugurate the unique news and entertainment radio program *Monitor*.

When Weaver departed Marvin left, too, and was immediately hired by Harold Di Voss for one reason only. As Marvin likes to tell you, "He couldn't get Pat."

"I'm looking for information about a guy," I told Marvin.

"He got a name?"

I hesitated, then decided, why not tell him? "An international assassin who calls himself Felix the Cat."

"Well, now," he said, grinning. He swung his big feet off the desk and got up from his chair. "Let's go see what we can dig up."

He led me back to the empty research room, where he sat at the nearest computer. Like a concert pianist, he popped his knuckles, flexed his long, thin fingers, and sent them flying over the keys, making his own electronic music.

"You've done this before," I said.

"It's like anything else," he said. "Once you figure out how it works, it's just a matter of refining your skills. Did that my whole career. No reason to stop now that I'm retired."

On the flat screen, I saw that he had signed off the person who'd been using the computer and signed himself on, using the ID MonitorMan. It was obviously a reference to his work on Weaver's weekend radio show.

"You're retired?" I asked.

"Nearly seventeen years now," he said. "Once I hit mandatory, I sure as hell didn't want to spend all day in the house staring at my wife, Celia, even though she was and is very easy on the eyes. A certain amount of absence is needed. So I cut a deal with young Vern." That would be the sixtysomething commander. Young Vern. "If he gave me an office to hang out in, I'd continue to advise him like I did his dad.

"Here we go, Billy."

The name InfoScoob appeared on the monitor, followed by the description: "a meta search engine with the option to contact users conducting similar searches." A line of type at the bottom of the screen read: "created by MonitorMan."

"This is your program?"

"I worked it out last year when I got tired of watching these kids in research putzing around with Google. That Felix the Cat name all you got on this guy?"

"Afraid so."

"We'll start with that. But we're gonna have to figure out a way to narrow down the search a little."

Marvin typed in "Felix the Cat" and was almost immediately rewarded with more than a million hits. Judging by the first page, ninety-nine percent of those were references to the cartoon and comic-book character Felix the Cat.

Marvin changed the search to "Felix the Cat" plus "murder." That brought the number of replies down to just more than one hundred thousand. "Felix the Cat" plus "assassination" narrowed the results to just eighteen thousand nine hundred.

Finally limiting the search to "Felix the Cat" plus "assassin," we were rewarded with eighty-nine direct hits.

Nearly an hour later, having clicked through all the newspaper, magazine, and video reports, printing whatever I requested, Marvin said, "You're not curious about who Minnie might be?"

"I don't understand the question," I said.

"You missed the notice that 'Minnie' had made a similar search last week," he said. "I added user history to the program so that people who share a similar info quest might correspond with one another if they cared to."

"I don't think I want to correspond with Minnie," I said. "But I wouldn't mind knowing her real name."

He tapped only two keys and the screen was suddenly filled with the user profile of . . . Trina Lomax.

"*Hmmm.* Looks like you and our executive producer share a common interest in Felix."

I nodded.

"And since she's already done her research, and since political assassination is a little off your beat, I take it your curiosity about Mr. Felix is personal rather than business. Right?"

"It's personal."

He nodded and closed down the session, logging the original researcher back on to the machine. "Why don't we go back to my office and talk about it?"

I stared at him, wondering if it had been his age or the whiskers or the tarpon cap and warm-up suit that had led me to so underestimate the MonitorMan. He'd been a bright guy all of his life, smart enough to have earned the respect and confidence of both the commander and his father, and he hadn't seemed to have lost any of his mental acuity to age. Still, I didn't want to get into a discussion of my problems with a guy I barely knew.

"Thanks for the offer and for your help, but I think these printouts will be all I need right now."

"Your call. As Vern will tell you, I give good advice."

"I'm not even sure what kind of advice I'd ask," I said.

"Well, if you figure that out, you know where to find me."

"There is one thing."

He eyed me, waiting.

"The commander sent Rudy Gallagher to Afghanistan on some kind of mission. I don't suppose he asked your advice before he did that?"

Marvin smiled. "I see where you're headed, Billy. You're hoping to convince the cops that Felix had a better reason to put Rudy down than you did. And you think that reason may have something to do with Rudy's trip to Kabul."

He was definitely a shrewd old boy. "What was Rudy supposed to do for the commander, Marvin?"

"You're going to have to ask Vern that question."

"I did."

"What'd he say?"

"That it had been a father's mistake. I assume that means it had something to do with his son Bud's death. Right?"

"I really can't address that point," Marvin said. "Good luck with your plan, Billy. But my advice is for you to abandon it and let nature take its course. If you didn't kill Rudy, it's gonna be damned hard for the cops to prove you did. Get on with your life and let Felix get on with his, until he slips up. They always do."

I thanked him again for his help and his advice, and headed down to my dressing room with the printouts on Felix. I snagged a cup of Billionaire Blend from the kitchen and settled in at Kiki's desk.

My assistant had left a reminder for me on the bulletin board: Lily Conover had scheduled the usual back-to-back *Blessing's in the Kitchen* tapings for tomorrow at the Wine & Dine building. I groaned. Even in normal times, the every-other-Thursday workday was a grueling one, but rather than dote on that, I focused on the printouts.

There were more than forty separate articles and reports referencing the assassin. Not one of them offered anything other than rumors of Felix's involvement. Nonetheless, I broke them down according to victims. Six piles. Six assassinations. The stabbing of the leader of the Moleta drug cartel in Bogotá. The long-range shooting of a Muslim firebrand with ties to Osama bin Laden in the Philippines. The bombing of an official in Yemen who was interfering with the investigation of another bombing, the one that took place on the USS *Cole*. There was a second stabbing that Henry Julian had mentioned, the Nigerian dictator General Santomacha. And finally, only a few weeks before, there had been an immolation of an ayatollah who'd been urging Iran's president to break off talks with the West. You gotta love a guy who keeps changing the menu.

There were no witnesses to any of the crimes. No clues, other than the presence of a rudimentary drawing of a cat, that had led to the presumption that Felix had been the perpetrator.

The truly disturbing thing was that the assassinations weren't just political, the victims had all been working against the interests of the United States. Could Felix be employed by the CIA? Or an agency even more clandestine than the CIA?

Marvin's advice was sounding smarter and smarter. What had I been thinking? Just let nature take its course.

I collected the printouts and the notes I'd made, ran them through the shredder, and left my dressing room/office.

The *Wake Up!* studio was almost vacant, the exceptions being Trina Lomax standing at the news desk with Arnie Epps, complaining about the dullness of the set. Was Trina's computer ID, "Minnie," a reference to Mickey Mouse's girlfriend, wife, whatever? Why hadn't I thought of that immediately? Minnie the Mouse, looking up info on Felix the Cat.

Was it an inside joke she was sharing with Felix? Could they be associates?

I decided to slink away before I was spotted, but that didn't work.

"Billy," Trina/Minnie called out. "Hold a minute."

She marched toward me, Arnie doing his best to keep up. "I was going to call you, but this is much better face-to-face," she said. "I want to personally thank you for the professional way you reacted to our benching you. It was a mistake I wouldn't have made if I hadn't been so new to the job. You've a whole lot of fans out there who missed you."

"Good to hear," I said, biting my tongue to keep from calling her Minnie.

"And that segment this morning, you and Gin discussing the Bruno fire with Lance, pure gold."

Arnie looked uncomfortable. "Ah, speaking of Phil, we, ah, got word a while ago that the, ah, remains in the burned building were definitely his," he said.

"I'm sorry," I said. "Any word about a funeral service?"

Trina looked blank. Arnie said, "Doesn't look like there's gonna be one. I spoke to Phil's sister. She's flying in from Miami. Plans to stay here just long enough to settle with the insurance company, arrange for the sale of the property, and have Phil's remains quietly planted next to his father. She said something about donations to the Shriners children's hospital in Manhattan."

"Thanks for the information," I said.

"Anyway, Billy," Trina said, "I think we should capitalize on all this brand-name attention you're getting. Arnie, I want you to fill Billy's dance card every morning. Let's put him to work and make his fans happy."

"We have Billy's segs with Mr. Turducken on our list," Arnie said. "I could schedule it for Monday."

"Mr. Turducken?" Trina said. "I hope that's a trade name?"

"Guy claims to be the ultimate supplier of turduckens in the U.S.," Arnie said. "Sends 'em out from his place in Fairview. You know the place, Billy?"

"Not exactly."

"You should drive over and check it out before Monday," Arnie said.

"I, ah . . . I'm not big on trips to Jersey," I said. "The Lincoln Tunnel freaks me out. If God had meant for us to travel underwater, he would have given us gills."

"Take the bridge," Arnie said. "It's a much longer trip, but if you—"

"I want you to give Billy some entertainment segments," Trina interrupted, evidently bored with our New Jersey discussion. "I'm growing more and more disenchanted with our resident showbiz diva, Chuck. In fact . . ." She appeared to be thinking. "Yes. The Friday Favorites remote from the Manhattan Museum of Culture and Art."

She turned to me. "They're opening a new exhibit. *The Mortal Superheroes: The Reality of Fantasy*. It focuses on the comic-book superheroes who've died."

"There are dead superheroes?" I asked.

"Quite a few, I gather," Trina said. "I think even Superman is represented."

"Sounds a little narrow and downbeat for our audience," I said.

"I disagree," Trina said. "Their thesis is that the comics mirror reality a little more than we think. Should make for an interesting discussion. And there will be plenty of eye candy. Arnie has talked them into letting us bring in some hot male and female models to wear those skintight costumes and show off some real flesh. It should be a fun segment with its touch of humanity, right?"

"Sure," I said, trying to put her possible involvement with Felix out of my mind. "Superheroes. Sex. Death. It's got everything."

"And after you're done there," she said, "you can go visit Mr. Turducken."

"You've been eating onions," Cassandra said as I entered the Bistro. Her tone wouldn't have been more accusatory if I'd broken several commandments.

"I was feeling deprived, so I treated Joe to a fine lunch at Le Haut Dog on Fifty-second."

"Well, you reek," she said.

"Thanks for sharing," I said. "What's your take on turduckens?"

She blinked. "You mean the chicken inside the duck inside the turkey? You're asking the wrong person. I don't even like mixing peas and mashed potatoes. Are you thinking of putting turducken on the menu?"

"No. I just . . . going to Jersey . . . Never mind. I'll work it out. How's business?"

"The weekend is looking good," she said, walking with me to the rear stairwell. "I think all the murder talk is starting to help."

"Say what?"

"It's not just our cuisine that's bringing them in. They're curious. They want to see what a murder suspect looks like up close, Billy. People love bad boys."

"Maybe I should wear a black turtleneck and an eye patch," I said.

"I said bad boys, not pirates. Anyway, we'll be at close to full capacity on Friday and Saturday nights," she said.

"What about tonight and Thursday?"

"We're at about seventy percent tonight, and your former squeeze's assistant just reserved a private room. We're in good shape."

"That's what I like to hear."

"I'm surprised Ms. Di Voss isn't still in mourning," Cassandra said. "Maybe she's like a praying mantis, strutting her stuff after the death of her mate."

"You're confusing your insects," I said as we entered my office. "Praying mantises sort of hop, not strut. And they eat their mates, so it's unlikely they'd feel the need to come to a restaurant."

"You're so literal, Billy," she said. "The checks are on your desk. Please sign them today. But try not to breathe on them or they may wither and turn to dust." She made an about-face and left me alone in my oniony literalness.

I slipped out of my jacket and draped it over the couch, rolled up my sleeves, and sat down at the desk to face the monthly stack of bills and accompanying checks. I booted up the computer and opened our accounting program. Then I began going through each bill and payment, double-checking Cassandra's figures.

She did not make mistakes. And I spent the next hour or so proving it.

When I was finished, I considered what it might be like being the bad boy. I don't think I qualified, even when I was younger and engaged in activities that were what some might call illegal.

I was momentarily distracted by the sight of my jacket, which I'd thrown carelessly on the office couch. I frowned, got out of the chair, and went to pick it up. I brushed the wrinkles away and placed it on a hanger. So much not the bad boy.

The coat's heft reminded me that the late Rudy's DVDs were still in the pockets. Before relegating it to the closet, I removed the jewel boxes, careful not to snag or tear the lining of the pockets. My plan had been to box and mail the disks to Melody Moon, but I decided it might be friendlier if I dropped them off myself when I had the chance. Do not misconstrue my motives. Melody was still seventeen, and I was not the bad boy. Though, I have to admit, I sometimes had bad-boy thoughts.

I opened a desk drawer and, to make room for the disks, pushed aside the junk I'd accumulated over the last half-dozen years. Dental floss, ear buds, an assortment of coins, Gem clips, key chains, a mirror, tiny knives, a plastic eyeball, nail clippers, triple-A batteries that were probably deader than Rudy, my business cards, hundreds of business cards from people with whom I'd never be doing business, ancient breath mints that were not so ancient that I didn't pop two to combat the onions, plastic spoons, a small airline-size bottle of single-malt scotch.

And Rudy's little black book.

I made a nest for the DVDs and picked up the black book. I'd just opened it when Cassandra returned to pick up the checks. She stared at the black book and shook her head sadly. "So old school, Billy. So depressingly old school."

"Is there anything else you wanted?" I asked.

"Do you know a man named Parkhurst?"

"Ted? Sure. Why?"

"He's in the bar. Says he's a friend of yours. But he seems a little seedy to me."

"Seedy?"

"Well, drunk." She grabbed the stack of checks and bills and carried them away.

Without thinking about it, I put Rudy's black book in my pocket, stood, grabbed my jacket from the hanger, and headed downstairs.

Chapter

TWENTY-EIGHT

At a little before five, the lounge was far from lively. Two regulars from an ad agency down the street were at one end of the bar, having their usual martini before hitting the Metro North to Darien. Ted was at the other end, staring into a tumbler of melted ice that looked like it may have once contained an old-fashioned.

Juan Lorinda was at his post behind the bar. He looked at Ted, then at me, and shrugged.

Since I'd never seen Ted drunk before, I wasn't sure exactly how deep he was in the bag. Deep enough that he wasn't bothering to brush back his forelock. I headed toward him, calling his name.

He was a little slow twisting on his bar stool, but the smile on his face suggested he was still partially aware. "Billy," he said, "nize place."

He leaned a little too forward on the stool and stumbled off it. But he kept his legs under him and, with minimal help from me, was able to sit back down again.

"Your mix-ologist makes a lovely cocktail." His voice was thick and slurry. "But he's very stingy."

I looked at Juan, who'd been watching us.

"Celebrating something?" I asked Ted.

"Not egg-zack-ly. I have been trying to work some-thing out in my mind, Billy."

"Want to talk about it?"

"Could I have another one of these?" he asked, holding up his empty glass. "Your mix-ologist cut me off. Even though I told him I was a per-sonal friend of yours."

"What's going on, Ted?"

"Does some-thing have to be going on?"

"You usually this hammered by five o'clock?" I asked.

"Oh, Christ!" he yelped, and lifted his arm to check his watch. "Is it five already? I'm sup-posed to meet Gin at the apartment at seven."

"Then you definitely don't want another of those," I said. I turned to Juan and pointed to the coffeemaker. He nodded.

"I'm a failure, Billy," Ted said. "I don't have any money saved. I'm in a dead-end pro-fession. Reporters ten times better than me are getting laid off. They could decide to-morrow to close down the mag-azine. It's just a matter of time. If Gin and I marry, I'll be one of those hus-bands who take care of the house and su-pervise the god-damn garden. When papa-razzi catch us on the town, they'll ask me to step out of the picture. I'll be good for nothing. Hell, I can't even hold my liquor. I'm god-damn James Mason in *A Star Is Born*."

"Let's focus on the most immediate problem," I said as Juan placed two mugs of hot black coffee in front of us. "Getting you sober enough to meet Gin in two hours."

The black coffee helped his sobriety, but it did nothing to lift his mood. He'd had lunch with a reporter who'd been let go in the course of the most recent downsizing at the *Chicago Tribune*. She'd come to New York hoping to find a job, but so far there'd been no takers.

"We both worked on the *Trib* about nine years ago," Ted said. "The reason I left that job was that she always got the best assign-ments. Because she was so damned *good*. Now she's out on the street."

Eventually he admitted that there'd been another reason he'd left the paper. She'd been his girlfriend, and his machismo or ego or sense of competitiveness had made it too difficult for him to stay in a rela-tionship where the woman was more successful than he.

At the moment, even though Gin was certainly more celebrated, their playing fields—television and print—were different enough and he was a respected investigative journalist, which more or less evened things up. But what if, after their marriage, he should find himself just another unemployed has-been?

"Have you talked with Gin about this?" I asked.

"Hell, no. She's in the clouds right now. Why bring her down? It's my problem, not hers."

It *was* his problem, and I couldn't think of even a Dr. Phil–level suggestion of what to do about it.

The lounge had attracted several other customers, at least one of whom was very loud. I looked at my watch. "It's about six-twenty, Ted. You steady enough to make it to the apartment?"

"I'd like to freshen up. Splash some water on my face."

"Use my bathroom upstairs."

"No stairs, please. There's a men's room down here, right?"

I pointed toward it. "It's well stocked. Soaps, colognes. All the comforts of home."

"Do me one more favor, Billy. Wait here for me. I'm a little wobbly. Might need help getting out and flagging a cab."

"I'll be right here."

He took a while. I occupied my time watching Juan work the bar. He was very good, attentive and polite, even to the loud jackass who seemed convinced that the whole room was interested in everything he had to say.

The early diners had arrived, and the waitresses were bringing Juan their drink orders. When Bridget Innes approached him with her requests, they exchanged quiet smiles. No problem with that romance. At least for the moment.

Ted was a little unsteady returning from the direction of the men's room. I gave him my arm and we made it out of the Bistro with a minimum of fuss.

I asked one of the valets to flag down a cab, but Ted wanted to walk a few blocks, to clear his head and get his legs working. So we took a stroll in the general direction of Gin's apartment. Ted didn't bring up his *A Star Is Born* problem again, and I didn't, either.

Instead we talked about the murders. Through his own research, he had put together a collection of articles and notices involving the mysterious Felix that sounded very similar to the printouts that

Marvin's magical software had produced. But his magazine also had access to informants who were convinced that the assassin was presently in the United States, presumably not on vacation.

Ted had found nothing to tie Felix to Deacon Hall, the murdered security guard, but was trying to make a connection from the other end. He was building a dossier on Hall, who was survived by a sixty-four-year-old mother, presently residing in Petaluma, California, and a four-year-old son who was living with Hall's ex-wife and her current husband in Los Angeles.

L.A. had also been the security agent's hometown. Hall had gone to UCLA on a football scholarship that ended when he nearly beat a teammate to death in a bar argument. He had spent six years in the Marines before joining Touchstone.

Somehow he became a favorite of the company's CEO, Carl Kelstoe, who sent him to oversee its operations in Iraq shortly after the invasion. More recently, he'd been reassigned to Afghanistan.

Ted had got a journalist friend to sniff around Kabul. Neither Gault nor Fredricks, the other two mercs who'd attended their associate's fatal dinner, nor any of Touchstone's other employees in Kabul, would so much as admit they'd ever even heard of Hall. Since the killers were themselves deceased, the Afghan National Police had no further interest in the murder.

As for homegrown law enforcers involved in Rudy's case, Ted had interviewed Philip Rodell, Cassandra's favorite district attorney, and my two favorite detectives, Solomon and Butker, and discovered, no surprise, that they'd made no progress on the investigation into Rudy's death. Their main course of action now was to wait for me to make some self-incriminating mistake.

I hoped they were holding their collective breath.

"Did Solomon say anything about Kabul?" I asked.

Ted grinned. "He mentioned you'd told him, in his words, 'a bullshit story' about Rudy's and Phil Bruno's murders being connected to Hall's murder."

"And you said . . . ?"

"I told him that it was true we'd all had drinks that night. Then he asked me if I had any evidence to suggest that the deaths were linked."

"And you said . . . ?"

"No. I don't, Billy. If I did, the story would be appearing in the next issue of *Now* under my byline."

We'd been strolling for about fifteen minutes when a vacant cab appeared, and Ted, feeling enough like himself, flagged it down, thanked me profusely for my help, and hopped aboard. That left me with a bracing predinner power walk back to the Bistro.

The dining room was filling nicely. And, Cassandra informed me, she had seated Gretchen and her guests in Private Room 1.

The guests, I discovered, were Trina Lomax; Arnie Epps; Vance Underwood, the VP in charge of the network's legal department; Heck Cochran, the promotion and publicity VP; Gregory Korshak, head of network security; and a stunning, exotic-looking woman whom Gretch introduced as Lee Franchette, a VP at InterTec Security. Markham Books had hired Lee and her staff to guard the health and welfare of Goyal Aharon, who was starting his U.S. book tour with Gin's interview on *Wake Up!*

In my time on the morning show and as a restaurateur, I've met supermodels and actresses and any number of the world's great beauties, but they all took second place to the tall and slim and graceful woman who now offered me her hand. Her straight, black shoulder-length hair framed an exquisite face. Glittering emerald-green eyes with a slightly Asian tilt, cheekbones that would have made Pocahontas proud, lips as full and sweetly curved as a Nubian princess's, all on smooth skin the color of café au lait. I had to force myself to stop gawking at Ms. Lee Franchette.

By an extreme effort of will, I released her hand and welcomed her and, when I thought of it, all of the others, to my humble little four-star restaurant. I informed them of our specials, adding a few suggestions of my own. I then left them to contemplate Duck à l'Orange and Venison with Pine Nuts and Scalloped Crab à la Blessing, while I was contemplating the extraordinary Ms. Lee Franchette.

I stopped off at the kitchen, where the delicious aromas moved me to order an early dinner of broiled venison cutlets with currant jelly.

I was feeling better than I had in weeks, eager to start the night off with that airplane bottle of single malt that I'd discovered in my desk. But I was distracted from that plan by one of the Bistro's expensive white cloth napkins that I'd had imported from Italy. It was spread out on the center of my desk. Someone had used my own black felt-tip pen to sketch a childlike drawing on it: a familiar stick-figure cat, standing on its hind legs, holding a pistol in one of its paws.

The cat was grinning. I was not.

I was, in fact, teetering on the edge of panic.

Unless someone was playing a very gruesome, cruel prank, Felix, a busy assassin, who slit throats and burned down buildings, had taken the time to drop by my office and leave a warning. Or even worse, a promise.

I took a few more deep breaths and began to wonder if the drawing might have been a diversion. That thought sent me hastily around the office, checking behind and under the couch, behind the books on the shelves, in the various drawers, in the closet that doubled as a walk-in supply cabinet.

There were no incendiary devices. No cats in either human or feline form.

I made the office tour again, slower this time, looking for something out of place. Nothing seemed to have been touched. Nothing seemed to be missing. Except . . . no, I remembered I'd put Rudy's black book in my pocket. I removed it and placed it back in a desk drawer, next to his DVDs. My growing collection of Rudy Gallagher memorabilia.

As long as I had that drawer open, I used my shaking hands to remove and pop the cap on the little bottle of single malt.

Then I called for Cassandra.

Since Felix had presumably dispatched numerous victims without a single witness to any of the crimes, I doubted that he would have been spotted sneaking into my office to leave his love note. After checking with the servers, Cassandra informed me that this was the case.

"I hope you're going to show that napkin to the police," she said.

"Solomon would just say I drew it myself."

"Well, this is not good." She frowned. "This cat killer could come back. We don't know what he looks like. The odds of him bumping into anyone in the hall below are negligible."

To prove the point, we both descended the stairs and headed toward the front of the house without seeing a soul. But as we passed

Private Room 1, the door opened and Trina Lomax stepped into the hall. She saw us, smiled nervously, and asked, "The ladies' loo?"

"Right past the stairwell," Cassandra said.

We watched her progress until she'd entered the ladies' room.

"If she'd been your Felix," Cassandra said, "all she would have had to do was to run upstairs, draw her picture, and run back down."

I wondered if, while I was on my power walk back to the Bistro, Minnie the Mouse might have done just that.

TWENTY-NINE

With *Wake Up!* and the back-to-back taping of two *Blessing's in the Kitchen* cable shows, my Thursday schedule was nonstop. And I was glad. Anything to keep the stick-figure cat and its deadly pistol out of my head.

Arriving at the Glass Tower, I discovered that per Trina Lomax's request, my increased on-camera presence on the morning show had been put into effect, much to Kiki's dismay. My assistant dutifully prepped me for a down-and-dirty three-minute survey of food-influenced bestsellers, from the latest by the Sweet Potato Queens to Robert B. Parker's new Spenser caper, *Sweet and Sour*. This was followed by a brief, almost improvisational, chat with Lance Tuttle about the current economy's effect on publishing, which lent credence to the rumor that he'd been trying to float an autobiography.

Next, Kiki physically removed a muffin from my fingers and, using language a bit profane for so early in the morning, explained that I no longer had ten minutes for breakfast. She then dragged me by the arm across the studio and out the door to meet the crowd waiting patiently on the sidewalk.

Nineteen minutes later, Kiki made sure I was on time to share the news desk with Gin and Lance for a discussion of "the president's plans for bailing out the recording industry," about which I knew nothing and cared less. As I stumbled glassy-eyed from that experience, my assistant declared that I was on my own while she prepared tomorrow's schedule.

"Hold on," I said, following her into office/dressing room. "While we have a second, maybe you'd better explain the attitude. I assume it's because I'm working more."

"*We* are working more," she said, tossing her clipboard onto the desk atop a pile of comic books.

"Looks like you've got time to read," I said.

"Those are research for the segment tomorrow at the Manhattan Museum of Culture and Art," she said. "The superheroes exhibit."

"Right. The dead superheroes."

"Arnie just threw them on the desk when I got in this morning. Then he handed me today's new schedule, leaving me less than half an hour to shift everything around. You might have said something about the museum assignment yesterday. Not to mention the increased workload. Or that you wanted me to set up a meeting tomorrow with Mr. Turducken in New Jersey."

"You're right about the museum thing. I should have given you a heads-up. But the new schedule was one of those 'suggestions' Trina floats. I had no idea it was going into effect so quickly. I thought we'd have time to talk about it today."

"Oh." She seemed only slightly mollified.

"About the Jersey thing," I said. "I may just pass on that."

"You will not," she said. "Arnie said it was a must, and I already set it up at ten a.m. Don't cause me any more grief, please."

"This isn't about my trip to Jersey," I said. "What's going on, Kiki?"

She took her chair and faced the computer monitor. "Nothing I want to talk about."

It was one of those statements that invariably means just the opposite.

I pressed my butt against the edge of the desk and looked down at her. "What's the problem, Kiki?" I asked. But from the tears filling her eyes, I already knew.

"Tuck left," she said.

Tucker Eldridge had been the third or fourth insignificant other in her life since I'd known her. I've never quite understood how a woman as smart, self-sufficient, and attractive as Kiki could wind up wasting her emotions on a gallery of such smooth-talking, self-centered jerks, but, as the waitress Bridget Innes had put it so insipidly, "The heart knows what the heart needs." Ignoring the advice of the brain, evidently.

"He stole fifty dollars from my purse and my iPod," Kiki added, bursting into tears.

"I'm sorry," I said, yanking a tissue from the box and handing it to her. "Good thing he was into music. He could have taken that flat-screen I gave you for Christmas."

"Damn you, Billy," she said, crying and laughing at the same time, and stopping both to blow her nose. "I just always seem to—"

She went from sorrow to panic mode, grabbing the clipboard and staring at it. "You've got less than a minute to get to Set Three."

I made it with twenty seconds to spare. This time I was serving as a human prop for Gin's interview with Mr. Z (not his real name), a former convict who was performing a public service by spilling the secrets of the pickpocket trade.

That completed, having checked my wallet to make sure it was intact, I moved on to the show's kitchen set, where Hollywood tough guy Stewart Gentry, in town to promote his new movie, demonstrated his skill at creating a baked Alaska. It turned out to be closer to half-baked. But it was one of those dancing-dog moments. The point wasn't how well the dog danced.

Gentry, who'd graduated from the soaps in the seventies to become a big-screen idol for the last three decades, proved to be a surprisingly good interview. In the course of prepping his dessert he briefly mentioned his current film, a comedy-thriller in which he played a middle-aged private eye helping a precocious teenage girl find her stolen dog. Then he delighted me and the audience with several candid, witty tales of the rich and infamous. As hilariously outspoken as he was about his fellow thespians, his best stories were self-deprecating vignettes that mercilessly undercut his gruff, macho film image. All of this was good news, because he, and yet another of his baked Alaskas, had also been booked on one of my cable shows that afternoon.

When *Wake Up!*'s closing credits began their roll, I found him in the green room, filling Kiki's pretty ear with more tales of the tinseled west. ". . . so this twenty-five-year-old jackass who was only producing the picture—which means he should probably have been on the phone somewhere and not bothering working people—says, 'Have I made myself clear? Grab-ass costs us money. There will be no more grab-ass on this set.'

"He storms off, and I turn to this grip standing next to me and ask, 'Who the hell was the little geek complaining about anyway?' And the grip busts out laughing and says, 'Hell, Stew, he was talking about you!'"

My assistant's tinkling laughter complemented the stars in her eyes. So much for the now hopefully unlamented Tuck.

I asked if she'd arranged for transport to the Wine & Dine building.

"Done," she told me. "Joe's waiting on B level."

"Can I bum a ride?" Stew Gentry asked.

"Sure, but don't you have a limo?"

"I suggested Ms. Kiki use it," he said. "She tells me you've loaded her up on work, and I want to make sure she can get around town fast enough to be ready for our dinner tonight."

I looked at my assistant, who grinned and shrugged. One door closes and another opens.

Stew was set for the second of the two shows we were taping. Lily Conover, by far the most amenable producer I've ever worked with, found the actor a couch to snooze on while we filmed show number one, then got an assistant to prep him for his appearance. Prepping Stew included picking up a new set of clothes from his hotel, waking him, and arranging for him to shower and shave in one of the executive bathrooms.

I met with him ten minutes before we were to appear on camera. He was sitting alone in the cable net's version of a green room, not much bigger than a closet but with comfortable chairs and a couch, an HD monitor, and a cooler for wine, water, or soda. I caught him in the middle of chasing down a pill with a Pepsi.

He seemed a little embarrassed. Not about the Pepsi. "It's something my doctor prescribed," he said, tossing me the little plastic bottle as if to prove the point. On it was the name Alprazolam, along with a warning strip not to take the drug with alcohol, since it could intensify the effect of the booze.

"What's it for?" I asked.

"Hate to admit it, Billy, but unlike you TV guys, I get a little up-tight going live before the public. One of those pills helps to loosen me up."

I was about to ask him more about the drug but was interrupted by the arrival of Liz Youmans, who handled publicity for the show, and a young woman carrying a camera. Stew looked a bit stricken but relaxed when I casually slid the pill bottle into my pants pocket.

Liz introduced herself and the camerawoman to Stew and asked if he'd mind if they took "a few shots to submit to the media."

I reminded Liz that we had less than ten minutes before showtime. She got what she needed in eight.

And the show began.

I don't know how much the Alprazolam had to do with it, but Stew was charming, funny, and entertaining. He even managed to get through several bites of my considerably less-than-best beef Welling-ton and spoonfuls of his not-even-half-baked Alaska.

After the taping I walked him to his limo, which was parked in front of the building with a very glamorous-looking Kiki on the backseat.

Stew and I shook hands and vowed to get together on his next visit east.

"Don't worry about Kiki," he told me. "We're just gonna have dinner and a few laughs."

"Keep it at just a couple of chuckles, then. She has to be at work at five-thirty," I said.

He grinned. "Hell, doesn't everybody? I'll be yawning over at CBS around that time."

His limo had melded into the nighttime traffic when I remembered I still had his pill bottle in my pocket.

Chapter

THIRTY

I arrived at the Bistro in the middle of the second seating. There were empty tables, but business was brisk enough for Cassandra to be in what, for her, passed as a good mood. "Two of the waitresses called in sick" were her first words to me. "I hope this isn't the start of some virus thing. We're almost completely booked for tomorrow night."

"You and I can always bus the tables," I said.

"To someone who once did that, it's not funny, Billy," she said, and left me to my meet-and-greet. Probably shouldn't have mentioned that I wasn't joking.

I worked the room and was just heading up to my office, hoping there would not be another cat drawing waiting for me there, when one of those odd feelings—in this case a tension in the room—caused me to turn.

A party of five—three young men and two young women—had just entered the restaurant. One of the men was standing a foot away from Cassandra, weaving a little, probably drunk.

She was in a combative stance, scowling at him. In that moment I realized who he was and headed their way as quickly as I could without disturbing the diners.

"Mr. Rodell," I said, and our illustrious district attorney turned from Cassandra with reflexes that resembled spasms.

He stared at me with eyes that were barely focusing.

"Blessing, huh?" he said, smirking. "I was jus' telling your girl, it looks like business isn't quite as good as the last time I dropped by."

"Billy, I—" Cassandra began, but I cut her off.

"We're doing fine," I said, talking to both of them.

"Thanks to me," Rodell said. "I could have kept the padlock on this place forever."

I smiled at him, placid as a pond. "What can I do for you and your party, Mr. Rodell? Dinner?"

"Jus' drinks," he said. "In the bar, where it's nice and dark." He smiled at the woman nearest him, adding, "And intimate."

The others in his group didn't look quite as drunk as he. They also seemed a little sheepish, like maybe they'd rather be a dozen other places than out drinking with an obnoxious asshole, which probably made them assistant DAs who were favoring job security over integrity.

"I'm heading home, Phil," the young woman who'd been the object of his "intimate" comment said. "It's been a long day."

"It's just starting. This is your night, Bess." He turned to me. "This beautiful young woman won her first case today."

"Congratulations," I said to her.

"So our drinks are on the house, right, Blessing? Unless you want the house locked up tight again." He grinned.

I sensed that Cassandra was about to deck the guy. And his loud talk was starting to annoy the diners. "Of course the drinks are on the house," I said, leading Rodell and his reluctant party into the lounge area, which was empty except for a couple sitting at the bar.

"Take any table you'd like," I told Rodell.

"We'll belly up to the bar, like real drinkers, if we can get those yuppies to move their big asses over one."

There were four empty bar stools to the left of the couple, two empty to their right. The man turned, frowned at Rodell.

"Nobody has to move," I said, grabbing one of the two unused bar stools and adding it to the unoccupied quartet. The man whom Rodell had insulted shrugged and returned his attention to his female companion.

"Sit," Rodell ordered the members of his party. He looked at Juan and said, "Barkeep, grog for my compat'rits."

Juan moved toward them. "Yes, sir," he said. "What can I get you?"

"Apple martoonies, all around," Rodell said.

"Yes, sir. Sweet or sour?"

Rodell blinked and turned to the young celebrant, Bess, patting her thigh. "What'd'ya think, honey? You feeling sour or sweet?"

"Whatever you want, Phil. I'm finished drinking."

"Finished? No way." He turned to Juan. "You're the bartender. Just make the goddamn drinks."

Juan looked at me, his face totally without expression. "Yes, sir," he said, a little white around the lips.

"Hold up," I told him. "Mr. Rodell and his friends are honored guests. I'll fix their drinks."

I lifted the gate and joined Juan behind the bar. He gave me a confused look.

"Could you put some ice into a shaker?" I asked.

"Sure."

While he did that, I robbed the glass shelf of bottles of Stoli, apple schnapps, and Midori liqueur, and deposited them in front of Rodell, then grabbed a lime and a crisp green apple from the small fridge beneath the bar.

"What you are about to see," I announced, falling back on a line of patter from the days when I'd used words as tools of distraction, "is the creation of the finest apple-tinis available in the Big Apple. And perhaps the free world."

I took the shaker from Juan and picked up the bottle of Stoli. "First we use the very finest, one-hundred-proof, go-to-the-moon vodka, guaranteed to make the cocktail seem as smooth as a magic carpet ride." To add a little excitement, I flipped the open vodka bottle end over end in the air and caught it by the neck, spilling not a drop, a trick I'd picked up working in a tourist restaurant-bar in the Bahamas.

Rodell and his minions, Juan, and the other two customers were all watching me with curiosity.

"Then we add the very heart of the drink, the apple schnapps. Not too tart, not too sweet. Now, while I use just a splash of Midori, watch carefully, Mr. DA. . . ."

"I am watching carefully," he said. "Lot of poisoning going on these days."

It had been a long time since I'd dealt with anyone as obnoxious as Rodell. When I didn't toss the liqueur into his face, I figured I'd passed another of life's little tests. Only slightly derailed, I continued my spiel. "Then just one squeeze of lime juice, one little kiss of citrus, and we . . . shake, shake, shake your booty."

As I worked the cocktail shaker, one-handed, I asked Juan to place six martini glasses on the bar. That accomplished, I handed him the shaker. "You do the honors," I said.

All eyes were on the cloudy green liquid as Juan poured.

By the time he finished, I'd cut up the green apple. I carefully placed one slice in each glass, then raised mine in a toast. "To justice," I said.

Rodell and the others raised their glasses. What else could they do? Mr. DA must've been serious about the poisoning, because he waited until I'd taken a healthy gulp of my apple martini before trying his.

The others in Rodell's party followed his lead. The girl whose name I didn't know said, "This is delicious, Mr. Blessing."

"Yeah," Rodell said, after he'd drained his glass. "Not bad. You're a good sport, Blessing. If somebody'd screwed me over, I wouldn't be so nice. I'd be planning a get-back."

"Revenge isn't all it's cracked up to be," I said, filling his glass.

"You shoulda thought of that before you killed Rudy Gallagher," he said. Gracing me with another of his blood pressure–raising smirks, he swirled the liquid and apple slice around in his glass and took another swig.

"Uh, Phil, this is getting a little weird," one of the young men said, "I'm gonna split."

"Nobody's chaining you to the bar stool, Joe," Rodell said.

"I've still got to prep for the Schwarz case in the morning—"

"*Via con Dios,* Joe," Rodell said. "Five's a crowd, anyway. This way it's boy-girl, boy-girl, right, Edmund?"

Edmund, the remaining male, shrugged.

"I should go, too," Bess said, getting to her feet.

Rodell grabbed her arm and pulled her back down. "Uh-uh. Not this time, ice queen. You barely touched your drink. You don't want to offend Blessing. You know how sensitive some . . . people are."

My smile felt like it was turning to stone as I watched him shoot his second apple-tini. I used the last of the shaker's contents to drown his apple slice. The cocktail would be a little watery, but I didn't think that would matter too much to Rodell.

He got two sips down before his head dropped sharply enough to cause whiplash, chin digging into his chest. He dropped the glass to the floor and slumped forward over the bar.

"Holy crap," the girl who was not Bess exclaimed. "Is he dead?"

I pressed Rodell's carotid artery. "No such luck," I said. "But I imagine he might settle for death when he wakes up in the morning. Think you folks can get him home, or shall we just roll him into the alley?"

The others were staring at the unconscious man as if uncertain what to do.

"I guess I could phone Mrs. Rodell," I said.

"I'll get him home," Edmund said. He was a big enough boy to handle it. Before he had a chance to move his boss, I took out my cell phone and snapped a shot of the unconscious DA.

"What are you doing?" Bess asked.

"For the website," I said. "You know, another satisfied customer."

I took a second shot of Edmund dragging Rodell off the bar, making sure to include the two ladies.

"You're not really going to put that picture on your website?" Bess asked.

"That'll be up to your boss," I said. "When you're dealing with a rodent as vicious as Rodell, it's best to have a rock handy."

She stared at me for a second, as if trying to decide something. Then she smiled. "You're a very interesting man, Mr. Blessing."

"I try to be," I said. "And it's Billy to my friends, Bess."

"Well, thank you for the drink and the entertainment, Billy."

"If I do use the shot, I'll Photoshop you out," I said, prompting another smile.

When the law folk had gone with their fallen chief, Juan took a dustpan and brush to the broken glass.

The remaining couple were curious about the little vignette. "Who was that creep?" the man asked.

"Just another bad drunk," I said.

"Sucker sure can't handle the sauce."

I nodded, though I knew that Rodell's sauce had been particularly hard to handle. It had been enhanced by three tabs of Alprazolam that I'd stuck in his green-apple slice.

I'd have to tell Stew Gentry that the warning on his pill bottle was correct. You really didn't want to mix alcohol with those bad boys.

Chapter

THIRTY-ONE

"Why devote an exhibit of comic art to deceased superheroes?" I asked at precisely eighty-forty-one a.m. the following morning.

It was the first question on the list Kiki had prepared for the bottom-of-the-hour remote. We were telecasting from the Manhattan Museum of Culture and Art, where the exhibit *The Mortal Superheroes: The Reality of Fantasy* would debut with a charity opening on Saturday evening.

"Well, first off," co-curator Marius Cathcart replied, "our exhibit actually covers all of the superheroes, including, of course, Superman, Spiderman, Wonder Woman, and Batman, although the Bat, as we all know, isn't really a superhero. That is to say, he's a normal human being, if highly intelligent and close to physically perfect, as opposed to the mutant X-Men. Or Superman, for that matter."

"You speak of these comic characters as if they were real."

"To some of us, they are," Cathcart replied. "And for those whose imaginations can't quite make the leap, films have provided the dimension of reality. These superheroes live and, as our exhibit points out, some of them die, the same as you and I eventually will."

Cheery thought, fanboy.

An hour earlier, when segment producer Jolie Durbin, cameraman

Gabe Farris, and I had arrived at ManMOCA, I'd discovered that the exhibit was a considerably bigger deal than I'd supposed, blessed by the governor, the mayor, several film studios, *People* magazine, assorted business and social groups, and, perhaps most important of all, Donald Trump.

Cathcart gave us a jiffy tour through five large showrooms filled with vivid comic art, panels, splash pages, and covers, along with statues and movie posters. There were photos of costumed crusaders shaking hands with presidents, sports figures, and other world leaders, entertaining soldiers in Iraq and Afghanistan, and helping out at the Special Olympics.

Placed in key positions in each room were video monitors on pedestals displaying documentary footage of comic artists at work, while live and animated versions of their creations did their superheroic stunts on white walls via projected imagery. One artist caught my eye. I blinked and said, "Is that Rita Margolis?"

"Rita? Sure," Cathcart said. "She draws *Funny Girls*."

"They're not exactly superheroes," I said.

Catchcart giggled. "Not exactly," he said. "But Rita's a good friend, and she's helped us put this whole thing together. You know Rita?"

I told him I did.

"She said she'd be here today," he said.

She hadn't arrived by the time we went live with Cathcart, his partner, Harris Whirley, and me seated on director's chairs in the midst of all the Slam! Bang! Pow! action art.

"I have to admit," I said, "I didn't realize that superheroes could die."

"Why not?" Cathcart asked, blinking into Gabe Farris's hot camera. "Death exists in the real world. Why not in the comic world, too?"

"It's what the fans want," Whirley added.

"They actually voted for it," Cathcart said.

"Right," Whirley said. "D.C. Comics asked them to decide whether Robin should live or die in the graphic novel *Batman: A Death in the Family*."

"And Robin died," Cathcart said. "Of course, like Batman, Robin wasn't literally a superhero, either."

Cathcart and Whirley were both bespectacled, pale, intense young men who could have been brothers or involved in any other kind of relationship one might imagine. Their fascination with comics seemed endless. I liked the idea of them batting the conversation back and forth, since I was clearly out of my league and, in truth, way beyond my interest level.

I continued to nod, letting them natter on, throwing in an occasional question, like, "How do you kill a superhero?"

"There are a lot of ways," Whirley said, "because all superheroes come with an Achilles' heel. Some, like Captain Marvel, revert to vulnerable flesh-and-blood forms. Superman has Kryptonite that renders him powerless, although, in truth, it was Doomsday's brute strength that killed him."

"Superman died?" I asked.

"Of course," Cathcart said. "It was well covered by the media."

"My subscription to the *Daily Planet* must've expired," I said. "Aren't there still Superman comics and movies?"

"He didn't stay dead," Whirley said, as if I was an idiot for asking. "He's Superman."

Our segment producer, Jolie, correctly sensing that we needed something more than sparkling badinage, cued the hunks and hunkettes standing by in their skintight outfits.

"We have a group of superheroes and, I think, supervillains about to join us," I said. "Give us a rundown on who they are, or, I guess, who they *were*."

As the models paraded in, flexing and posturing, the two curators provided the introductions. First to appear was Blue Beetle (murdered by someone named Maxwell Lord), followed by Black Canary (who died of "natural causes"), the first Captain Marvel (who died of the same "natural causes"), Silver Sorceress (killed by sniper fire), and Batgirl (killed, "as we all know, by the Joker").

"A lot of deaths for so early in the morning," I said. "But they all look healthy enough."

"Well," Cathcart said, "some comic characters may die . . ."

". . . but comic art lives forever," Whirley said.

"Especially in the case of the superwomen, good and evil," Cathcart said.

"Because they're super-hot," Whirley said.

He wasn't exaggerating, I thought, as more models sauntered past Gabe's camera. Cathcart gave them names that meant nothing to me. When, on Jolie's cue, we cut to a commercial, one of the models approached me, a truly stunning redhead with golden eyes, wearing a chamois bikini and skin painted in tiger stripes. *Her* comic-book name I remembered from Cathcart's list. Tigra.

"I have something for you in the dressing room, Mr. Blessing," she said. "Don't run away, now."

"I wouldn't dream of it," I said. Tigra smiled, gave me a cute little growl that I hoped wasn't just in character, and pranced away.

"On in ten seconds," Jolie yelled. "Then wrap it up."

I struggled through the wrap-up, trying not to speculate about what Tigra might be bringing me, while Cathcart and Whirley plugged their opening-night gala, dropping the names of celebrities whom they expected to be on hand and inviting fanboys and fangirls to visit the exhibit during the weeks ahead.

I sent the show back to Gin and Lance at the news desk and we were clear, at least until the final wave to the audience under the eight-fifty-nine a.m. credit crawl.

Grinning like a goose, I watched Tigra jiggling back my way. She was carrying an envelope. "As promised," she said, handing it to me.

My name was on it.

"Thank you, Tigra," I said, amused, thinking it was a setup from Jolie or Arnie back at the studio. I opened the envelope and slid out the card. The grin froze on my face when I saw the childish cat drawing and the scrawled words *I have nine, but you only have one. Pity.*

"Who gave you this?" I asked Tigra, trying to stay calm.

"Nobody. I found it in the box with my costume," she said.

"And where did you get the costume?"

"Here. We had a fitting yesterday at the WBC building. And the costumes were waiting for us here today. I think the wardrobe people must have brought them. Maybe one of them put the card in. Is there a problem?"

"No. No problem," I lied. Nothing to get upset about. Just being stalked by a killer. No big deal.

"Good," she said. "I was thinking, maybe a friend of yours at the network happened to see me yesterday and thought this might be a sort of meet-cute. I am a fan."

As if to prove there are more powerful emotions than fear, I immediately stopped worrying about Felix and started wondering what Tigra might look like without the red wig and body makeup. "Are your eyes really gold?" I asked.

"Only when I wear these contacts. Tigra isn't my real name, either."

"What is?"

"It's Maureen Bet—"

"Ten seconds to credit wave," Jolie called, and began the countdown.

Tigra joined the group of models gathering behind the curators and me, any one of whom, I realized, might be the mysterious Felix under the costume. On cue, we all faced the camera and waved, and I verbally bid the audience farewell.

When the little red light on the camera blinked off, I thanked God, silently, that I was still alive, then thanked the curators and the models for all their efforts. As much as I wanted to, I forced myself not to take the envelope from my pocket for another look. Better to keep my eyes open on what was going on around me. Like Tigra/Maureen Bet–something approaching.

"As I was saying before we were so rudely interrupted," she said, "I'm Maureen Bettenhaus. I'm in the Manhattan phone directory under the name Moe Betta. In case you might want to call me sometime."

With that, she did an about-face and walked away. Slowly.

That woman can't be involved with Felix, I told myself. God wouldn't be that cruel.

But who's to say God doesn't have his playful moments?

Jolie and Gabe were waiting for me by the front door. I told them I wouldn't be going back to the tower with them in the van. Mighty Joe was picking me up for the trip to see Mr. Turducken. In fact, I could see him in the dirtmobile, parked in front of the museum.

Instead of exiting, I returned to the main exhibition showroom, where I found Cathcart and Whirley going over the plans for opening night. "Where are the dressing rooms the models are using?" I asked.

"I'll show you," Whirley said, heading toward an exit that led to the rear of the museum. "What did you think of the Owl?" he asked.

"Which one was that, exactly?"

"Lavender bodysuit. Owl face, big eyes. Beak. A rather obscure hero from *Crackerjack Funnies* in the 1940s," he said. "But some of his adventures were written by . . . wait for it . . . Jerry Siegel."

When I didn't fall down on the floor, writhing, he said, "Jerry Siegel? Co-creator of Superman?"

"Oh, *that* Jerry Siegel," I said.

"Yes. We're quite proud of bringing that little-known fact to light. Too bad you didn't see the Owl."

"See the Owl." It sounded like a euphemism for some sort of indecent behavior.

Two portable dressing rooms—black curtains on metal tube frames—had been hastily constructed in the museum's shipping area. I wasn't interested in them. It was the wardrobe mistress I wanted to talk to.

It turned out to be a wardrobe mister. Simon ("just Simon, surnames are superfluous") informed me that "the costumes, once they had been fitted and adjusted, were either put on hangers or, in the case of tiny little nothings, wrapped in tissue and placed in cardboard boxes, all of it labeled, of course."

"And where were the hangers and boxes kept overnight?"

"In Wardrobe."

"Locked up?" I asked.

"Not well enough, evidently," Whirley said.

"I think the costume was simply misplaced, though frankly I don't see how," Simon said.

"What costume?" I asked.

"The Cheetah," Whirley said. "From *Suspense Stories,* 1965, Charlton Comics. Very, very sexy lady. Costume was skintight, yellow with black spots, a sort of bookend to Tigra. Marius and I were so looking forward to seeing both of them together. Though I must say Tigra was pretty impressive on her own."

"Who had access to the costumes?" I asked Simon.

"There weren't that many who knew about them. People from *Wake Up!,* mainly."

"Who specifically?"

"The show's producer, who was wearing a Hawaiian shirt that I would have killed for. Some woman with a skunk-tail streak in her hair. But you know, anybody could have just walked in."

We thanked Simon for his information and made our way to the front of the museum.

As we crossed the main hall, Cathcart called out, "Did you see her, Chef Blessing?"

"Her?"

"Rita," he said. "Rita Margolis. She was here just a few minutes ago. I mentioned you'd asked about her." He looked around the large exhibition hall. "I don't see her now. She's probably off on some errand. Rita never seems to stand still."

"Like a hummingbird," I said.

I thanked the two curators again for hosting us and was heading away when Cathcart called out, "Rita will be back shortly. Would you like me to convey a message?"

I told him not to bother. I'd probably be running into Rita myself before too long. Actually, I couldn't imagine anything I'd have to say to Rita or she to me that would be of any consequence. Not exactly a perceptive forecast, as it turned out.

THIRTY-TWO

"What's that perfume?" I asked Joe when I stepped into the Volvo.

"I don't know," he said, clearly upset. "I left for just a minute to—you know—walk the dog. Come back. Stinko. Stinko."

"It's almost toxic," I said.

"Be okay with window open, once we get going," he said.

"Do we have to use the Tunnel?" I asked him.

"For you to get to the address in Fairview by ten," he said. "We take bridge, far out of our way, maybe make it by eleven. Another hour of stinko."

"Okay," I said.

"This guy you go see, he put chicken inside duck?"

"And both of them inside a turkey," I said.

Joe started giggling. He didn't do it very often, but it was kind of infectious.

We both were still grinning as he took the right turn at Eighth Avenue, then a left on West Thirty-ninth Street. But as we followed a huge beer truck into the Lincoln Tunnel, the grin left my face.

In the moments before we lost daylight, I decided to just close my eyes until we could see the slate-gray skies of Weehawken. With the windows open, the noise was intense. The air was close. I felt the pressure, real or imagined, from being underwater and wondered how long it would be—and I was sure of the inevitability of it happening—before the tunnel would crack and cave in.

I was entertaining myself with that thought, my eyes squeezed shut, when Joe said, "Billy, anybody else from show going to see this turkey man?"

"Not to my knowledge. Why?"

"Hummer following us. Been there from the museum."

I opened my eyes to a nightmare of car headlights reflecting off the walls and ceiling of the tunnel. Horns blaring. Big rigs zooming. Angry traffic.

I twisted in my seat to look through the rear window. More headlights. But I saw the vehicle Joe had mentioned. A bloodred Hummer about two car lengths behind us. It was difficult to see into the Hummer, but I could make out the image of a big man behind the wheel and at least one figure on the rear seat.

I told Joe I saw nothing to cause any alarm.

It was frightening enough just being in the tunnel. The whole tube full of cars seemed to be traveling at warp speed, but maybe the noise had something to do with that.

I noticed a slip of paper on the rubber mat near my feet—unusual, because Joe kept the interior spotless. I picked it up, knowing it would contain another cat sketch. In this one, the stick-figure cat was accompanied by a little friend, a skunk, radiating squiggly lines that cartoonists use to indicate odor.

"He coming up fast," Joe said.

As point of proof, the Volvo was suddenly bumped from behind. I was jerked forward as far as the seat belt allowed. If the bump had been any harder, the airbags might have gone off.

Joe was yelling in Vietnamese. I assume he was cursing the guy in the Hummer.

I looked back. The big vehicle had returned to its previous position. Then, with absolutely no warning, it leaped into a small space in the left lane, causing the suddenly alert driver of a Mercedes sedan to risk a pileup by tapping his brakes.

The Hummer was coming up on our left. Its side windows were dark-tinted.

Joe gunned the Volvo, but thanks to the big rig in front of us, there was no place for him to go.

When the Hummer was side by side with us, its right rear window lowered. Then the bad freakiness began and I stopped worrying about being in a tunnel under the Hudson.

A full-size cheetah glared at us from the rear seat of the Hummer. Not a cheetah, of course. Cheetahs don't ride in Hummers. They don't wear gloves. They don't point space guns out of car windows.

The cheetah aimed its weird-looking gun at Joe. I suddenly realized the significance of the cheap perfume and the cat drawing.

"Shut your win—" I began.

Too late.

The back of Joe's head seemed to erupt in red, and he was thrown toward me. He continued screaming as the Volvo veered to the left and kissed the side of the Hummer with a grinding screech, the cheetah leaping back from the window. I reached over and grabbed the wheel, bringing us back into the right lane.

Joe pushed me away and regained control of the wheel. "I got it, Billy," he said.

"You okay? The blood . . ."

"Head hurt like hell," he said. "No blood. Paint."

Paint?

"Got some in left eye. Right eye okay."

The Hummer was ahead of us now. The cheetah shot at us again. This time the Volvo's windshield went red, cutting off the view from even Joe's good eye.

He popped his seat belt and, keeping his right foot on the gas, stuck his head out of his window, screaming as he steered us forward.

The Hummer swerved again, this time into our lane, ahead of the big rig.

Joe maintained his awkward position until we emerged from the tunnel and he was able to pull over to the far left, past the safety cones, into a non-traffic area underneath a giant American flag that was occupied by the vehicles of the tunnel crews.

One of the crewmen was kind enough to provide us with solvent and a rag to clean most of the paint off the windshield, and rubbing alcohol to clean Joe's face. He carried his own bottle of water that he used to wash out his eye. But my diminutive driver remained in despair over the damage done to the side of the car and the dent in the rear bumper. He stared at the long scratches and gouges. Then he ran his hand over them tenderly, as if soothing a wounded animal.

"I see that Hummer again," he said, "I destroy it."

"You see that Hummer again, it'll be in a police impound yard," I said. "It's bound to have been stolen."

"Then I destroy woman in catsuit."

"You sure it was a woman?" I asked.

"You not know difference?" he said. "I explain. Women got these, but much bigger." Joe was holding his hands out in front of him. "Even Mrs. Joe, though not that much bigger."

"It wasn't just a catsuit," I told him. "It was a Cheetah costume, stolen from the Glass Tower."

"Then you know who woman is?"

"Not a clue," I said.

"Car a mess," he said. "Interior got paint, too. Like my jacket."

I noticed splotches of red on my jacket, too.

"You still want to see turkey man?" Joe asked.

I wasn't that wild about it to begin with. "No way," I said. "Get me back to Manhattan as soon as you can, even if we have to take the Tunnel."

"Then we need to get car repaired," he said.

"Well, it won't be a total loss. They'll have to wash it, too."

I let Kiki handle the whole car-repair thing.

While she made the calls and the arrangements, I slumped on the only soft chair in my office, brooding as I dabbed at the red spots on my jacket with lighter fluid. That's where Arnie found me.

"Your presence is requested in Gretchen's office," he said.

"What's up?" I asked, getting to my feet and following him through the door.

"Something about a car accident."

"How'd she find out about it?"

"She passed your car on the way back from lunch," Arnie said, leading me to the bank of elevators.

"It's not that big a deal," I said.

"Gretchen said the car looked like crap," he said.

"What's the big deal? It always looks like crap," I said.

Gretchen was at her desk, a coffee mug at her elbow and a concerned look clouding her handsome face.

"Sit down, Billy," she said. "I want to hear what happened."

During my brooding, I'd more or less decided that as Henry Julian and Cassandra and, especially, Felix had been telling me, it was not in my best interest to continue to annoy the killer. Yes, mine was still the only name on Detective Solomon's suspect list. But that was something I could live with, at least until the cop realized the error of his ways or Rudy Gallagher's murder became an official cold case.

So I told Gretchen that we got sideswiped in the Tunnel. "The other car got away. End of story."

"What about the costumed figure shooting paintballs at you?"

"How in God's name do you know about that? Don't tell me Joe—?"

"Joe . . . tell me *anything*? Of course not. Billy, this is the era of information. Nothing goes unreported."

She spun her desk monitor around. There was a grainy but clear-enough photo of the Volvo being fired upon by the Cheetah in the Hummer.

"Damn," I said. "I wouldn't have thought there'd been enough light."

"Your car has been identified by the plate," she said, "and there has been speculation on two of the gossip sites that the cat person is a fan of Rudy's, attempting to avenge him."

"Did I hear you say 'cat person'?" Trina Lomax asked from the doorway.

"Trina, come in," Gretchen said. "I heard there was some problem at your apartment this morning? Everything okay?"

"False alarm," Trina said, taking a chair. "What's this about a cat person?"

Gretchen showed her the photo.

"Fascinating," Trina said. She turned toward me, her blue eyes shining with delight. "I definitely underestimated you, Billy. Playing paintball in the Lincoln Tunnel with a cat. Hard-core."

"I wasn't playing anything," I said. "Gretchen, has anybody checked the plate on the Hummer?"

"Owned by a Scarsdale dermatologist," she said. "He claims it was stolen sometime during the night."

"A cat shooting at you," Trina said. "Ring any bells, Billy?"

I gave her my best blank look.

"You know something about this, Trina?" Gretchen asked.

"I know about a very dangerous man who calls himself Felix the Cat."

Could Joe have been mistaken about the Cheetah being a female? The wardrobe guy, Simon, had said it was a woman's costume, and the cartoon character had been a woman. But Trina seemed convinced Felix was a man. Perhaps an androgynous one?

"You remember the assassination of a drug kingpin named Tumetello in Bogotá four years ago?" Trina asked.

"Vaguely," Gretchen said.

"My memory is a little more vivid," Trina said. "I was working on a story about the Moleta cartel for International News and got to the crime scene early enough that the body was still warm. Tumetello wasn't what you'd call a wonderful guy, and his death eventually brought about the end of the cartel. But his killer had disemboweled him. And left a calling card of sorts on a wall beside the body. He'd cut off Tumetello's finger, dipped it in the dead man's blood, and used it to draw a stick figure of a cat on the wall beside the body, signing it 'Felix.'

"Six months later, another cat drawing turned up in Nablus near the headless body of a Hamas heavy who'd reputedly organized, but not attended, a suicide attack on Israeli security forces. That's when I talked my boss at INN into putting me on the Felix story.

"What I discovered was amazing. The name and/or the stick drawing were connected to at least nine key assassinations in a three-year period. But Felix remained a total enigma."

"No witnesses?" Gretchen asked. "No clues?"

"A few months ago, I heard about a *Paris Match* reporter who'd told friends he was about to expose Felix as a Frenchman with a mistress in Marseilles."

"I assume you contacted the reporter," Gretchen said.

"I didn't get the chance," Trina said. "He and an unidentified woman were burned to death in a car crash."

"The woman being Felix's mistress?" I asked.

"That's as good a guess as any," Trina said. "It seems the reporter's files had also been burned in the crash. That fire ended my investigation as well as his. The big dogs at INN sent word that I was to concentrate on subjects that were less dangerous and offered a quicker yield. It wasn't my welfare that concerned them. They just didn't want to throw a lot of money into a project that could wind up as ashes, along with a reporter whose death would probably result in higher insurance rates for the company.

"So I quit. And thanks to Felix, here I am."

"Billy, is it possible the person in the Hummer . . . ?"

"Was this Felix?" I asked. "Why would an international hit man waste his time on me?"

"That's funny," Trina said. "Gin told me you were very concerned about Felix."

I had to give her props. It was the perfect interviewer move. You hold out key information, let your interview subject crawl out on a limb of lies, then use it to cut the limb.

"She says you called her attention to one of Felix's personal touches, the stick drawing of a cat on the sidewalk near Phil Bruno's burning building. She also said you took a picture of it. I'd love to see it."

I wondered if she'd already seen it. Perhaps even drawn it while we were in the building almost getting burned with Phil. Something about her Felix vignettes bothered me. I couldn't put my finger on it, but it left me with the feeling that I shouldn't trust my life to Trina Lomax.

"I don't have the picture anymore," I said. "I had no reason to keep it. And I'm not even sure it was a cat."

"You told Gin it was and that the person all of you saw leaving Bruno's building probably was Felix."

"Let's just slow down and review the bidding," Gretchen said. "We're talking about an international assassin who may have killed one of our cameramen and who now has his sights set on you, Billy? Are you in some suicidal state of denial? Or is it some equally suicidal macho I-can-handle-it pose?"

What the hell! Felix the Cat was out of the bag.

I got out the card Maureen "Tigra" Bettenhaus had given me at the museum and placed it on Gretch's desk. "Is this the kind of drawing you're talking about, Trina?"

"My God, yes," she said. "And this comment about your one life. Billy, this is a threat you should take very seriously."

"I've got a driver with red eye and a car with its side bashed in," I said. "I take it seriously."

"Do you know why he's threatening you?" Trina asked.

"He may have the mistaken idea that I want to cause him trouble," I said, staring at her. "That is something I definitely do not want."

"Rudy," Gretchen said, her normally full-throated voice going up an octave or two. "My God, this Felix may have killed Rudy. Rudy and Phil and . . . he attacked you and poor Joe. We have to do something."

"Just hold on," I said. "Let's not . . ."

But Gretchen had rushed from the room.

Trina looked at me. "Where'd you get this card?"

Why ask that question if, as I suspected, she knew the answer? Would a lie or obfuscation suggest I hadn't given up the Felix hunt? Would the truth cause Tigra/Maureen harm? My head was starting to hurt.

Fortunately, I was saved from Trina's inquisition by Gretchen's return. Her father was with her. And Marvin, dressed in his usual warm-up outfit and flying-dolphin cap. He gave me a wink and stayed in the doorway, leaning against the jamb.

The commander looked pained. "Gretchen has just apprised me of the situation, Billy. I'm damned sorry, but I may have brought this on you."

"I don't understand," I said.

"Against the good advice of the smartest man I know"—he nodded to Marvin—"I did a very foolish thing. I can't do anything to undo what happened to Rudy and Phil. But I can get someone to see to your safety."

"Thanks, Commander, but if this Felix wanted me dead, he wouldn't have used paintballs. I don't need a bodyguard."

"Yes, you do," the commander said. "Gretchen, call InterTec. Talk to that woman VP who's handling the Mossad guy's security."

"Lee Franchette," Gretchen said.

"Whatever. Tell her we need a twenty-four-seven on Billy."

The beautiful and exotic Lee Franchette? 24/7? The combination had its appeal. Still . . . "I really don't think it's necessary," I said. "I'll just be careful and mind my own business and—"

"What do you think, Marv?" the commander asked.

"I think a protector's a fine idea," the old man said. "Get Billy somebody like Robert Vaughn in that series he did in England."

"Make it happen, daughter," the commander said, and marched out of the room.

Marvin stayed at the door, observing.

Gretchen picked up her phone, but before she could dial, I said, "I don't get it. How could your dad have anything to do with Felix?"

She hesitated, her eyes shifting to Trina, who seemed to be on ultra-alert.

Marvin said, "Why don't you and I take a walk, Billy, and leave these executives to their multitasking?"

Chapter

THIRTY-FOUR

The walk was a short one, just down the hall to an office nearly the size of my entire restaurant, only with more expensive carpeting and the look and smell of wax-polished pale wood. To my right was a wall covered by a looooong floor-to-ceiling bookcase with a matching rolling half-ladder, the better to reach even the highest glass-covered leather-bound scripts and books. The wall to my left featured two large oil paintings—of a crusty old bird in a general's uniform that seemed to be giving me the stinkeye no matter where I stood in the room, and a truly handsome dowager in a pale-blue ballgown who looked remarkably like I imagined Gretchen would in her sixties. The commander's father and mother.

Farther down the room was a waist-high cabinet constructed of the same wood as the bookshelf, its surface jam-packed with shiny industry awards, along with framed accolades and certificates of merit.

At the far, far end of the room off-white draperies had been drawn, exposing a bank of six windows. The commander sat at his massive desk with the windows to his back. He was staring at a framed photograph in his hand.

He raised his head suddenly and said, "That you, Marv?"

Marvin gave me a stay-there hand gesture and walked toward the commander. "Billy's with me," he said, "but we can come back later."

"No, it's okay," the commander said. He placed the photograph on his desk, pulling his display handkerchief from his pocket and dabbing at his eyes.

Marvin waved me forward.

I dragged my feet, trying to give the commander more time to pull himself together. He blew his nose and put the handkerchief away. He managed a wan smile, but his eyes were red and wet as he looked at us expectantly.

"I think we owe Billy an explanation for putting him in the crosshairs," Marvin said. The metaphor sent a chill down my spine, and I quickly scanned the multi-window space with some apprehension. All I saw were empty rooftops and workers in their offices going about businesses probably more conventional than ours.

"I suppose we do owe you that, Billy," the commander said, bringing out his handkerchief again, folding it, and wiping his eyes. "Please sit."

Marvin had already taken a soft leather chair on the commander's right. I sat on its twin to the left of the huge desk.

A silence settled on the room. The commander lowered his head, apparently gathering his thoughts. Marvin was staring at me. He gave me another of his winks, this one seeming to say, *Relax, everything will be fine.* I'd known other men and women who could chase away your fears and worries with just a simple gesture. They were usually on the con. But as cynical as I'd become, especially the last few days, I thought Marvin was exactly what he appeared to be, a wise old man.

The commander cleared his throat and, looking straight ahead, began his explanation. As I'd assumed, it involved his son, who'd died in Baghdad five years before when his vehicle lost a battle with a land mine. "Bud's death was . . . devastating," the commander said, his voice weakened by emotion. "But time does have a way of dulling the jagged edges of painful memories. Until something happens to sharpen them again."

He paused, pressed a button on his desk, and asked someone for Evian water. He turned to Marvin, who evidently communicated a soundless request, "And a Yoo-Hoo," the commander added, turning to me and raising his eyebrows. I thanked him but declined both water and Yoo-Hoo.

The room was silent again, until a young man wearing a blue blazer with a WBC patch on its breast pocket brought in the liquids in two tall glasses and departed.

"I prefer my Yoo-Hoo straight from the bottle," Marvin said, frowning at the chocolate drink in his glass. "It's the curse of the underprivileged. But don't mind me, Vern. Please continue."

The commander took a sip of water and turned to me. "Last month, I received an overseas call from a man who told me he had information about my son's death. He said that Bud had thrown some Touchstone civilian soldiers off of his base after they were caught acting as enforcers for a Baghdad moneylender and black marketeer. Three weeks later, the vehicle carrying Bud exploded. My caller said it had not been an accident, that Touchstone's CEO, Carl Kelstoe, the son of a bitch who was in my studio just a few weeks ago, personally ordered Bud's death and arranged to have the dismissal of the five mercenaries expunged from the logbook."

"Let me make a wild guess," I said. "Your caller was a Touchstone merc named Deacon Hall."

The commander looked surprised. "That's right."

"What kind of proof was he selling?"

"Recordings of telephone calls he received from Kelstoe, one of them ordering the death . . . the murder of my son."

"Recordings can't be used as courtroom evidence."

"I don't care about that. They can be used to destroy Kelstoe's reputation and, with luck, his business, leaving him in disgrace and ruin."

"If Hall was leveling with you," I said, "he had to have been involved in your son's murder. Wasn't he concerned that some of that disgrace and ruin would rub off on him?"

"He said the money would make up for that," the commander said. "But I was suspicious, and I wanted to be certain the recordings were authentic. That's why I sent Rudy to meet with Hall. He was familiar enough with recorded material to know if the phone calls had been faked or edited."

"What kind of price tag did Hall put on the recordings?"

"Three hundred thousand dollars," the commander said. "It would have been cheap at that price. Once Rudy authenticated the recordings, I was to wire the money to an account Hall had in Belize. But we never got that far. Hall was murdered before he had a chance to show Rudy the recordings."

I wondered about that. The blurred shiny object Phil Bruno and I had seen on his film footage could have been a flash drive containing copies of the phone calls. In that case, Hall had passed them on to Rudy. And Rudy had lied about it. He'd told Melody Moon he was coming into money. He'd scheduled an important meeting the night of his murder. And Carl Kelstoe had been in the city. It all seemed to fit, but it was still much too speculative for me to suggest to the commander that his prospective son-in-law, now deceased, may have been a liar, a thief, and a sellout.

"I doubt we'll ever know what happened to the recordings," the commander said.

"They may not have even existed," Marvin said. "I never put much stock in what that Hall fellow had to say. Why'd he record his boss in the first place? And why'd he wait so long to put the bite on you?"

The commander nodded. "You're right, Marv. If I'd listened to you, I'd have told Hall to go fly a kite and Kelstoe wouldn't have sent his pet killer after Rudy and Phil Bruno." He shifted in his chair and faced me. "And now you, Billy."

"You're making a lot of pretty big assumptions, Commander," I said.

"It seems pretty cut-and-dried," he said. "A: Kelstoe found out about his man Hall's betrayal and had him killed. B: Once he learned that Rudy and Phil had spent time with Hall that night, he couldn't take the chance that one of them might have the phone recordings. And C: From what Marv tells me, you've been collecting information on this Felix, hoping to clear your name with the police."

Marvin looked a little sheepish. "I was worried you might be buying trouble, Billy."

"Marv wants me to tell the police about . . . everything," the commander said. "Get you clear of this mess. As loath as I am to provide fresh food for the gossip hounds, I see now that this is the correct course. I'm glad it isn't too late."

Without any physical proof to back it up, I wondered how much his statement would matter to Solomon. Well, it wouldn't hurt.

"I appreciate this, Commander," I said.

"As I mentioned, Billy, until this Felix thug is brought to justice, you'll be given 'round-the-clock protection."

"After your session with the cops, you'll be needing some of that protection, too, Vern," Marvin said.

"We'll see," the commander said. He stood, which was a signal for me to be going.

He walked me all the way to the door. Probably needed the exercise. "Soon this whole ugly mess will be behind us," he said.

I doubt he believed that any more than I did.

Chapter

THIRTY-FIVE

At a little after five, while I was on the phone haggling with the body shop that Kiki had chosen to repair the Volvo, Cassandra opened my office door and marched in. She stood at my desk, shifting from one foot to the other until I'd cradled the receiver.

"Two people downstairs to see you," she said.

"Don't suppose you caught any names," I said.

"Did my job description change without you telling me, Billy?" she asked. "If people are going to be constantly dropping in on you, maybe you'd better hire a receptionist to handle the flow."

"I'll take that as a no on the names," I said.

"They're from InterTec Security," she said, pouting now.

"Was one of them the most beautiful woman you've ever seen?"

"No. But the guy's kind of hot."

"Send them up anyway," I said.

It wasn't easy to climb the stairs noiselessly, but the two security agents appeared at my office door as if by magic. They entered moving casually and quietly, surveying the room and me with admirable nonchalance before introducing themselves.

Bettina Noor was an attractive, diminutive East Indian woman who, even in a beautifully tailored business suit of charcoal gray, looked young enough to be in high school. Straight black hair cut just above shoulder length. Dark eyes. No makeup. Carrying a black leather purse that, I presumed, contained a gun and a cellular phone, at the very least.

Her partner, A.W. Johansen, was in his mid- to late twenties, with the tan face and curly blond hair of a surfer. He was two or three inches taller than me and a pound or two lighter. Well, maybe five pounds. Okay, fifteen, but that's it. He was wearing a rumpled dark-blue blazer, khaki slacks, and a white shirt open at the neck, no tie. His blazer bulged near his right hip.

Ms. Noor quickly assumed the lead, explaining in a fast singsong patter that they would be accompanying me in twelve-hour shifts. "I understand from Ms. Snell that you are to be at the WBC building at six a.m. on Monday."

Ms. Snell, an InterTec employee, had called a few hours before with about a hundred and fifty questions, all of which I had dutifully answered.

"She said that you travel by chauffeur?"

"Usually," I said. "But my car's in the shop. And my chauffeur prefers to think of himself as a driver."

"I will remember the distinction," she said. "I assume you leave for work at approximately twenty minutes to the hour?" I nodded. "Fine. On Monday I shall arrive here at five-forty a.m. to relieve A.W. I will remain on duty until five-forty p.m., staying as unobtrusive as my duty will allow. At that time, A.W. will take over. That will be our weekday schedule."

"Sounds excellent," I said.

"What about the weekend, tomorrow and Sunday?" she asked. "Shall we, for the sake of simplicity and continuity, maintain that same schedule?"

"That'd be between you and A.W.," I said. "I'll be lolling about in bed until at least eight a.m. tomorrow morning."

"Same schedule's fine with me, Betts," A.W. Johansen said.

"Excellent," she said, consulting the large round watch on her slender wrist. "Then you will officially be on duty in exactly nineteen minutes."

I successfully avoided laughing, but I did smile.

Young Mr. Johansen grinned back at me and said, "I've got a bag downstairs in my car. I'm not sure what kind of extra sleeping setup you've got, but I don't need much."

"There's a guest room you can use," I said.

"Is it near enough to your bedroom for A.W. to maintain constant surveillance?" Bettina Noor asked.

"Right across the hall," I said.

She nodded. "You are unmarried. If there is someone else who will have access to your bedroom, now would be the time to notify A.W."

"I doubt that will pose a problem," I said.

"We can't be too careful," she said. "You told Ms. Snell that the building had been compromised last week by a man disguised as a policeman. Someone will be here within the hour to change the locks on the doors and to readjust the alarm system. Please notify the lady downstairs."

"Her name's Cassandra," I said. "I'll talk to her. I assume your alarm guy will let me pick my own key code."

"Of course. And as for the incident in this office, I would like to see the napkin with the perpetrator's warning."

I still had the napkin, folded, in my out basket. Ms. Noor studied it for a while, then passed it to her partner, who eventually handed it back to me.

"I think we can assume he is a better assassin than he is an artist," Ms. Noor said. "In any case, I shall be here tomorrow at five-forty a.m."

"I'll be up and waiting to let you in," Mr. Johansen said.

"Have some dinner before you leave," I said to Ms. Noor. "Consider meals a perk."

"I appreciate the offer," she replied. "But I have assayed your menu on your website and find it lacking in nutrition and health. In fact, I consider your food long-term suicide. Good evening, Mr. Blessing."

Both Mr. Johansen and I watched her go.

"Wow, that is one crazy party girl," I said.

"Bettina is a vegan," he said.

"She seems a little uptight, even for that," I said.

"She's kinda by-the-book," he said. "But she's also the best agent I've ever worked with."

"Good to know." I liked this A.W. Johansen.

"About that dinner offer . . ." he said. "I'm definitely not a vegan. In fact, I'm a big fan of yours, Chef Blessing."

"Thanks," I said. "And 'Billy' works for me. Do I call you A.W.?"

"Everybody does."

"What do the initials stand for?"

He hesitated. His tan face reddened and he half mumbled, "Andy Warhol."

"Come again?"

"My dad was Piet Johansen, the silk-screen artist. Mom used to be an actress. Vera Sweet's her real name. She was billed as Very Sweet in a couple of Warhol movies. She and Dad met at The Factory back in the sixties. Warhol was my godfather, but I only met him once, when I was seven. This was just before my dad passed away."

"Your mom still with us?"

"Very much so. She and my stepfather left the city a while ago. They run a bed-and-breakfast on the West Coast. In Topanga Canyon, kind of near L.A. Both doing great."

"And you were just out there on a visit."

He blinked. "How . . . ?"

"Elementary, my dear A.W. The suntan."

He grinned again, showing perfect, very white teeth.

"Why don't you get your bag," I said, "and I'll show you the spare room. Then we'll see about getting you dinner."

"Great," he said. "I'm starving. I had lunch with Bettina at one of her faves. Hummus and wheatgrass soup really doesn't do it for me."

"I think I saw a twenty-two-ounce bone-in rib eye ready for grilling," I said.

I could've sworn he did one of those zip out and back moves like Wile E. Coyote. I wouldn't have been surprised to find ACME stenciled on his bag.

I showed him the spare room, pointed out the bathroom, and left him to unpack while I went down to give Cassandra a heads-up about the arriving locksmith and spend a few kitchen minutes observing Chef Maurice and his merry band preparing for the evening.

Chapter

THIRTY-SIX

Looking at the little man with the tobacco-stained gray beard, the porcupine gray hair, and the oily blue denim jumpsuit sitting on his personal folding stool while adjusting the Bistro's front door latch assembly, I finally understood the rationale behind the proverb "Love laughs at locksmiths."

At my urging, Cassandra managed to hustle the lock-fiddling leprechaun, his folding stool, and red toolbox decorated with the Rolling Stones' big lips to the rear exit just as the first wave of customers hit.

I welcomed the diners, congratulated them on their good taste in having chosen one of the finest restaurants in the city, and showed them to their tables. When Cassandra returned, I retreated to a deuce at the rear of the room where A.W. was studying the evening menu. He placed it on the table and informed me that he would be passing on the rib steak in favor of the more imaginative squab with oysters, a combination I'd blithely stolen from one of the great chefs, Jasper White, though I did create my own sauce.

I complimented him on his choice, took one more look at the tables being filled, and, satisfied that all was well, liberated a bottle of Grand Cru Beaujolais and a wineglass from the bar and retreated to my office intending to at least glance at the morning show's temporary schedule that Kiki had prepared. But I couldn't focus on it. I felt . . . what? Vaguely depressed? Frustrated? Annoyed with myself? Why?

I should have been at peace with the world. If Trina Lomax was connected to Felix, she would have informed him by now that I was definitely off his case. And even if that didn't work, I had people with guns protecting me. Assuming the commander had talked to the cops as he'd promised, that should have at least given Solomon something to think about other than me. These were good, positive things. So why was I feeling so blah?

I took a sip of the Beaujolais. Then another. My stomach growled, but I wasn't quite ready for dinner. I picked up the morning-show schedule and put it down again. It was the damned vagueness of it all that was getting me down.

I had no real basis for thinking that Trina was connected to Felix. By her own admission, she'd made him a special project, which explained why she'd run his name through MonitorMan Marvin's super-search program. It also explained why she knew so much more about some of Felix's murders—the severed head, for example, and the full, grisly story of the Colombian cartel boss's death—than had been in the news reports. She could have uncovered facts that other less-aggressive reporters would have missed.

But there was something . . . and I suddenly realized what it was that had bothered me at that meeting in Gretchen's office. When Trina was talking about Felix, she seemed to be almost a different person. Gone was the unsympathetic professional who treated Arnie Epps like a lackey and used the murder of a coworker as a promotional tool. She'd seemed obsessed. Passionate. Felix was definitely more to her than just an elusive story.

Then there was the whole Rudy Gallagher thing. The commander had explained Rudy's presence in Afghanistan, and even provided a motive for the murder of the security guard Deacon Hall. But the old man was assuming that Touchstone CEO Carl Kelstoe had sent Felix to New York to do a mop-up.

That didn't seem to make sense. If Felix's goal had been to recover Kelstoe's recorded phone message and kill whoever might possess it, wouldn't the commander have been number one on the hit list? He'd made the deal with Hall. Rudy was just the transporter. And why Phil? All he did was inadvertently videotape the information transfer.

Why had Rudy been killed? Regardless of what he'd told the commander, he'd been in possession of the recording. Since he'd said to Melody Moon that he was coming into money, it was safe to assume he was planning on selling it. To whom, if not to Kelstoe?

Maybe paying for a hit was cheaper than paying Rudy. Or Kelstoe wanted to make sure that Rudy wouldn't be coming back at him with copies for future bargaining. Or, Rudy being Rudy, maybe he just pissed Kelstoe off. In that case, was it possible that Kelstoe, not Felix, had killed him? No. Kelstoe might have beaten Rudy to death, but I couldn't see him using poison.

But I also didn't see why a smart guy like Kelstoe would have been hanging around town on the night that his hit man was going to kill Rudy. He had to assume that the commander could link him to the murder. Except that the commander hadn't . . . until today. And why was that?

Well, the old man's consigliere Marvin had only recently told him about Felix. Maybe, in spite of what he'd said to the contrary, the commander had thought I'd killed Rudy. A lot of people did. Was that the point of using a Bistro meal to kill Rudy? To send the cops toward me and away from Kelstoe?

So many questions.

I opened the drawer to my left and got out Rudy's little black book to see if it might provide any answers.

Judging by a date scribbled on the third entry, he'd started this particular record of his horndog adventures just three years before. Of its two hundred pages, one hundred and eighty were filled with scribbled entries. Two to a page. Approximately one hundred and twenty women a year. Talk about your multitasker.

Gretchen Di Voss's "G.D.V." entry was near the end. My guess was it had been added approximately four months ago. That's about when Gretch, to use her term, became his "back-door romance."

There were thirty-six entries after Gretchen's. At the rate the Love Shepherd had been gathering his flock, as many as twenty-five or twenty-six little lambs could have made it into the book before the Gretch-Gallagher relationship had blossomed into what she'd assumed to be its monogamous affianced stage. That left ten or so post-fiancée flings.

I scanned those initials. M.M., Melody Moon, was the second to last, right after S.Y., H.H. and B.I. But unlike the other entries, Melody's had no ratings. Instead, Rudy had drawn a dark line through that section of the page. Indicating what? That he hadn't slept with her? He had. Melody wouldn't have lied about that. That she hadn't been worth rating? Doubtful, since he had continued to court her and was considering marrying her. Maybe he'd felt she was too special to rate? More special than Gretchen?

In that case, why was there one entry after Melody's?

I gave it another look and realized it wasn't an entry at all. It was a message from Rudy to himself: *Call C.K. after nine.* Not Clark Kent, I assumed. Nor Craig Kilborn, or any other C.K. except the most obvious one. Two telephone numbers were listed.

I flipped back through the book but could find only ratings. That he'd started using the pages for notes was probably another indication that he'd convinced himself Melody was the One.

I picked up the phone and dialed the first of C.W.'s numbers: 212-744-1600. Even before I'd hit the final "0," I knew who'd be answering.

"This is the Hotel Carlyle. Good evening."

"Sorry, wrong number," I said. I pressed the disconnect for a few seconds and then tried the second number. *"We're sorry, but you've dialed a number that is no long—"*

I hung up the phone.

The Carlyle. It wouldn't be hard to find out if Kelstoe had been staying there the night of Rudy's death . . . whoa. What was I thinking? This was exactly the sort of thing that would put me back on Felix's hit list, assuming I'd ever left.

I replaced the black book into the drawer for what seemed like the hundredth time and picked up the bottle of wine. Still two-thirds full. Polish it off or have dinner? Finally a decision I could make.

I had the beefsteak plate delivered from the kitchen. With potatoes au gratin and petit pois. It was a dish I loved, comfort food, but because of my mood, I was working my way through it listlessly when A.W. arrived and took the chair across the desk from me.

He seemed so energized, it picked me up a little.

"That was the best meal I've had in months," he said. "The combination of meat and oyster was brilliant. Reminded me of M.K.F. Fisher's essays about the oyster, which I guess you've read."

"To be honest, I haven't really read as much of Ms. Fisher as I should," I said. "And I sort of stole the idea of squab and oysters. But the sauce is mine."

"The sauce? Awesome! Melted butter, of course. Vinegar. Minced shallots. Pepper. Beef stock?"

"Close enough," I said. "Unsalted butter and defatted meat drippings. What else?"

"A dry white wine and, I don't know, something briny I couldn't quite . . . maybe anchovies?"

"Caviar," I said, carving a forkful of beefsteak. "It was thoughtful of InterTec to send me a cross between Vin Diesel and Bobby Flay."

"Too much hair for one and too little talent for the other," he said. "But I love to eat. And I do a little cooking."

"How'd you wind up in the security game, A.W.?"

"Just lucky, I guess."

"Seriously," I said.

"I was an MP in Yemen when the USS *Cole* got bombed," he said. "That'll give you an idea of how well loved we were in that part of the world. Anyway, I just happened to be in the right place to help a car full of embassy workers avoid being captured by terrorists. This CNN reporter interviewed me, and a day later I got a job offer from a guy named Ken Foster at InterTec.

"I told him I had another year to go on my tour of duty and I was thinking of re-upping. But after the Towers came down and Bush started his war in what seemed to me to be the wrong place, I figured it was time to get my butt out of uniform. With Ken's help, I managed to free up at the end of my tour, even as some of my buddies were being hit with mandatory reenlistments."

"Foster a big dog at InterTec?" I asked.

"He was my supervisor, in charge of domestic assignments," A.W. said. "He had a heart attack behind the wheel and drove his Lexus into a wall three months ago. A good man and a good friend."

He stared down at the carpet.

Nice job, Billy, I thought. *Now he's as bummed out as you. Way to go!*

"This is pretty good wine," I said. "Have a glass."

"No, thanks," he said. "On the job." He checked his wristwatch and stood. "I'd better check on the lock guy's progress," he said. "Then I'll take a quick tour, just to see if anything looks hinky."

In the time it took me to finish my dinner and have another glass of Beaujolais, he was back. Rushing in, a little flushed.

"Something going on?" I asked.

"No. It's all fine." He was pacing back and forth. "The locks and the alarm are finished. He tested the silent alarm and it worked. I didn't think you wanted your customers to be disturbed by the non-silent."

"Definitely not."

"So it's all good."

I looked at him expectantly, waiting for whatever the other shoe was to drop.

"Billy, is Cassandra . . . hooked up with anybody?"

"Not that I've heard," I said, leaning back in my chair. "But I'm not sure you want to go there."

"Why not?" he asked, sitting down. "She's beautiful. And she's got a great sense of humor."

I stared at him. "I'm with you on the beautiful thing, but humor . . ."

"Just now, a guy was leaving the bar and he stopped to ask her what it would take for her to come back to his hotel room with him. And she said, 'A lobotomy.' Tell me that's not hilarious."

I had to admit it was funnier than her usual two-word reply.

"Any objection if I ask her out?"

"That's really not my call," I said. "But it might be smarter for you to wait until our business is finished. Otherwise it could get complicated. Especially if it doesn't work out and you end up killing either her or yourself."

"Right. I get it," A.W. said, very serious now. "So until we're clear, it's okay if Cassandra and I just . . . talk?"

It occurred to me at that moment that he and Cassandra might not be such an odd match after all.

Chapter

THIRTY-SEVEN

The next day was relatively uneventful, at least until nightfall. After that, well . . .

I didn't wake up until nine-twenty-five a.m., so I'm not sure Ms. Noor, who begrudgingly allowed me to call her Bettina, arrived at five-forty, but knowing her, I assumed she did. As I emerged, showered and shaved, from my bedroom suite, she was in the hall, sitting on a chair she'd taken from the guest room, pinning me with her dark-brown critical eyes.

She was listening to music or news or, for all I know, a Bollywood soundtrack, via an MP3 player. The device, I later suspected, was like the book I always took with me on commercial flights, an excuse to avoid conversation.

She followed me, two paces back, as I went downstairs for a breakfast of a smoked salmon, onion, and capers omelet, two slices of toast, and two cups of fully caffeinated coffee, dark as sin. She refused to join me in anything but the coffee, which she had the good grace to say was delicious.

She continued following me on my power walk and on my quest for Traditional Fit Boxers at Brooks Brothers on Madison Avenue. She followed me to the Village, where, in a little hole-in-the-wall tobacco store that will not be named, I purchased an illegal box of Cuban cigars for a friend. There she faltered, in a room so filled with cigar smoke that a gas mask should have been required. But she stuck to the task, saying not a word.

At the Bistro, while I devoured a roast-beef sandwich, she settled for a mixed green salad. Dry. Okay, I can understand her refusing the dressings we have, since most had been made with some dairy product or other. But she also gave oil and vinegar a thumbs-down. No point in enjoying anything, right?

Shortly after two p.m., my cellular played its little tune—the first several notes of "The 1812 Overture," if you must know. No personal significance, just happened to be on the phone when I bought it.

The sound of the first note put Bettina on alert. She got up from her chair and approached the desk. I picked up the phone, clicked it open, and said hello.

"Hi, Billy," Ted Parkhurst said. "Just calling to thank you for taking care of me Wednesday evening."

"Don't give it a thought," I answered, smiling to let Bettina know the call was from a friend, not a foe. "You and Gin okay?"

"So far so good," he said. "What about you? I understand, via the WBC grapevine, that you were attacked yesterday."

"Paintballed. Joe and the car took the brunt of it."

He'd heard pretty much the whole story of my adventure from Gin, of course, who'd heard about it from Gretchen or maybe Trina.

"Think it was Felix?" Ted asked.

"Probably," I said. "What are you and Gin up to tonight?"

"What we've been up to the last two nights," he said. "She's working on her interview with Goyal Aharon like a brainiac studying for a final. And I'm watching bad TV."

"If you guys can break away, have dinner with me here at the Bistro."

"We'll break away," he said. "Eight okay?"

"Perfect."

I closed the phone and stared at Bettina. "What are you listening to?" I asked.

"An audiobook," she said, unblinking. Poker-faced. "It's a fascinating study of why some people succeed and others don't."

"Sounds like something I should read," I said.

"It may be too late for you," she said.

THIRTY-EIGHT

That night, romance was definitely in the air at the Bistro. An engagement party was occupying one of the larger private rooms, with a mainly young crowd celebrating the prospective bride and groom with drinks and laughter. In the bar, I spied Juan and Bridget staring starry-eyed at each other while she awaited her cocktail orders. And A.W. seemed to have mistaken his purpose for being on the premises, spending more time guarding Cassandra's body than mine.

Gin and Ted arrived at eight on the dot.

I'd decided we would dine in the small room upstairs at the front of the building, where, if a table is placed in exactly the right spot, the diners might get a glimpse of moonlight on the Hudson through the surrounding buildings.

Ted and I had duck breast with port sauce, and Gin, weight-watching, settled for scallops sautéed with garlic and herbs. I was happy to note that Ted's condition on Wednesday had been a one-shot. Gin and I were doing the lion's share of the wine drinking.

We were sipping after-dinner coffees when she asked, "Who's that big blond guy who's been pokin' his head through the door every twenty minutes?"

"My bodyguard," I said. I was feeling full and satisfied and considerably mellowed by more than a few glasses of French red Rhône.

"Then everything I've been hearin' is true," Gin said. "The guy who killed Rudy and Phil is now gunning for you."

"At this point, the only gun has been loaded with paintballs," I said. "If Felix really wanted to kill me, I'd be in a wooden box by now. So I don't know if I'm worried or not."

"Billy," Ted said, "I'm going to need some quotes from you for the piece I'm writing."

"I'm not that drunk," I said. "In fact, everything I say from now on about anything is off the record."

"I thought we were pals."

"We are. And because of that, I don't think it's healthy for you to pursue this piece on Rudy's murder. In fact, you probably need a bodyguard more than I do."

"What are you talking about?" Ted said.

"Keep turning over Rudy's bones and you'll eventually catch the attention of some nasty people. If you haven't already."

"Meaning what?"

"Nothing you don't know," I said. "Three of the guys who were at your table at that Irish pub in Kabul are dead. That leaves just you and the other two Touchstone guards."

Ted brushed the hair from his forehead. He opened his mouth to say something, then changed his mind.

"What?" I asked.

"I found out yesterday. Fredricks was killed in a sniper attack. Okay, I'm scared now. Billy, if you've got any idea what the hell is going on, tell me. Off the fucking record, if that's how you want it."

"That's how I want it," I said, and told him what I'd learned from the commander about Rudy's mission and what I'd surmised.

"You're saying Carl Kelstoe hired the infamous Felix the Cat to kill Rudy," Ted said, brushing his hair back from his eyes for the hundredth time that night.

I nodded.

"Why murder Phil Bruno?" Gin asked. "And why threaten you?"

"I can't figure the Phil connection," I said. "He taped Hall passing something to Rudy in the Irish pub. But I don't see how Kelstoe or anybody else would have known about that. Phil himself hadn't been aware of what he'd shot until he and I discovered it two nights before his murder. And I don't know why that video would have made Kelstoe nervous enough to turn Felix loose on Phil."

"Maybe Felix had his own reason," Ted said. "Phil was in Kabul for several days. From what I've heard about Felix, nobody knows what he looks like. What if he just happened to step into one of Phil's pan shots and wanted to make sure nobody ever saw that footage?"

"Not bad," I said.

"And let's say Felix has been stalking Phil and saw him with you," Ted said. "That would have put you on Felix's list, too."

"Lucky me."

"Maybe ah'm missin' something," Gin said, "but assuming Felix set fire to Phil's building to destroy all of his tapes and films, why didn't he set fire to Rudy's building? Why'd he go to all the trouble of poisoning Rudy's food? And how'd he get the food, anyway, Billy? Wouldn't that mean that Felix had to come to this restaurant, buy the dinner, treat it with poison, and then get Rudy to let him into his condo with it? How did he get into Rudy's building without the security camera picking him up or the doorman seeing him?"

"Here are some of the answers," I said. "I've been told that when Rudy was expecting a visitor and he didn't want the guard or the camera to notice, he'd leave the building's alley service entrance unlocked. Let's say that night he was expecting Carl Kelstoe with the cash to purchase the recordings. Felix picked up the dinner from here, doctored it, and handed it off to Kelstoe, who made a gift of it to Rudy."

"Or Felix went in Kelstoe's place," Ted said. "Rudy lets him in and surprise, surprise! Felix takes the so-called evidence and, instead of paying Rudy money, forces him to eat the poisoned food."

"I don't think so," I said. "According to the detectives, Rudy ate quite a lot of the dinner and washed it down with wine. Doesn't sound like he was forced."

"Another thing the cops told us," Gin said, "the killer trashed Rudy's apartment. Like he was looking for something. So maybe Rudy died without telling Felix or Kelstoe or whoever where the recordings were. And they tried to find 'em. And maybe they didn't."

Thanks to my brush with the fake cop, I tended to agree with "didn't." What I still found puzzling was the sequence of events on the night of the murder.

Rudy had an appointment to meet someone who was going to make it possible for him to quit WBC and marry Melody. That someone—probably Carl Kelstoe or Felix—purchased the food from the Bistro, poisoned it. Rudy was expecting a visitor, had told the visitor about the unlocked alley door. Had trusted the visitor enough to devour the food that was brought. For some reason the visitor had left after his death. When Gretch arrived, the place was still relatively in order. But when the cops showed up the next day, it was a mess.

I couldn't think of a reason why Gretch would lie about the condition of the apartment, even if she had killed Rudy because he'd been unfaithful. That left only three possible conclusions:

1. Whoever poisoned Rudy didn't know or care about the recordings, and, consequently, whoever cared about the recordings arrived after his death and after Gretchen's visit to trash-search the place. *Or* . . .

2. Whoever killed Rudy and cared about the recordings was in the condo when Gretchen arrived and waited for her to leave to trash-search the place. *Or* . . .

3. Whoever killed Rudy cared about the recordings but for some unknown reason left the apartment and came back later for the trash-search.

"Well, what about it, Billy?" Gin said. Her face was flushed, eyes glistening. I'd evidently tuned out of the conversation.

"*Hmmm*," I said, wondering what I'd missed.

Ted filled me in. "You really think it could still be hidden in Rudy's apartment?"

"Let's go see," Gin said.

"Bad idea," I said.

"Why?" Gin asked. "The cops are through with the crime scene by now. If they'd come across anything like a recording of somebody settin' up a hit in Iraq, they wouldn't still be on your case, Billy."

"But they are. And they're saying a prayer each night for a reason to arrest me. Finding me at the scene of the crime would be like Christmas for them."

"Okay, you stay here and be a good boy," Gin said. "We'll go find the flash drive, won't we, Ted?"

"I don't know, Gin. I can see the headlines now: 'Fifteen-Million-Dollar Woman Arrested at Crime Scene,' and in much smaller type, 'Hack Reporter Boyfriend Also Apprehended.' "

"You guys are wusses," she said, getting up too quickly and wobbling a little. "I'll go by myself."

Ted and I watched her weave toward the door. "I can't let her do this alone," he said, and went after her.

Sighing, I got up and joined them.

"Here's the deal," I said. "We go to the apartment. If there's still police tape on the door, we turn around and call it a night. No police tape, we'll go in and look around."

"We'd still have to break in," Ted said.

"Not literally," I said. "I know where Rudy kept a spare key." Thanks to Gretchen.

"Well, that's perfect, then," Gin said and hiccuped.

The dining room was nearly deserted. Just the busboys trying not to look daggers at the couples at two tables who were lingering over their after-dinner drinks.

As we headed toward the front door I spied A.W. sitting at the bar with Cassandra. I'd decided to bring him along, just in case we were to run into a shadowy, self-promoting hit man. But as I took a step toward him, both he and Cassandra, totally engrossed in each other, suddenly roared with laughter over something she'd just said.

It was the first time I'd ever heard her laugh.

Instead of disturbing them, I led Gin and Ted away from the happy couple to the exit at the rear. I considered my decision romantic, but, as I would learn, sneaking out on my bodyguard was an act of wine-induced hubris and sheer stupidity.

THIRTY-NINE

Maxwell Sucony was at his post near the front door of the late Rudy Gallagher's building. He had a shiny, silver-colored thermos in one gloved hand and a plastic coffee cup in the other. When he saw us approach, he put both on the tile floor behind a pillar and walked toward the door, grinning. His uniform looked as neat as if he'd just put it on.

He unlocked the door, opened it wide, and said, "This a real surprise."

"Hi, Maxwell," I said. "Could you join us out here for a minute?"

He looked puzzled, but he went along with it, letting the door swing shut behind him. "What's goin' on, chef?" he asked.

"These are two friends of mine, Maxwell," I said, and introduced Gin and Ted. He allowed as how he'd seen Gin on *WUA!* once or twice. "I'm usually asleep that time of morning, but I sure been reading about you in the papers."

"I'm going to ask a big favor, Maxwell," I said.

"Must be big, you not wanting to discuss it in view of the lobby camera."

I hadn't wanted to discuss it at all, but the service door had been locked.

"We'd like to take a look at our late associate's apartment."

Maxwell frowned. "That's one big favor, chef. There's a lot of back-and-forth been going on about six-D. Tenants on that floor been complaining about the condition of the apartment. Management wants to clean it up, but the police say they gotta wait until they finished."

"The police are still going over the place?" Ted asked.

"Not so I noticed," Maxwell said. "Maybe during the day. Must be some reason they don't want it messed with."

"Is it still taped shut?" I asked, hoping he'd say "Yes" and we could all go home.

"I know it isn't, 'cause one of the managers got me to go in there with some air fresheners. It's one creepy place. I figure whoever inherited it is gonna have some trouble unloading it, no matter how much they fix it up."

"Think you could look the other way for a minute and let us go up?" I asked.

"Why you wanna go up there?"

I put my arm around his shoulders and moved him away from Gin and Ted. Softly, I said, "Ms. McCauley thinks she may have left something of hers up there a while back. She works with Ms. Di Voss. It might be embarrassing if Ms. Di Voss should find it."

"I understand," he said immediately. "The man surely was a playa."

I took a previously folded fifty-dollar bill from my pocket and slipped it to him. He started to object, but I said, "She asked me to give you this."

He took the bill. "The apartment's locked. You gonna need my key."

I shook my head. "I've got a key."

"Then excuse me, chef, but I got to go to the office. That security camera's been actin' up. I'm gonna turn it off and then back on to see if that helps."

We waited by the front door. In just a few minutes, the red light on the camera flickered off and we went in.

Initially, I figured the occupants of the sixth floor must have had more sensitive sniffers than I. The hallway near Rudy's apartment smelled of nothing more unpleasant than carpet cleaner and air spray. As Maxwell had noted, the door to 6D was bare of police tape.

The key that Gretchen had mentioned was under the carpet. I used it to unlock the door, then wiped it with my handkerchief and replaced it where I'd found it.

I'd left the door cracked only an inch or two, but it was enough for me to get a whiff of what the neighbors had been complaining about. We got the full blast when I pushed the door open. Rudy's body and his bodily fluids had been removed weeks ago, but there remained a ghastly smell of sickness and spoiled food and general mustiness that the sweet aroma of lemon air freshener could never dissolve.

I ran my hand along the wall beside the door until I found the light switch.

The place was a shambles. To our right was a small dining room where Rudy had expired, judging by the taped outline of an upper body. The doors to an antique cabinet were hanging open, displaying the broken pieces of what had once been expensive glassware and dinnerware.

To our left, in the living room, a knife or razor had sliced open the cushions and the back of a maroon love seat, a cream-colored stuffed chair, and an assortment of throw pillows that rested on the carpet like little gutted animals. Next to them were books that had been tossed from a now-empty case.

A bearskin rug lay rumpled on the carpet in front of a fireplace that, judging by the stirred ash and disturbed logs, had also been searched. I pointed at the sliced and ripped bear head and said, "If there was something here worth finding, it was probably found."

"Well, this is still pretty damned excitin', isn't it?" Gin said.

"If that's what you want," I said, "try bungee jumping. Let's get out of here."

"Oh, don't be a poop," she said.

"Where do we begin, Billy?" Ted asked.

"I don't think it matters," I said.

"I'll check out this room." He hunkered down to look under the ruined love seat.

"Well, ah'm gonna find the bedroom," Gin said. "That's where ah hide mah valuables."

"Good to know," I said, and headed for my favorite room, moving gingerly past the kill site.

The smell of rotten food was much stronger in the kitchen. Maxwell hadn't thought to give it the benefit of one of his air fresheners. It was not the kitchen of a man who did much cooking. The gas stove was too small and looked like it had barely been used. The refrigerator was small, too. I used my handkerchief to open its door. It was dark and warm inside. Unplugged. The shelves were empty. Ditto the freezer.

Like the other rooms, the kitchen had been powdered for prints and, one presumed, thoroughly searched by both the unknown trasher and the police. Drawers were pulled out, their contents emptied on the black rubber–matted floor along with pots and pans. The cabinet doors were open, exposing empty shelves. Dishes, cups, and saucers were on the counters. One dish rested alone and unused beside an empty frozen-food carton with a familiar smiling face on it. Mine. It had contained Blessing's Own Complete Tex-Mex Dinner for One.

Curious, I used my handkerchief to pop open the microwave's door. The bad food smell nearly put me down. As cooked beans will after a period of time, those in the Tex-Mex Dinner had erupted inside the machine, coating its walls with not just odiferous bean paste but particles of taco and chicken enchilada now mottled with green fungus.

Using my elbow, I slammed the microwave door shut on the mess, my duck-breast dinner starting to come alive in my stomach. But I now knew that Rudy had planned on a frozen-food dinner that night and ignored it in favor of a take-out meal he hadn't been expecting.

On my way out of the kitchen I noticed a framed blackboard, approximately one foot square, screwed to the wall just to the right of the entryway. Next to it was a piece of blue chalk on a string. The board was filled with scrawled blue notations, apparently a running list of things Gallagher was reminding himself to do. "P/U hed let, pk cher tomats." "Omeg o, lipo at drug." "Furn polish and air fresh."

Yep, a little more air fresh would have come in handy.

The list was long enough to suggest that Gallagher hadn't gone shopping since his return from the Middle East. I struggled through every abbreviated note. Only two stumped me, the bottom entries on the board, "Jewel for Berry9" and "Check: 1 or 2, F or OC?"

I got out my phone, planning to take a snapshot of the board, but it began to vibrate in my hand. The call was coming from the Bistro. A.W. or Cassandra, or both. I let the call go to voice mail. Then I took my snapshot of Rudy's bulletin board and exited the odiferous kitchen to see how the others were faring.

The apartment seemed a little too quiet.

"You guys off somewhere necking?" I asked.

No reply.

I moved down the hall. The light from an open door brightened the far end. Approaching the door, I saw a portion of a stripped bed. And then . . . Ted sprawled on the pale green carpet, facedown.

I rushed to him.

He was breathing effortlessly. I was about to try and revive him when my attention was drawn to Gin in the corner of the room, draped gracelessly across an overstuffed chair. The collar of her blouse was bright with blood.

I moved past Ted and went to her.

She had a steady pulse. The skin behind her right ear was broken and starting to swell. It had been the source of the blood. As gently as I could, I lifted her from the chair and placed her on the carpet, being careful with her damaged head.

That was when I sensed rather than heard movement directly behind me. A shifting of air, a shadow. Something. Then I experienced the sensation of my skull being pierced and the room was thrown into darkness.

No. Not the room.

Chapter

FORTY

I was alone in a milk-white kitchen. It was immaculate. The counters were spotless. The pots and pans shined. The black and white tiles on the floor glistened. A small door at the far end of the room opened, and a black-and-gray alley cat sauntered into the kitchen, trailing muddy footprints across the tiles.

It was joined by another cat, a cinnamon tabby, its fur fluffy from a recent bath.

The cats moved apart. The scruffy feline rubbed against a polished chrome cabinet, leaving a trail of dirt. It grinned at me and leaped up suddenly onto the counter, landing gracefully. Purring now.

I was shocked to see that its paws were covered not in dirt but in blood.

So intently was I focused on the gray cat that when the tabby leaped upon my back, sinking its claws into my flesh, it caught me off guard and off balance. I stumbled, my feet slipping on the polished tile floor. I was barely able to raise my hands to guard my face as I fell forward, hitting the tile floor with a solid thud.

The tabby's claw was caught in the material of my coat. The cat tugged at the coat, trying to free itself.

To my surprise, it began talking in a human voice. "C'mon. C'mon now, chef. Wake up."

It was Maxwell Sucony, his round, black face looking stressed. "C'mon, chef. No time to snooze. You gotta get out of here. Cops on the way."

Somebody had stuck a razor blade in a tennis ball and was bouncing that around in my skull. But I was awake enough to go along with Maxwell's effort to get me to my feet.

I was still in Rudy's bedroom.

Just me and Maxwell.

"The couple who came in with me. Where are they?"

"Beats the hell out of me, chef. All I care is they gone. And that's where I want you before the cops show and we have to explain how you got in here."

I was woozy. Staggering. Maxwell was all but dragging me to the front door. "Jesus, the smell of this place could gag a maggot," he said. "All my wasted effort."

Somehow we made it to the hall. Maxwell closed the door to Rudy's apartment and used his master key to lock it. "What exactly's been goin' on up here?" Maxwell asked.

"I wish I knew."

"Your friends didn't leave past me. They musta used the service stairs. You'd better do that, too. The cops'll be coming through the front, if they're not down there already. You navigate the stairs by yourself?"

I nodded. A mistake. That razored tennis ball started bouncing again.

"I better get down to deal with the cops," Maxwell said, moving to the elevator he'd locked there with its door open.

"Why did you call 'em?" I asked.

"I didn't. They phoned me on the night line. Said they got an anonymous call reporting a break-in at six-D. Did I know anything about it? I told 'em I didn't know nothing, and they said to keep an eye out but not to go investigate myself. They were sending some officers to check it out.

"Gotta go, chef," he said, running to the elevator. "Good luck."

I thanked him, then slid along the wall to the door leading to the service stairwell.

It was dimly lit and smelled of disinfectant.

I grabbed the handrail and descended the stairs slowly and carefully. I felt like such a fool that if I'd had a spare foot, I would have used it to kick my own ass on every step. Down all six floors.

FORTY-ONE

A.W. was in my office at the Bistro.

"He just walked in," he said into the cell phone pressed against his ear. He stared at me while whoever was on the other end of the line had their say, then added, "Okay, Lee, I'll take care of it."

He closed the phone and slipped it into his jacket pocket. His expression showed more disappointment than annoyance. "You put me on the bad side of my boss," he told me.

"That's because he's an inconsiderate bastard," Cassandra said. She was sitting to my left in the corner of the room. Her eye makeup was smudged.

"Have you been crying?" I asked.

"You didn't answer your phone. I thought you'd been killed, you asshole."

"Well, I did get my skull cracked, if it's any consolation."

"Damn you, Billy," she said, rising quickly from the chair and walking toward me. Studying my head, she added, "You could have a concussion. Move under the light."

I moved near the light, and she stared into my eyes for a few beats. "Looks okay, but you can't always tell. You feeling dizzy?"

"I'm feeling pain."

"Turn," she ordered. I obeyed, and she examined my wound. "There're two lumps here, one small and one big and bleeding slightly."

"People seem to like hitting me on the head lately," I said.

"I'm next, you pull another stupid stunt like this," she said. "Where the hell is your first-aid kit?"

"Down the hall in the bathroom," I said. "Under the washbasin. And some aspirin, please."

Watching her go fetch, A.W. asked, "What the hell happened, Billy?"

"Aspirin first," I said. I sank to the nearest chair and waited for Cassandra to return. When she did I took the pill bottle, knocked a couple into my palm, and slapped them down with tepid water that had been sitting in a pitcher on my desk for at least five days.

While Cassandra poked at my scalp with a peroxide-soaked Q-tip, I told them of my misadventures of the past several hours, at least the conscious portion.

"Think it was Felix who took your friends?" A.W. asked.

"I don't know. Getting two unconscious bodies out of that building was at least a two-man job," I said. "I only got a glimpse of Felix that night at Phil Bruno's, but he seemed a little too slight to be able to handle any heavy lifting."

"So Felix and a helper," A.W. concluded. "Your fake cop?"

"Maybe." I felt something greasy on my scalp. "What're you doing up there?" I asked Cassandra.

"Neosporin. I put it on everything, just in case," she said. "The finishing touch."

She returned the various oils, unguents, and no-stick strips to the plastic box and placed the box on the desk. "You can put this away, Billy," she said. "I'm going home. I've had enough excitement for one night."

"Thanks for being my administering angel," I told her.

"Fuck you, Billy," she said. Then she turned to A.W. and, to his surprise, kissed him hard on the lips. "I'll see you tomorrow, Andrew."

We both watched her strut from the office.

A.W. was in something of a daze, as well he should have been.

I snapped my fingers an inch from his ear. "Back to reality, Andrew," I said.

"Right. Uh, reality. You should try to phone Ms. McCauley."

"I did, on the cab ride here. Wound up with her voice mail. Good recovery, by the way."

"Yeah, well, I wasn't exactly . . . Why do you suppose they took your friends?"

"I have no idea. It can't have been anything planned. We decided to go to Gallagher's place on the spur of the moment. Either somebody was watching the apartment or it was just our bad luck." But an egotistical, if not paranoid, reason did come to mind. Felix could have decided to take them just to put me on the spot.

A.W. got out his phone.

"What are you doing?" I asked.

"Calling Lee. I have to report this, Billy."

"She'll bring in the police, right?"

"She's not big on that. She'd rather we clean up our messes ourselves. But we now have a kidnap situation involving a celebrity, so I don't know."

"Calling in the cops won't accomplish anything except to get me arrested," I insisted. "The doorman at Rudy's building, a nice guy who helped me, will lose his job." I got to my feet. "And I don't think it'll help Gin and Ted."

"If I don't call her, I'll lose my job," he said.

"Your job, as I recall, is to care for my well-being," I said. "That won't be served if I wind up in the slam."

He looked at the phone in his hand.

"Lee might go along with keeping the police out," he said.

I was weary, but the aspirin had done some work, reducing the ache to a mild throb. Or maybe it was the thought of Lee Franchette. . . . "Why don't I invite her here for a talk," I said, removing the white display handkerchief from my jacket pocket and handing it to him, "while you try and remove your new girlfriend's lipstick?"

FORTY-TWO

Lee Franchette arrived looking as if she'd just awakened from a beauty nap. Judging by the combative stance and the flashing green eyes, she'd been hoping for a rest of longer duration.

"Well, here I am, Chef Blessing. What is so important?"

"Can I get you something to drink? I've got a forty-year-old cognac—"

"I accept the fact that you are charming and a good host, chef. My usually dependable agent is proof of that."

Behind her, A.W. slumped and dropped onto a chair.

"But it is nearing one a.m.," Lee continued. "I've had a very full day. I'm tired and a bit out of sorts. So let us cut to the chase. What is it you want?"

"First, about A.W.," I said. "It would be a mistake to blame him for not keeping me on a tighter leash—"

"I have no intention of blaming A.W.," she interrupted. "What happened is in no way his responsibility. Your life has been threatened by a world-class assassin. A.W. had no reason to suspect you might be foolish enough to leave these premises without him. Are you suicidal, chef?"

"No. On the contrary. I enjoy my life, such as it is. And I enjoy

freedom, which is why I asked you here. Why don't we sit down"—
I pointed to my prize piece of furniture, a Goetz sofa of ebonized
oak wood and ultra-comfortable cushions covered in Herman Miller
Aztec material—"and I'll try to explain."

Lee removed her shiny black knee-length coat and draped it on a
chair. That left her in a white silk blouse with a spread collar, tight
faded jeans, and black running shoes with red stripes.

She descended gracefully onto the sofa. As I sat beside her, she
stared at me. "What's that greasy mess behind your ear?" my goddess
asked, wrinkling her nose in distaste.

"Um . . . Neosporin," I said. "I . . . was hit . . . knocked out."

"I was hoping for a more detailed account," she said.

I nodded, untied my tongue, and told her about our visit to Rudy
Gallagher's and its unfortunate consequences. When I'd finished, she
shifted her glance from me to the carpet.

She sat there in silence for nearly a minute. I looked at A.W., who
raised his shoulders in a quick shrug.

Lee Franchette's emerald eyes were suddenly focused on me again.
It was like the hard drive in her brain had re-engaged and she was
ready. "So rather than have A.W. merely report this information by
phone, you wanted a face-to-face. Why?"

"Surely you've looked in a mirror," I said.

"Another time, I might be flattered," she said. "Right now, I expect a serious answer."

"I was concerned you might go to the police," I said.

"Why would I do that, when that's precisely what your attacker
would want?"

Her answer surprised me. "Yeah," I said. "I just wasn't sure . . ."

"Wasn't sure I'd understand the situation? I am not an idiot."

Even though I could detect no hint of an accent, her precise manner of speech made me think that English was not her first language.
"There is only one possible reason your friends were removed from
the crime scene. To incriminate you."

"What about ransom?" A.W. asked. "Ms. McCauley is the fifteen-
million-dollar woman."

"That may be a secondary reason," Lee said. "But if it were the
prime reason, they would have left Mr. Parkhurst and taken our
client, since his redeemable value is considerably higher than Mr.
Parkhurst's."

"And they wouldn't have bothered calling in the police," I said.

"Correct," she said. "Their intent was to add to your woes, chef. Which is what we are trying to avoid."

"What happens now?" I asked. "Gin and Ted are out there somewhere, probably with a guy whose business is murder. How do we find them?"

"We don't," Lee said. "This is not Deadwood, chef. It's New York City. And they could be in a suburb or out of the state by now. The only reason I would consider the police is because of their informants. Someone may have seen something. But my feeling is that it is too late for the police to be of any practical use. By now these miscreants have realized you have escaped arrest. I can think of no reason why they would kill your friends, unless they believe the deaths could be attributed to you somehow. It seems more likely they will settle for some other way of using them. Or, best scenario, they will release them."

"So all we do is stay put," I said.

"Exactly," she agreed. She cocked her head and seemed to be studying me. Not with distaste this time. A slight smile brightened her exotic, exquisite features. "You know, I do think I would like that cognac now."

I went down the night-lighted stairs, through the dark and silent restaurant, and into the bar, where, in the glow of the bubbling neon sea-horse clock, I grabbed a half-filled bottle and three snifters and carried them back to the office.

Lee was roaming about, looking at plaques and photos on the walls. I placed glasses on the desk, removed the bottle top, and was starting to pour when A.W. appeared with his overnight bag.

"Going somewhere?" I asked.

He looked toward Lee.

"No sense both of us doubling the hours," she said. She was studying an autographed photo of the first great television chef, Julia Child, taken just after she had been presented the French Legion of Honor award. I'd picked it up at an auction.

"So . . . do I come back tomorrow evening?" A.W. asked Lee.

"I can't think why not," she said, turning to face him. She smiled. "Sleep well."

"You, too," he said, then winced, realizing that the reply may not have been entirely appropriate.

"That will be up to our villain," she said. "I expect we may be hearing from him shortly."

"Then maybe I should . . ."

"Go," she ordered.

A.W. looked at me, bemused, and gave me a two-finger salute.

"See you tomorrow," I said, equally bemused, and watched him make his exit.

I finished pouring the cognac.

"Is that for me?" Lee asked, indicating one of the snifters.

"Of course," I said. "But they say we should let it breathe a half-minute for each of its years."

"How boring," she said, walking toward me to claim the glass. I lifted mine, trying to think of a toast that would be provocative but not totally obvious.

But she was walking away, toward the hall leading to my living quarters. "I assume, chef, that your bedroom is in this direction."

"Let me show you," I said, moving toward her. "And all things considered, 'chef' seems a little formal, don't you think? Call me Billy."

"Don't make too much of tonight, chef," she said. In her thick rubber soles she was almost my height. I put my arm around her waist and led her down the hall, wondering exactly *what* to make of it.

She stopped suddenly, turned, and pressed against me. "Oh, hell," she said, and we kissed. A good long kiss.

I guessed our cognacs would be getting more time to breathe than they really needed.

Chapter

FORTY-THREE

It was barely dawn when I felt someone shaking the bed.

"Huh. What . . . Lee . . . ?"

I blinked awake and saw Bettina Noor standing bedside, looking at me with open-eyed surprise. "Lee . . . left hours ago," she said.

"Oh. Must've been dreaming," I croaked. Judging by her expression, she was stunned by the probability that her supervisor and I had engaged in a relationship more intimate than professional.

She was studying the bed. With a groan, I sat up. At the sight of my naked chest, she looked away. "We have to go," she said. She seemed disillusioned.

"Go where?" I asked. "What time is it?"

"Seven-forty-two." She was heading for the door. "We have to drive to the WBC building. Hurry."

"Why?" I asked, throwing back the covers and easing onto the carpet. My headache had returned, in high-def. "It's Sunday, the day of rest. I don't work today."

"This is not about work," Bettina said, her back to me. "Ms. Franchette just notified me that ransom instructions regarding your friends have been received. Your presence is requested, immediately, in the network conference room."

Within fourteen minutes, I was sliding onto the passenger seat of her gray Camry hybrid, a considerably more comfortable vehicle than I'd imagined. And certainly more spick-and-span than Joe's rolling dustball.

Not that I was in any condition to be thinking about cleanliness. I'd performed only the most basic hygienic necessities. I felt unclean, uncomfortable, emotionally perplexed, coffee-starved, and ill-prepared for whatever awaited us at the Glass Tower.

Bettina, on the other hand, looked fresh as a daisy, a disdainful, determined daisy, as she drove at upward of seventy mph through the slowly filling Manhattan streets. What usually took Joe twenty minutes on the best of mornings, she accomplished in twelve, roaring up to the underground parking gate, clicking it open with a wireless device, zooming in, and braking in an empty slot within ten yards of the elevator bank.

"Before we go up, I should convey a message from . . . Ms. Franchette," Bettina told me. "She advises you to say nothing about your involvement in the events leading to the kidnap. If it should come out, do not deny it. But don't mention it otherwise."

"Did she happen to say why?"

"I believe it is because you are still under the shadow of Mr. Gallagher's murder and she would prefer to minimize your participation in an incident involving his apartment," she replied. "I am surprised you and she did not already discuss this last night. Presumably you were otherwise occupied."

I was thinking of how to politely phrase the suggestion that whatever had or had not transpired the previous night was none of her goddamned business when she said, "I apologize. I have not the right to subject you and Ms. Franchette to my standards. Please forgive me."

I wasn't sure I forgave her for that backhanded apology, but I took the easy way out and nodded my forgiveness. "I guess we'd better get upstairs," I said.

"My instructions are to wait here for you," she told me.

"Okay," I said. "Just don't do anything I wouldn't do."

FORTY-FOUR

Four people were in the conference room. The commander was seated at the far end of the table, his white hair sticking up in cockatoo fashion. The collar of a yellow pajama top with powder-blue piping showed behind the open neck of his starched white dress shirt. I guessed he was still wearing the matching pajama bottoms under his gray woolen trousers. Lee sat at his right, looking lovely and relaxed in an ivory silk shirt and black slacks. Trina Lomax, on the commander's left, was in jogging gear, her skunk hair tucked under a Yankees baseball cap. Gretchen, in slacks and a tight T-shirt that read I'D RATHER BE WATCHING WBC, stood by the coffee urn, pouring what I guessed was not her first cup of the morning.

"Billy, finally," she said. "Billionaire Blend?"

"Oh, thank you, yes," I said, not ignoring the display of bagels and pastries.

I selected a Danish and took it and my coffee to an empty chair beside Lee. She gave me a smile that made the day seem a little more tolerable. I took a sip of coffee and saw that Gretchen was staring at me, then at Lee, and frowning.

I like to think of myself as a man of the world, but, in fact, I'm probably too much of a romantic to qualify. A player I am not. So being in the same room with two beautiful women I'd known intimately left me with mixed emotions. Male pride, of course. But also regret, as if, by spending the night with Lee, I'd closed the door on whatever Gretchen and I had shared. A foolish notion, I told myself, since that door should have been slammed shut, with a padlock or two slapped on for good measure, when she threw me over for the arrogant horndog Rudy. And as for any kind of relationship with Lee— she'd made it abundantly clear that that door was never going to open.

Gretchen carried her coffee to the table and placed it beside her laptop computer. She plugged a cord into one of the computer's USB ports, and almost immediately the large monitor at the far end of the room was filled with her inbox page. It contained a single piece of e-mail.

"Move it along, daughter," the commander said.

"I'm doing that, Daddy," Gretchen said in exasperation.

"The phone woke me at a little after seven this morning," she continued. "An electronically disguised voice told me to look in my e-mailbox for 'an interesting message' from Felix. As you can see, it was sent at six-forty-five a.m."

Nearly seven and a half hours after the kidnap.

At a mouse click, the e-mail sprouted into a message from "Felix" to "Gretchen Di Voss."

In the space for a subject title was the instruction: "Left-click on the insert."

Gretchen positioned the cursor to do that.

"Just a minute," Lee said. "Click on 'Felix' and see the e-address he's using."

Gretchen obeyed and, to my dismay, I saw bbless@WBC.com flash on the screen.

They were all staring at me.

"That's my address," I said. "But I can assure you, at six-forty-five this morning I was not sitting at any computer."

"I imagine our agent can testify to that fact," Lee said. "Do you lock your computer here at the building?"

"I don't know," I answered truthfully. "I rarely use it."

"We'll check it out," Lee said. "Please continue, Gretchen."

Gretch moved the cursor to the insert icon and left-clicked. Her computer's media player took over, displaying a small, dark screen with a gray play arrow at its center.

"Make it bigger," the old man ordered.

Mumbling to herself, Gretchen popped the screen to a size that filled the monitor. Then she clicked on the play arrow.

The scene went from black to a blurry, too-bright medium shot of a groggy Gin, posed against a mottled ivory wall, wincing at the lights or her damaged head or both. Clearly it was cold where she was. She was shivering in her light jacket and her breath was visible. At the moment, outside our building it was a gray sixtysomething degrees.

"Hold up the paper, please." The speaker sounded like one of those infuriating, affectless, automated answering devices you get when you phone a customer-service line. The request finally penetrated Gin's mental fog, and she raised her right hand, which was holding the front page of the Sunday *New York Times,* proof of her being alive and well, at least when the paper had hit the streets that morning.

"Read this." A gloved hand thrust a sheet of paper toward Gin. She dropped the *Times* and took the sheet.

Ever the pro, even under those conditions, she scanned the sheet to make sure she understood what she was about to read. "'Do not speak to the police,'" she began. "'We have not been harmed. Our captor wants fifteen million dollars, the same amount as my well-publicized annual salary, or he will kill us. As the world knows, he has killed before.

"'Later, I will provide you with details on where to wire the money. Notify my good friend, Billy Blessing, to be standing by. The arrangement for our release will involve him.'"

The screen went to blue and then, as Gretchen closed down the file, to black.

"Christ," the commander said. "Fifteen mil, and they treat it as if it were carfare. That's what all this blather about saving the economy has done. When you hear of trillions being thrown at failing banks and corporations, millions seem like loose change."

"I do not see that you have a choice," Lee said. "You know what Felix is capable of."

"I have to agree with Lee," Trina Lomax said. "Felix wouldn't think twice about killing Gin and Ted."

"Perhaps Mr. Parkhurst's publisher would contribute part of the ransom," Lee suggested.

"No way," Trina said. "He's closed down three of his twelve magazines and fired half of his staff. He'd think paying ransom would be self-defeating, because Ted's death would let him avoid the possibility of severance pay. And it would sell magazines."

"A man like that would probably not agree to keep the kidnapping a secret," Lee said.

"Fifteen mil," the commander repeated, running his long, pale fingers through his white hair. "Well, I suppose I must. Gretchen, get the new bank guy. . . ."

"Grey Wilfred," she said.

"Whatever the hell his name is, get him and Ralph (that would be Ralph Whitman, the company's chief financial officer) and, of course, Marv, and have them in my office in an hour."

"It's early Sunday morning, Daddy," she said.

"Oh. Right. Well, get 'em here in two hours. But first I want you to come with me to fix up my couch so I can take a little nap before they get here."

Lee, Trina, and I watched the father and daughter leave the room.

"It ain't easy being the princess in this castle," Trina said.

"Easy or difficult, we make our own lives," Lee said. She turned to me. "Well, chef, will you participate in the recovery of your friends, as requested?"

"You tell me," I said. "Speaking as an expert charged with my safety."

"Excuse me for interrupting," Trina said, "but I have a more immediate concern: How exactly do we handle the news report of this kidnapping?"

"You don't," Lee said. "We say nothing until the participants are safe."

"That may work for a Sunday," Trina objected. "But tomorrow morning I'm responsible for two hours of live television. If Gin hasn't been released by then, how exactly do we handle her absence?"

"How would you handle it if she came down with pneumonia?" Lee asked.

"I'd have her coanchor say precisely that at the top of the show."

"Then do that. Say she's come down with pneumonia. Or migraines or whatever malady is currently in fashion."

"Lying to our audience," Trina said. "A lovely way to maintain their trust." She picked up the notepad in front of her, stood, and started to leave.

"A minute, please, Trina," Lee said. "Assuming Ms. McCauley will be unavailable on Tuesday to interview my client, Goyal Aharon, who will take her place?"

"I will," Trina said without hesitation. "Why?"

"Just curious," Lee said, as if she wasn't curious at all.

Trina continued to stare at her for a beat, then turned on her heel and left.

"What was that all about?" I asked.

Lee smiled. "Just a wager I had with myself."

"Did you win or lose?" I asked.

"To reply to a more serious question of yours," she said, "as someone responsible for your safety, ordinarily I would advise you to avoid any involvement in the kidnapping."

"But?"

"If we fail to meet any of Felix's demands, it is probable he will kill your friends."

"There's no guarantee he'll let them live even if he gets his way. He may be luring me to a location where he can either kill all of us or kill my friends and leave me in a position to pay for their murders. Kind of a lose-lose situation, wouldn't you say?"

She reached out a hand and patted my cheek. "Such negative thoughts."

"How about some positive ones?"

She moved her hand to my ear, tracing it with her index finger. It was very distracting. Not that I was complaining.

"The best scenario would be for Felix to honor his contract with the commander and not harm any of you," she said. "After all, fifteen million dollars for a few days' work should trump whatever his employers are paying."

"That brings up another question," I said. "Why did Kelstoe hire him to give me trouble? I don't even know the guy."

"Ah, but is Carl Kelstoe Felix's client?" she asked, almost playfully, as if she knew the answer to the question. She moved her chair closer so that her knees nudged mine.

"You don't think he is?" I imagined I could feel a current running from her knees to mine.

"Let me explain something, my dear, sweet chef." She moved even closer. Her finger continued to play with my ear. Her voice was soft and almost lyrical. But she was not singing love songs. "A decade ago, the company I work for, InterTec, was the largest and most respected security agency in the free world. It had achieved that position by hard work and fair play. At the time, Touchstone was a little one-room automobile repossession and home-guardian business in a shopping mall in Bismarck, North Dakota.

"When Carl Kelstoe retired from the U.S. Marines, he purchased Touchstone. Almost immediately, he took advantage of political cronyism, the bungled war effort, and the failure of conscience among America's leadership to transform his company into Touchstone International, currently this country's leading supplier of mercenary thugs, provocateurs, and torturers.

"I loathe the man and everything he stands for, Billy. But I have no reason to think that he has ever condoned premeditated murder."

I reached up and took her hand away from my ear. "Then you don't believe he had the commander's son killed?"

"No." She leaned back away from me, pulling her hand free of my fingers. "It's possible that young Di Voss was assassinated and that one of Kelstoe's hired thugs was involved. But I don't believe he himself was."

"Well, you're the expert on crime. I'm just a guy who chats up celebrities and makes soufflés."

"That's not exactly true, is it?" she said.

"No?" I knew where this was headed.

"InterTec wrote the book on background checks. Which means, chef dear, I am aware of a time when your skills were more criminal than culinary."

"You had me investigated?"

"No offense meant. Tell me you've never Googled anyone of interest?"

"I'm 'of interest'?"

"All InterTec clients are of interest," she answered. "I know of your . . . association with the late Paul Lamont, a confidence man and thief."

"Paul was like my father, and, as thieves go, he was a fairly moral one. None of his marks were straight or his scams wouldn't have worked. And he'd still be alive. Hell, if I'd been with him when . . . But I wasn't."

"I'm sorry," she said. "It was not my intent to stir up unpleasant memories."

"Really?" I said. "My guess is you thought that reminding me of my failure to save Paul's life would soften me up when it came to saving Gin's. I'd say you're something of a con man yourself, Lee."

"Perhaps," she agreed.

"I'd already made up my mind to do whatever Felix wants."

"So you were testing me." She brightened. "That's why we get along so well, chef. We are both con artists of a sort."

"I'd rather put it that we think alike."

"Then you must know that right now I am thinking that A.W. will have another night to himself."

"You mean I'll probably be dead by nighttime?" I said.

"No, you fool. I mean we—"

I kissed her to indicate I knew exactly what she meant.

Chapter

FORTY-FIVE

Bettina Noor drove me back to the Bistro, staying within the speed limit.

After a period of silence, she asked, "Am I not flexible?"

"Beats me. Maybe a yoga demonstration—"

"I just had a telephone discussion with A.W., and he accused me of being too inflexible. I have heard this before. Ken Foster, whom Ms. Franchette replaced, told me that I needed to be more flexible, that, in this business, it is something to be cherished. If, as I fear, I have been guilty of this criticism, I should adapt, don't you think?"

"It couldn't hurt," I said. Events would prove me wrong, of course. They always do.

At the Bistro, Bettina took a deliberate circuit through the building, making sure all was secure. By the time she arrived at the kitchen, I had prepared eggs and sausages for our breakfast.

"I don't eat flesh or feathers," she informed me. "Anyway, I had my breakfast at five o'clock this morning."

"Then it's time for brunch," I said.

"I do not eat brunch."

"Just out of curiosity, what did you have for breakfast?"

"Vegetarian lentils and a gluten-free potato-flour biscuit. And one cup of tea, unsweetened."

"Damn, girl. You know how to party!!" I said, using my fork to spear a section of egg and a chunk of sausage. "You bake that biscuit from scratch?"

Ignoring the question, she sat down on a high stool beside me at the kitchen counter and stared at the plate I'd prepared for her. "It seems absurd for us to keep people from trying to kill you," she said, "while you're killing yourself with cholesterol and fats."

She pushed the plate away. "Anyway, I thank you for the breakfast, but I wish you had asked first. With so many starving, I hate to see any food, even this, go to waste."

"I assure you it will not." I drew her plate closer to me. "Tell me a little bit about Lee. What's her story?"

"Her 'story'? I should think you'd know more of that than I."

"Humor me."

"She's a strong, dedicated woman of Asian and African ancestry who has achieved great success in a business not known for sexual or racial equality. I consider this a great opportunity to observe and learn from her firsthand."

"You've never worked with her before?"

"I'm assigned domestic cases. Until quite recently, she's been global. She was reassigned when our previous supervisor died. She seems considerably more adept at leadership than her unfortunate predecessor, judging by the security arrangements she has made for the Goyal Aharon book tour."

"What's so special about them?" I asked.

"Aharon's book is fiction, and is therefore frivolous," she replied. "However, because of his candor in discussing the many Mossad operations in which he participated, his life has been threatened by both pro- and anti-Israeli groups."

"Sounds like nobody loves Goyal, except maybe his publisher. How many InterTeckies are assigned to him besides Lee?"

"Lee *does* the assigning," she said, as if I'd insulted her boss. "She has designated the coverage as a four-and-four."

"As opposed to my one-and-one?"

She nodded. "His security will be much more difficult, since the dangers are limitless and unknown. For example, bookstore signings would require from ten to twenty agents, depending on the size of the store and the number of exits. Therefore, his promotional appearances will be limited to only key stores and on-air interviews that can be carefully controlled."

"Beginning on Tuesday with *Wake Up, America!*"

"Yes." As if to stem further conversation, she hopped from the stool and said, "Excuse me, but I have reports to prepare and submit. And we may be summoned back to the WBC building at any moment."

I finished my breakfast and most of hers, and left the dishes in one of the sinks for the dinner crew to deal with. Then I climbed the stairs to find her seated at the desk in my office, working at her laptop. Rather than disturb her, I backed away and went to my living quarters.

The bedroom looked sad and empty, as they do on those mornings. I felt tired but didn't think I could sleep. Especially since I was on call. I replaced the linen and gave the blanket what Paul Lamont used to refer to as a "Navy tuck." Then I shaved, showered, and dressed in gray slacks and a charcoal wool pullover.

I picked up my cellular, checking to make sure I hadn't missed THE call while in the shower, as if Bettina would have allowed that. There were no messages.

I sat down on the newly made bed and stared at the phone in my hands. With nothing better to do, I brought up the photo I'd taken of the blackboard in Rudy's kitchen. The reminders he'd left for himself seemed no less enigmatic then than they had last night. "Jewel for Berry9." "Check: 1 or 2, F or OC?"

Could the F have been Felix? Then what was I to make of OC? There'd been a television show called *The OC*. About Orange County in Southern California, I thought. Hadn't one or more of the actors dropped by our show? As everyone kept telling me, Rudy had not only lived TV, he'd loved it. Had he been planning to check for some connection between Felix and that show? Or maybe he thought Felix was born in the real Orange County. Or maybe the F didn't stand for Felix at all.

"Ahem."

Cassandra was standing in the doorway. "I just got the third degree from Little Miss Bollywood in your office," she said. "What happened to Andrew?"

Andrew. A.W. to the world, but Andrew to Cassandra.

"He's off-duty. You're here a little early for a no-lunch day, aren't you?"

"I was up. I figured I might as well . . ."

". . . have breakfast with Andrew?"

"I was just . . . never mind."

"You blushing?" I asked.

"Abso-fucking-lutely not!" she said, storming off down the hall.

How juvenile. To prove I was above that kind of childish behavior, I called out after her. "Cassandra and Andrew sittin' in a tree . . . K-I-S-S-I-N-G . . ."

In response, one of Cassandra's shoes came sailing back in my direction, just missing my head. She could've gone after our last President with an arm like that.

"Gonna be hard, walking around on one shoe!!"

It was nearing eleven a.m. on what was starting out to be the longest day of my life. I've never been very good at waiting, especially for a phone to ring. When it finally does, it's never the person you want.

I went to the office to do busywork. Since Bettina was still using my desk, that consisted of straightening picture frames, gathering newspapers and tossing them, collecting scattered magazines into piles, and putting books back on their shelves.

"Did you want to sit here?" Bettina finally asked, after I'd opened the desk drawer on her left to put away a bunch of business cards I'd collected from the various shelves.

"Not really," I said.

That's when I noticed the stack of Rudy's DVDs still in the drawer. I wondered how late Melody and her roommate slept in on a Sunday morning.

Chapter

FORTY-SIX

"Who is this Melody Moon?" Bettina asked as she parked her hybrid in front of Melody's apartment building.

"A friend. I'll just run in, drop these off, and come right out."

"These" were the Rudy DVDs.

"I'm coming in, too," Bettina said.

"It'll go quicker if you don't, and you might get a ticket," I said, leaving the car before she could argue about it.

Melody answered the buzzer wearing tan slacks, a bright-red sweater with silvery dots circling the neck and wrists, and a puzzled expression.

"Sorry to bother you on a Sunday morning," I said, holding the DVDs behind my back.

"That's okay," she said. "Rita and I were just getting ready for a drive to Sag Harbor."

"I won't keep you, then," I said, bringing the disks around and handing them to her. "I just dropped by to give you these."

"Ohmigod," she said, "Rudy's shows. Come in, please, chef. Have a cup of coffee."

She opened the door wide and I saw Rita Margolis perched on the maroon pressed cardboard sofa, glaring at me, a cup of something in one hand. She was dressed in white slacks and a matching white jacket over an orange T-shirt with a comic character I didn't recognize at its center. A little winged man smoking a cigar and wearing a brown porkpie hat and a brown suit.

"Hi, chef," she said. "Get those paint stains off your car yet?"

"Paint stains?" I repeated stupidly.

"I've seen the picture on the Internet," she said. "I never would have guessed you for a run-and-gunner."

"I'm not," I said.

"Well, the Cheetah sure is. I was wondering what she was up to, sitting parked in that Hummer at the museum. I mean, the superheroes were supposed to be inside."

"You got a good look at the Cheetah?" I said.

"I . . ." Rita paused, distracted by something behind me.

Bettina. "Hi," she said. "I'm Billy's . . . friend."

"Please come in," Melody said, ever the perfect hostess. "I was getting Billy a cup of coffee. Can I get you one?"

"We won't have time," Bettina said. "I got the call, Billy."

"Just a minute," I said, turning back to Rita.

"This the Cheetah?" Rita asked. "I thought she was taller."

"You think the Cheetah was a woman?" I asked.

"Oh, yeah. Don't you know who it was?"

"Billy," Bettina said, "we're wanted."

"Right," I said, keeping my eyes on Rita. "No. I don't know who was wearing that costume."

"Weird. Fact is, there was something weird about the costume, too. I'm not sure what. I'm not the world's greatest Cheetah fan, like the boys at the museum. But there was definitely something off."

"Like what?"

"I'd have to check the original art."

"Would you?"

"We have to go, Billy," Bettina said.

"It's very important," I said to Rita.

I must have gotten the point across, because she said, "They have some art at the museum. I'll check it out when I'm there. Call me tomorrow afternoon."

"Thanks," I said. "We've got to run."

"It was sweet of you to bring the DVDs," Melody said. "How much do I—"

"No, they're gifts," I said. "My pleasure."

"Come on, Billy." Bettina grabbed my arm and almost dragged me from the room.

"You were rude up there," I said to Bettina once we were back in her Camry.

"Really," she said, zipping through the Sunday-morning traffic. "Tattooed people make me uncomfortable. And besides, she's much too young for you. Both of them are."

"Rita saw Felix," I said.

"Oh," Bettina said. "The figure in costume you were talking about?"

"If she and my driver are correct, and I suspect they are, Felix is a woman."

"That might explain why she has been so successful," Bettina said.

"And as for the ladies being too young for me," I said, "I believe you're only as young as the woman you feel."

"All you old men believe that," she replied.

FORTY-SEVEN

The assembly in the conference room included those who'd been there earlier—Gretchen, the commander, Trina, and Lee—and the commander's guru Marvin in his familiar warm-up suit and cap. A wardrobe that simplified must make getting dressed in the morning a breeze.

We walked in on the heels of another newcomer, a short, male fireplug in a conservative three-piece suit named Ralph Whitman, the Di Voss Company's CFO. Judging by his sour expression, he'd already been apprised of the kidnapper's demands. "Let's get on with this," Whitman said, taking a seat next to Lee, the one I'd been heading for.

I settled for an empty chair beside Trina. Bettina remained standing near the door, as if guarding us from intruders.

The new video had been sent at eleven-nineteen a.m., not from my office computer—which had been under the scrutiny of InterTec—but from a display laptop at a local electronics store. Another agent had been dispatched to that location to see if any of the floor salespeople had noticed anyone using their machines. If my experience with electronics-store employees was any indication, they wouldn't even have noticed if the building had been on fire.

The video began to play on the big screen.

Again Gin was featured, blinking into a harsh light while standing in front of the mottled wall, looking even colder than before. The difference this time was that the city had awakened. There were background noises—the low rumble of traffic, a church bell gonging, and a couple of other distinctive sounds, including circus music.

Gin seemed oblivious to the city sounds as she read from a sheet of paper, informing us that "'the fifteen million dollars should be wi-ayd to account number S325469554 at Bank Austria Cayman Islands at any time between the present and precisely noon on Tuesday.

"'At noontime, assumin' the transfer has been made without incident, Bill Blessin' will be notified, via his cellular phone, of the address where he can find Ted Parkhurst and mahself. He is to travel alone. We will be alive and well, merely bound and gagged.'"

She looked directly into the camera. "An', Billy, if you're watching this, please hurry, 'cause it's cold enough heah to freeze champagne."

The back of a large figure suddenly entered the frame, its gloved hand lashing out to slap Gin across the face. "Say only what is written," the odd mechanical voice ordered.

Alone on camera again, mouth red with blood trickling from one corner, Gin glanced at the paper in her hand with moist, frightened eyes. She read in a halting voice, "'S-should you involve police awh FBI, awh should you fail to follah these instructions in any way, ouah captors will be forced to k-k-kill Ted and mahself.'"

The screen went to blue, then black.

"Will there be any problem wiring them the money?" the commander asked Whitman.

"Wiring the money is not the problem," Whitman answered. "Getting the money back from Gibraltar is the problem. Insurance companies tend to balk when they find out you refused to notify the FBI or even local law enforcement. According to the security people you hired"—he pointed to Lee—"I can't even call Gibraltar's CEO to get a reading on it."

"We can worry about the insurance claim after the fact," the commander said. "Right, Marv?"

Marvin raised both hands, palms up, indicating two plates of a scale. "Money or people's lives?" he said, moving his hands up and down. "You can always get more money."

"If the kidnapper is as dangerous as everyone seems to think," Whitman pointed out glumly, "there's no reason to believe that money will make any difference to him."

"We *are* wiring the money, Ralph," the commander said with a finality that shut the CFO up like a clam.

"Did anyone hear the background noises?" I asked. "Not just the traffic, I mean."

"The church bells," Gretchen said.

"Dogs barking," Marv said. "Sounded like a whole pack."

"What was that music?" asked the commander.

"I can't begin to count the times I ran behind the source of that music waving a quarter," I said. "The Mister Softee soft-serve ice-cream truck."

"I'll get someone to find out the morning routes," Lee said, "as well as the addresses of kennels and dog parks. Perhaps we will discover an intersection."

The commander stood up. "Thanks to each of you for your cooperation. And thank you, daughter, for the presentation."

As everyone headed for the door, I stopped Trina. "Could you ask someone to put the footage Gabe Farris took at the superhero exhibit on a disk for me?"

She gave me a half-smile. "Working on your talent reel, Billy?"

"Never know when you're going to need one," I said.

Lee was standing with Bettina at the door, both of them watching me approach.

"What was that about?" Lee asked, pointing her lovely chin at the departing Trina.

"Shop talk," I said.

"We should have some of that right now," she said. "I'm sure Bettina will excuse us."

"Of course," Bettina said, and left us alone in the room with Gretchen. We waited while she powered down her computer, snapped its lid shut, and, giving us a curt nod, departed.

"I have a long list of things to do regarding Mr. Aharon's arrival," Lee said, "but if you so desire, I will tell A.W. to expect to spend the night in his own bed."

"I so desire," I said.

"At about ten?"

"Or even earlier," I said. "I've got to be on the set at the crack of dawn tomorrow."

"I'll make it nine," she said. "I wouldn't want you to feel hurried."

Then, in a sudden display of compartmental dexterity, she lost her sexy smile and it was back to business. "You are prepared to go through with the plan on Tuesday?"

"Sure. But I'm a little curious why Felix wants me to come alone."

"You won't be alone," she said. "I'll make sure of that."

"There's something else I'd like you to do. Treat Trina Lomax to one of your famous InterTec background checks."

"Why?"

"Earlier today, when you asked who'd be interviewing Aharon if Gin weren't available, she didn't even have to think twice," I said. "Lance was the obvious second choice, but Trina didn't even give him a moment's consideration. She had the answer on the tip of her tongue, almost as if she'd known for some time Gin wouldn't be free."

"As fond as I am of your devious mind, chef dear, I think Ms. Lomax was simply establishing a backup plan. From what I've seen of Lance, I can understand her decision to do the job herself."

"Maybe. But why are they holding Gin until Tuesday afternoon? It'd be much more efficient and less risky to close the deal today or tomorrow. Why wait, if not to keep Gin off the show? What's scheduled for the show? Let's see. *Hmmmm.* Isn't there an appearance by a controversial guy some people would like to see dead?"

"I'll get that background done at once," Lee said.

"Make sure it includes the INN assignments she's had over the past couple of years. I know that she was in the same locations as some of Felix's kills. It would help to know if she was nearby for all of them."

"You're saying Trina could be Felix?"

"Why not?"

"Felix—a woman? You are a wonder. Whatever gave you that idea?"

As much as I would have liked to tell Lee about Joe and Rita Margolis both claiming the figure in the Cheetah outfit was feminine, I didn't want to drop any names on Lee. I didn't want her or her minions bothering Rita or Joe, or dragging them into this mess.

"Everybody knows you females are deadlier than us males," I replied.

"Don't you forget it, Mister Softee," she said, giving my face a none-too-gentle pat.

Chapter

FORTY-EIGHT

"Pull up over there," I said to Bettina, pointing to a section of empty curb on Central Park South.

"Why?"

"Why not?"

"I thought you wanted to get back to the Bistro," she said, maneuvering the hybrid into the parking space.

"Cassandra's on duty," I said. "Could you use that phone gadget of yours to Google dog parks and kennels in the city?"

Instead of replying, she took out her phone and began tapping at it.

I looked past her to a couple of horse-drawn carriages clopping along to the park. It was a nice sunny Sunday. Great day for a carriage ride. Or jogging in the park. Or strolling along. Or thinking about absent kidnapped friends.

"Google says there are over four thousand kennels in New York City."

"That may be more than we can handle today," I said. "Let's limit our search to Manhattan. The sections of the city near water."

"Why water?" Bettina asked.

"Gin mentioned champagne. I assume she was telling us she's in a wine cellar. An old wine cellar, judging by the wall behind her, and one that's permanently cold and damp. A lot of the city's old mansions that were constructed near water had wine cellars dug deep to take advantage of the natural cooling."

The limitations left us with eightysomething dog hostels.

We spent a little under an hour driving to the first twenty locations. Then we stopped for food, or what they pretended was food at a Bettina choice, Café Carrot on the Upper West Side. Another hour to cruise the second twenty canine conclaves, and for my stomach to digest roasted seitan, grilled onions, and soy cheese. We were in the beginning of the third group of listings when I asked her to park the car again.

To our right was the Dawn of the Dog Hotel and Spa, where a collection of overpampered pups was resting quietly in a gated pen where once a lovely lawn and garden grew.

"Well?" Bettina said. "We have dogs, but they make no noise. So?"

I looked at my watch. "Let's wait a bit."

"Is there something special about these dogs?"

"To paraphrase the great Sherlock Holmes," I said, "the thing that makes them special is that they are not special."

"I don't understand," she said.

"Wait for it . . . wait . . . right . . . about . . . now."

Church bells began to ring in the hour. Could have been St. Bartholomew's or St. Peter's Lutheran over on Lex. The dogs were now singing along at full bark.

"Two out of three on our city-sounds list," I said.

"But I still don't know why you thought—"

"At the end of the block," I said. "The abandoned stone-and-brick monstrosity we drove past."

She looked back. "Chain fence," she said. "Three-story with boarded windows. Totally overgrown with bushes and vines. What about it?"

"It's the Vosburgh mansion," I said. "A classic city eyesore. Built back at the tail end of the nineteenth century by an old crook named Joe Vosburgh, who still holds the record for the number of times he sold the Brooklyn Bridge. The mansion cost nearly half a million dollars, which was a whole lot of ill-gotten loot back in those days."

"I appreciate the history lesson," Bettina said. "Is there a point to it?"

"You tell me. A year ago, Gin and I did a segment covering more than a dozen of the city's old mansions that are so tied up in legal red tape they just sit there gathering greenery gone wild and dust and rodents. The Vosburgh was on our list. The thing that added to its uniqueness is that the old con artist spent a hunk of that half-million digging a double cellar so deep in the ground that because of the proximity of the East River, the temperature was a natural forty-five degrees. That's where he kept a gazillion bottles of French champagne that he bought when he saw that Prohibition was soon to become the law of the land. While everybody else was swilling bathtub rotgut, Vosburgh's friends and clients were enjoying *vin extraordinaire*."

Bettina frowned. "So you think that when Ms. McCauley was talking about freezing champagne, she was telling you she was being held at the Vosburgh mansion?"

"I'm jus' sayin'."

Bettina nodded. "Logical. We should see."

She reached for the door handle.

"Whoa," I said. "That's not smart. Could be a dozen guys inside. With Uzis."

"You watch too much television," she said. "Besides, I have a gun."

"One thing I learned from TV, the cop who goes in without calling for backup ends up in trouble. You have a phone. Use it to call the troops."

"Your friends could be in there at great risk," she said. "Waiting for more agents may be the proper procedure. But this is a situation that demands . . . flexibility." She handed me her cellular. "I will enter the building and you call A.W. Press button three."

"Let's go in together," I said. "I've been in there before."

"No. You are under my protection."

"Wait . . ." I began. But I was talking to myself.

She moved down the block at a swift pace. I fired up the phone, and A.W. answered on the second ring.

While giving him the situation, including our location, I watched Bettina find a loose section of the chain-link fence that surrounded the Vosburgh. She pulled it back and squeezed past it onto the property.

"Sit tight," A.W. instructed me. "I'll be there with backup in ten minutes."

Ten minutes, I thought, as I put the phone away. Too much could happen in ten minutes. I felt like a jerk just sitting there. But Bettina was a trained professional. She was armed. I was a guy who ran a restaurant and talked to people on TV.

Then I heard popping noises coming from the mansion. Two, then silence.

With great reluctance, I got out of the car.

Another pop.

I did not take my time getting to the weak link in the fence. It wasn't as easy for me to squeeze through as it had been for Bettina. My jacket pocket ripped and a pant leg caught, tumbling me onto my knees in a jungle garden of overgrown shrubs and bushes, some of them with thorns.

Our crew had cut a path through the jungle a year ago. Somebody—the kidnappers probably—had removed whatever growth there had been since then. I had no problem moving past the branches and brambles.

At the rear of the mansion, the greenery had really taken over.

I suddenly froze, staring at a pale hand poking through the shrubbery. There were people hiding among the weeds and vines and plants. No, not people, I remembered with relief. Ivy-covered statues of Greek gods and goddesses that the old con man had imported to give his estate a "classic look."

A broken brick path led me to a slightly ajar basement door.

I'm not a particularly brave man, and I really didn't want to go through the door. Not empty-handed. I looked around for something that even remotely resembled a weapon. A hoe, a rusted hammer. Even a big rock. Nothing.

With pounding heart, I entered the building.

To my right was a short stairwell that, as I recalled, headed up to a dayroom in the main house. To my left was a much longer set of creaking, partially dry-rotted stairs leading to the deep basement.

With a sinking feeling, I turned to the basement stairs. I had no weapon. I had no flashlight. And I had even less courage.

I closed my eyes and concentrated on sounds from down below. All I heard was my own panicked breathing.

There was enough reflective light from the open back door for me to see the first several stairs. A dim glow down below indicated that I'd be able to see the bottom steps. But in between . . . darkness.

Well, hell. I'd come this far.

I descended cautiously. The wooden stairs were old and weak. And very noisy. I probably sounded like a golem stomping down. Halfway, the temperature dropped and there was a dampness to the air that couldn't quite mask the unmistakable firecracker-plus odor of gun-smoke. There was another aroma, too, almost as pungent. Gasoline. Not good.

I could see that the faint illumination came from a round, battery-powered Stick 'Em light lying on the ground just past the bottom step. Somebody had probably tried to adhere it to the moist wall and it had fallen and rolled downstairs. Instead of concentrating on it, I should have noticed the sponginess of the stair under my left foot.

The rotted wood gave way and I tumbled forward, banging my left elbow against the wall, hitting the stairs on my right shoulder, and sliding to the cement floor on my back, totally disoriented.

A jolt of pain from my elbow helped to clear my head. As I reached to comfort that aching joint, my shoulder reminded me that it, too, had taken a hit. I lay there on the cold cement, feeling very sorry for myself, until I heard someone moving around in the base-ment.

The Stick 'Em light was only a foot away from my face. I reached out to press the little button that turned it off. My elbow stopped me halfway. It wasn't broken, I didn't think, but it definitely didn't like sudden movement. Breathing heavily, I eased the arm out and turned off the light.

With just the faint glow from the top of the stairs, I was in nearly total darkness. I rolled over and crawled painfully into the pitch-black basement.

Another rustle.

I had to assume that whoever was moving around had gotten a good look at me when I stumbled into the Stick 'Em spotlight. That they hadn't shot me was a good sign. But if it was Bettina scurrying around in the darkness, she probably would have identified herself. So the best I could do was stay quiet and still and wait for A.W. to arrive with the cavalry.

My left ankle was hurting now, too. What fun. I lay on my back and tried to mentally catalog my injuries. I got as far as the elbow that wasn't broken and the shoulder that was definitely bruised.

Then the shooting started.

There was a tiny flash of light and a bullet smashed into the wall near me. About where my head would have been if I'd been sitting up. I quickly rolled farther away from the stairwell. Another bullet. Another roll.

I was about as panicked as a man can be without peeing his pants . . . or worse.

I lay there, listening to my own breathing. Waiting for the bullet that would find its mark.

Instead there was the sound of rushed motion. Footsteps heading toward me, then past me, and moving quickly to the stairwell and up.

I prayed that whoever it was would hit that rotten stair and get trapped there, screaming in pain. But like so many of my prayers, it went unanswered.

When I'd heard the shooter's footsteps moving up and away, I sat up and turned on the Stick 'Em light. I used the nearby wall to stand. My ankle hurt but took its share of my weight without giving way.

I aimed the light at the rest of the basement. It wasn't much, but it was enough for me to see Bettina, lying on her back on the cement floor.

I hobbled to her.

She was alive. Unconscious, shivering, but with a strong pulse. Blood glistened in the dark hair above her left ear. A bullet wound, I assumed. How serious, I had no idea.

I was afraid to move her, even if my damaged limbs would have allowed it.

I struggled out of my coat and tucked it around her. Not much help, but all I could do for the moment.

I scanned the room again. Where the hell were Gin and Ted?

Bettina's gun was several feet from her right leg. I picked it up and, using the Stick 'Em light as a lantern, limped into the darker section of the basement. The gasoline smell was stronger.

That's when I saw the other body. A big white guy, pitched forward on his face. Very dead. His left hand seemed to be reaching out in Bettina's direction. I was reminded of Lee Marvin's famous death scene in the remake of *The Killers*. He'd been shot before he could draw his gun, but, with his last breath, he made a kid's imitation gun with his thumb and index finger and pointed it at the person who did him in.

I held the Stick 'Em light close to the dead man and saw that a bullet had entered the back of his head. I had no interest in turning him over to see the exit wound. But there was something . . . Yes, along with the cordite and the gasoline, there was a faint, familiar odor. I moved the Stick 'Em light down his body to a pair of brown shoes I'd seen before.

Hello, Clove Boy.

Staring at his corpse, I wish I could say I felt sorrow or even revulsion, but I was too concerned with the fate of my friends, and what he'd done to them, to give a damn.

His gun lay on the floor a few yards away. I hesitated about picking it up. I'd probably screwed up the crime scene evidence already by taking Bettina's weapon. I left this one where it had fallen.

Thanks to the Stick 'Em, which was rapidly becoming my favorite infomercial product, I saw the spotted wall that had served as a backdrop for Gin's video. The Sunday *New York Times* was still where she'd dropped it and, though no camera was in evidence, the portable generator that had been used to power the video light rested on the cement floor. It was the source of the gasoline smell.

The Stick 'Em helped me find another stairwell, this one short and made of stone, leading down to a lower, colder second level. This was clearly where old Joe Vosburgh had kept his imported bubbly. To my left were empty wine racks and a faded and flaked painting of a bevy of cancan girls popping out of a giant champagne bottle labeled VOSBURGH'S CRISTAL.

The House of Roederer had created Cristal for Russia's Czar Alexander II, but, just as the United States was about to lower the boom on booze, the keepers of the House decided that the rest of the world should also get a taste of the classic champagne. And Vosburgh, the old pirate, had somehow got his hooks on the first cases of the stuff. God, a case of that Cristal today would go for—

An impatient squeal drew my attention to a very female figure lying on the cold concrete about ten yards away. A blackout mask had been duct-taped over her eyes. More duct tape had been used on her body—to seal her lips, to secure her wrists behind her back, and to hold her ankles together.

Ted Parkhurst was lying against the far wall, similarly bound, blinded, and gagged.

"Gin. It's me, Billy," I said, as I painfully hunkered beside her.

She made a series of *"umm-umm"* noises while I placed the gun and Stick 'Em light on the floor. I got out my trusty Swiss Army Knife and sliced through her wrist tape.

"I'm gonna let you do the rest," I said, "while I help Ted."

The knife did its job there, too.

I was amused to see that no sooner had Ted torn the mask from his eyes and the duct tape from his mouth than his unruly hair flopped onto his forehead.

"Is that it? Are we free?" he asked me, unconsciously pushing back his hair.

"Like the birds in the trees," I told him.

"Are you okay, baby?" he called over to Gin.

"Yeah, sweetie," she said, working on her ankles. "We're all okay."

Except for the big white guy in the other room, who was about as far from okay as you can get.

And poor Bettina.

Chapter

FORTY-NINE

We were entering the upper basement when flashlights blinded me. A gruff voice shouted, "Drop the gun."

"No problem," I said, placing the weapon on the concrete floor. "Dropping the gun."

"It's okay," I heard A.W.'s voice shout. "They're friendlies."

"Is the area clear, chef?" Lee asked.

"Yes," I said, shading my eyes. "Think your guys could lower the flashlights?"

When they did, I saw that Lee was kneeling beside Bettina. "Who did this?" she asked as I approached.

"Over there," I said, pointing at the corpse.

"Killing him was good work, chef," she said.

"I didn't do it," I said.

"Then Bettina . . ."

"Maybe, but there was somebody else here," I said. "Too dark to see. Could have been Felix. The guy over there took a bullet in the back of his head. I don't know how Bettina could have managed that."

"We can sort that all out later," Lee said.

While A.W. and the others wrapped Gin and Ted in blankets and led them upstairs, Lee wasted no time sending for paramedics for Bettina and arranging for her hospitalization. Then she turned to me. "You okay? You look like you've been through hell."

"I, ah, fell down the stairs," I said. "Some aches and pains, but I'm ambulatory."

"Good. I think you should leave here now. And take your friends. A.W. can drive you."

"The police will want to talk to us."

"Not if they don't know about you," she said. "I'll take care of it. You do not want to be involved. Neither you nor your friends. But especially not you. We're paid to handle things like this."

She called out to A.W. and, when he arrived, instructed him to take us away from there immediately. But before I left she asked, "What did you touch?"

"The handrail along the stairs, this." I handed her Bettina's pistol. "And the Stick 'Em light. That's about it."

"You touched nothing else? This is very important."

"The strips of duct tape."

"The sleep masks?" she asked.

"Maybe."

"We'll have to collect and destroy all of that, anyway," she said. "Now that there was no kidnapping."

She held up Bettina's gun. "I'll take care of this, too. You should go now and let me summon the police. We will talk tonight."

I nodded.

As I reached the stairs, I heard her say into her phone, "I wish to report a trespass and a fatal shooting at . . ."

Chapter

FIFTY

"Mah head's still sore as a boil," Gin said as A.W. chauffeured us through the darkening city toward her apartment on Riverside Drive. She and Ted were sharing the backseat, her sore head resting on his shoulder.

She'd already told us about being whacked on the noggin by person unknown at Rudy's suite and waking up thinking she might be paralyzed and blind before realizing she was bound and gagged and wearing a blindfold.

"One of the bastards woke me and freed mah ankles and walked me to the upper basement, where he took the tape off mah mouth. He was surprisingly gentle about it, careful easing it off my lips. Then he released mah hands and gave me stale-tasting doughnuts and a cup of lukewarm, weak coffee."

After that pathetic excuse for breakfast, she'd been placed in front of a wall where "they peeled the blindfold from mah eyes."

She reached up suddenly to touch her eyes. "Damn, ah hope they didn't pull off mah eyelashes?"

"Your eyelashes look beautiful," Ted reassured her.

"Thank God. Well, anyway, when they took off the blindfold at first ah couldn't see much more than the bright light in mah face. But slowly other things came into focus. A cheesy little camera was sittin' on a tripod pointed at me. Theah were two men that looked jus' like shadows. Later, ah saw that they were wearin' black raincoats, buttoned, black pants, black hat, black shoes. They wore stockings over theah faces to disguise theah features. The thinner one stood beside the tripod pointin' a gun at me. The other, a big man, was near me, just off camera, holding a white paper in one hand and a copy of *The New York Times* in the other.

"That fella handed me the *Times* and the other fella, speaking in an odd, throaty voice, ordered me to hold it up close to mah body with the front page showin'."

"You remember his exact words?" I asked.

"He said, 'Hold the paper up when the camera's red light goes on.' And ah said ah knew all about hot cameras, since ah have spent most of mah adult years standin' in front of one.

"Then he said, 'Fine, only when ah cue you, drop the newspaper and take the sheet of paper from mah associate.' The guy near me showed me the paper.

"'You jus' read what's on the paper,' the thin fella said. And ah asked to look at the paper and he said, 'No. Ah want a cold reading.'"

"Wait," I said. "He used the words 'cue' and 'cold reading'?"

Gin nodded. "So ah read it cold. Well, actually, ah kinda screwed up the first take. Which is a good thing, because that gave me a chance to look around. The bright light really lit the place up, and ah realized ah'd been there before, with you, Billy, talkin' about the old man—Vosburgh, right?—and his champagne cellars. So ah threw in that line about champagne hopin' you'd catch it.

"It kinda ticked 'em off. The big guy hit me. But they kept the camera going. Ah was afraid they might do another take, but they must've thought the comment was innocuous natterin'."

"Did you hear both kidnappers speak?" I asked.

"No. Jus' the thin one. The big guy coulda been a mute. Anyway, they stuck the blindfold back on and ah was led back to the lower, colder cellar, where mah wrists and ankles were taped again.

"Later, they put me through the same routine, except they substituted a dry cheese sandwich for the doughnuts and there was no newspaper prop and the words on the paper were different.

"Ah was led back to the lower cellar, and that's where ah stayed until the shootin' started, and then you cut me loose, Billy."

"Any idea how many kidnappers there were?" A.W. asked.

"Ah only saw the two, but it was kinda weird. Ah had the feelin' somebody else was there, watchin'. An' another thing, now that ah think of it, the thin one coulda been the same person we saw leaving Phil Bruno's building just before the fire."

"Could the thin kidnapper have been a woman?" I asked.

"Ah guess, Billy. He, she, whatever, wasn't feminine exactly. But there was . . . somethin'. I picked up a definite he-she vibe."

Ted's abduction story was similar to a point. At Rudy's, he'd gone looking for Gin, had seen her lying unconscious and started toward her, when he, too, had been hit from behind. He'd awakened in the basement and remained bound, gagged, and blindfolded until I'd freed him, except for a brief period when his gag was removed and he was fed a ham sandwich and a soft drink.

He was telling us that he neither saw nor heard his captors when A.W. suddenly grabbed a headset from a niche beneath the dash and slipped it on. We listened in silence as he mumbled several yesses and noes and uh-huhs. Finally he said, "I'll check and get back to you," and removed the headset.

"News about Bettina?" I asked.

"She's on her way to Manhattan-Presbyterian. Still in a coma. Lee wants me to pass along some info on the dead guy. He's been ID'd as a Steven D. Gault, from Chicago. Mean anything to anybody?"

It did to me and, I assumed, to Ted. I looked at him.

"Gault?" he said. "Holy Jeez. One of the Touchstone mercs in Kabul. From that damned pub."

"Kinda makes you the last man standing," I said.

"Thanks for pointing that out, Billy," he said. "So that's why."

"That's why what?" Gin asked.

"I could see why they grabbed you, honey. You're a very valuable lady, in every sense of the word. But why bother with me? Now I'm thinking it was because I was sitting at the wrong damned table at the wrong damned time."

"I'd better pass this info along to Lee," A.W. said, slipping on the headset again.

The ensuing telephone conversation with his beautiful boss did not seem to interfere with his driving. He was still listening and mumbling when we arrived at Gin's building.

We sat there for a minute or two with Gin's doorman eyeing us suspiciously. Finally A.W. broke the connection and removed the headset.

"Lee's sending some agents to stay with you folks," he said to the couple in the backseat. "Shouldn't take longer than fifteen or twenty minutes. We'll just hang here until they arrive."

"Nooo," Gin said. "My head hurts. I need sleep. I wanna go in now."

"I guess we can do that," A.W. said, though his body language said he'd have preferred not to.

He got out of the vehicle, circled it, scanning the area all the while. He opened the rear door, then mine, and ushered us into the building, where he left his car key and a five-spot with the doorman.

A.W. insisted we stay in the hall while he checked the apartment for unwelcome visitors. Gin leaned against Ted and said, "Honey, ah'm so worn down ah'm not even considerin' havin' sex tonight."

"TMI," I said.

"Ah'm sorry, Billy. Ah didn't mean to offend. You find sex talk offensive?"

Thankfully, I was relieved of having to respond by the reappearance of A.W. giving us the all clear. We filed into the apartment. Gin and Ted wished us a good evening and retired to the privacy, one hoped, of their bedroom.

A.W. and I occupied the living room, staring at a television show about a smart-talking crime scene investigator who, judging by his choppers and the fact that he worked the night shift, made me suspect he was a vampire.

"Geez, they have all this realistic autopsy stuff," A.W. said, once the hero's penchant for blood was disclosed, "and they throw in a vampire."

"Yep," I said. "Hard to take the living dead too seriously. But zombies now . . ."

My sore elbow shot a pain arrow up my arm and I winced.

"You okay?" he asked. "You got pretty banged up back at the old house. Maybe we ought to get you checked out."

"I'll heal," I said.

The InterTec agents selected to guard Gin and Ted arrived before the vampire forensics expert had sunk his teeth into the villain, but we got out of there anyway. I was anxious to see how the Bistro was faring on a Sunday night. And A.W. . . . Well, he had a different kind of fare on his mind.

Chapter

FIFTY-ONE

Cassandra was at her post just past the front door, presiding over a full house.

She'd been staring at the diners with a scowl that vanished as soon as she saw A.W. When she finally acknowledged me, the scowl returned in triplicate.

"My God, Billy. You look like you've been rolling in a gutter. Your coat's ripped and filthy, and you're limping."

"It's good to see you, too, Cassandra. Oh, and I fell down a flight of stairs," I said.

"Well, you certainly don't want to stroll through the dining room looking like that."

She was right. In spite of the twinges of pain, I'd forgotten how I looked. I left the two of them, ducked into the lounge, and took the hall exit that led past the kitchen to the rear stairwell. Heading up, my ankle reminded me of every step I took.

In my bedroom, I removed my tattered coat and slacks and shirt and limped into the bathroom to observe the damage. Nothing terrible. Just bruises. I washed my face, wrapped an athletic bandage around my ankle, and put on a fresh mock turtleneck and slacks. I eased my sockless feet into a pair of black loafers and was ready to greet the evening.

I wasn't quite up to a waltz through the dining room, but I did work my way down the stairs to visit the kitchen, where the unexpected turnout of customers was testing the endurance levels of Maurice Terrebone and his staff.

The usually unperturbed Maurice paused briefly to say, "We must give the coq au vin a rest, Billy. Take it off the list of specials. Everybody wants coq au vin. The waiters tell me they call it the 'killer dish.' Can you imagine? They're crazy, these New Yorkers."

Maurice was a native of New Orleans. Swept to our Eastern shores by Katrina, he was one of those poor, displaced souls who weren't happy in their new environment but were too pragmatic to return to a place of such woeful impermanence.

He rushed away to count his remaining chickens, and I made my creaky and aching way back up the stairs to my office, feeling surprisingly alert, considering all that had transpired during the day.

I'd just eased my rear end to the chair cushion and was starting to check my e-mail when A.W. appeared to say that the building was secure. He'd also managed to get in a call to the hospital. Bettina's condition was unchanged.

"Cassandra says there's a book on your shelf about my namesake," he said. "Okay if I check to see if my folks are mentioned?"

"Be my guest," I said, gesturing to the slightly sagging bookshelf. I didn't know which surprised me more—the fact that I didn't remember owning a book on Warhol or that Cassandra knew that I had one.

A.W. was a professional detective, and it didn't take him long to find *The Warhol Papers*. While I clicked through my e-mail, he stretched out on my prize couch, skimming through stories about Nico, Edie Sedgwick, Paul Morrissey, and, as it turned out, his mother and dad. He looked over and said, "Listen to this. 'Piet asked Paul not to use Vera in *Flesh for Frankenstein* but wouldn't say why.' This is so cool. I bet I know why. It's right around this time Dad was asking Mom to marry him, and he didn't want her to be in Paul Morrissey's movie because of the nudity. He wasn't a prude, but she was going to be his wife.

"I'll be right back, Billy."

He hopped from the couch and headed toward the stairs.

"Take your time," I said. "I'm not going anywhere."

I got out my cellular phone and dialed Melody Moon's number. Maybe her roommate had some new thoughts about Felix. No answer. Just before I was switched to voice mail I remembered that they'd gone somewhere . . . Sag Harbor, was it?

I sat back in mild frustration, glaring at the phone as if it were to blame. Then I picked it up again. I clicked to the image of the enigmatic scribbles from Rudy's blackboard.

"Jewel for Berry9." "Check: 1 or 2, F or OC?"

Check: Felix or OC? . . . Felix . . . or Other Cat? Then why OC in caps? Felix. And initials? Osgood Conklin? Otto? Orson? Let's think about this a minute. Rudy was a TV guy. . . .

The solution that suddenly occurred to me was so obvious I couldn't believe I hadn't seen it at once. And if I was on the right track . . .

I used the phone for its original purpose.

After several rings, Gin answered, sounding half asleep.

"Sorry to wake you," I said.

"You didn't wake me, Billy. It was the ringin' of the phone."

"Can I speak to Ted?"

"Sure. Hold on. Uh. No." She sounded fuzzy. "Oh, that's right. He went out about twenty minutes ago."

"Any idea where?"

"No. He jus' said he was goin' out fo' a while."

"He signs his columns 'TOP.' What's his middle name, Gin?"

"He hates it," she said. "Oscar."

I thanked her and clicked off the phone. I grabbed my coat and opened the middle drawer of my desk, where I kept a pistol, a Smith & Wesson 625 that I'd purchased after a break-in long ago and never used.

It wasn't there.

There wasn't even a bare spot in the drawer to suggest it had been there. I tried to remember if I'd moved it. But I didn't have time to waste thinking about it. A.W. had a gun and knew how to use it.

I hop-walked downstairs to the main dining room. Cassandra was guiding a couple toward an empty double. A.W. was standing near the entrance, holding his book and watching her. Waiting for her to return.

"Close the book, Romeo," I said. "We're going to the hospital."

"Something up with Bettina?" he asked anxiously.

"I hope not," I said. "But we'd better get there fast."

In his car, heading for Manhattan Presbyterian, he tried to phone the InterTec agent who was supposed to be guarding Bettina.

The agent didn't answer.

Chapter

FIFTY-TWO

We burst from the elevator onto the hospital's third floor. Well, A.W. burst. I hobble-walked.

"Room three-seventeen," he shouted at the group of startled hospital attendants gathered at the nurses' station.

"Hold up," one of the men said.

A.W. paused to show him his ID.

On the wall beside the elevator was an arrow pointing to rooms 301–321, and I limped in that direction.

A.W. was several paces behind as I rounded the corner. I was aware of visitors and patients in robes walking in the corridor, gawking at us, and people shouting. But I was focused on finding room 317.

It was on the left, near the end of the corridor, just off the stairwell. An empty chair was beside the closed door.

"We're too late," I said.

But as I pushed through the door, I realized that wasn't the case.

Ted Parkhurst was standing beside Bettina's bed, holding a pillow with both hands. "Billy?" he said, only mildly surprised. Considering the situation, he was way too cool for anyone but a true sociopath.

"Back away, Ted." A.W. had joined us.

"I was just going to give her another pillow, make her more comfortable."

I noticed with relief that the monitor near Bettina's bed was registering regular heartbeats.

"What's all this about, guys?" Ted asked, the picture of innocence.

"You're in a no-visitor hospital room, beside an unconscious woman, holding a pillow you were going to use to suffocate her," I said. "The best con man in the world couldn't smooth-talk his way out of this."

"I swear, Billy, I just—"

"Stop it, Ted. You're caught. It's over."

A.W., gun drawn, moved past me. "Keep holding the pillow, Mr. Parkhurst, but turn around and face the wall, please, sir." His words were almost a parody of politesse, but there was an angry edge to them that Ted obeyed. A.W. pressed his gun against the back of Ted's head and reached past his shoulder to take the pillow from him. He tossed it on the empty bed against the far wall. Then he searched Ted and found a thin leather-covered object about six inches in length, with a loop strap on one end.

"Is that a blackjack?" I asked.

"A palm sap," A.W. said. "Fits in your palm so people can't see it, but when you slap somebody with it, they sure as heck feel it."

"That must have been what the bastard used on Gin and me at Rudy's apartment."

Ted was looking at the object in A.W.'s hand in wonderment, as if he'd never laid eyes on it before. "Did you see that, Billy?" he said. "He tried to plant that on me."

A.W. ignored the comment. "Mr. Parkhurst, please turn and exit the room slowly, sir."

Ted offered no objection, just did as he was told.

I looked down at Bettina. Her head was wrapped in a neat white bandage. She seemed to be sleeping peacefully. Thank God.

I left the room to find a mildly disturbing tableaux—A.W. and Ted surrounded by a group of orderlies or possibly male nurses, bull necks and muscled arms protruding from their pale-green scrubs. Past them were female nurses and a few odd visitors and patients, all alarmed but also fascinated.

"This man's got a gun and he's crazy," Ted was shouting. "He's trying to kill me."

"Drop the gun, bud," one of the orderlies growled.

A.W. kept the gun right where it was, pointed at Ted. "I'm a security agent with InterTec," he said. "This man—"

"He's lying!" Ted shouted over him. "He's a hired killer."

"That's the lie," I said. "He's the killer. The man with the gun is a security agent."

The orderly who was the spokesman for his group gave me that "how do I know you?" look that never goes out of style.

Another of the men in scrubs said, "It's the guy from the morning show."

"What the devil is going on here?"

This came from a middle-aged dark-skinned woman in a crisp white uniform. The head nurse, was my guess. She marched through the others to park her wiry five-foot-five body in front of me.

"We just caught this man trying to harm our friend in three-seventeen," I said. "Could you check to see if she's okay?"

"I take my orders from doctors," she snapped. She turned to A.W. "Mister, you got identification to go with that gun?"

A.W. used his free hand to find his wallet. Continuing to keep his eyes on Ted, he flipped the wallet open and held it in the direction of the nurse.

She glanced at it and said, "You can put it away. Where's the fella from your company supposed to be guarding my patient?"

"I don't know, ma'am," A.W. said. "I'm sure this man does, but he's not talking."

She gave Ted a disgusted look, then faced the assembled crowd. "You people have work to do, right?"

When the group started to disperse, she gave me a fierce glare, then moved past me into Bettina's room.

Several orderlies remained, still unconvinced of who was lying about whom. But they didn't object when A.W. ordered Ted to face the wall, extend his arms, and press his hands against it. Before obeying, Ted managed to brush his errant hair out of his eyes.

"I . . . I called the police," a nurse at the rear of the group said.

Ted turned his head to me, his lank hair flopping down again. "You're making a big mistake, Billy," he said.

"Shut up, Ted."

A red-faced young man, sweating profusely, entered from the

stairwell and pushed through the crowd. He had a plump hand pressed against the back of his head.

"Where the hell have you been, Sistrom?" A.W. asked angrily.

"I . . . somebody called for help out on the stairs," Sistrom said. "I went to see and . . . whammo. This the bastard who hit me?"

"He tried to kill Bettina," A.W. said.

"Shit. Is she . . . ?"

"She seems to be okay," I said.

"Thank God," Sistrom said. "Then you won't have to make too big a deal about me leaving my post, right, A.W.? I mean, it sounded like somebody was real hurt. I had to go see, right?"

"You're on your own on that," A.W. said.

Ted was still staring at me. "I did nothing wrong," he protested.

"Just for starters, attempted murder and assault," I said.

"You're nuts," Ted said. "I came here to see how the lady was doing. Everything else is in your head, Blessing. I'm not even going to need a lawyer on this."

I turned to the sound of footsteps hurrying our way. Lee Franchette, beautiful even while frowning. She strode past the still-curious nurses, then suddenly wheeled to face them. "I know some of you can't wait to phone your favorite gossip hotline or blogger scum about what you're seeing here tonight. Try it and I assure you you'll be joining the growing unemployment line so fast it will make your heads swim. Be sure to pass the word."

Then she turned her attention to us, mainly to Agent Sistrom, who still had his hand pressed to his head. "What's your story?" she asked, in a way that suggested she wouldn't buy it, whatever it was.

He was saved from having to explain himself by the head nurse exiting Bettina's room and closing the door behind her. "I don't know what's going on here," she said, "but the condition of the patient in that room is unchanged. From this moment, she is to remain undisturbed, pending the arrival of her doctor. Do I make myself clear?"

"Of course," Lee said.

"It's about time the police were notified," the head nurse said.

"One of your nurses said they're on the way," I said.

"Good." The little woman stared at me. "You know, you look a lot like that man who's on TV in the morning. The one who's always grinning like a hyena."

"I get that a lot," I said.

"Ah, Nurse . . ." Lee said, studying the nameplate pinned above her right breast. "Nurse Cuttler, is there someplace we could wait for the police in privacy?"

"And who might you be?"

Lee slid a black leather ID case from her coat pocket. It had a tiny metallic Prada inverted triangle stuck into the leather that impressed the nurse about as much as a used bedpan. She seemed to find the information on the ID only slightly more impressive. "Miss Lee Franchette. Then you would be the lady I talked with on the phone, arranging for the guard over there with the red face."

Lee nodded.

"Okay, I'll show you to a room the interns use when they're on call overnight. Then maybe my people"—she glared at the orderlies and nurses still lingering in the corridor—"can GET BACK TO WORK!"

Chapter

FIFTY-THREE

The intern room consisted of two cots and a washbasin. It smelled of disinfectant and something funky but unidentifiable. Intern perspiration, maybe. I sat on one of the cots, taking the weight off of my ankle. My shoulder felt stiff.

Sistrom was holding a wet paper towel to his wounded head, looking at Lee eagerly to see if she had bought his tale of woe.

"Is this the man who attacked you?" she asked, pointing to Ted, who was lying on one of the cots, his wrists and ankles handcuffed together so that they forced his body into what might have passed for a new yoga position. He looked uncomfortable and angry, and tossed his head in an unsuccessful attempt to flip his bangs away from his eyes.

"I didn't see who it was, but it musta been him."

"Thank you, Mr. Sistrom," she said. "Now please go and get your head examined."

"Uh. Then you want me back on guard, ma'am?"

"Definitely not," Lee said. "A.W. can handle that. And when the NYPD finally arrive, I imagine they'll have their own ideas."

Sistrom rewarded us with an attempt at a brave smile and made his awkward exit.

"That idiot didn't see me hit him because I didn't hit him," Ted said. "I didn't do anything wrong."

"You were in Bettina's room," A.W. said, "moving in on her with a pillow in your hands."

Lee stared at Ted, who repeated his absurd excuse that he was only trying to make Bettina more comfortable.

She turned to me. "Well, chef?"

"Well what?" I said, rubbing my shoulder. "Like A.W. just told you, we caught the guy in the act."

"But what made you rush here, thinking Bettina might be in jeopardy?"

I told her about the blackboard note I'd seen in Rudy Gallagher's apartment.

"'Check: 1 or 2, F or OC'?" she said. "And from that you surmised that Mr. Parkhurst would try to kill Bettina?"

I didn't blame her for being skeptical.

"There's a little more to it than that," I said. "What I think the note means is that Rudy saw or heard something that made him wonder if F, the assassin Felix, was working alone or with a partner, forming an OC, Odd Couple."

She seemed puzzled. Too young and too European. "You mean gay?" she asked.

"It was a play, and a movie," A.W. said. "A comedy about a prissy guy who gets divorced and moves in with a divorced friend who's a slob. We put it on in high school. I helped make the sets."

"It was also a long-running TV show in the 1970s, before you were born," I said. "Rudy loved old TV. He would have known the names of the odd couple. You remember them?"

"I should," A.W. said. "I heard those guys practicing every day for about a month. The neatness freak was Felix. And the slob was . . . Oscar, but I don't see how that name fits in."

I looked at Ted. "You want to tell him?"

He closed his eyes and said nothing.

"Ted's byline on his articles is TOP," I said. "Theodore *Oscar* Parkhurst. OC, Odd Couple, was Rudy's shorthand for Felix and Oscar."

"So it is your assumption," Lee said, "that Gallagher was about to explore the possibility of Ted being Felix's little helper?"

"It might have been what got Rudy Gallagher killed," I said.

"That makes me a hit man, my middle name?" Ted said. "What bullshit."

"It plays," I said to Lee. "Like a fool, I told Ted that Phil Bruno had video footage of the night in Kabul. Less than an hour later, poor Phil was burned to death and whatever his video could have disclosed about that night was gone forever."

"This man is delusional," Ted said. "I was with him every minute of that evening. When could I have set fire to the building?"

"Not you. You phoned your partner, Felix, who did the arson job."

"That's just fucking crazy. I'm not the friend of a killer. I'm not a killer. If anything, I'm a victim. I was kidnapped, for God's sake."

"You're a liar," I said. "And I can prove it."

"Good, that would be appreciated," Lee said. "But first, the one thing we know for certain is that Felix is still out there somewhere. A.W., please go see to Bettina's safety."

The young agent nodded. He leaned over Ted to make sure he hadn't slipped a cuff, then left the room.

"Now, about that proof . . ." Lee said.

"There is none," Ted said. "It's fantasy."

"Let's see if I can run it down," I said. "First, the kidnapping. How could the kidnappers have known you and Gin would be there that night? How did they get past the doorman? Why weren't they on the security tape?"

"I can only guess," Ted said. "There are crooks who specialize in looting the remains of the recently deceased. Gallagher's address was spread everywhere by the media. The robbers had to be in the apartment before we arrived. They came out of hiding, knocked us out, recognized Gin, and decided to kidnap us."

"And one of them happened to be the same guy you had dinner with in Kabul," I said. "It makes much more sense if you were the kidnapper. All you had to do was call in your mercenary buddy Steve Gault to drive a car to the alley behind the building to help you cart Gin off to a secluded hideaway."

"Why would I do that, Blessing?"

"Ignoring the fifteen million bucks for the moment, I'd say the main point was to stop her from interviewing Goyal Aharon on Tuesday morning. For some reason I haven't quite figured out, this was a necessary part of Felix's plan to assassinate Aharon."

"Aharon being Felix's target because . . . ?" Lee asked.

"I'm no political strategist," I said. "But I'm thinking that Felix has a benefactor who isn't too keen on Aharon trekking across the U.S. with his new novel, tarnishing the Israeli image by spilling the beans on the Mossad's darker deeds."

"Who do you think is paying Felix?" Lee asked. "And don't tell me the Mossad or the CIA."

"The dead guy worked for Carl Kelstoe," I said.

"And Kelstoe is engineering all this because of his political convictions?"

"You're asking who the guy is behind the guy behind the curtain? Hell, I don't know."

"It's a bit speculative," Lee said. "Well, Mr. Parkhurst? Care to fill in the blanks for us?"

"What are you talking about?" Ted said. "You're as mental as he is."

"This would be the time to unburden yourself," Lee told him, "while you can still put some spin on the facts."

"You don't expect . . . What is it you want from me?"

"The truth," I said.

He was staring at Lee. "The truth is what you *don't* want to hear, that I'm an innocent man."

"Why would an innocent man try to kill Bettina?" I asked. "We've got you cold on that. What made you risk that? Did she see you untied and roaming around that basement? Maybe Gault didn't shoot her? Maybe it was you?"

"I was bound and gagged, you stupid hash slinger. You had to cut me loose."

"There was somebody else in the basement," I said. "Your partner had just enough time to put on your blindfold and gag, wrap a strip of duct tape around your ankles and wrists. Or you could have done it yourself, saving your wrists for last, wrapping the tape loosely and giving your wrists a final twist to make it look tight.

"But however you got tied up, just before you did, you made a stupid mistake."

His eyes glared at me from behind his bangs.

"It was a thing you do a hundred times a day," I said. "You brushed your hair back."

"My hair?"

"When I found you on the ground, supposedly where you'd been for hours, your hair was pushed off your forehead. How could you have done that with your hands tied behind your back?"

He blinked, then said, "Gee, Billy, I think even Perry Mason would have turned up his nose at that kind of 'evidence.'"

"They probably won't need much evidence, Ted, with Bettina as an eyewitness."

Ted looked at Lee. "There's no proof of anything," he said.

"We'll just have to see how it all plays out, Mr. Parkhurst," she replied. She leaned over him and used her left hand to brush his hair back.

His body stiffened, and he jerked his head away from her. The forelock flopped forward again.

Lee made a *tsk-tsk* sound and grinned at him.

FIFTY-FOUR

The first police to arrive were several officers in uniform whose names I didn't catch. They were followed by a pair of detectives. One of them, a young Hispanic-American woman named Juarez, read Ted his rights. She and her partner, an older black man named Gideon, asked the basic who-what-where-why questions. Then, satisfied that such action was appropriate, they and two of the uniforms took Ted off to the lockup.

A Detective Hawkline, a middle-aged white woman who was a dead ringer for the late Spencer Tracy, and her equally white partner, Detective Seestrunk, a thirtysomething beer keg with ears and blood-shot eyes, took more detailed statements from Lee, A.W., and, finally, me. Hawkline and Seestrunk, it turned out, were the lead detectives investigating the shoot-out at the Vosburgh mansion.

Since I had no idea how Lee had spun that situation, it was a good thing the detectives were working under the assumption that I had not been involved. They knew who I was. They knew I was a person of interest in the Gallagher murder investigation. They did not know why I wound up being a witness in what appeared to be an attempted murder in the hospital. That was the focus of their questioning, which was done primarily by Hawkline.

I kept my story as close to the truth as I could. Because I had received threats on my life, my employer, Commander Vernon di Voss, had hired InterTec to make sure I came to no harm. Bettina Noor was one of my bodyguards. When I learned of her misfortune, I decided to visit her in the hospital, where I and my other bodyguard, A.W. Johansen, interrupted Ted Parkhurst attempting to smother Ms. Noor.

Seestrunk seemed satisfied with my explanation. He appeared to have something more important on his mind, like hitting the nearest bar and grill. Hawkline, on the other hand, was one of those dog-with-a-bone investigators.

"Any idea why Mr. Parkhurst should want to kill Miss Noor?" she asked.

"No idea."

"But you knew Mr. Parkhurst? Had what might be described as a friendly relationship with him?"

"I'd thought we were friends."

"Was he a friend of Miss Noor's, too?"

"I don't know," I said.

She changed the subject, asking if Detective Solomon would corroborate my "story" about the death threats. I replied that I had not bothered to tell him about the threats, since we were in an adversarial situation and he didn't seem to believe anything I had to say.

She nodded and looked at Seestrunk, who was focusing on a spider in a corner of the ceiling. She nodded again and asked if I knew why Bettina Noor had gone to a deserted mansion earlier that day.

I said that I did not.

She asked if I knew a man named Stephen Gault, and I replied that I did not know him.

"Could Miss Noor's trip to the mansion have had anything to do with your death threats?" she asked.

"I don't know," I said.

"What about this Parkhurst guy? Think he might have been the source of the threats?"

"He'd be near the top of my list," I said.

"Why do you think he's got it in for you?"

"You'd have to ask him."

"And why would he have it in for Miss Noor?"

I was beginning to like Detective Hawkline and the way she threw those questions right across the plate. I actually wished I could lay it all out for her—Felix, the kidnapping, the whole works. Just unburden myself. But that would have been foolish. Instead I said, "I don't know."

"This gonna take much longer?" Detective Seestrunk inquired.

Detective Hawkline told him she thought it would and smiled when she said it.

Shortly after that, she got a phone call. She listened awhile, emitting little grunts of mild surprise. She made a few whispery comments behind her hand that I couldn't hear, being neither a dog nor a teenager. Then she put away the phone.

"Good news for the bars in town, Seestrunk, you're through here," she said, rising. Her body was a little like Spencer Tracy's, too.

"What's up?" I asked.

Detective Hawkline gave me a look of bemusement. "Good-bye, Mr. Blessing," she said. "I imagine Detective Solomon may be checking in with you to talk about those death threats."

"I'd rather talk with you," I said.

"I appreciate the compliment, if that's what it is," she said. "But we have nothing more to discuss."

"I'm not sure what that means."

"The case against Theodore Parkhurst is no more. It expired with Mr. Parkhurst."

"Say what?"

"Mr. Parkhurst died. Dead. Taking a dirt nap," Detective Hawkline said over her shoulder as she followed Seestrunk out the door. "Good night, Chef Blessing."

FIFTY-FIVE

"You sure you're up to this, chef dear?" Lee asked as she stopped her gleaming black Lexus in a passenger loading zone in front of Gin McCauley's building.

"It's better she find out from me than see it on the news."

But we were too late.

Gin opened her apartment door, red-eyed, sniffling, and in her nightgown. The sweet-stale odor of whiskey floated on the air. A large TV monitor had taken over the living room since my dinner there just weeks ago. Filling its screen was footage of Ted Parkhurst in the Middle East chatting with soldiers, accompanied by voice-over biography.

Gin staggered back to the couch where she'd been watching her late fiancé's life being picked to pieces by whatever gleeful talking heads the news channels had been able to round up during the dinner hours.

She muted the narration but continued to stare glassy-eyed at the roughly edited film clips. "What the hell, Billy?" she said. "They're callin' it a heart attack. Ted didn't have any kind of heart trouble. And as for the other stuff, this talk about him tryin' to kill somebody, where the hell is that comin' from, anyway? It's gotta be some kinda horrible mistake, right?"

"You have anything here to help you relax besides the booze?" I asked her.

"You mean drugs?" she said. "No. Ted got rid of mah stash. Called it mah pharmaco . . . pharma . . ."

"Pharmacopoeia," I said.

"That," she said, her eyes tearing. "Ted's very anti-drug. *Was* very anti-drug. It's all a mistake, Billy. The cops made a mistake. They arrested him by mistake and they did somethin', you know, like, they overreacted and . . . did something that . . . caused him to . . ."

She shook her head. Then she grabbed a glass half-full of a very dark brown liquid and tried to down it in a gulp. I sat beside her and stopped her from inhaling the whole thing by twisting the glass from her grasp. Globs of whiskey hopped from the glass and spilled down her face and neck, staining her gown.

She didn't seem to notice. "Why would he try to kill a friend?" she asked me.

"A friend?"

"He said the phone call was from a friend," Gin said.

"What phone call? You didn't mention a phone call when we talked earlier."

"When we talked earl— Oh, yeah, we did talk. You asked about his middle name. That was a weird question, Billy." The whiskey was slowing her down, sending those neurons on to the big sleep.

"About the phone call Ted got?" I prompted.

"Uh-huh. We'd just gone to bed when his phone rang. Ah was kinda groggy, only caught a little of what Ted was sayin'. Somethin' like, 'Why can't you handle it by yourself?' And then he was out of bed and gettin' dressed.

"Ah asked him where he was goin', and he said a friend needed help an' he'd be back in an hour if not soonah."

"You have any idea who the caller was?" Lee asked.

"A friend was what he said." She started crying again. "Ah don't even know who his friends are. Maybe ah didn't even know him."

Gin was in a bad place and was going to be there for a while. Once Bettina awoke, Hawkline or some other investigator would probably put together the full story of the kidnapping and Gin would become the main course in a media feeding frenzy, until the next hot story broke.

"Is there some place you can go to . . . rest for a while?" I asked.

"Go? Ah can't go anywhere, long as Ted needs me . . ."

With that, she slumped against the couch. The whiskey had done its job.

"Well, what now, chef?" Lee asked.

"We put her to bed," I said. "And I look for her cellular."

The latter required no effort. It was on her bedside table. I pressed the number she'd designated as "Hildy."

Gin's manager, Hildegard Fonsica, arrived at the apartment within twenty minutes. She seemed curious about Lee and how she fit into the picture, but she didn't let that get in the way of her concern for her client.

She leaned over Gin's now-snoring body, sniffed the air, then wrinkled her nose. "This was just booze?" she asked. "No pills?"

"She said no. She'd thrown them all away."

"Good. Booze is bad enough. Thank God you called, Billy. I've had the goddamned TV off, plowing through some crappy scripts. Missed the whole mishegoss about Ted. Caught some of it on the cab over. Tell me all."

I told her if not all then at least most, including the kidnapping and the part Ted played in it.

"That friggin' buttlick," she growled. "I never liked that smart-mouth prick."

Note to self: Hildy not standing by to give Ted's eulogy.

I told her why I thought Gin should drop out of sight for a while. Hildy took only a few moments to ponder the problem. "I got a client with a fully staffed getaway home in Bermuda," she said. "She's stuck in L.A. filming the world's unfunniest sitcom. A hit, naturally. Which means the place is just sitting there. Leave it to me. I'll get Ginger on her feet and out of here."

"The police will want to talk to her," Lee said.

"They'll have to find us first." Hildy looked down at Gin. "Just leave everything to Mama."

Gin was lucky to have someone like Hildy in her corner. I sighed and decided the next time I saw Mr. Wally "pay me to watch you on TV" Wing, I'd kick him in his karmic ass.

Chapter

FIFTY-SIX

The Bistro was dark and had been for at least an hour when Lee and I arrived at the rear door. Since I'd received no call or message from Cassandra, I assumed that the evening had progressed much less eventfully at the restaurant than it had out in the real world.

Inside, I tapped in the alarm-canceling code, but the warning beeper continued. Then I remembered—new code. My second try did the trick.

The cooking aroma was chased away from the main rooms and the kitchen by the cleanup crew, but it tended to linger in the alcove where Lee and I stood. My stomach growled. "You get anything to eat at the hospital?" I asked.

"Some kind of pudding," she said. "White. Very sweet."

"Tapioca," I said. "A hospital favorite. I could whip up something a little more substantial."

"It's late," she said, and headed up the stairs.

I cast a lingering look in the direction of the kitchen, then followed. That's when I noticed she was carrying a slim briefcase. "What's with the luggage?" I asked. "Planning on a work night?"

"It's something you asked for," she said. "Trina Lomax's background check. I put an agent to work on it right after we talked."

At the top of the stairs, to my dismay, she didn't even hesitate in selecting the office over the living quarters. She clicked on the light and placed the briefcase on my desk. From it she removed several sheets of paper.

"This is just a quick first hit, but it includes some significant information."

The biographical high points began with Trina's birth on October 12, thirty-six years ago, in Tokyo, where her father, a designer in the automotive industry, had relocated. She'd attended the American School in Japan briefly before being sent back to the United States to board at Miss Porter's in Farmington. There she did well academically, edited the school newspaper, played varsity tennis, yada, yada, yada.

I glanced at my watch. A little past midnight. The day had been a wearying one. I'd hoped that if I arrived on the set in a few hours yawning, it would be for reasons more romantic than reading up on Trina's bio.

"What's this note, 'Farid Qedir at Avon'?"

"Qedir was a student at Avon Old Farms, a boys' school near Miss Porter's. He and Trina seem to have . . . bonded at joint socials," Lee said. "They both spent their junior year abroad in Paris, cohabitating. They also attended Brown University."

"And this is important because?"

Her face registered a mixture of sadness and regret. "It's on the sheet, if you read further. Trina went on to join the news staff at CBS in Paris, and Farid Qedir returned to his homeland, Saudi Arabia. Am I boring you, chef? Would you prefer to discuss this in bed?"

"I would prefer to be in bed *not* discussing it."

"This is important," she insisted. "But I can summarize. While Trina's star rose in the television news firmament, Farid was placed in a key position in Islamic World Health, a charity funded by a number of oil-wealthy Saudi sheikhs, chief among them his father.

"In 2002, customs agents in this country raided a web of so-called charities based in Herndon, Virginia, that were suspected of helping to finance Islamic extremists here and in the Middle East. Many of these 'charities' had strong ties to similar Saudi organizations, including Islamic World Health. The following year, documents surfaced, including correspondence between Yasser Arafat and IWH, that linked the Saudi charity with several in the West Bank identified with Hamas. IWH was summarily closed down."

I felt the yawn coming but was helpless to block it.

"Am I keeping you up?" Lee asked.

I was so tired I almost used the old punchline, "That's what she said at the picnic." But instead I managed, "No, please go on."

"Well, here is the crux. The reason the documents surfaced is because a Mossad team captured an official of IWH and 'convinced' him to surrender them. That official was Farid Qedir. He died two days after he was released. A year later, to the date, the leader of that Mossad operation, Reuhen Fromm, a six-foot-two-inch muscular brute, was found in his home near Tel Aviv. His eyes, testes, tongue, and hands had been roughly removed. While he was still alive."

Suddenly I was wide awake. "He just sat there?" I asked.

"He'd been injected with a drug. Vecuronium, of the curare family. Administered as it was there, without the proper sedation, it left its subject paralyzed but wide awake and in constant pain even before the 'operation.'

"According to our sources, which are impressive, this marked the first appearance of the childish cat scribble, left in Fromm's blood on his bed linen. The debut of our friend Felix."

"I thought assassins were supposed to be dispassionate," I said.

"I will spare you the description of what had been done to Farid Qedir," Lee said. "Not that it justifies what Felix did."

"I'm guessing that Trina was on assignment near Tel Aviv when Fromm was murdered?"

"She was preparing the special report on the West Bank for CBS that established her reputation," Lee said. "It ultimately resulted in her being hired by INN as a sort of international roving reporter, given carte blanche to create her own documentaries. And to travel wherever she chose."

Lee suggested I look at the final two pages she'd given me.

"On the left are the cities Trina Lomax visited for her INN special reports. On the right are cities where key political figures, most of them InterTec clients, by the way, were murdered during that same period."

I scanned the lists. "It's not a one hundred percent matchup," I said.

"No. But remember, she was not working alone. I bet we will find that Ted Parkhurst's schedule put him near the other assassinations, like the Touchstone guard in Kabul. I'm convinced she is our Felix. And there's one more thing you should know."

"What more could there be?"

"A month ago, when Goyal started his European tour, he was asked which of his Mossad assignments had made him the most proud. Among those he mentioned was the capture of a little 'mouse of a man' who was easily 'convinced' to provide his team with proof that a Saudi charity was funding Hamas."

"Like the song goes, it's a small world after all," I said.

"And unless we act, Felix will most certainly find a way to avenge the torture and death of her little mouse."

"We should take all this to the police," I said, placing the papers on the desk next to her briefcase.

"As you know, the police will do nothing without evidence. All we have is conjecture."

She stopped talking, a reaction to the sight of me nearly falling asleep on my feet. "Forgive me," she said. "You are exhausted and you must be alert for your broadcast. We should go to bed. In the morning, we can both think more clearly."

I discovered something that night: Sleep was not at the top of my physical necessity list. Later, mentally, physically, and sexually exhausted, with her warm, naked body pressed against mine, I was just drifting off when Lee whispered in my ear, "I have thought of a plan to trap her."

Pillow talk.

FIFTY-SEVEN

I don't know if Lee slept at all that night.

I woke at four-thirty a.m., alone in bed. I tested my various damaged areas, expecting the usual day-two increase in pain. But they actually felt improved. Could sex be the ultimate painkiller? It certainly beat Celebrex.

At a little after five, showered, shaved, suited, and lured by the smell of fried bacon, I found Lee in the restaurant kitchen. She'd prepared breakfast for us. Scrambled eggs and coffee to go with the bacon. It looked lovely. But as they say, there are no free meals.

I'd barely nibbled a forkful of egg when Lee said, "It is not just a question of saving Goyal's life. I do not want that bitch to slip away where she can kill more of my clients. I want her nailed tight to the prison floor. I think we can do that."

"'We'?" I said.

"My plan requires your participation."

"Why? You've got a whole army of agents, Lee."

"You are part of this, chef," she said. "You have a more personal reason than I."

"Yeah?"

"Self-preservation. Felix gave you a warning that you foolishly ignored. Besides, I'm not asking you to do anything you aren't capable of handling."

"Whoa. Flip that over and serve it up again."

"I need you to do the interview with Goyal Aharon."

I ate a piece of crisp, dry bacon, took a sip of coffee, and mulled that over.

"Assuming you could somehow derail Trina Lomax's plan to interview him, there are quite a few people next in line, including Lance Tuttle and our news anchor, Tori Dillard. I'd be in that line somewhere after the entertainment guy."

"You're wherever Gretchen Di Voss wants you to be. And I don't think it will take much to convince her you're the man for the job."

"But I'm not," I disagreed. "I know my limitations. To begin, my knowledge of international politics comes mainly from James Bond movies. I don't know anything about Aharon, except that he talks too much for his own good. And I haven't even read his book."

"As if any of your associates bother to read the books of the authors they interview. These things are of no importance."

With that she stopped talking and concentrated on devouring her breakfast. I, on the other hand, had lost my appetite. I picked at the egg and sipped a little more coffee and wondered what one said to an ex–Mossad agent. "Hey, how are things in the Holy Land?" "How about that Hezbollah?"

There was a noise just outside the kitchen door.

If Lee heard it, she seemed to ignore it as she continued consuming the remains of her breakfast. I turned to see the door swing inward as A.W. stepped into the kitchen. "About time to hit the road," he said.

"Give us a minute, A.W.," Lee said.

"Sure. I'll be out in the car, Billy."

"I'd better be going," I said. I started to rise, but Lee placed a hand on my wrist, indicating I should remain seated.

"Goyal's flight arrives at a little after eleven. We'll give him a while to shake off the jet lag, then get you two together."

"I don't understand where you're going with this. What's the plan?"

"I thought you could figure that one out," Lee said. She stood, picked up our plates, and carried them to the sink. "Goyal may be Felix's primary target, but she has her own reasons, whatever they may be, for wishing you harm, too. Putting both of you together in a seemingly accessible location—like Goyal's hotel suite—should be an opportunity she'll be unable to resist."

"In other words," I said, joining her at the sink with the glasses and coffee cups, "for you to get the hard evidence you need, Felix will have to make a self-incriminating move. Pull a gun. Set fire to the room. Stab one of us in the chest. Something like that."

"I'll be near enough to ensure your safety," she said, taking the glasses and cups from my hands. "Don't worry about the dishes. I'll put them in the machine and lock up after I'm through. You just get to work on time, chef dear."

"This is no little thing, Lee," I said.

"You and Goyal will be safe as houses," Lee said. "Trust me. At the first hint of trouble, we'll close Trina down."

Outside, a car horn sounded.

"You should go," she said. "And don't worry. Tonight we will celebrate."

She stepped into my arms and we kissed. It was very nice, but it didn't stop me from worrying.

Chapter

FIFTY-EIGHT

As we drove to the Glass Tower, the night was dragging its feet on the way out of Manhattan. The streetlights were still bright, but the black sky was showing streaks of purple and a pale orange line was barely visible on the horizon. Nautical twilight.

A.W. asked, "Did Lee mention, ah, how she wanted to handle things tonight?"

Ordinarily, I would have been amused by the unintended double entendre, but I was too worried about Lee's plan. "For one reason or another, by tonight I doubt I'll be needing a guard."

"Why's that?" he asked.

So I told him about the proposed showdown in Goyal Aharon's hotel suite. "What do you think?" I asked.

"Lee's the boss," he said.

"Leaving that aside."

"She's been at this a little longer than me, Billy, but I don't know as I'd put two clients at risk like that. 'Course, the risk would be minimal, since she'll be controlling the situation."

"Explain."

"I assume that since we're setting up the location, the hotel suite will be wired for sight and sound. InterTec will take over that section of the floor, with agents in the suites next to you and across the hall. Both you and Mr. Aharon will be armed. And presumably we'll have surprise on our side."

"That's all comforting to know," I said.

"And Lee will probably be in the room with you," he said. "I doubt Ms. Lomax could come up with an innocent-sounding reason for keeping her out."

"Even better," I said. I was almost starting to feel okay about the whole thing.

Making a turn into the tower's underground parking, A.W. said, "And just in case Ms. Lomax tries something funny with you before this evening—like maybe while you're in the studio—don't worry. I'll be sticking close."

Whoa. Me? In danger before *the meeting? Now?* I hadn't considered that.

"Trina's been looking for you," Kiki said as soon as we'd set foot into my dressing-room suite. "And who's this gentleman, Billy?"

My mind on Trina, I did the introductions almost by rote.

"So now you're keeping him from harm, A.W.," Kiki said. "What happened to the Indian lady?"

"She's in the hospital," A.W. said.

"Oh, no. Hope it's nothing serious."

"She was shot, but they say she'll recover."

"Oh my God," Kiki said. "Is she the one I was reading about in the paper? Gin's fiancé tried to kill her in the hospital? What in the world . . . The article was a little fuzzy on the details."

I somehow doubted the details would ever be unfuzzied.

"I want to hear all about it, Billy, but it'll have to wait," she said. "Trina wants to see you pronto. In Rudy's, I mean, her office on six."

"On my way," I said, heading out, A.W. beside me.

As I stepped off the elevator on six, there was a flurry of motion to my left. A.W. pushed me and, as I stumbled forward, I saw Chuck Slater, the boy movie critic, frozen in his tracks, gawking at us, face drained of blood, eyes and mouth wide open in fear.

"Drop the gun," I heard A.W. say.

Chuck did have a gun in his hands. A weird-looking, sinister thing with two barrels lined up horizontally, the top one slightly shorter.

He dropped it to the carpet.

A.W. stepped forward and kicked the gun away from Chuck.

"Holy Christ," Chuck said, his voice several octaves higher than usual. "You guys nuts?"

The others in the area—the receptionist, a brunette named Maude, a couple of assistants I didn't know—seemed equally startled.

A.W. kept his weapon aimed at Chuck while he bent to pick up the strange firearm. Straightening, he shook his head and holstered his weapon. He handed me Chuck's gun.

"It's a RAP-four," A.W. said.

"Whatever it's called," I said, "it shoots paintballs. I learned that the hard way. What were you doing with it, Chuck?"

"Doing with it? Taking it home, asshole. This guy could have shot me."

"He still might," I said. "Why were you carrying a paintball gun in the office?"

"I . . . I just gave it to him," Maude said. "I found it in the trash and it looked like something . . . Chuck might like." She was on the verge of tears.

"It's okay," I told her. "We're all a little on edge. I'm sorry."

"I'm sorry, too, ma'am," A.W. said.

He looked at the gun. "This the one used on you?"

"Why else would it be here? In the trash?"

"Everybody and his cousin have probably had their hands on it," A.W. said, "but we should probably check it for prints."

I shook my head. "Waste of time and effort. The one set of prints we'd want won't be there. The Cheetah was wearing gloves."

"You wanna give me my gun back, Bless-sing?" Chuck's arrogance had returned. "It's mine. She gave it to me."

I threw it to him. He juggled it, finally caught it. "I oughta report you guys to security," he said.

I saw that Trina was now standing in the doorway to Rudy's old office, watching us with an angry expression. "If you're through playing with Chuck, I want to talk to you, Billy."

As I moved past her into the office, I could smell the pleasant odor of her shampoo or hair spray. She entered the room behind me and started to close the door, but A.W. stopped it and stepped in.

"I'm sorry," she said to him, "but this is a private conversation."

"It's okay," I said. "He's my bodyguard."

"I don't plan on harming you," Trina said, her eyes flashing. "But the hell with it."

The office was a mess. Floor littered with cardboard boxes, some opened, displaying framed photos and other bits of memorabilia. Foam peanuts and packing tissue scattered everywhere, strips of Bubble Wrap popping under your feet. A joke stress-o-meter. Little comedy statues of cameramen tearing their hair out and golfers doing dumb things with their clubs.

"Gallagher's world," Trina explained. "The cops took it all away and now they're sending it back, box by box. And the building cleanup crew is taking their time . . . Well, that's neither here nor there."

"You didn't throw away a paintball gun, did you, Trina?"

"Of course not. What would I be doing . . . Is that THE paintball gun?"

I shrugged.

"Here? On this floor? I saw the damn thing in the trash. Didn't give it a second's thought. But I was right."

"Right about what?" I asked.

"Never mind. The reason I asked you up here, Billy, is that Gretchen called this morning to say that she wanted *you* to do the Aharon interview. WTF?"

"I don't know," I said. "What did Gretchen say?"

"Some bullshit about keeping the interview light. Why would we want to do that when we have a chance to make some real news? Since when do you keep it light with the former head of a secret intelligence agency?"

I stood there looking as helpless as I felt.

"Well, crap, I'm stuck with this bullshit decision from on high. So here's how it goes. At your meeting with Aharon later today, I will be there. It's my understanding that he's agreed to answer anything we ask. I want to make sure that hasn't changed. And I've created my own set of questions that you *will* ask during the interview. And he doesn't see the questions before we roll tape. Understand?"

"Sure. I imagine you'll let *me* see those questions before the interview."

She gave me a cold smile.

"A few minutes before. Billy, if you ever pull this kind of bullshit again, going behind my back to grab a get, one of us is going to be leaving this show. And frankly, if this is an example of how things work around here, I won't care if it's me."

She opened the door and gestured with an arm wave that suggested we leave.

"Feisty," A.W. remarked as we headed down in the elevator.

"I'd be angry, too," I said.

"'Course, if Lee is right—and the appearance of that paintball gun in the trash near her office is another indication that she might be—the anger is probably just an act."

I looked at him.

"I mean, she's just using it to explain why she's going to be in that hotel suite with you and Mr. Aharon."

Chapter

FIFTY-NINE

That morning's show played out pretty much as planned. I interviewed a veterinarian who'd written a diet book for dogs and cats. I tried my damnedest to keep a paddleball going for at least ten paddles while the U.S. paddleball champion kept his ball bouncing throughout the whole segment, simultaneously offering his reasons why the sport should be considered for the Olympics. On the street, I talked to some nice folks from Utah who wanted to remind our viewers that it was one hundred sixty-two years ago that Mormons settled in their state. They also wanted to express their dismay at the way so many people seemed to approve of same-sex marriage while disapproving of polygamy. (But they had no comment one way or the other about same-sex polygamy.) And I did a human-interest chat with twin sisters who were celebrating their one hundredth birthday and were looking forward to a meeting later that morning at NBC with their "dream man," Willard Scott.

From time to time throughout the show, the camera and I checked in on Mr. Turducken, with whom I'd finally connected. He was spending the morning demonstrating the creation of his namesake dish with a four-pound chicken stuffed into a five-pound duckling stuffed into a twenty-pound turkey. All deboned, of course. I had expressed my concern that certain stages of the turducken preparation might not be appreciated by viewers at breakfast, notably, those involving close-ups of the various birds in their boneless but very bloody repose. In high-def yet. This warning had gone unheeded, and by the time the show headed into the homestretch, with the turducken on its back, trussed up to keep from falling apart in the oven, the switchboard was aglow with complaints.

As he'd promised, A.W. had hovered just off camera during the two hours. When the network headed into the nine o'clock news, we headed to my dressing-room office.

He was saying something about checking on Bettina that I didn't quite hear. I was too distracted by the familiar form of Detective Solomon slouching in my dressing-room doorway.

"Hiya, Blessing," he said. "Miss me?"

"Not really," I said. "Where's your sidekick?"

"It's our day off and he's home with his family. Which is where I'd be if I had a family. Instead I'm talking to you, as suggested by Detective Hawkline. She mentioned threats."

"Come on in," I said, moving past him into the room.

"Messages," Kiki said, thrusting a neat stack of little salmon-colored slips at me. She was at her desk, working on a personal laptop. "In case you're wondering," she said, "we're missing the office computer. I've notified building security."

"Oh, gee," A.W. said. "We've got it. I'll see about having it delivered back to you, maybe today."

Solomon was intrigued by the conversation. "And who might you be?" he asked A.W.

I stuffed the message slips into a coat pocket and did the introductions.

"So you're his bodyguard? The one who was at the hospital last night?" Solomon asked A.W.

"Yes, sir."

Solomon studied A.W. briefly, then turned to me. "What's up with your missing computer, Blessing?"

I knew what was up with it: It had been used to send the first kidnap note, and InterTec was checking it for prints, bugs, you name it. I definitely did not want Solomon to add kidnapping to my list of major crimes and was racking my brain to think of an alternative explanation when A.W. said, "We're installing some of our software on it."

That seemed to satisfy the detective. He anchored his butt on the arm of a plump green chair and asked, "So maybe if your associates here will give us some quality time alone, you can tell me about these threats you don't believe I'll take seriously."

I told A.W. that I was in good hands. He helped Kiki gather her laptop and papers, and they left together. All that had taken about two or three minutes, which I used to remind myself about exactly which threats I should or should not mention. While I described the former, Solomon used a thin gold pen to scribble notes on a small pad that could have come from a hotel stationery kit.

"I don't suppose you kept any of this stuff," he said. "The napkin, or the message you got at the museum?"

"InterTec has 'em," I said. "I think they checked them for prints, DNA, whatever."

He seemed surprised. "Any results?"

"Not that I heard."

"I'll want to take a look at them."

"I can probably arrange that," I said. "You might want to check the Internet for a photo of my car being attacked in the Lincoln Tunnel. Just Google my name and hit Images."

"Nothing I love more than cruising the Internet," he said, "unless it's getting my prostate checked."

He put the pen and pad away, a gesture that was supposed to make me think the official part of his visit was over. "You mind telling me what that deal was at the hospital? The Hawk—er, Detective Hawkline—said she got the distinct feeling she was being played by everybody involved. Including you."

I told him the same story I'd told Hawkline.

"You didn't happen to mention to Hawkline that you and the dead guy, Parkhurst, were at that arson-murder scene together?"

"I don't think I did."

"Or the yarn you told me about him and Gallagher and a murdered Touchstone merc all having a night out together over in Afghanistan?"

"So you *were* paying attention," I said.

"Oh, yeah. I pay attention. So when I hear that an ex–Touchstone employee got himself shot in the same basement as your bodyguard, I start wondering if there might not be some validity to that story of yours. Care to enlighten me further?"

"I've told you everything," I said.

"Uh-huh," he said. He pushed himself off the chair. "Lemme tell you something, Blessing, I'm not slow and I'm not stupid. I make mistakes, and when I do I try to correct 'em. In all the years I've worn the shield, I've put the arm on maybe three hundred perps. I can only think of four or five times when a subject looked good for a crime but didn't do it. I don't know about you yet. In spite of all the weird bullshit piling up around Gallagher's death, I still think you might have killed him. But I'm not gonna put on blinders and ignore evidence to the contrary. And I fucking well resent your suggesting otherwise to a fellow officer."

I didn't think I'd told Hawkline that he ignored evidence, but I apologized to him all the same.

On his way out, he said, "Detective Hawkline wanted me to tell you she'll be calling you shortly."

"Why?"

"The case she's investigating."

"I thought that was closed when Ted Parkhurst died," I said.

"That was the old case. Her new one is Parkhurst. His heart attack wasn't what you'd call natural. The M.E. found a tiny puncture on his upper back and a drug called clar, claramycin—something like that— in his bloodstream. Looks like whoever did it ripped the stuff from the hospital's supply room.

"According to Detective Hawkline, everybody at the hospital that night is on her list. Including you, of course."

He was trying to make me feel uneasy. And he had succeeded beyond his wildest dreams. Not with talk about Ted being a murder victim. It was his use of the word "blinders" that did me in.

Chapter

SIXTY

Of the nine message slips Kiki had given me, eight required no immediate action. The ninth was from Rita Margolis, saying she'd made some drawings I should see.

I phoned her. She'd be at her apartment for another hour. I said I'd be there shortly. As soon as Kiki and A.W. filed back in, I told him we had to get moving.

But not before Kiki connected her laptop to the printer and ran off several copies of the Tuesday-morning schedule, one of which she presented to me. "Check the special note," she said.

In addition to the highlighted Aharon interview, there was a cooking segment requiring me to wear a chef's jacket and toque. The jacket I had no problem with. But the toque was another matter. "Whose idea was this?" I asked Kiki.

"Trina's. It's not smart to get in bad with your boss," she said.

"Be good for you to keep that in mind," I said.

The toque would not be a problem. Whatever happened that evening in Goyal Aharon's suite, I wouldn't be wearing one on tomorrow's show.

"Let's go, A.W.," I said.

As we cleared the underground parking garage, he asked, "To the restaurant?"

"Eventually. There are a couple of stops before that," I said, and gave him the first address.

"What's the deal with the toque?" he asked.

"I don't wear them."

"Why not?"

"A matter of personal vanity," I said. "I've been told that a toque makes me look like the guy on the Cream of Wheat box."

"Oh," he said. "Yeah. I guess I can see that."

"Thanks for the confirmation," I said.

It was not until he'd squeezed us into a parking space a block away from Melody Moon's building that he asked the purpose of our visit. "To get a look at an artist's concept of Felix," I said.

"Who's the artist?" he asked as we got out of the car.

I told him Rita's name.

"Sure, Rita. She draws *Funny Girls*," he said.

"You've read *Funny Girls*?"

"I've seen copies. Rita's part of the Chelsea art scene."

"You're into art?" I asked as we entered the building.

"You have to ask, knowing my background?" he said.

My being with A.W., whom Rita called "the best part-time silk-screen artist in the city," put me back in her good graces, at least temporarily. Enough for her to include me in her offer of soft drinks. I politely declined. A.W. accepted a Diet Dr Pepper.

"Melody not home?" I asked.

"Working today," Rita said. "Modeling cosmetics. She needs to do more of that. She's still moping around. Those disks are a mixed blessing." She pointed to several of Rudy Gallagher's DVDs resting beside the TV monitor. "Watching the guy seems to make her happy, but they just reinforce her memory of him, and when she turns the set off, she gets moody again."

"I wouldn't have brought them if I'd thought they'd cause her pain," I said.

"I know," Rita said. "Like I said, she's happy when she's watching them. I'll go get the drawings."

I strolled to the TV stand and glanced at the disks in their jewel boxes. *USS Huckleberry,* disk two and disk five. I wondered if Rudy had recorded the shows in chronological order. Of course he had, the anal-retentive jackass.

Rita returned from the general vicinity of the bedrooms with two sheets of art paper on which she'd sketched detailed full-figure drawings in colored pencils of the Cheetah.

"I did these more for myself than for you," she said. "This one is the model in the costume that I saw getting out of the Hummer to stretch herself."

A.W. moved behind me, lured by the drawing. "Solid work, Rita," he said. "I bet this beats the original art."

"Well, I'll show you."

She held up a much-less-complex comic-book version of the Cheetah. "They didn't go in for shading in those days," she said. "And with the other I was working from a model. I'd say they both reflected the subjects."

The two drawings looked more or less the same, except that the comic-book Cheetah had gloves that looked like paws, while the dimensional, shaded Cheetah was wearing ordinary gloves. And more important, as I said to Rita, "The masks are different."

"Exactly. That's the thing that caught my eye," she said. Both were wearing similar Cheetah cowls surrounding the face, but the original 1940s comic-book version was wearing the standard domino mask. And the model's mask was more elaborate. The eye section was part of the cowl. And there was a lower mask of white with a slit for the mouth. It even covered the neck area.

"Curiouser and curiouser," I said. "What do you think, A.W.?"

He studied the drawings. "Beautiful work, like I said."

"The model remind you of anybody?"

"Not really," he said. "Could be anybody under all that."

"That's what makes it so interesting," I said.

I got out my cellular and dialed Arnie Epps.

The *Wake Up!* producer was still at the Glass Tower, putting together tomorrow's show.

"Is Trina with you?" I asked.

"No. She said she had things to do before the meeting tonight with you and the Mossad guy."

"Ex-Mossad," I said.

"You've got her spitting nails, Billy. How the hell did you swing that interview, anyway?"

"I think it must have been that segment I did at the museum comic-book exhibit," I lied. "Remember that?"

"Of course. That was a good job."

"What did Trina think of it?"

"Trina?" He sounded puzzled. "I think she liked . . . No, wait a minute. She didn't even see it. Yeah, that was the morning . . . She got a weird phone call. Guy said he was her super and there was smoke coming from her apartment. She left before we cut to your segment."

"How bad was the damage?" I asked.

"No damage. It was a crank call. Her building's super hadn't phoned her. And her apartment was fine."

"Glad to hear it," I said. "Catch you later, Arnie."

"Huh? Oh, sure. And Billy, try to be at the Ritz-Carlton by five. Don't be late. Trina's really on the warpath."

"That the time and place of the meeting with Aharon?" I asked.

"Yeah. Didn't Trina call you?"

"I imagine she will," I said.

Chapter

SIXTY-ONE

"Miss Noor is feeling a bit groggy and not too talkative," Detective Hawkline told A.W. and me when we arrived at the hospital. "The doctor says it might be good for her to see some familiar faces."

We'd been driving back to the Bistro building when A.W. checked in on Bettina and discovered she'd awakened in the early morning. Her nurse was concerned that she had refused to eat. Detective Hawkline was annoyed that she had also refused to talk.

They both thought we might help.

Bettina was sitting up in bed when we walked in. If the bandage on her head had been made of gold, she'd have resembled a Hindu priestess. "Hi, Bet," A.W. said. "We thought these might brighten the room a little." He placed the yellow tulips we'd brought on a bedside table.

"Lovely," she said.

She seemed neither happy nor sad to see us. But when Detective Hawkline followed us into the room, she frowned.

"Feeling better, Miss Noor?" the detective asked.

"Until a moment ago, yes."

"I was hoping you might be able to tell me a little more about what happened at the old house."

"There is nothing more to tell," Bettina said.

"Miss Noor says she didn't see anything in that basement," Detective Hawkline said.

"Too dark," Bettina said.

"But not too dark for you to shoot and kill a man." To us, the detective said, "The bullet we recovered from Mr. Gault came from Miss Noor's weapon."

"Someone fired at me," Bettina said. "I fired back."

Detective Hawkline looked skeptical. She knew, as did I, that Gault had been shot in the back of his head.

"Any sense of how many people were in the basement?" the detective asked.

This would be the time that Bettina might be tempted to mention the kidnapping, not knowing that we all would prefer to forget that particular element. But she said, "As I told you, I just saw the one man while I was driving by. He was entering the grounds through a broken section of the fence. The way he did it made me think he was trespassing. I parked and followed him in because I thought he might be up to no good."

"Can you describe the man?" the detective asked.

"Big."

"That's it? Big? How about height, age, body type, race? Wearing what? A tux? A swimsuit? How about a clown costume?"

With each question, Bettina seemed to be withdrawing a bit, physically sliding down under the covers, turning away from Hawkline.

"Could we talk for a minute, Detective?" I said.

Hawkline stared at me, then turned her attention back to Bettina, who had closed her eyes. "Sure," the detective said. "Talk? Why not?"

"We'll be right back, Bettina," I said, and held the door open for the detective. "Care for a cup of coffee?" I asked her.

"Sounds great. My nerves are still asleep, because I've only had five or six cups today."

Her partner, Seestrunk, was at the nurses' station, chatting up a busty administering angel. Just as Hawkline opened her mouth to call out to him, he leaned in close to the nurse and said something, causing her to draw back in disgust. Hawkline mumbled the words "What a dick" and led me away in the opposite direction.

In a nearly empty waiting room, we sipped bitter machine-dispensed coffee and I explained that Detective Solomon had suggested I inform her of a few things I knew that might help her investigation of Ted Parkhurst's murder.

"Yes," she said, "he mentioned something you told him about a mysterious gathering in Afghanistan."

So once again I described the infamous meeting of the toe-tag gang in Kabul, embellishing it a bit to give A.W. as much time as possible with Bettina, which was my purpose in distracting the detective. I ended by asking her about the man shot in the old mansion's basement. "You said his name was Gault. Steve Gault?"

"Stephen. You knew him?"

"No. But he was at the Irish pub in Kabul, too."

She smiled. She had that Spencer Tracy rueful grin down cold. "You make my head swim, Chef Blessing," she said. "So let's see what we've got. Six men shared a table in a bar in Kabul about a month ago. Now all of 'em are dead. And what should I deduce from that fact? That a serial murderer is at work? That'd be interesting. I've never investigated a serial-killer case. Probably because we don't get many serial killers in real life. Certainly not any with IQs higher than Stephen Hawking's who like to play tricky games with us."

"What about Zodiac?" I said.

"Well, that's the West Coast," she said. "They live the fiction out there. Here, we're a little more down to earth. We get Son of Sam. No criminal genius. Just a homicidal nutjob with a talking dog who had a lucky streak that eventually ran out."

"I'm not suggesting all those guys were killed by the same person," I said. "But now that we know that Ted Parkhurst was capable of murder, I think it's possible he did away with one or two of them."

"Not to put too fine a line to it, chef, I really don't give a rat's ass who he killed, unless it helps me find out who killed him. That's my assignment."

"I'd be looking for a partner in crime," I said.

"Well, thanks for that suggestion, chef. I've been thinking along those lines, too. What I need help with is figuring out who the partner is."

"And how Parkhurst was injected with the stuff that killed him."

"That I know. A hospital is a great place to commit murder with a hypodermic needle and get away with it. How hard would it have been for somebody in a white or green uniform to brush up against

Parkhurst as he was being taken out? Maybe standing behind him in the elevator? And the beauty part is, you toss the needle in a hazmat bag, and no cop I know of is going to go rooting around in there looking for a weapon. No. I'm not concerned with the how. Just the who. I don't suppose you might have been Parkhurst's partner?"

"If that's a serious question, the answer is no."

"Solomon thinks you killed Gallagher," she said. "Why shouldn't we add Parkhurst to your bill? You were here last night. You had opportunity."

"But no motive."

"Unless you were his partner and you didn't want to risk him giving you up."

"You're just playing with my head, aren't you, Detective? You don't really think I killed anybody."

"I'd be a fool if I went by what I thought," she said.

"If you seriously suspected me of anything, you'd have invited Detective Seestrunk along and read me my rights."

"Has Detective Solomon read you your rights?"

"No."

"That's because he doesn't have enough evidence. I have even less."

She looked at her watch. It was a big, silver retro Swatch. "We've been chatting for about fifteen minutes. Anything else you feel compelled to tell me?"

I shook my head.

"Well," she said, "I think your friends have had enough time to compare notes, don't you?"

I told her I did.

"I like the story about the Irish pub," she said.

"It's true," I said.

"That's why I like it," she said.

Chapter

SIXTY-TWO

"How did Bettina know not to mention the kidnapping to Detective Hawkline before you clued her in?" I asked A.W. as we drove away from the hospital.

"She's pretty intuitive," he said. "And we were lucky that it was Detective Hawkline's partner who was on duty when the doctor said she was well enough for visitors. Before he began to ask her questions, she started throwing questions at him about how she'd wound up at the hospital and what exactly had been going on.

"He told her just about everything he knew. But he never once mentioned the word *kidnapping*. And later, when Detective Hawkline arrived, she wanted to know what Bettina had been doing at the boarded-up mansion, which meant none of us had said anything about the search for Ms. McCauley. So she improvised."

"She wasn't improvising about not seeing anything in that basement," I said. "I know from personal experience it was too dark down there to see anything."

"If Parkhurst hadn't been so paranoid," A.W. said, "he wouldn't have gone after Betts and messed himself up."

"Going after her wasn't his idea," I said. "Felix phoned him and sent him to the hospital. She's the one who's paranoid. Or maybe she wanted to set him up."

"Whatever, it worked for her," he said. "He's dead and she's still at large."

"For now," I said, with more hope than conviction.

Trina had left a message for me at the Bistro. It read, in Cassandra's delicate hand, *Meeting five p.m. at the Central Park Ritz-Carlton, room 601.*

There was another note. *Call Lee ASAP.*

"Chef Blessing, dear," Lee said, answering her phone. "I am still at JFK with two very uninteresting agents, awaiting the arrival of our client from London. The flight is forty minutes late, and we are not amused."

"You called earlier?"

"Yes. To ask you to arrive at the hotel a little before the meeting. Say four-forty-five. There are a few things we should prepare."

"No problem."

"I assume A.W. is with you," she said.

"He's in the building. Want to talk with him?"

"No. Just tell him that he is to drop you at the hotel entrance. I will be waiting for you there."

"I'll tell him," I said.

"Till four-forty-five, then. Are you still worried?"

"A little."

"Don't be. Everything will go as planned," she said.

"Just like your client's arrival time," I said.

A.W. was having a late lunch in the main dining room at a table for two that provided a clear view of Cassandra at her hostess perch near the front door. I wondered which of them had picked that table.

Business had been brisk, and there was a fair amount of after-lunch dawdling. Middle-management types engaged in office talk, some well-dressed wedding-ringed ladies taking time out from their shopping, a tourist couple, a table of ten twentysomethings celebrating a birthday, and a few reliables from the nearby ad agencies, who ate with us three or four times a week and would return later for a pre-commuter cocktail.

I took the empty chair across from A.W.

He was halfway through his meal, a baby-lamb–shoulder salad, accompanied by, it pains me to report, some kind of soft drink. He was, after all, on duty.

I told him Lee's request that we arrive early for the meeting. "You're going to be in on this, right?" I asked.

"No. There's a special team for takedowns."

"We have to talk about that," I said. "And I'm going to need a few things that you know more about than I."

"Like what?"

I checked my watch. We had about three hours before magic time. Long enough for me to talk him into a slight adjustment to Lee's plans that would make me feel a little less vulnerable. I smiled at him. "That salad looks good," I said. "Maybe I'll have one, too."

Chapter

SIXTY-THREE

Lee must have been standing just inside the Central Park South entrance to the Ritz-Carlton. When A.W. pulled up behind an idling horse and carriage, she stepped through the door and waved to me.

"Here goes nothing," I said to A.W.

He gave me a concerned look.

Lee took my arm and led me through the hotel lobby without paying much mind to its heralded antique/contemporary ambience. "How are you holding up, chef dear?" she asked.

"To reference an old joke: Like the suicide jumper said as he passed the fifth floor, 'So far, so good.'"

"Relax. Everything is in place. And you will appreciate Goyal."

"Appreciate?"

"I am sure you two will get along famously."

"If you say so," I said.

Of the three men in the suite's almost too antique-y sitting room, Goyal Aharon was the last I would have picked to be ex-Mossad. His hair was blond, almost white, cut short and neatly brushed to the side. His eyes were gray. He was clean-shaven and tanned. He was on the thin side and maybe two or three inches shorter than me, six inches shorter and fifty or more pounds lighter than the two rugged InterTec agents who were guarding him. He was wearing pressed khaki trousers, a black Polo pullover, soft black leather loafers, and a crooked grin. He resembled an actor playing a young professor in a TV show set on a 1950s campus.

"Glad to meet you, Mr. Blessing," he said, with only a mild accent. It was his handshake that offered the main hint of a rugged past. There was callused strength in it.

"Call me Billy," I said. "Everybody does. Almost." I glanced at Lee, who rewarded me with a smile.

"I understand you are a famous chef, Billy," Aharon said. "Will we be talking about food tomorrow? I learned from my grandmother the Ashkenazk cuisine, but I am also conversant in other styles. I worked in a bakery in my youth. Perhaps I could demonstrate how one prepares sufganiot?"

"I think we'll have plenty to talk about other than food," I said.

"Where are you going, Lee?" Aharon asked, suddenly distracted.

I turned to see Lee and the two security brutes heading for the door.

"Just giving my men their final instructions," she said. "As I mentioned, we have a specific plan that will be going into effect in just a few minutes."

He turned to me and shook his head. "I do not quite understand what Lee expects to happen. Do you?"

"I get most of it, I think."

He gestured toward an armchair with a red-velvet seat. It was part of a gathering of furniture surrounding a coffee table containing a French Limoges tea set. He waited until I was comfortable, then sat across from me on a Victorian love seat with a pale-blue silk padding. "So explain it to me," he said.

"What don't you understand, Goyal?" Lee asked as she joined us, sitting next to him on the love seat.

"To begin," he said, "if I am in danger, as you keep telling me, why have you dismissed my guards?"

"They are not dismissed," she said. "Merely less visible. They're in the suite across the hall, watching everything we do and listening to everything we say via state-of-the-art visual and audio equipment hidden in this room."

"Hidden where?" I asked.

"There are cameras in that enclosed bookcase," she said, "and in the chandelier. Tiny transmitters have been placed in key positions. For example, the pen on that desk is a transmitter, but you can also write with it."

"It seems so odd," Aharon said. "You have reason to believe this Felix has been hired to kill me, and we are supposed to just sit here, bait for your trap. Why are we taking the chance she may succeed, when there is a much safer and more efficient way to handle the problem? Why not just remove her?"

"As the Irish have said for centuries, it is better to deal with a devil you know than a devil you do not know," Lee said, filling our cups with tea. "If we merely remove Felix, we probably would have to face a new, unknown replacement. What we must do is get Felix to tell us who hired her so that we can stop the threat at its source."

Aharon nodded. "I suppose you are right. Actually, I am interested in meeting this murderous lady I've heard stories about. Call me a chauvinist, but I had assumed Felix to be a man."

"We have Chef Blessing to thank for that bit of clarification," Lee said.

Aharon turned to me. "Ah. Then you are not only a chef, a restaurateur, a television performer, and an interviewer, you also dabble in crime?"

"Only when forced," I said.

Aharon took a sip of tea and settled back on his chair. "So what do you expect, Lee? That she will try to remove me with you and Billy sitting here?"

"I think she will try to remove all of us. But we will not let that happen."

"Good," he said. "I was hoping to write another book."

"This might make an interesting chapter," I said.

"In fact—"

Whatever Aharon was about to say was preempted by the chirping of Lee's cellular.

Aharon and I stared at her as she brought the phone to her ear. "Yes?" she said, and was silent for the next several seconds. "Good" was her next and final word before she put away the phone.

"I've had a team shadowing Trina," Lee informed us. "She is on her way up."

We sat there, silently staring at the door to the suite.

It couldn't have been more than a minute or two, but it seemed like an eternity until an electronic *bing-bong* sounded.

Lee rose, adjusted the purse strap on her shoulder, and went to open the door.

After a brief sharing of hellos, Trina Lomax entered the sitting room carrying a worn leather briefcase. Lee was a step behind her.

Aharon and I had risen.

I was staring at Trina, trying to decipher her expression. Curiosity, perhaps. Maybe a hint of annoyance. But no sign of suspicion. "Billy," she said. "Early and eager?"

"Something like that," I said.

"And this must be Mr. Aharon." She stepped forward, hand extended. "I'm Trina Lomax, executive producer of *Wake Up, America!* on Worldwide Broadcasting."

He hesitated for only a millisecond before shaking her hand. "A pleasure," he said, smiling. "But, please, I prefer for beautiful ladies to call me by my first name, Goyal."

"That's very sweet, Goyal," she said, putting the briefcase on the glass top of the coffee table, beside the tea service. "I hope you'll call me Trina."

She took the remaining chair, one similar to mine but with a purple-velvet seat. Aharon and I followed her lead.

Lee filled Trina's cup, then raised her own. "To a successful tour," she said, and we toasted Aharon.

Trina scanned the room and frowned. "Shouldn't there be people guarding Goyal, Lee?"

"I am here. Others will be joining us shortly."

"Good. Then I guess we should get to it," Trina said, reaching for her briefcase. "I have something I hope we can agree . . ."

She seemed surprised when Lee grabbed the briefcase from her hands, opened it, and dumped its contents on the empty section of the coffee table.

"What the hell, Lee?" Trina said as printed sheets of paper, photographs, creased little notepads, and other bits of reporter paraphernalia flopped and fluttered to the table, some of them sliding to the carpet.

Lee looked inside the briefcase and, evidently satisfied that it was empty, tossed it aside.

"What's going on?" Trina asked, looking at Aharon and me for answers.

"Tell her, Lee," Aharon said.

"Just wanted to make sure you were not carrying something . . . lethal."

"What are you talking about?" Trina asked, starting to rise. "What's going on here?"

Lee removed a .44 Magnum from her handbag. "Sit down, Trina. Before you fall down."

"What's with the gun, Lee?" Trina asked.

Lee pointed the .44 at Trina's midsection. "Sit. Down," she demanded.

Trina obeyed. Once seated again, she blinked her eyes and gave her head a shake.

"Who has paid you to kill me, Trina?" Aharon said.

"Is everyone here crazy?" Trina asked.

Aharon looked at me. "I expected something more," he said, "considering Felix's reputation."

"Beware what you ask for," I said, looking at Lee.

She rewarded me with a smile of delight. "Oh, chef dear, you recognized my weapon."

"All of them," I said, "including the gun in your hand, which used to be in my office."

"A gift to me from Teddy. He found it the evening he left the napkin drawing for you."

"Considering how lame he was at the hospital," I said, "I'm surprised he fooled me so completely with his drunk act."

"I am now confused, too, Lee," Aharon said. "What is happening here?"

Lee ignored him, continuing to address me. "Does your devious mind tell you why I have your revolver?"

"I suppose it's because you're going to shoot these two people and blame it on me."

"Not at all. But you will be playing a big part."

"Why me? What did I do to get involved in all this?"

"Don't play coy," Lee said. "It's because you caused me so much trouble."

"How did I do that?"

"You killed Rudy Gallagher."

I was momentarily stymied. "Why would you think that? Even the detective assigned to the case is having doubts."

"Then he is a fool. Gallagher took your woman, though I personally feel you are well rid of her, and he was about to destroy your career. Of course you killed him. But, unfortunately, he was in possession of an audio file that a smart investigator, or an obsessed journalist"—she bowed her head to Trina—"might use to endanger Felix's anonymity. A purchase had been arranged with Gallagher. But you murdered him before that came to pass. And the file is still out there somewhere. Such trouble you have caused."

"I didn't kill Gallagher," I said.

Trina made a little strangled cry and suddenly fell forward onto the carpet.

"One down," Lee said, shifting her position to cover both Aharon and me with the gun.

He stood and reached for the weapon. But his reflexes were slow and Lee merely rose from the love seat and took a step backward. Aharon tried to follow, but his leg gave out and he fell very close to Trina. They both lay motionless on the carpet.

"My own little teapot brew," Lee said.

"Is it fatal?"

"No. Basically a variety of flunitrazepam—what you Americans call a roofie—but with a special something that will keep them awake so that they will see the bullet coming. And the drug will be out of their systems long before your overworked forensics people will find time to examine them.

"And how are you feeling, chef dear? A little off the mark?"

"I feel . . . fine," I said, blinking a little.

She looked at Trina's scattered papers. "I'd love to read those, to see how close she's come. I know for a fact she was snooping around Baghdad for information about the death of Di Voss's son. I think that's why she went to work at your network, for more background."

"Did you kill him?" I asked Lee.

"Plastique attached to a vehicle's undercarriage. To the geniuses trying to cope with the violence in Iraq, there is no difference between that and a road mine. Almost too easy."

"Who . . . hired you?" I asked, as the teacup fell from my fingers to the carpet, spilling its contents.

"What difference does it make? Dead is dead."

"Lee is . . . nickname, right? For Felice. Close enough to Felix."

"Lee, Felice, Felix. They are all of my own creation. As is Franchette. That one may be too literary for you, chef. It's a tribute to Colette's favorite feline."

"How many . . . have you killed?"

"Not so many," Lee answered. "Nine, actually, including Lieutenant Di Voss. Teddy killed four, including that oaf Gault, who'd become something of a burden. Teddy was a talented amateur but needed supervision."

"Who . . . hired you to kill Di Voss?" I asked again.

"That is of no consequence," she said, "since, in a little while, Felix will be no more. The thing about enigmas is that almost anyone can be made to fit the image. As you once suggested, Trina is an excellent choice." She reached into her handbag and removed an ugly serrated knife. "She will have the double satisfaction of using this, the same weapon that Felix has employed in the past, on the Mossad thug and you, chef dear. But before you die, you will, with your last strength, shoot her."

"And what happens . . . to you?" I asked.

"I drink a lot of that tea and fall unconscious at the same moment the security guards across the hall, alarmed by the gunfire, break down the door."

"It will take . . . perfect timing," I said, just before my head fell forward.

My eyes were open. I could see her walking around the table to stand before me. She placed a hand under my chin and lifted my head. She leaned forward and kissed my motionless lips. Then she straightened and took a step toward the coffee table.

She placed my gun on the table, then, knife in hand, stepped over Aharon. She prodded his body with one pointed toe, rolling it so that he was lying on his back. She raised the knife. . . .

And I cleared my throat.

She turned swiftly and reached for the gun she'd placed on the coffee table.

It was no longer there.

It was in my hand, aimed at her lovely chest. "I spent a year at Gidleigh Park in Devon, working in Michael Caines's kitchen," I said, "but I never developed a taste for tea."

She smiled and shifted her hold on the knife.

"Put the knife on the table," I told her. She hesitated. "You're too smart to bring a knife to a gunfight."

She placed the knife on the table.

"Now what? You still have no proof. I can claim you were Felix, partnering with Teddy."

"What about them?" I indicated the narcotized couple. "I think they might just back me."

"They've been drugged. Unreliable. In the end, chef dear, it will be your word against mine. The word of a murder suspect against the word of a respected executive of an international security agency."

I didn't buy any of that, but it didn't really matter. I undid the buttons of my shirt and showed her the transmitter taped to my chest.

She sighed and said, "So Felix will not be dying today after all."

"Nobody will," I said. "Time to come in, A.W."

Lee continued to smile at me as we heard the click of the suite door unlocking.

A.W. entered the room, followed by the other InterTec agents, all with guns drawn. "Well, Billy," he said, "that was some show."

One of the agents knelt beside Aharon and Trina to check their vital signs. A.W. holstered his weapon and removed a set of cuffs from his coat pocket.

Lee put out her hands, but A.W. reminded her that company policy required behind-the-back cuffing.

While that was being accomplished, she continued to look at me. "Would it not be amusing, chef dear, if they find you guilty of murder and we wind up in the same prison?"

"I didn't kill Rudy Gallagher," I said.

"That makes two of us," she said.

Chapter

SIXTY-FOUR

"Here's to Chef Billy Blessing," Detective Hawkline said, rising for the toast, "for helping us close at least three murder books."

We were in my favorite of the Bistro's private dining rooms, brightly lit by crystal chandeliers, with framed mirrors nearly covering the walls, a décor influenced by a stint I served at Galatoire's in New Orleans. Two long tables, each running nearly the length of the room, had been joined in a U shape. Being of a humble nature, I'd elected to sit at the bottom of the U or the top of the table, depending on your point of view.

I'd planned the dinner to begin at eight, a multicourse affair built around haunches of venison soaked for twenty-four hours in a marinade of burgundy, brandy, and olive oil, crushed peppercorns, bay leaves, and cloves, and cooked for five hours.

We were, by and large, a cheery crowd, made even more so by predinner cocktails and wine. Gretchen and the commander were there, of course. And Marvin, whom I hardly recognized in a suit instead of his warm-up clothes, and his considerably younger wife, Celia. Trina, Arnie, and the on-camera team from *Wake Up, America!* were present, with the exceptions of Gin McCauley, who was still blissing out in Bermuda, and the boy-wonder movie critic Chuck

Slater, who'd broken his leg that morning racing to work on his motorcycle.

Kiki arrived with a new beau, a junior executive with the wholesaler that distributes our sponsor, The Daily Brew coffee. He didn't strike me as the kind of guy who'd steal her iPod, which could mean that their romance would be short-lived. My coproducer Lily Conover stepped into the room, took one look at Detective Hawkline, and said, "Billy, what a literary coup. A dinner party with Gertrude Stein."

Goyal and A.W., who was now responsible for *his* security, showed up a little late. The new author had been flogging his book on the Stephen Colbert show, an experience he found so perplexing he demanded an immediate shot of Gold vodka to clear his head.

The only two participants not totally enjoying the evening were the NYPD's finest, Solomon and Butker. Like Detective Hawkline, they'd been a bit miffed when they heard the full story of the kidnapping. But Hawkline more or less forgave the cover-up. Her investigation into the murders of both Gault and Parkhurst had been successfully closed by Lee's arrest. On the other hand, Lee was continuing to claim neither she nor Ted had poisoned Rudy Gallagher, which meant that Solomon and Butker were still stuck with an open case.

"Not that I don't appreciate a good feed, Blessing," Solomon said when he and Butker arrived, "but I'm not sure why you insisted we show up here tonight. As suspects go, you're not quite in the same league with this Franchette woman. But until she gives up on Gallagher, it's probably inappropriate for us to be here."

"For tonight at least," I told him, "think of me as your host and not a murder suspect. Relax and enjoy the dinner. Please."

From the look they exchanged, I suspected it was less my plea than the promise of a free venison feast that convinced them to take their seats at the table next to Detective Hawkline.

As the dinner progressed in stages, presented by our waitress, Bridget Innes, and a phalanx of busboys, the conversation drifted to a variety of subjects. A remark about the balmy evening resulted in a much-more-information-than-needed response from *Wake Up!*'s resident meteorologist, Professor Lloyd Sebastian. Lance Tuttle chatted with Marvin about the never-ending disclosures of steroid use by many of our highly respected professional athletes. Marvin idly wondered why there was so little time devoted to sporting events on the morning show. Lance, stumped for a reply, passed the question on to Gretchen, who suggested they "take a look at the demos and see who's watching."

Arnie emerged from his teen TV fanboy closet to engage Lily, an admitted fangirl, in a spirited discussion of the relative merits of *Gossip Girl* over the refurbished *Beverly Hills 90210*. Mrs. Marvin asked newswoman Tori Dillard if she was married and Tori replied, "Not exactly."

And so it went. But as might be expected, eventually the talk of the table turned to Lee. Tori said that while driving to the dinner she'd heard that the question of jurisdiction had been raised. Lee, or Felix, or whatever her real name would turn out to be, was suspected of having committed murders in many countries, and each wanted the pleasure of putting her on trial.

"The dreadful woman should be tried, convicted, and incarcerated right here where she was caught," the commander stated.

"I don't know," Trina said. "There are places in the Middle East where she'd be treated to a justice more appropriate to her crimes."

"We can tie her to at least three murders in this city," Detective Hawkline said. "My two and your former coworker, Mr. Bruno. That should be enough for us to hang on to her."

"What was it exactly that made you suspicious of her, Billy?" Gretchen asked.

"I have Detective Solomon to thank for that," I said, noting with amusement the surprise on his dour face, "and, not incidentally, for saving my life. Several hours before Lee planned to kill us, the detective and I had a chat. He used the term 'put on blinders.' That reminded me of something Lee said in the basement of the old mansion. She asked if I'd touched any of the materials the kidnappers had used to keep Gin McCauley bound, gagged, and sightless. She specifically mentioned 'sleep masks.' Later, Gin used the more general term 'blindfold.' I doubt she even knew she'd been wearing a sleep mask. And there was no possible way Lee could have known it at that particular moment, unless she'd been one of the kidnappers."

"It's the little stuff that catches the smarties," Solomon said.

"Once I considered the possibility of Lee being Felix, I realized there were other signs that I'd been ignoring," I said. "For a while I was dumb enough to think you were the assassin, Trina, and Lee tried to encourage that folly in several ways, including the planting of that paintball gun near your office. She also put together a report that indicated you were in the vicinity of most of Felix's known assassinations."

"I was collecting material on Felix," Trina said. "The murders are what drew me to those places. In most cases, I arrived after the crimes had been committed. Maybe just hours after, but still . . ."

"The thing is, Lee also said that many of the victims had been InterTec clients. I think she told me this in case I happened to come across reports that placed *her* at Felix's crime scenes, too. But the point is, she *was* there. And as the person responsible for security, she had both access and opportunity.

"Then there was the incident in the Tunnel that most of you know about. After sending me a written threat when I was doing a segment for the show on comic-book superheroes, she followed my car into the Lincoln Tunnel and did her best to involve me in an accident by shooting my driver and the windshield with a paintball gun. She wasn't trying to kill me, just scare the hell out of me. She didn't want to be recognized, so she got the playful idea of wearing a catlike comic-book costume. But the comic-book version of the character she was portraying wore a harlequin mask. The mask she wore covered her whole face and neck. I can think of only one reason for that. She wanted to hide the beautiful but distinctive color of her skin.

"And, finally, I remembered something that happened at the hospital. Lee moved near the handcuffed Ted Parkhurst, apparently to brush back his hair. When she did, his body jerked slightly. I should have realized the brushing motion had been a misdirection. The hand I wasn't looking at administered the fatal injection, removing the only remaining associate who might be pressured to give her up."

"It was still all conjecture," I said, "but I was spooked enough to bring my concern to A.W., who got me fixed up with a wire and kept the other agents on hand after Lee had dismissed them."

"I don't suppose she's given up the name of the villain who was financing her?" the commander asked.

"Not as of three hours ago," Detective Hawkline said.

"Of course we know who he is," the commander said. "Carl Kelstoe. The bastard was ingratiating himself with certain morally bankrupt members of the so-called power elite by eliminating people perceived as troublesome to America."

"But why were you on her list, Goyal?" Gretchen asked.

He looked at me. I'd told him about Farid Qedir, the Saudi who Lee had claimed was a former lover of Trina's. But, of course, it had not been Trina's story at all.

"An enmity as old as time," he said, answering Gretchen's question. "I doubt that anyone had to pay her to kill me."

When dinner ended and the last bite of fresh fig-and-strawberry soufflé had been consumed, Bridget returned with busboys to clear the table. She took requests for after-dinner drinks, and I suggested she add a couple of pots of coffee to the list.

"Speaking of Kelstoe," A.W. said, "there's a secondary benefit he got from Felix's work, the embarrassment of his closest rival. As you mentioned, Billy, InterTec was responsible for the safety of several of the victims. Every one of those deaths cost us goodwill points. And with a VP of ours exposed as the assassin Felix, the company stock's in free fall."

"And Kelstoe's stock is on the rise," the commander said.

"I thought the congressional committee found those Touchstone mercenaries guilty of starting that riot," Lily said.

"They did," the commander said. "But the bastard has simply changed the name of the company. And Wall Street is rewarding him for his duplicity."

"Excuse me, folks," Detective Solomon said, "but before this turns into a depressing discussion about Wall Street, I've got a question for Chef Blessing."

"Shoot," I said.

"What I gather from some of the people here tonight, you spent a lot of time with this Felix. Do you think she's telling the truth when she says she didn't kill Rudy Gallagher?"

Everybody was looking at me. Gretchen's stare was particularly intense.

"It's the truth," I said. "She killed a lot of people, but she didn't kill him."

"How sure are you?"

"Sure enough," I said. "That's one of the reasons I invited you and Detective Butker here tonight." I looked at Gretchen and said, "This might be a little rough, Gretch."

"Don't worry about me, Billy. I've shed my last tear for Rudy."

I reached into my pocket and withdrew Rudy Gallagher's little black book. I tossed it to Solomon, who snagged it with one hand.

"I've seen this before," he said, flipping the pages. "So what?"

"It's Gallagher's."

"You told me this was yours."

"No. You assumed it was mine, and I didn't correct that assumption."

"I won't argue the point," he said. "So if it belonged to Gallagher, how'd you get it?"

"It was mixed in with some DVDs you guys allowed the network to remove from his apartment."

"Don't give me that. We wouldn't have missed something like this."

"You could and you did," I said.

He stuck his lower lip out in a policeman's pout and studied something in the black book. "Looks like Gallagher tore a couple pages out," he said. "Rejects, huh?"

Gallagher hadn't torn the pages. I had. Gretchen's and Melody Moon's. They wouldn't be needed for my show-and-tell.

Bridget arrived with the drinks and the coffee. She moved along the table, placing the brandies and the cognacs, then made a more complete tour with the coffee carafe.

"Check the entry right before the last torn page," I said to Solomon.

"Okay. Got it."

"Read out the phone number."

When he did, Bridget's hand jumped and she spilled coffee on the tablecloth.

"You okay?" I asked her.

"Sure," she said. "I just . . . sorry."

"You look a little upset," I said. "Maybe you should sit down for a minute. We can get you a chair."

"I'm okay. I prefer to stand."

"That was your phone number, wasn't it?"

"I'm sorry, what?"

"The phone number the detective just read. It's yours, right, Bridget?"

"The detective?" Her head jerked toward Solomon. "I wasn't listening."

Solomon read the number again.

"It's mine."

"So you knew Rudy Gallagher," I said.

"Sure. He came in a lot."

"And you went out with him."

"Once or twice."

"Didn't you break off your romance with Juan because you thought you were in love with Rudy Gallagher?"

"No. Not at all. I'm still with Juan."

"But you told me that you ended your affair with Juan because you'd found true love. 'The heart knows what the heart needs,' I think you said. Weren't you talking about Rudy Gallagher?"

"No. It was . . . somebody else."

"Who?"

"I'd rather not say."

"Where were you the night Rudy Gallagher was murdered?" I asked.

"I don't . . . Here, I guess, working."

"No. Cassandra says you felt ill and left early."

"Right. Yeah. I remember now. I was sick one night. That night, I guess."

"But not so sick you didn't take one of the night's specials home with you."

"I'm sure I didn't do that."

"You were seen carrying the white bag."

"Whoever says they saw me is mistaken."

"That would be Juan. He likes to keep an eye on you, and he is very certain."

"Well, he's wrong."

"Bridget, if Detectives Solomon and Butker were to go to your apartment right now, wouldn't they find the cleansing liquid you used to poison Rudy Gallagher?"

"What? No. Of course not. I didn't kill Rudy." She was edging toward the door. "I was at my apartment. Sick."

"We all can understand why you did it, Bridget. Rudy hurt you."

"No. No, he didn't. I barely knew—this is all wrong."

Solomon and Butker were standing now, flanking the waitress.

"Thanks for the dinner, Blessing," Solomon said. "I think we better take this young lady to where we can have a somewhat more official chat with her."

Bridget's face was chalk-white, her eyes locked on mine. "Help me," she said. And as the detectives escorted her from the room, I really wished I could have.

Chapter

SIXTY-FIVE

There is nothing like the arrest of your waitress for murder to bring a dinner party to a close.

One minute the room was filled with people thanking me and saying good-bye. The next I was standing there alone with Gretchen, who had tears in her eyes.

She hugged me and kissed my cheek and whispered in my ear, "Thank you, Billy. For the dinner, but especially for the closure."

She stepped back and said, "You may not believe me, but my heart goes out to that poor girl."

"Why wouldn't I believe you?" I said.

As she made her exit, Cassandra entered the room, one eyebrow arched.

"The princess was sniffling," she said. "Crocodile tears."

"I don't think so," I said.

"Clearly, you don't," she said. "Well, no one can say you don't throw one hell of a party."

"Thank you. I assume you know what just happened."

"It is my job to know what happens here during the hours of operation."

"The customers in the main room didn't . . ."

"No. The detectives took her out the back way. You know there's something you have to do now."

I nodded. "I don't suppose you could help—"

"As I've said a hundred times, I draw the line when it comes to HR issues."

With that, she did an about-face. Considering the spikiness of her heel, I was a bit surprised she didn't screw herself into the floor. I looked back at the empty, partially bused table and saw that there was one liqueur that someone—the commander, I think—had left untouched.

I picked it up and shot it, barely experiencing its syrupy kick.

Then I headed to the bar to tell Juan that the woman he loved had just been arrested for murdering Rudy Gallagher.

Chapter

SIXTY-SIX

Several weeks after that night of nights, I had just finished the Friday edition of *Wake Up, America!* when I received a phone call from Melody Moon.

It was good to hear from her, even better when she told me the reason she called.

She'd been playing Rudy's old television shows and she'd found a CD mixed in with the DVDs. "It could be, like, a movie or TV soundtrack," she said. "But it sounds pretty real. And one of the men has this soft voice, like Clint Eastwood's, only much creepier, and he's telling the other man he wants him to assist some . . . I hate the word, 'bitch,' but that's what he said . . . some bitch he'd hired who was coming to the other man's military base to kill an Army officer.

"The other guy says he's not sure he can help, and the creepy-voice man gets angry and tells him to make up his mind, that the . . . bitch can bring a guy named Oscar to help, but that would cost him almost double the amount."

Felix and Oscar. Rudy's "Odd Couple." I recalled the other note he wrote for himself on his kitchen blackboard. "Jewel for Berry9."

"Was the CD in the jewel box that was supposed to contain *USS Huckleberry,* disc nine?" I asked.

"Oh," she said. "Then you already know about it. I guess it was silly of me to think it might be important."

"It's very important," I said. "Can I come over now to pick it up?"

"Please," she said. "I don't like having it here. It's ugly. What's it all about, anyway?"

"In a word: karma," I said.

ABOUT THE AUTHORS

AL ROKER is known to over thirty million viewers each week for his work on NBC's *Today* show, a role that has earned him ten Emmy awards. He also has his own show on the Weather Channel, *Wake Up With Al.* He is a blockbuster *New York Times* bestselling author for his book *Don't Make Me Stop This Car!: Adventures in Fatherhood.* An accomplished cook, Roker also has two cookbooks to his credit, including the bestselling *Al Roker's Big Bad Book of Barbecue. The Morning Show Murders* marks his first foray into fiction. Bantam Dell will publish the second Billy Blessing mystery in 2010. Al resides in Manhattan with his wife, ABC News and *20/20* correspondent Deborah Roberts, and has two daughters and a son.

DICK LOCHTE is the author of a list of popular crime novels including the award-winning *Sleeping Dog,* named one of the "100 favorite mysteries of the century" by the Independent Booksellers Association. His crime fiction column that ran for nearly a decade in the *Los Angeles Times* earned him the 2003 Ellen Nehr Award for Excellence in Mystery Reviewing. He lives in Southern California with his wife and son.